DAWN RISING

Books by Lisa M. Green

The Awakened Series

Dawn Rising
Darkness Awakening
Midnight Descending

Standalone Novels

The First

See the rest at *lisamgreen.com/books*

Newsletter

Sign up for updates and information on new
releases at *lisamgreen.com/newsletter*

Some spells were meant to be broken…

DAWN RISING

AWAKENED ~ BOOK ONE

LISA M. GREEN

TRIDENT PUBLISHING

ISBN: 9781952300004 (hardcover) / 9781952300011 (paperback) / 9781952300028 (ebook)

Library of Congress Control Number 2020910605

First edition published in the United States of America in September 2020

Trident Publishing
Atlanta, Georgia
tridentpub.com
contact@tridentpub.com

In memory of Justin

If heaven has cake, it almost certainly has books. I'm sorry I made you wait so long for this one. I'll sign a copy for you when I see you again, friend.

The train was always for you.

ERESSEIA

THE KNOWN WORLD

Mare Dolor
(Sea of Sorrow)

Mare Dolor
(Sea of Sorrow)

Vanito

Eadon

Rasenforst

Ramolay

Perdita Bay

Enchantress's
Tower

Imperium

Menos

Bramosia

Mare Dolor
(Sea of Sorrow)

A glossary is located at the back of the book.

AWAKENED

In waking dreams I glide on thorny paths
Trampled upon by those who wish to harm.
The briars all but broken in their haste
To rid the world of what must come to pass.
The roses dying, dying in their bed;
A thankless death to purge the unseen past.
An unknown path I take through the darkness
To reach the grail I do not wish to seek.

Through sylvan screen, I know he's waiting there,
An unwilling specter in my dark thoughts.
Never seeking, always finding, poor soul.
He does not want this, a burdensome crown
Upon his weary head, crushing down hope
And freedom from what he knows he must do.
This fearful dance will set the world ablaze;
Embers ignite, dreams fading into dust.

But dreams are shadows of the waking world,
Weaving a web of whispered promises.
In the end, pricks may sting and thorns may bite;
The spell was cast, but death did not take me.
Fumbling, stumbling, crumbling mind.
In death I'll not be someone's rotting corpse.
In sleep I lie in dreams that do not die,
Awakened by one who knows my true name.

Part One

In Waking Dreams

In waking dreams, I glide on thorny paths
Trampled upon by those who wish to harm.
The briars all but broken in their haste
To rid the world of what must come to pass.

Chapter 1

AURIANNA

Hoist and march, heave and drop.

Today of all days, Aurianna longed to be almost anywhere else. She desperately wished she could avoid looking at both Damon and at the burdens they shared.

He kept grinning at her like an idiot as they carried one corpse after another down the hallway in the depths of the Consilium to the burning pit of magma. Approaching those who guarded the flames, Aurianna and Damon heaved and tossed their load before hurrying away, eager to leave behind the horror and the smell of burning flesh—but reluctant as well, knowing they were just going to have to haul another to the same fate.

Hoist and march, heave and drop.

Aurianna always hated seeing this, hated being a part of it. She knew the people were criminals. Aunt Larissa had been telling her the story since Aurianna was a little girl.

"Once upon a time, not so long ago, people began to fall from the sky," she would begin. *"Dark shadows erupted into dazzling shards of light*

as the night sky was filled with bodies pouring from the clouds. Everyone stayed away, terrified of the strange beings who fell from the heavens but did not die."

When she was younger, the words didn't always make sense to her, but as she grew older, Aurianna began to understand and appreciate the horrible truth they revealed.

"A group we call the Carpos was assigned to hunt down and question them. Eventually, they reported back, claiming the strangers were trespassers from a distant future who'd come to steal our resources and take them back to the future, along with as many of the people as they could capture—to be their slaves."

The woman was a masterful storyteller, always conveying more than she said.

"Horrified at this revelation, everyone let go of their doubts and curiosity, no longer questioning the need for the strangers to be rounded up and put to death. They became numb to the smell, the sight, the sounds...."

But for Aurianna, the fear and anger of her people was never enough to dissolve her own revulsion at having to take part in all of it. Something in the way her aunt told the tale gave Aurianna a sick feeling deep in her core. She couldn't overlook the fact that only hours before, these corpses had been living, breathing individuals. When the bodies were ready to be taken to the burning pits, they were just a pile of discarded refuse.

Hoist and march, heave and drop.

Despite these feelings and without any choice in the matter, Aurianna continued in the morbid dance, grabbing the arms as Damon grabbed the legs, awkwardly moving down the hall with— quite literally—dead weight between them. And still, he beamed stupidly at her, prattling on in a conversation he was unknowingly having with himself. Aurianna was in no mood for lighthearted banter. All her mind could do was focus on the memories of the morning and the undesirable task at hand.

No, it hadn't exactly been a grand start to the day, getting the absolute worst labor assignment. And this day was no more grim than all the rest, but for some reason her patience had worn thin lately. No one harbored much patience these days, with the Darkness seemingly intoxicated on the joy it lapped from the air.

Even standing in line to receive her work detail for the day had been an exercise in frustration. The Praefect on duty had been working by himself that morning, causing the line to stretch down the street and wrap around the nearest corner. The Consils, the governing body of her people, usually kept the number of Praefects to a minimum in order to maintain the position's prestige, but typically at least three of them handed out labor assignments in the mornings. The Praefects were nothing more than an extension of the Consils, performing whatever tasks were asked of them by their esteemed leaders. There was, however, a fair bit of bowing and scraping required to obtain the coveted role. The Praefects were tasked with anything from running errands for the Consils to guarding the flames of the burning pit.

When the nasty little Praefect with the balding head and clammy palms had slapped the service docket in her hand early that morning, she hadn't even looked at the details of her assignment for the day until she had almost passed the Consilium.

The brightly lit Consilium was an alien monstrosity among the low-lying homes and shacks scattered in tiers across the rolling hills of the land. Within the walls of this imposing structure, the Consils met to govern and rule over the people of their small community. The structure beamed with an unnatural glow from an abundance of what the Consils called "electric power." No one knew where it came from or why it only existed at the Consilium.

Stopping in the lee of the building as it loomed before her, she'd looked at the paper in her hand, silently cursing. She hated any assignment that brought her even close to the building. Something about it struck her with a sense of foreboding, even though everyone who worked and lived there seemed happy and content. Of course they were. They had electric-powered everything.

Still, something unnerved her about it.

Hoist and march, heave and drop.

Aurianna came out of her dark thoughts to focus again on Damon's expectant smile. She had wished over and over throughout the morning that he would stop looking at her like that. They were adults now, not children. The one kiss they had shared years ago had been innocent, and she had regretted it the moment it happened. Damon had been like a brother to her for almost twenty years now. Nothing would ever change that fact. Aurianna had been attempting to avoid one-on-one time with him ever since "the incident" and had succeeded quite well until today.

She sighed, reaching up to her headscarf and pushing a stray lock of her light copper-brown hair back up into its folds. She yanked the knot tight with a quick jerk of her hands before bending to take up a new burden. Heavy physical labor had never suited her, particularly when it came to the horrid business of transporting dead bodies to the burning pit.

"So, how is your aunt doing these days?" Damon attempted to smile at her despite the unfortunate load they carried between them. The sweat sticking his dark-brown hair to his forehead threatened to run down into his eyes.

Aurianna gave a half smile back, certain he could see through the feigned gesture. "She's doing well. About the same as always, I guess. Never seems to age as fast as the rest of us." Thinking of her aunt made her laugh. "I bet she'll be running around attending to me in *my* old age." The image brought another smile—this time genuine—to her face.

Hoist and march, heave and drop.

It wasn't until she heard another voice—more a raspy whisper—that she returned to reality.

"Help!"

The stench of burning flesh permeated the air, suffocating and choking her. Yet it faded from her senses as she registered that one simple word—a plaintive cry that tilted her world into something unrecognizable to her own eyes.

Aurianna pivoted her upper body around, looking for the source of the voice—anyone who might be passing by—but the empty hallway revealed nothing. She peered back at Damon to see if he had heard it as well. Eyes wide with some unknown emotion and half-covered by his long hair, Damon had his focus locked on a point just below her waist—an odd and uncomfortable gaze.

She was about to ask him just what the hell he was staring at when she heard the whispered plea again. Looking down, she saw two deep pools of pale-green staring back at her. The intensity of the man's gaze seemed to bore a hole into her lungs, stealing away her breath.

Dead bodies were one thing. The not-so-dead one in her arms caused her grip to tighten as she tried, in vain, to inhale. His cracked lips parted, opening myriad fissures where dried blood had stained tiny rivulets of red.

When it—*he*—spoke again, her entire body froze, and her paralyzed hands lost their grip on the man's arms. He fell in slow motion, the action feeling like a lifetime in her confused mind. She refused to believe her eyes, to believe the impossible.

The dead normally lacked the desire—and capacity—for speech.

But the dead wanted company.

7

For one sharp moment, Aurianna froze and let her senses return. The man's eyes were slightly open and gazing intently at her. That word, that plea for help, was all she heard in that instant. Damon had also forfeited his grip on the man's legs and was slowly backing away, so she grasped the stranger's arms again and proceeded to drag him into the nearest open room, mindful of the possibility of a Praefect walking by at any moment. Damon was in a daze but followed as if he were attached to them by an invisible thread.

Aurianna laid the man on a faded oval rug in the middle of the room and ran to close the door. The sound of the door slamming shut roused Damon from his stupor. He looked at her, then at the half-dead man lying on the floor.

As she knelt to speak with the man, Damon grabbed her upper arm and screeched in her ear, "What the hell are you doing, Aurianna? That man is dangerous! We must tell someone. Now." When she refused to move, he backed away, shaking his head. "You can't be serious?"

Steeling her amber gaze on him, Aurianna spoke with calm determination. "Damon, the man is *alive*. He spoke to us. You heard it, right? I will not take a living being to the flames, Damon. Do you hear me? I will not do it." When he started to answer her, she stopped him. "Haven't you ever wanted to talk with one of them, to find out what they're like? The future, Damon! Aren't you even a little bit curious?"

All the time she was speaking, the man lay gasping on the floor, blood-streaked clumps of sandy-blond hair clinging to his pallid face, death tugging at him mercilessly. Aurianna turned to him, a desperate question in her eyes. Instead, she said, "I won't hurt you. But I can't help you."

The man answered in the same raspy whisper, "I know. But I want to tell you something. Someone needs to know so this can stop. My people are dying, and there's no way to warn them, to tell them it's a trap."

"A trap? No one asked you to come here."

"No. But they knew we were coming."

"What is that supposed to mean?"

"Your Consils have more at stake than they let on."

"That doesn't surprise me, but why come here? Stealing resources from your past seems incredibly stupid." Her uncertainty building, she deflated, settling next to him on the floor, thinking about all the things they were told by the Consils regarding these people, these invaders from the future. None of the stories had ever made sense to her. How could someone change the past by taking resources—taking *people*—and not risk major changes to their own reality in the future? She'd spent many nights mulling it over but had always come to the same conclusion: she couldn't understand time travel unless she experienced it herself.

"I don't...I don't know anything about stealing resources. I just came here to escape." He paused, gasping for one more breath, seeming determined to hang on long enough to reveal his secrets. Sudden realization dawned on his face. "Our past? You think we're from your future. Is that what you're saying?"

Now it was Damon's turn to sag to the ground, the confusion in his eyes dragging his entire body down in exhaustion. His words were barely more than a whisper. "But you can time travel. You have to be from the future." He shared a look with Aurianna, both dreading the man's answer.

"No. No. Not the future. The past. Everything went wrong. We thought it was safer here. And there's no one to tell the others..."

Aurianna straightened. "What others? What are you talking about?" The other part—the part where they were from the *past*—did not want to register in her brain just yet.

"The other Kinetics. They will keep coming. And dying. They'll all be killed. Someone has to warn them not to come."

"Kinetics?" She shook her head. His words confused her, making her head spin with a thousand unspoken questions.

"You don't know." A solemn look of realization came over the man's face, followed by a moment of mirthless laughter. At least, she thought it was laughter. He didn't make a sound, but his chest shook, and the corners of his mouth tilted upward almost indiscernibly. "I guess they've won, then. Our names, our existence. Erased from memory." The man silently wept as his stunned audience looked on.

Damon clutched his arms to his chest, rocking back and forth on his heels. He glanced her way, mirroring the dread Aurianna felt in her heart. She chewed her bottom lip, no idea what to do or say. Cold fingers inched up her spine as the stranger's tears edged down the side of his face, disappearing into the fabric of the rug beneath him.

Finally, he spoke again, the air rattling in his lungs with his dying breaths. "We—Kinetics—have control over the elements. Some call us mages, but we possess no real magic. Our gifts lie in manipulating what is already there." He paused again, his face pained with the effort of breathing. "Some hated our powers. Then one of our own hurt a lot of people. So they sought to destroy us. Hunted us down. This was our escape, our plan to regroup and fix everything. But they were waiting for us. We should have known."

"Who? Who was waiting for you?"

"The ones who did this to me."

"The Carpos? They're trained to find and bring back anyone like you. They work for the Consils. What exactly did they do?"

"Drained my powers, what little I had left. Drained me over and over. I must have passed out. I guess they thought I was dead." He gave a small smile. "They were just over-hasty."

"We'll get you some help. I know I said we couldn't, but we will. Right, Damon?"

Damon only stared at her, not moving. Finally, he said, "Yeah. We'll get you some help. I'll go find a Healer."

A series of racking coughs shook the man violently. This went on for several moments. When he regained the ability to speak, he said, "No. That's not necessary."

"Of course it is!" Aurianna cried.

"Just don't let them erase us. If you can find a way to warn the others... But no. They lie in wait for us. There's no time. Just... help my people, please. If you can. Promise me that."

"What can I possibly do? The Consils control everything here!"

"Promise me you'll try. That you'll tell my story to others."

"Of course! Of course. We promise. But we need to get you some medical attention."

"Too late, I'm afraid. Thank you." He took Aurianna's small hand in his own, his grasp weak and cold to the touch. When he locked gazes with her, his pupils dilated, and a look of recognition crossed his face for the briefest moment before it was gone. His small smile was unmarred by derision or pain now, a faint look of joy that was wholly unnatural on the face of a dying man. Aurianna was puzzled by his sudden change in demeanor and wondered if he was simply becoming delusional in his last moments. "I feel it in you, girl. It's going to be alright, some day. Maybe the Essence still hear us. You might be..."

His last words were lost as the life left his eyes and his body went limp.

As they sat in silence, stunned beyond words at the revelations still swirling like tiny cyclones in the charged air around them, Aurianna realized she had never asked him his name.

Chapter 2

AURIANNA

They called it the Darkness.

Not the black of a moonless night or a room devoid of candles, full of shadows born from the creeping unseen. This was the Darkness of choking death—overwhelming, consuming, suffocating. Raw and complete. Total and utter oblivion.

And rain. When the Darkness settled in, the rain often began, weeping for those whose names were washed away in their own innocent blood.

Chewing anxiously on her bottom lip out of habit, Aurianna sighed as she sat by the window and stared off into the inky blackness of the night. Back at home, the events of the day seemed almost surreal. She kept reminding herself that she hadn't imagined them, that Damon had been there as well.

She saw the rain merely as a backdrop to the loneliness she always felt deep down in her thoughts and dreams. The downpour might as well have been a solid wall for all the isolation it caused.

Daytime wasn't much better, but when the Darkness seized

hold, the world stood still. Yet it had not always been so. Some still lived who remembered the sunlight—brilliant rays that had been diluted but still enough to live with happily. The dark of night did not pervade the very air back then. Night was simply a time to rest, a time to think.

But now it refused to leave. One day, the sun had turned its back on all of them, and the Darkness had taken over.

Aurianna could sense something. A change was coming. For better or for worse, she couldn't tell. The only thing she knew was she was as unhappy as the rest of the small society of people who inhabited her world, no matter the forced smile she plastered on her face whenever she left the house. Aunt Larissa could see it, she was certain. She couldn't hide her pent-up emotions from the woman. Larissa seemed to possess some sixth sense about her, an uncanny way of knowing Aurianna's mind without her even speaking.

She turned to Larissa, who was busy cooking in the kitchen. "Auntie, do you think it will be warmer soon? I'm thoroughly miserable in this chill."

"Well, throw another log on the fire, child! You know very well there's little hope of it getting warmer." A sudden emptiness entered the woman's eyes for a moment, but when she blinked, it was gone. "Nonsense. I'm speaking nonsense. Of course there's hope. There's always hope." Suddenly, she smiled. "And what would you hope for on your birthday? You've only got one more day to decide."

Her birthday. Normally, she would have been thrilled, but ever since the cold of the Nivalis season had stubbornly refused to leave and make way for the warmer days of Solaris, she had felt the melancholy creeping in further. Without the warm season between the long expanses of chill, every day brought them closer to a constriction on the rations. Even with everything else, that was one thing they hadn't had to worry about before. Everyone had enough to get by, and the daylight hours had normally offered slivers of sunshine peeking through the solid mass of gray clouds overhead—clouds which never moved.

Aunt Larissa had told her tales of the days when the sun shone bright upon the land. No one seemed to know why the sky had abandoned them to the Darkness below. Exactly half of every day was spent in complete and total black, the other half in murky gray. Only the candles and glowing hearths offered a respite from the inky blackness. No one was allowed out of their homes during those hours. No one was even tempted. The Darkness was an ever-present fear stroking their hearts, occasionally squeezing hard enough to provoke someone into embracing a tightly woven noose.

Aurianna hadn't known any of those people personally, but she'd heard stories. The elderly lady across the way had an older daughter who'd been married off years before Aurianna's memory. The young woman had taken her own life with a newborn babe in the next room lying innocently in the arms of the husband she also left behind to grieve. Some people said it was the melancholy many mothers felt following the birth of a child. But the old woman insisted the Darkness had gotten to her, that her daughter had spoken of strange dreams, a sign of the Darkness taking hold of the mind and crushing all hope.

Hope was all that was left to them. Without it to cling to, it was no wonder some felt the only way out was at the end of a rope.

Trying desperately to shake the morbid thoughts from her mind, Aurianna pulled herself up from the floor and went to feed the fire in the hearth, their only source of warmth. Little comfort there. She stoked the dying embers, trying unsuccessfully to switch her brain into thinking about what she would like to do for her birthday.

Without warning, the fire crackled, sizzling and churning out of control in a matter of seconds within the small nook and threatening to engulf the entire area, stone and all. Aurianna leaped backward, fearful she'd set the place afire.

Her aunt was standing beside her in an instant. "I told you to put *one* log on. What happened?" The threatening inferno had already settled back into a cozy radiance. The image was still seared into her brain, however, as if the flames themselves had crept inside her mind, unbidden.

"I didn't put any on it yet. I was stirring up the coals first, and it just... happened. I don't know." She looked at her aunt, trying to make sense of the situation.

Larissa was staring at her with an enigmatic expression, leaning on the back of a chair and breathing heavily. The woman's intense gaze was making Aurianna feel awkward and uncomfortable. Even though she wasn't Aurianna's blood relative, Larissa had always treated her and obviously cared for her as a daughter. Finally, her aunt said, "Yes. Fire is a funny thing." Then she turned and looked at the fireplace, adding, "You must be careful in the future. Keep it under control. Always remember control is the key." And with that cryptic statement, she returned to the kitchen. Aurianna began to feel very, very small as she stood in the tiny room, all alone with her thoughts. She felt as if the world were caving in on her.

She turned back to the fire with no thought of the extra wood now, deciding the chill was, in fact, rooted deep within her.

And there was only one thing to do.

Chapter 3

AURIANNA

On the morning of her twentieth birthday, Aurianna woke up early to the sound of nothing.

On warmer days, the sounds of children playing and people out on the streets could be heard. But this day was just like the one before, and the one before that.

The bitter cold seemed to have no end, a fact that put Aurianna into a sour mood the moment she opened her eyes. She remembered the days when the Solaris season lasted for almost half the year, the pleasant breezes cooling off the heated land instead of this damned bone-jarring wind and snow. She missed the balance. Not too warm, not too cold. It made the long days of Nivalis, the cold season, far more bearable knowing even a small bit of warmth was coming their way.

Now it seemed as if those days were merely fleeting dreams, with the reality of what life truly was only now hitting them all. She *did* dream of Solaris from time to time, and with sharp clarity—a bittersweet reminder of what they once had and might never see again.

No, she refused to allow herself to think that way. This was merely a hardship to endure, like any other. The clouds would move again, and warm rays would radiate down. Soon. Very soon.

Looking in the mirror, she decided running a brush through her hair would be a good idea before she saw anyone. At all. She dressed quickly, with little thought given to which tunic and pants she put on. All muted shades, all similar designs—it was all the same. And the thin, shapeless material was never quite enough to keep the chill out.

Treading softly in case her aunt was still asleep, she grabbed her overcoat and headed off into the crisp, early morning air. She and her friends had all agreed to meet at Kareena's home that morning before going to pick up their labor assignments. Kareena had promised them all a cup of warm spiced cider, a rare and welcome treat on a morning such as this. Aurianna had agreed to come, as always—especially since it was her birthday, and they would all be expecting her.

She didn't hate them. She had no desire to push them away completely. But she would never trust a single one of them again. No one seemed to sense the distance between them, though, so she carried on as normal—careful to hide her feelings, if only to keep some sort of connection.

Aurianna hesitated as she opened the door to leave, wondering for a moment if perhaps it would be better just to cut all ties with them.

When she had set out to leave that night almost a year ago, a bag filled with everything she owned on her back and a head full of the desire to explore, she had never expected to be the only one to show. She had waited at the edge of town for over two hours past the time they had agreed to meet. They planned to all set out together to see what their world had in store for them, to test the boundaries placed on them and find a better way of life, collectively dreaming of other lands, other climates, other anything.

But no one else had shown up. Not one.

Aurianna had tried to push the emotions down deep, to swallow the disappointment and hurt. She had finally gone out to explore on her own. Determined to find a better way—the others be damned.

She had gotten as far as the group of hills just beyond sight of the village before the Praefects caught up to her. The journey back was made in silence. She had nothing to say, and she had known her punishment would be severe. But none of it compared to the pain of betrayal.

They had all betrayed her. How else would the Consils have known?

The sudden appearance of Praefects had signaled a trip straight to the Consils' audience chamber. And that never ended well for anyone.

Her punishment had consisted of a special mark they gave to anyone attempting to escape—a very rare occurrence, but it did happen. The mark was a small finger-length branding of the word *effugere*—a word meaning "runaway" in the old language—on the top of her right shoulder blade.

She had been treated to an entire moon cycle in solitary confinement as well, a small room dedicated to "reeducating" the lost. Each day she had been forced to listen to a different Praefect drone on and on and on and on. All about how dangerous it was to leave, how well taken care of they were, how swift the Darkness would get them. All the things they had drilled into them as children and throughout their school years.

She had known. But she hadn't been afraid. She had followed curfew her entire life, but dreadful stories notwithstanding, she hadn't been afraid. At least, not of the Darkness. Something chilled her to her core. Something that was *not right*. But it wasn't the Darkness.

The only emotion she had felt at the time was rage—a burning anger for the ones who had given her up to retribution, to a justice that was anything but. How could they have done it? Their cowardice had been the first betrayal. Leaving her to journey alone, after all their talks, all their plans. All their dreams.

Then, the ultimate betrayal: they had snitched on her. Every last one of them had gone to the Consils, begging them to find and stop her before it was too late. But that revelation came later, Faethe pleading with her to understand they were only trying to help her and that it was *just too dangerous*.

Dangerous. Danger had already invited itself in. Danger was lurking everywhere as their crops slowly dwindled. Promises of a better way of life from the Consils never amounted to anything but words swept away with each passing day. Who were they to tell her—a grown woman—where she could go?

But Aurianna had conceded. Mostly because she knew her aunt was thoroughly disappointed in her, and she hated upsetting the only person in the world who truly cared about her. She knew how lucky she was.

Thinking about Aunt Larissa as she stood at the front door, Aurianna reminded herself that today was her twentieth birthday. Yet she briefly considered skipping the cider altogether. It wasn't that good anyway.

To hell with all of them, she thought as she stepped outside.

But the wind, which seemed to have gained in intensity since the previous evening, spurred Aurianna on, grumbling the entire way to her friend's house. *If they want to keep pretending nothing happened, so will I*, she thought. Her birthday didn't seem like the best day to start a fight, especially since the meet-up had been, at least in part, organized to celebrate it. And there would be a fight if she didn't show up, at least with Faethe, who would certainly want to know the reason. If Aurianna told her the truth, Faethe would immediately get defensive. And if she lied . . . well, Faethe could tell when she was lying. And, really, there was no excuse for not stopping by on her way to the labor lines. Not a good one, anyway.

She'd lost some deep connection with all her friends, even Faethe. No matter how hard she tried, the connection seemed to dissolve faster and faster. Faethe was still the best friend she had, but even still, that bond had been broken the day her trust in all of them had been shattered.

She was so absorbed with her inward brooding she didn't see the old man in time, colliding with his slight frame at a pace that nearly knocked him off his feet. Naked fear ran through her. She didn't recognize him, but he could have been a Consil in town on business. His age and bearing certainly heightened the possibility.

He stopped, staring into her eyes so intently she almost forgot her manners. "My apologies, sir." Quickly lowering her gaze, she continued on her way. Several paces down the road, she could still feel his eyes on her back. Terrified he was indeed someone quite important, Aurianna practically ran the rest of the way. She forced herself not to look back, keeping her eyes on the path in front of her, careful to avoid making the same mistake twice.

When Kareena's home came into view, Aurianna sighed with relief. Surely if the man had wanted to punish her, he would have caught up to her already. She quickly ducked into the house and the waiting heat within.

*   *   *

"You're joking, right?" Faethe said as she pushed another clump of golden hair back behind her ear.

Aurianna watched as her friend reached across for another basket of wool. Surrounded by the textile machines, she was thankful that fate had decided to go easy on her today. Spinning wool was paradise compared to lugging corpses around. "I keep telling you to tie your hair back. I'd hate to see it caught in the spindle. Again."

Faethe blushed at the memory. "Okay, Aurianna. You're changing the subject. How can I take you seriously?"

"Because I'm being dead serious."

"And your only witness to back you up is . . . *Damon?*" Faethe's eyebrows shot up knowingly, a hint of mocking amusement in the gesture.

Aurianna glared at her semi-best friend, embarrassed and hurt at the insinuation. It was one kiss. One stupid kiss she now regretted with every ounce of her being. There was nothing wrong with Damon, and the kiss hadn't been bad.

But it had felt like kissing her brother.

Growing up, they were both part of the same group of friends, and although Faethe had been her closest friend since before she could remember, Damon had always been someone she could count on. In her naivete, she had thought things could remain that way.

Then time did what it's best at. It passed. And they grew up.

Damon decided a few years ago that they would fall in love, get married, and have kids. Aurianna had no idea what to say to him. She didn't want to hurt his feelings, but she had always known he would never be more than a friend.

She certainly had never led him on at any point.

Did I?

Either way, the chasm that would have opened from that little confession would have been the end of their friendship. Aurianna knew this. She saw it in the way he looked at her, his hazel eyes gazing with something she wished he didn't feel. Silly, stupid boy.

Not a boy, she sighed to herself, any more than she was still a girl. Despite Auntie's protectiveness of her, they both knew Aurianna was now a grown woman. Almost. Some days she felt much older than nineteen—*twenty now*, she reminded herself—but some days she still felt like a child lost in the wilderness.

Her birthday was turning out just *peachy* so far. Grinding her spinning wheel down to a halt as she lifted her foot from the pedal, she said, "I'll have you know he's the first one who noticed the man wasn't dead."

This was a mistake. She could see that already, but it was too late to take it back now. Despite her distrust of Faethe, Aurianna had decided to take a chance, hoping she would back her up this time. The past had shown Faethe's true colors, but Aurianna was desperate. She didn't want to do this alone, and asking Damon was out of the question. He would no doubt get the wrong idea.

"Says you. Come on! He would agree to anything you say. Not exactly a reliable witness."

"Why are you insisting I'm lying?" Aurianna whispered furiously.

Faethe sighed. "It's not that I think you're lying, Aurianna. I'm sure something happened. The guy probably did say some things, but he was clearly out of his head. The whole business about them being from the past and all? That's just crazy talk. How does it even make sense? If people in the past could travel through time, wouldn't we already know about it? Think about it, Aurianna. Doesn't add up, does it?"

She knew her friend had a point, the very nagging point that had been bothering her since she and Damon had spoken to the man—the *Kinetic*—in the Consilium. If time travel already existed, why wouldn't they know about it? But the man had been so sincere. And Aurianna had felt a pity she could not explain, deep down where her darkest thoughts lay, buried under ashes and smoke.

Why would the Consils drain their powers? Is that how they got the electrical power for the Consilium? If that was the case, considering the number of bodies being burned regularly, wouldn't they have enough for everyone? What were they doing with all the power they took? It simply didn't make sense for them to hoard it since the factories and the mills kept everyone alive, including themselves, and the ancient machines standing motionless inside those buildings would help increase productivity on a massive scale. Presumably. If electricity worked the way she thought it did.

Shaking her head in frustration, she realized exactly what she needed to say. "No, Faethe. No, it doesn't add up. That's why I want to go watch."

"Watch what?" The trepidation in the girl's eyes glittered on the surface as a raw form of nervous energy.

Aurianna glared at Faethe for a moment, then in a whisper so soft she barely heard her own words, she said, "A culling."

* * *

Aurianna had never seen a man fall from the sky before. She'd heard the rumors. But never did she think she would actually witness something so incredibly surreal. Despite being an almost daily occurrence, the actual reality of witnessing a culling made her skin crawl for some reason.

Yet here she was, creeping silently into the largest warehouse on the edge of town, snaking her way through columns of stacked containers. She trembled despite her layers of warmth, ecstatic yet fearful to be a witness to such a thing, wondering if she should have stayed at home in bed.

Birthdays being what they were, she was exhausted. She had insisted she wanted nothing at all for her birthday: no party, no cake, no gifts. So—after the party which, of course, consisted of cake and gifts—she had gone to her room, only one thing on her mind. Faethe had followed close behind—at least no one else had shown up—sighing in resignation. The girl knew exactly where Aurianna had been headed as they'd slipped out her bedroom window.

Now here they were, hunkered down in a huge agricultural shed.

She heard a small shuffling sound behind her. She turned and watched as Faethe, having changed her mind, wound through the maze of piled containers. Aurianna laid a hand on the girl's shoulder to reassure her. Faethe was undoubtedly terrified, as was she. But this was an opportunity to witness something Aurianna was dying to know about. Were these men and women able to transport themselves from a past or a future time? And how did they do it?

Why were they really here? Was it for the reasons she'd always been told, or had the dying man spoken true? She had to know.

Unable to explain, even to herself, why she had such a deep desire to know the truth, she stood motionless, barely breathing, waiting for the inevitable moment.

The Carpos were Praefects who had been delegated as soldiers for these very occurrences. They would arrive soon. They always did.

Curiosity got the better of her as she—ever so slowly—began to slither her way around the corner of the box in front of her to the column just ahead. The stack of boxes provided cover to shield her from the eyes of the Carpos yet offered a much too tempting vantage point for viewing the strange being. She peeked through the open gap in the wall of the warehouse where the two sides of an enormous sliding door had been pulled apart.

A swarm of Carpos had gathered on the horizon in the distance like a murder of crows, flocking to the scent of doomed flesh, hungry for action and thirsting for blood. The streaks of lightning that could be seen from town whenever one of the "visitors" arrived were blinding up close. The timing usually seemed to be around dusk, a fact she had been counting on. And she wasn't disappointed.

The clouds spat a human-shaped figure out over the field before them with a force so powerful it made her teeth rattle in her head. The resounding echo clattered off the walls of their shelter into the area behind them.

Before the man had even touched the ground, the Carpos were bearing down upon him with a fierce swiftness.

He—for it was most certainly a man—fell from the sky, only slowing his descent a meter from the ground then landing softly on his feet. He was a man like none she had ever seen. There was certainly something different about him, something unknowable yet unquestionably distinct from any person she'd ever known. A fierce energy flowed from him in waves that rolled across the expanse between them, nearly knocking her over in its intensity.

That other man—the one who had exacted a promise from her, the man who had died on a faded rug in the heart of the Consilium with two strangers by his side, the man whose name she would never know—he had possessed that same unique quality, though whatever it was had been fading even before he had spoken. If his power had once been like this, she truly pitied the frail creature he had become. This was raw power. She didn't understand it, but she could feel it emanating from the vicinity of the being before her.

Upon landing, the man crouched, his head swiveling and trying to take in his surroundings. Then he turned, spying the figures of the Carpos heading in his direction and looming closer every second. Their gait was purposeful, their faces intent on their prey.

A frantic whisper at her back broke her focus, but Aurianna kept her eyes on the tense scene playing out. "Aurianna, please. Can we please go home now? You've seen it. He'll be captured, and you can't be considering following him to the Consilium, right?"

Faethe's eyes reflected the hidden plea in those words: *Please don't drag me any further into this insanely dangerous plan!*

Considering, yes. But even hearing the word *Consilium* shook her resolve to its core and withered any ideas she'd had of doing that very thing. *Faethe is right*, Aurianna realized. Following them would be reckless and stupid and would probably end up getting them killed. They would watch the arrest but go no further.

The stranger finally seemed to realize his immediate danger. A look of sheer terror eclipsed his face, followed by one of morbid resolve. He began to move, sprinting away from the Carpos and . . . straight toward their hiding place in the warehouse.

Faethe uttered a muffled squeal before Aurianna gripped her forearm, dragging them both sideways through the maze of boxes, praying the man would continue straight through the warehouse.

When he flew by on the other side of their cover, Aurianna breathed a sigh of relief. But now they were trapped. The Carpos would follow the man until he was captured. Aurianna and Faethe's only avenue of escape was now the open wall in front of them leading out into the field where the man had landed. If they went that way, they would risk being seen by anyone out in the fields.

Staying where they were was not an option. The rhythmic plodding of heavy boots signaled the imminent arrival of the Carpos. Any moment they would enter the labyrinth of boxes in pursuit of the trespasser, eager in their search but not so focused on him that she and Faethe were likely to go unnoticed. They could only hope the group would stay close to one another and allow them to scuttle across the room, away from the ensuing chase and around the front of the boxes to safety. If even one of the Carpos strayed from the pack, the odds would increase that they would be caught.

And being caught at a landing zone was a death sentence.

Faethe was squirming in her grasp, a look of mute horror on her pale face. Aurianna took off in the direction of the side wall, pulling her friend along, both of them keeping their heads far below the tops of the containers. Weaving among the scattered rows, putting as many layers of cover between them and the path of the Carpos as possible, they finally reached the wall and began to sneak forward to open sky.

At the last moment, as if pulled by an unseen hand, they both ran forward out of the stifling building, a haven turned prison in a moment's time. Aurianna slid her back against the front of the structure, collapsing on the ground, panting from their exertion.

"Well, that was fun," she said between staggered breaths.

Faethe stared at her friend with a mix of awe and indignation. "How can you joke at a time like this? Your stupid curiosity almost got us killed, Aurianna! And for what? We barely got a glimpse of the man, much less the arrest that's probably occurring at this moment. We're lucky it isn't *our* arrest after what just happened."

"I know. I'm sorry, Faethe." Aurianna was panting as she yanked the girl down into the shadows with her. "But weren't you just a little bit curious, too? I mean, a man just appeared out of the clouds and fell to the ground without breaking a bone in his body. If the Consils are right about them being travelers from the future, why are they here? What do they want? And what if the man I spoke with was right? Something *is* different about them. I could sense it. A raw kind of power that—"

"Does it matter? They can detect them coming now. The Consils say they're bad news, Aurianna. Isn't that enough? They get here, they're captured, so no harm done. But we almost got caught in the middle of it. Is this worth dying for? Hasn't your aunt repeatedly warned you and told you to stay away from them? And was this really how you wanted to spend your birthday?"

She was right. And wrong. Aurianna felt the deep rift between them widening as old resentments rose to the surface, threatening to choke her in their intensity. She'd made a mistake in bringing the silly girl, thinking she could make her see and sense what her indifference and fear had blinded her from. "No, of course it's not worth our lives! I just…I just feel like something's…wrong with all of this." If the man—the Kinetic as he called himself—was telling the truth, something was indeed very wrong.

"Well, doesn't everyone? I mean, hell, Aurianna, this is serious stuff. No one wants to mess with it. Including me, in case you couldn't tell." Faethe's eyes suddenly traveled over the slowly darkening ground at their feet, flitting up momentarily to throw a pointed gaze in Aurianna's direction. Then she tilted her head with a puzzled look on her face, the enveloping dimness of dusk casting strange shadows around her dark untethered locks. The effect made the hairs on the back of Aurianna's neck stand on end even before she heard the boom and turned to witness the flash of light in the far distance, followed by an eerily familiar scene of something falling, falling through the dusky sky.

* * *

Aurianna told Faethe she needed time to think and begged the girl to return home without her. Faethe immediately protested, fearful she planned to follow the Carpos and their captive to the Consilium. But Aurianna insisted and swore she would do no such thing. This was a promise she did not intend to keep.

The irony was not lost on her. Her friends hadn't kept their promises on that fateful night they had betrayed her, so she couldn't find it in herself to feel any guilt.

As soon as Faethe rounded the corner up ahead, Aurianna turned back, heading toward the bright lights of the Consilium.

Rumors flew that the electricity was used for more than just lighting. Supposedly, the cooks in the kitchens had functional electric ovens for cooking, something Aunt Larissa would love to have. But the electric ovens in their houses had no power, just a forlorn look from years and years of being completely useless, sitting in a corner gathering dust. The Consils said they were working on getting power beyond their own structure, but after a long time of promises with no results, the people had given up hope. The old ways were just fine with them.

Staying in the shadows of the approaching Darkness, she slipped around the sides of homes and buildings with surprising ease. Most of the residents were already indoors, mindful of the curfew. Soon, only she and the patrolling Praefects would be outside.

The Darkness was gathering into itself, blackness creating nothing where objects and structures once were. She stumbled in the inky void, occasionally bumping into walls, falling over unknown objects left in dark corners. The cobblestone streets were gone, replaced with a dark cloud. She would have had no sense of direction if it weren't for a muted glow in the distance. All she knew was the silence of everything, save the occasional laughter or bit of loud conversation from within a home.

Eventually, the electric lights of the Consilium revealed vague shapes among the shadows. Aurianna made toward those lights, grateful for their existence this once, relieved they pinpointed her destination.

Upon reaching what she thought was probably the left side entrance at the far back, the access closest to where the prisoners were kept, she stopped and listened. Sounds of muffled conversation met her ears, but she could not discern words. Creeping closer, she was finally able to see once again.

Aurianna knew the warmth she felt upon walking inside the building was another offering from the strange energy. Again, only the Consilium enjoyed this luxury. She assumed the mechanism for circulating the geothermal heat was hidden far below the structure.

Deep in the bowels of the premises—somewhere apart from everything else—dwelled the Arcanes. They kept the old records and rarely emerged from among the ancient books and scrolls. But on the rare occasion she'd run into one during her duties, they had been polite and cheerful—unlike some of the Praefects. Those who earned *that* title seemed to have a natural penchant for discourtesy.

All around her were statues of unknown and long-forgotten people lining the walls. To her right, the wall ended halfway down the length of the structure. The hallway straight ahead of her continued for some time before rounding a corner. She had never been down that way. Nevertheless, she knew to avoid it. She'd heard rumors that Praefects stood guarding the door back into the main entrance hall and audience chamber. The entire structure existed as a circle within a square, one level above ground and one level below. She was on the left side of the square, near the back of the building's interior, and only Praefects would have any business being here or going through the door.

Each top-level corner possessed an entrance and a staircase, but she had known the one opposite her on the back right would have given her away to the guards immediately. Consils, Arcanes, and anyone else who worked at the Consilium could come and go as they pleased, as far as she knew. The only doors the rest of them were supposed to use were the main one for official business or the front right entrance to report for labor duties.

Her objective was the staircase on her left, located in the corner of the square. Aurianna made her way down to the bottom level. The burning pit was in the very center on the bottom level, just on the other side of the stone wall of the narrow hallway she had entered. The larger area with the pit contained four holes spaced evenly around the circumference of the ceiling, allowing the air to travel up through identical holes in the top floor, all the way to the roof of the structure. Long tubing stretched the height of the upper level, at least as far as she had ever seen, allowing most of the foul air to eventually leave the building. The walls and floors protected them from the boiling magma which churned just below the surface of the planet and continued down into the unknown depths of its core. It was all around her now. The thought of all the raw power just beyond the stone barrier nearly suffocated her. Despite the lack of the stench from the burning pit, the atmosphere in the hallway was almost unbearable. Yet she *was* able to bear it when she was assigned to move the corpses and face the horrid smell of burning flesh, so she told herself she could do it for this.

This? What was she even doing here?

A heartbeat later she had her answer as she craned her head to the left and saw the row of caged cells spanning the length of the narrow hallway, all along the outer wall. Scores of them.

She couldn't move. She couldn't speak. She forgot to breathe. Her heart almost forgot to beat, the shock lasting much longer than the space of time required for it to do so.

Another heartbeat passed, and then the frantic whispers began.

CHAPTER 4

AURIANNA

The people in the cages knew not to cry out, knew they'd risk alerting the guards who were most likely just inside the room at the far end of the hallway. They couldn't have this many prisoners without someone close by.

A few enclosures down, a man with the kindest eyes Aurianna had ever seen was sitting on his knees, his hands outstretched beyond the bars keeping him imprisoned. He brought his fingertips together, fingers spread apart, a strange gesture that caught her attention.

Those kind eyes suddenly exploded into raw, naked fear the moment he took a closer look at her. The man backed away from the bars, shaking his head violently. He nestled into the corner of his cage, trying to make himself as small as possible. Aurianna quietly edged her way closer to him, ignoring the whispered pleading from the others. She could not help them.

As she approached, the man continued to stare at her, fear paralyzing him even as his eyes followed her every movement.

Gradually, a forced but knowing smile crept onto his dirt-smeared face. His voice was barely audible. "You're here."

"I . . ." Suddenly, she felt a fierce desire to run. She couldn't risk being punished. Again.

The man scooted forward and grabbed her arm through the bars as she hesitated and started to head back toward the stairs. "It's alright. I understand, I think. But, just tell me, why are you here? Surely not to rescue dozens of prisoners. Not by yourself. You can't help us." He craned his neck to look behind her. "Is someone with you?" he added hopefully.

His fear was contagious, her inclination to run nearly overwhelming, but she pushed it down and whispered, "No, I just came for answers. I want to know the truth."

The man just nodded his head slowly, dropping his gaze from her face to stare at the floor beneath him.

"What's your name? I'm Aurianna." The image of the nameless, dying man floating before her eyes.

"Lucas," he replied.

Aurianna began again, hesitantly. "There was a man. He . . . he told me your people are Kinetics and you come from the past? I didn't want to believe him—that the Consils were doing this just to drain you of your . . . your power." She said the last part awkwardly, unsure of how to feel or talk about the strange new concept. "Is it true? You have magic?"

He shook his head. "We don't personally refer to it as magic, but control over the elements, yes. My strength was with earth. Rock and stone."

"Was?" she asked, already knowing what he was going to say.

"As soon as we're captured, they drain us enough to keep us from using our powers. We're then taken one at a time into the room down there. The screams are awful, worse than the initial draining."

33

He looked at her again with woeful eyes. "The ones who go that way don't come back."

Aurianna thought for a moment, frowning. "Well, one did. For a moment, at least. He was alive long enough to explain some things to me. Why you're here. What the Consils and the Praefects are doing to your people." She choked on the last bit, trying not to imagine the smell of the burning pit and the bodies as they went up in flames.

"Please don't cry. There is hope, of that I'm now certain. You're here. None of this will matter if things are changed."

"I don't understand."

The man sighed deeply. "Listen to me. The Consils of your time are doing this because they're scared. Scared of what we might do here. Scared of our power. They think we've come to take over your tiny group of survivors." He shook his head. "This world was once filled with people. In my time, Eresseia was a thriving place with many regions and many opportunities. You and your people are all that's left because of . . . something . . . our kind did. Something terrible happened that caused the Consils, and the world, to fear us, to hunt us down like animals and rid Eresseia of anything they deem "magic." I know it sounds terrible—and it is—but it all started because one of our own decided to do something reprehensible, and the rest of us have paid dearly."

When he stopped to take a breath, she asked, "Eresseia? Is that the name of this world?"

"Ay, it is. I'm not surprised you didn't know. The point is this must be stopped. It will be, and none of this will matter."

"But how is it going to be stopped? It already happened a long time ago."

"The Arcanes said it could be stopped. But only when the prophecy is fulfilled. You see, right now we can't go back to our time without a piece of the Aether Stone. We can't warn our brothers and sisters not to come here. But once the prophecy is complete, all of this will melt away into the Aether, and none of it will have happened."

Aurianna's head hurt. It was too much. Too much information. Too many questions. After listening again for sounds from the guard room, she finally whispered to him, "I don't know what I can do. You were right before. I can't help you. I wish like hell I could, but I just can't."

The Kinetic smiled at her. "Doesn't matter. Like I said, none of this will have happened."

"But it is happening!" She peeked back down the hall as her voice started to rise despite her attempts to stay calm.

"Yes, but only in this reality. In my time, everything will be fixed, and I'll still be there."

The realization finally hit her with a sudden chill, like a bucket of cold water. "That means I won't be here, most likely. If this horrible event that occurred never happens, then whatever happened as a result won't have happened, and my time—my reality—won't be anything like it is now. Meaning I'll probably never have been born. You're talking about trading my life for yours." Not even sure if she was making any sense, Aurianna felt her anger trying to seep around the edges of the wall she kept in front of her deepest emotions.

A look of shame spread across the man's face like a shade being pulled, his concern apparent. "Oh, child, I didn't mean to upset you. That's not necessarily the case. No one can know the future. Not the one that hasn't happened yet, anyway. Besides, you're going to be just fine this time."

"What?" she hissed, shaking her head and backing away.

Enough. She had had enough.

Aurianna took off down the hallway, making far more noise than she intended. But she *had* to get out of there. She knew Larissa would be furious with her for being out after curfew, but there was nothing to be done about it now.

None of this made any sense to her befuddled brain. Was any of it true? Could her existence really be wiped out? How could he think it was okay to erase the lives of so many people to save those of these Kinetics she'd never met?

But was any of it true? Was it possible to go back and change the past? If they could travel forward in time, why couldn't they go back? He said they needed a stone. An *Aether Stone*, he'd called it. Time travel? Could her brain even accept that basic piece of the puzzle? The Consils claimed it was true, but considering they were obviously not to be trusted…

Yes. She definitely believed in the time travel part of this man's story. The rest was a big question mark. But why would he lie? He gained nothing from it and hadn't even encouraged her to help him.

It was going to be a long, long journey home with the weight of the world on her mind and in her heart.

Aurianna left the confines of the Consilium and started on the long, winding road which was the most direct path home. Lost in thought, she was startled by the appearance of a large shadow before her, the details of its form lost in the Darkness. Frozen by a nameless fear, she stood rooted to the ground, unable to move or speak, certain the Darkness had finally caught up with her.

The figure continued to move toward her, gradually becoming more distinct.

His facial features were suddenly clear in the scant light emanating from the electric lights of the Consilium. Dark hair fluttered in the gentle night breeze. Stubble covered the man's chin in the same hue. He had pale skin with strikingly blue eyes that shone nearly violet in the glow from the Consilium.

As he came closer, she noticed he was dressed strangely. *Like the people in the cages. The Kinetics.*

She ran.

* * *

As she attempted to sneak by the kitchen and into her room, she was accosted by a wooden spoon and a petite, middle-aged woman who looked for all the world like a crazed mother hen.

"Are you out of your mind, child? Do you have any idea what time it is? Of course you do. The Darkness cannot have escaped your notice." The spoon was a deadly weapon in her hands, swinging wildly in Aurianna's direction with each gesticulation her aunt made. "How many times do I have to remind you of the importance of following the rules, of avoiding their notice, Aurianna? Do you want to be punished again? How is breaking curfew avoiding their notice?"

Not knowing what to say, words began to tumble from her mouth. "We saw one of them, Auntie. One of those men who—"

Her aunt covered her mouth with her free hand, her eyes wide. "I know bloody well who you mean, girl. No need to speak the words. You never know who's listening. Follow me." She grabbed Aurianna's hand, guiding her into Larissa's bedroom, the innermost room in the house. Picking up the nearly spent candle from her bedside table, her aunt began to pull her in the direction of the closet.

"What are we doing, Auntie?"

"Hush, child! Just follow me."

The woman dragged Aurianna into the tight quarters, pulling back a rug and lifting a section of floor to reveal a ladder. Aurianna had never noticed the odd placement of the rug before. Complete darkness lay beyond, and a sensation of dread began to creep up the back of Aurianna's neck again. As she tried to back away from the dark opening, Larissa shook her head.

"Now, you can trust me, seeing as I've taken care of you your whole life. Or you can walk away and tell me you've got no faith in what I'm doing here. The time is coming, my dear. And I'm afraid I've again failed miserably in preparing you for it. So perhaps your hesitation to trust me has its merits, but you've got few alternatives, I'm afraid."

Aurianna was shaken by the woman's words—especially that word *again*. "Larissa, what is going on? I don't understand. I'm sorry for breaking curfew. I know it was dangerous and all kinds of stupid. But right now, you're scaring me."

Aunt Larissa sighed as her shoulders sagged. "Aurianna, I don't know how to explain things other than to show you. But you have to trust me."

Hesitantly, Aurianna offered her hand to the woman who'd raised her, who'd made a promise to her mother and taken on the responsibility of a child with no blood connection. This woman now pulled her to the edge of the gaping maw and held the candle as far down into the space as she could reach. Aurianna closed her eyes for a second before clambering into the pitch-black space. She felt her way down the rungs of the ladder until she felt the solid ground beneath her. Larissa passed her the candle and made her own way down, promptly shutting the trap door above them.

When Aurianna turned, candle in hand, she could see the space was small and sparsely furnished. A chair nestled beside a round table with a collection of small objects Aurianna did not recognize. A cot lay in the corner, and cobwebs grew from the ceiling in various shapes and lengths.

Larissa was watching her take in the meager surroundings. She smiled sadly. "This was our first home. Back then, we were lucky to have a bed to sleep in, much less anything else. And it was safe. Safe for you, safe for me."

"I, I don't . . . but why, Auntie? Why did we live here? And how could we? I mean, there isn't even—" As she spoke, she noticed an amethyst-colored stone on the table, and a vague memory took shape. She pointed at it. "I remember playing with this when I was very young. No, wait. No, I didn't play with it, but I wanted to." It reminded her of something, something she couldn't quite place.

Her aunt nodded. "You were enthralled by the thing. It was a constant nightmare trying to find new hiding places to keep it out of your reach. But you were so determined. Try explaining things to a toddler that would be hard for even an adult to understand." She stared at Aurianna then, her eyes glassy and unmoving, a thought forming behind them, then it was gone. "And here I am, still trying to figure out how to explain it to you."

"But I remember it was shiny. Like it glowed or something. That's why I wanted it, I think."

"Yes, it used to work. But not anymore. Not that it would have mattered. I put things in place myself, so I certainly couldn't be the one to mess it all up and start things in motion prematurely."

"What does that mean?"

Again, a sigh. "It means, child, the time wasn't right then. I knew it, yet I still kept watch over that thing, hoping for a sign everything was alright, and we could go home."

"But you said *this* was our home."

Larissa paused to consider her words carefully. "Yes, this was our home for a few years. The elderly couple who lived upstairs were very kind. They recognized a need, even if they didn't understand it. They kept us fed, clothed, and basically happy. There was no danger of anyone hearing you crying from this place. But when they died a few years later—within moon cycles of each other, in fact—they had no heirs, so the house was declared vacant. Things were safer then, so I paid the Praefects the housing fees for the first year with money I made from sewing clothing for the neighbors, and we moved into the house proper. You were still too young to remember much, I'm sure. You were only a small infant when we first came to live in this room." She scanned the small space, a touch of wistfulness in her glances despite its current state.

"What did you mean by *go home*, then? Go home where?" Her confusion turning to anger, Aurianna felt it taking over the longer she stood there. The candle's flame danced wildly around as if it, too, were resentful of her aunt's guarded words.

"I know I'm not doing this very well. But I can't . . ." Larissa's voice faded to a whisper, her eyes sinking to the ground. Suddenly, the woman lifted her gaze again, and placing the stone in Aurianna's hand, she waited expectantly.

She remembered then. The necklace. A deep shade of sapphire, it had belonged to her mother, a memento her aunt had given her years ago. She had never seen color that vibrant anywhere else. Until now. Though the oblong crystal in her palm was more purple in hue, and most of its intensity had faded, it somehow reminded her of the dark blue stone in her mother's necklace. Light and dark, dark and light.

After several minutes, the woman took the stone back and held it in the air. "It used to glow . . . because it's made from—well, what you would call magic."

Aurianna just stared for a moment at the woman, struggling for words. When she finally spoke, her voice was low, almost a whisper. "Magic doesn't exist anymore."

"That's true, for the most part. As you can see, the magic within this stone is gone. I had hoped . . . It doesn't matter. I wanted you to see. To remember."

"But why? Why bring me here to show me some rock I fancied as a baby?" She hadn't even been aware she was backing away from her aunt until her back hit the wall behind her with a sudden thump. Aurianna was shaking her head, willing the conversation to be over, terrified someone would hear the secrets being let loose in the small space.

"To prepare you for what's to come, child. And for what has already come to pass. Today is your twentieth birthday, Aurianna. And here I am calling you 'child,' as if you haven't been a grown woman for several years now. A storm is coming, and you must be ready to embrace it."

"I don't even understand what you're talking about. What storm? And what does it have to do with me or my birthday?"

A weary silence followed. Aurianna couldn't tell if her aunt had heard her or not until the woman sat down on the edge of the chair and looked up at her.

"That man you spoke to is a danger to us both. You mustn't go near any of them again, or you risk everything. Both of our lives. Do you understand?"

"I understand." Only she didn't. Not even a little bit. And what had Larissa just said? The part of her mind that drowned in distrust and suspicion immediately went to thoughts of Faethe. She hoped she was wrong. Aurianna narrowed her eyes. "Wait, which man? And how do you know I spoke to them?"

"Them?" her aunt cried.

Wincing, Aurianna turned back to the ladder, hanging her head. She hadn't meant to give away the fact that she'd spoken to *another* Kinetic. How had her aunt known exactly what she meant when she had said "one of them" unless Faethe had dropped in on her way home and told the woman?

A sigh echoed in the space behind her. Larissa placed a gentle hand on her shoulder. "It doesn't matter now. It's getting late. Let's just get out of here."

As they slipped back out of the closet, Aurianna's mind was full of questions she didn't know how to ask. She finally decided to at least tell her aunt about the man with the blue eyes who had accosted her on the way home. Well, perhaps *accosted* was a bit strong, but...

Upon hearing the revelation, Larissa froze in place, a lifetime weaving itself into an instant.

"It's time, then. Go quickly. I'll draw you a bath so you can get ready."

Ready for what?

"But...wait...I thought you said they were a danger to us!"

"Things have changed, dear. And...happy birthday, Aurianna." Larissa held the same purple stone out to her, palm up. "I had thought to see you earlier this evening, and I was going to give you this." Aurianna hesitantly took it, unsure of what to do with it. Her aunt continued, "I know it isn't much, but I think you might want to take it with you. It is, after all, a piece of your home. Our home." With tears in her eyes, she grabbed Aurianna into a fierce embrace.

Larissa pulled back and said, "Just in case I'm wrong about the timing, you can't speak of the hidden room, the stone, or *magic* to anyone." In a daze, Aurianna merely stared. Larissa shooed her in the direction of the bathing room. "Go on then!"

In a way, having the knowledge—even if she didn't understand what it meant—made her feel special. But in a world where being different could prove disastrous, if not fatal, it was certainly best to keep it secret.

Still reeling with her unspoken questions, Aurianna nodded in agreement. She needed to think about everything, and a bath was the perfect setting to ease her tired mind and body.

Stepping into the steaming bathing tub a while later, her muscles already thanking her, Aurianna had hoped for a reprieve from all of this for more than a few minutes.

Destiny had other plans.

Chapter 5

PHARIS

The falling was not unexpected. But the moment Pharis saw the faint outline of the bridge soar upward on his left, he knew there had been a grave miscalculation.

Twisting his body to glance down, Pharis braced himself for the impact with the swirling water below. He felt a moment of blinding pain, the water so cold as to force his eyes open in shock. Next, the lungs screamed for attention, for the next breath, any breath. He aimed for what he presumed was the surface. When his head broke free, he gulped down a blessed lungful of air and glanced wearily at the cliffs above.

So, that's what cliff diving feels like. He had always envied those who could enjoy those luxuries of leisure.

But never again.

He began to swim toward the closer rocks of the small island he knew as home, thinking how much easier this could have been if the need for secrecy had not been so great. He would make his way up the cliff face on this side and . . . but perhaps it would be more prudent to avoid the risk of being seen while crossing the bridge in the open?

No. The night was now black as ink, no moon in sight. He thought it odd but counted himself lucky for once.

Lucky, ha. Luck hadn't been on his side a moment ago when he'd been plummeting down at breakneck speed, his jaw clenched as he braced for impact with the water below. He had tried to reach out and grab at something—anything—but the nothingness below had pulled him down toward the frigid water. The water that was now seeping through every one of his pores as he fought against his body's silent screaming.

Caution was of the utmost importance, but he'd had no choice but to disobey that order and slow himself down just enough to avoid death. If his father and the Arcanes couldn't understand his need for self-preservation, then perhaps they should have chosen someone else.

Or at the very least calculated his landing correctly.

He continued to swim until he reached the bottom of the island's craggy cliffs. He looked up, and even though only the barest outline was visible, Pharis knew he would never make it without the proper tools. The only option was to scale the bridge supports.

He made his way over to the base of the bridge. The trestle soared upward to a dizzying height of over three hundred feet. The only benefit to climbing the metal bridge supports was the availability of handholds, something the cliffs were sorely lacking.

Pharis eventually dragged himself up onto the bridge and trudged, still dripping, toward the edge of town. The darkness would have been disorienting for someone not familiar with the area, but he knew that behind him the bridge led to a building that perched atop the rocky island. Ahead of him, the foot bridge intersected the railroad that ran parallel to the cliff edge on the mainland. The tracks, like the foot bridge, were supported by an iron lattice that crisscrossed down into the waves crashing against it below. As he stepped over the first rusty rail of the abandoned transit system, buckled and in disrepair, the signs of neglect were a punch to his chest.

Abandoned. *How did that even happen?* he wondered. The Arcanes had warned him to expect differences, but still, it made this place seem like a completely different world.

He paused, suddenly feeling the full reality of his situation. This was home. Yet it wasn't. The juxtaposition of the two thoughts left him feeling unnerved. It was going to be an exhaustingly long night.

Muttering to himself, he pushed on. When he reached the mainland and entered the town, Pharis wandered down the first few side streets without encountering a single inhabitant.

The strangeness did not bother him. The only thing that mattered was his target. Everything else was irrelevant. After his long, arduous climb, the fear had vanished, to be replaced with the contempt he had felt at the beginning of the whole endeavor.

This is their plan, not mine. Honestly, he didn't care if he succeeded or not.

But if he succeeded in this mission—which was, in his opinion, going to be more trouble than it was worth—he would have even more trouble when he returned. His horrid bastard of a father had finally gone too far...waiting until the last moment to tell him.

Coward.

He had known Pharis would balk at the mere suggestion, much less an official decree. But no one else knew, other than the Arcanes. He wasn't sure which had formulated the addendum, but his father and the Arcanes seemed to agree on this, for some unimaginable reason. Pharis would never allow it to happen.

Pharis clenched his jaw and shook his head. He crept along in the dark with his even darker thoughts, treading carefully to avoid tripping over his own feet—or something else. Up ahead, a few flickers of candlelight forced their way through the shadows. Cautiously, he peeked around a corner. Seeing no one, he continued slinking down the avenue between houses standing empty and forgotten. Another reminder this was not really his home.

When he reached the area where the candles flickered through curtained and shuttered windows of homes, he realized everyone seemed to be indoors. Not surprising, considering the lack of visibility, the cold, and the evident lateness of the hour.

But there were no guards about, no drunks staggering home, no passersby furtively participating in clandestine adventures. All was still and quiet. And so dark.

This, more than anything, unnerved him to the point of anguished desperation. Why did they send him here? Why him? This was too much to bear. Too much reality to take in.

His uncharacteristic self-doubt and anguish quickly turned to the all-too-familiar anger and frustration. *Where the hell is she? How am I supposed to find her?*

They had warned him not to be seen, not to be spotted, not to let a single person know he was there. His life depended on it. He believed them. Knocking on doors was out of the question. Besides, he had no idea what she looked like.

He continued, less cautious now he knew the streets were empty. Pharis headed onward through town, picking up speed. He had spotted the giant building, a familiar sight at least. The Consilium was the only thing emitting any real light. Not having any concrete objective, he made for the structure with the hope of finding some clue . . . or at least the relief of being able to see his hands in front of his face again. All they had told him was he would find her. No specifics, no guidance, no help of any kind.

The main road sloped upward, bending to the right toward his current goal. Pharis followed the path, his hopes of finding the girl sinking with each trudging, squishing step.

What felt like a lifetime later, as he drew closer to the Consilium, Pharis heard faint scuffling sounds up ahead. Slowing his steps, he listened attentively to confirm his suspicions.

They were definitely footsteps.

Shooting ahead, he turned the corner and stopped almost as quickly. A figure approached, the lights of the Consilium behind casting the dark form in silhouette.

The figure either wasn't aware of his presence or didn't care. It continued moving forward until almost colliding with him. A momentary stillness brought the features of the person into stark relief.

A sharp intake of breath. Pharis wasn't sure which of them had made the sound but had no doubt he had found his quarry.

Amber eyes.

The girl's eyes were literally *glowing*, even in the darkness. A smattering of freckles was visible along her cheekbones and across her nose.

Bloody hell.

She stood frozen, fear etched into those golden orbs that lit up her face. Before he could gather his senses long enough to form any words, the girl turned and peeled down a side street at breakneck speed—hopefully, not literally.

Pharis took in a deep breath and watched the girl's retreating form dissolve into the inky darkness. *What the bloody hell was that?*

It made no sense. Even with limited vision, as close as he'd been, he could clearly see her wildly terrified reaction and something else (anger, perhaps?) on her face. She *had* to know who he was. Well, not exactly who he was. They'd made sure to dress him in a plain style of clothing to ensure his safety and protect his identity. The change was a bit freeing—no one able to recognize him, no responsibilities—

But he still had to find this stupid girl. It had taken Pharis hours—assuming that *had* been her—and now . . . well, now he'd managed to lose her a moment after he'd found her. The description seemed right. The age. The *eyes*—bright flecks of gold glowing against a backdrop of pure amber. Her eyes seemed to give off an unnatural glow, a light all their own. They had been very specific in this respect. And despite her being lit from behind at the time, he had noticed the prominent freckles sprinkled across the pallid skin of her nose and cheeks.

These thoughts flashed through his mind until his legs took over and recognized the need to pursue her before she disappeared completely. The fact that he was the only other living soul out on the streets should have made it a fairly easy job to accomplish. But it was pitch-black, so his vision was useless. He would have to rely on his hearing, willing his steps to fall as silently as possible and his breathing to blend into the background.

Up ahead, he was sure he heard the pitter-patter of footsteps on the surface of the hard-packed ground. Pharis took an instant to stop and listen, then he took off again down an alley just in front of him, veering right. After a moment, he stopped again when he heard the muffled creaking of a door opening. Sure that he'd found her, Pharis moved quickly toward the sound, but by the time he reached the area, a dozen identical doors stared at him, daring him to enter.

Which one?

Pharis turned in circles, hoping for a flicker of movement to guide his path. Nothing. Candles flickered behind curtains and between cracks in shutters, winking beacons that taunted him, mocked him. Well, at least he'd narrowed the mission down a bit. However, he needed to find her tonight. The morning wouldn't do. They had told him it must be tonight, and well before the dawn broke. He wasn't going to argue with the Arcanes. And speaking to his father would have been impossible without his anger taking over, so Pharis had merely nodded his agreement like he had for all the other parts of the plan. It was a detailed plan attached to the emphatically stated importance of the girl: an importance he didn't understand, didn't care about, and didn't wish to waste time arguing over.

The *other* issue was most definitely still up for debate. A conversation his father would not appreciate, but he didn't give a damn how his father felt, considering the man hadn't taken *his* feelings on the matter into account. Not one bit. As he stood mired in his anger over the decision made without his knowledge or consent, Pharis realized he'd lost his focus on the task at hand.

Later, he thought grimly. At the moment, he needed to find the girl and bring her back, leave her at his father's feet, and walk away with the certainty he would play no further part in any of this.

Pharis risked a quick glance through a front window of the closest home. Nothing. Next, he tried each of the windows in the back rooms. The sleeping forms in the beds weren't visible enough to be certain his quarry wasn't there, but they all seemed to be sleeping normally. If she had gone in immediately to her bed without stopping to undress, perhaps she could be clever enough to fake it, but he didn't think this was the case. Plus, she had no reason to assume he would follow her. He hoped.

Pharis repeated the process for every house in the vicinity. Some people were still awake, but, thankfully, no one spotted him. The thought of trying to explain his way out of being caught peeping into windows, especially being dressed as he was, made his blood run cold. Who knew what these people might do to a stranger? Or even one of their own, for that matter.

A few of the houses stood empty. One of them, vines entwined along every outer wall, crisscrossing in a complex pattern, had several candles burning inside. Surely someone was about if candles had been lit, but where? He'd checked every room via the windows. Not a soul was within the home. Could she have taken off again before Pharis had reached her door? Had she noticed him lurking around and taken an opportunity to run when he was behind one of the buildings? He didn't think so, partly because of the noise, but mainly because she was supposed to be living with an older woman who was taking care of her. A woman who was supposed to know exactly what to expect and when.

But hadn't he just seen the turmoil in the girl's eyes? Was the fear that had caused her to run from him based on knowledge or ignorance? He'd been told the girl was being prepared for her part in this game, that she would go with him willingly. Had the Arcanes been wrong? Had the woman never told her anything, or was the truth the very thing that had caused her flight? He'd drag her back against her will, if need be, but he hadn't prepared for that option.

The night was sure to be exhausting either way.

Then Pharis heard sounds coming from the vine-covered house with the candles, sounds of muffled voices followed by water being poured. He rushed over, careful to keep his head down, and peeked through the front window. A woman—slightly bent with age, her long brown hair a stubborn contrast without a hint of gray—was walking into the room carrying an empty bucket. She turned and made her way into the adjacent room, a kitchen by the looks of it. It was hard to tell with the briefest of glances he allowed himself.

He began to walk around the structure again, this time with slightly higher hopes. As he passed under a back window, the sound of a female voice reached his ears. A young female, he thought. Pharis smiled to himself and tilted his head slightly up and to the side in order to investigate the room.

There she was, the girl with the amber eyes. The Arcanes had only told Pharis to search, and he would find her. No description other than the eyes. When he had run into her on the street, Pharis had hoped he'd found the object of his mission before he even saw her eyes, but when he had seen those shining golden orbs staring back at him, he had known.

And now, here they were again, those liquid amber eyes. The girl was muttering to herself it seemed, in an obvious state of anxiety. Her skin wasn't as pale as he had originally thought, but it wasn't quite as dark as his own. The shade was light enough to provide contrast for the freckles that danced across her skin, but...

Stop.

Pharis could only see her face from the mouth up, the only other feature he could distinguish was hair the color of copper.

This was it. Now or never. He had to bring the girl back *tonight*. The Arcanes, and his father, had been adamant about that fact.

Sneaking back around to a side window, Pharis checked to make sure no one was in the room before silently opening the window, pulling himself up and crawling over the ledge. Now he needed to locate the room where he'd just seen her. Carefully, he crept across the floor and peered around the doorway. Nothing in the hallway. Pharis stepped around the corner and moved down to the next door, the door to the room the girl was occupying.

The door was partly open. Pharis could hear nothing over the beating of his heart. Why was he nervous? He had no idea. He wanted to go home. He was tired of playing someone else's game. Tired of catering to his father's wishes. This would be the last time.

Pharis pushed the door further open as he strode into the room, fully aware the girl would be frightened again. But his patience had worn thin, and he was fully prepared to snatch her up and walk out the front door. At least he had her cornered now. There was nowhere she could hide.

The moment he was fully in the room, taking in the layout as he proceeded further, he realized his mistake.

Then the screaming began.

Chapter 6

AURIANNA

The last place Aurianna expected to meet the strange man again was in the bathing room. Despite her initial shock, she handled the situation quite well.

She screamed.

Afraid to take her eyes off the man, she reached blindly to a nearby shelf, all the while yelling for her aunt. Aurianna grabbed the first thing she touched. While attempting to cover her mortification, she quickly realized her mistake: the towel she had managed to grab was woefully undersized. She sank deeper into the water, holding the small towel underneath the surface, trying at least to hide the most important bits. She hoped the water surface would disrupt his view enough to provide some cover as well.

No amount of coaxing from the stranger would calm Aurianna down from the precipice of sheer terror she was facing. The young man was clearly distressed by the sudden earsplitting shrieking, but he managed to maintain at least a semblance of decorum as he attempted to patiently await its demise.

She had no intentions of granting that wish until help arrived.

Larissa entered the room, slamming the partially open door against the wall, and brandishing her deadly wooden spoon. She stopped abruptly in front of the man as an expression of dismayed resignation replaced the protective fierceness on her pale face.

The Kinetic—or whatever he was—moved from his position near the bathing tub. With a slight bow of his head to Larissa, the man then gestured toward Aurianna. He finally spoke. "Please tell me she isn't prone to such annoying outbursts. I'd rather not be treated to that torture ever again."

Larissa continued staring at the young man with eyes that conveyed a melancholic depth of despair. Aurianna, shocked into silence at her aunt's reaction to the man, forgot her embarrassing lack of attire for a moment as she looked between the two people in a silent standoff before her. The man sort of loomed intimidatingly, while Larissa crossed her arms in a gesture of stubborn defiance, the wooden spoon still clenched in her fist. An unspoken battle waged between them.

But why would Larissa even consider the idea of antagonizing one of these strangers, a so-called Kinetic? Who knew what powers they possessed, not to mention the danger he represented by association if the Consils found him here? Her aunt seemed to fear them, of all people, most.

Aurianna stared at the confrontation occurring in their bathing room, certain no one she knew had ever even seen a Kinetic in person, besides Faethe and herself. And Damon. No one alive at least.

And now one of them was standing in her home, glaring with an odd lack of intensity, almost as if bored by the entire ordeal. She waited expectantly for the inevitable crackle, the sizzle of magic in the room.

Yet nothing happened.

So she decided to speak, whispering, "Larissa, what's going on?" She desperately hoped this was simply a dream, some manifestation of her sleep-deprived brain. It would not be surprising after the last few days.

The woman slowly turned to face her, features frozen in a state of mixed emotions, but her shoulders now slumped in resignation. She drew in a deep breath and, almost in a daze, Larissa walked over and picked up a large towel from the top shelf, handing it to Aurianna. The man at least had the decency to turn around without being asked, an inscrutable look on his face, while she stood up and wrapped herself in the towel.

Larissa signaled for him to turn back around. "Aurianna, dear, this is . . . there's no easy way to say this. I did try to warn you. It's time for you to go home. I told you it was time, but I thought we might have a little more of it. Your twentieth birthday, and it's all flown by so fast."

Aurianna continued to stand, stunned into a momentary silence, dripping water back into the tub. The implications of *time for you to go home* still reverberating in her ears, she replied—a hint of irritation in her voice, "What are you talking about? What home? This *is* home."

At her words, the man glanced sharply at Aurianna and then at her aunt. "You mean, you haven't told her? You've had twenty years to prepare her and didn't say a word?"

Larissa hung her head. "I didn't." She sighed deeply then looked up. "I tried to, many times. But trust me, it's better this way. Having the weight of that knowledge on her shoulders wouldn't have been helpful, to her or anyone. You of all people should be able to understand that." She aimed a pointed look at the man before another sigh escaped her, and her eyes were drawn back to the young woman who was like a daughter to her. All the words Larissa wasn't saying seemed to freeze within that sigh and float between them, pulling the air from the room. Then she hastened to reassure the stranger. "But don't worry. She'll go with you. I've explained enough to her."

Aurianna said, "What exactly have you explained to me? I don't understand what you're talking about. Who is this man? Do you know him? I mean, you seem to, and you don't seem all that surprised that he's here. *In our bathing room.*" She eyed both of them suspiciously, unsure of what to do. She needed to repair her dignity before she could continue the conversation. "Never mind. I'm getting dressed first. Can I have some privacy?"

They both nodded to her and left the room. Aurianna went through another door which connected to her bedroom. Larissa had prepared the hot—now tepid—bath for her in the bathing tub, and all she had wanted was to sit down and relax for a moment after the events of the day. Her birthday, and she couldn't even have the luxury of a lukewarm bath. Fighting the temptation to slip back into the tub and block out the swirling thoughts for just a little while, she plopped herself on her bed and fell back, staring up at the ceiling and wondering if any of it was real.

The brief reverie wasn't going to bring her any answers. The thought spurred her back into action. After changing into respectable clothing (deciding it best to forgo her nightclothes), Aurianna found her aunt and the young man sitting in the main room. She took a seat opposite them on a chair facing the kitchen. It was only then she noticed his disheveled hair and damp clothing—odd considering the lack of rain that evening.

Larissa was the first to speak. "To answer your questions, perhaps in the wrong order..." She paused for a few seconds. "First of all, this man's name is Pharis. He is, in fact—"

With a quick shake of his head, Pharis looked at Larissa pointedly, his nostrils flaring.

Her aunt looked confused for a moment but continued, "Well, I know him, though he's never met me. Pharis has come to take you back home, I'm assuming. Where you belong. You remember the things I told you earlier? About the purple stone and our first home?"

Pharis looked at Larissa questioningly when she said this, but he didn't speak. When Aurianna nodded slowly, Larissa hesitated, then continued, "Everything was true, but the little room wasn't technically your first home."

"Yes. I gathered that." Aurianna's deadpan retort was just the tip of the frustration building within her. "How about we stop talking about what *isn't* and start talking about what *is*?"

"Alright then. Aurianna, I brought you here." At that point, the woman began to stumble over her words. "I know how this will sound, but you'll just have to trust me for now." She stopped again, glancing at the man with a hopeless look in her eyes. "I brought you here from the past. You were born a hundred years ago. Technically. For reasons that will eventually become clear to you, I had to travel to the future with you when you were a baby, to keep you safe and protect you from a horrible fate."

Aurianna sat still in her chair, staring in mute confusion.

Her aunt, seeing no response was forthcoming, said, "Aurianna, there are so many things you need to know. But only when the moment is right. I know it sounds unfair, but you'll figure it all out in time, and most importantly, at the *right* time. I will say this: you were born in an era when something akin to magic existed, and more than just that of the Kinetics." At the mention of that word—*Kinetics*—Aurianna's head snapped up. *So, she does know.*

Larissa continued. "Even greater powers were held by some. The point is, when you were born, you were cursed by a horrible spell, a spell meant to ensure you died. But you were rescued from that fate by another spell, one that saved your life. Lifting the death curse was impossible, but the second spell changed it, allowing you to leave instead, to disappear in a way. That's how I was able to take you forward in time."

A deafening silence filled the space—every inch covered in an invisible film of *what the hell is happening*—and the room became very, very small.

Aurianna blinked.

She blinked again.

No words. There were no words.

Eyes narrowing, skepticism of the highest magnitude weighing heavily in her voice, Aurianna finally spoke, the staccato rhythm punctuating each syllable like an accusation. "So . . . we're time travelers. From the past. We zipped along a hundred years into the future." The sarcasm dripped from her words like honey.

Larissa smiled, but the gesture did not reach her eyes. "Eighty years, technically. The counter-spell that saved your life required a hundred years to run its course. Today is your twentieth birthday, so it's been one hundred years since we left. And now it's time for you to return."

Aurianna sat for a moment in silence, staring at her hands resting on the arms of the chair, willing herself to wake up from this horrible dream. Was it horrible? She had wanted answers, to know more, to uncover the truths that had always seemed just out of reach. This wasn't what she had expected, not by a long shot. "I'm sorry, but this is crazy. You know that, right?" Aurianna blocked the emotions rising within her, but her frustration was now threatening to spill over.

Pharis cleared his throat. "What I want to know is why you keep referring to 'spells' when Kinetics don't do anything of the sort? That's a leftover vestige from Fae lore, right? Stories to tell children and whatnot."

Larissa shook her head. "It's not that simple, and I wish I could tell you more without risking a break in the timeline." She turned to Aurianna. "I don't know what all you saw or heard tonight, but I know you spoke to that Kinetic the other day. Damon told me."

And there it was. All Aurianna needed to let the dams burst forth with the force of her anger and yet another betrayal of her trust. Not Faethe this time, but Damon...

"And why would he do that, Auntie? To *tell* on me for helping a man? The Kinetic was dying! He needed someone to talk to, someone to listen. I couldn't just let him die alone or burn alive in the pit!" Aurianna leaped to her feet to cross the short space between them.

Larissa looked up at her, nodding. "Yes, I agree. It would have been cruel and horrible to toss a dying man into a heap of bodies. It's just as cruel and horrible for those bodies to have been tortured and drained in the first place."

"Of course, but you've always seemed so afraid of these strangers. Why talk of helping them now?"

"Because they need it. Aurianna, I was never afraid of *them*. I was afraid for *you*. If one of them ever saw you and recognized you, this day might never have come." Larissa began tapping her fingertips against the arm of the chair, no longer able to contain her nervous energy. "It was my duty to keep you safe and prepare you for your twentieth birthday, when the spell would be broken by someone who would travel here to take you back. I already knew this would happen, so ... so I've been waiting. But I didn't tell you because it wasn't necessary. It would've only caused you more pain and created even greater walls between you and everyone here. I had to keep you hidden until your twentieth birthday. Hidden in plain sight, perhaps, but I wanted you to stay away from those men. Who knows if they're all here for the same reason? What if one of them were sent to look for you, and not with good intentions? I never thought you'd find one on your own like you did. But maybe it was still part of the plan."

"What plan? What exactly are you hiding me from? Is this . . ." Aurianna began to chew on her bottom lip, but her aunt interrupted her before she could continue the thought.

"Listen, Aurianna. Can you trust me? I know I've hidden so much from you, but I've done so to protect you. You will discover the answers, eventually. You must go with Pharis. You *can* trust him, I promise you. But you have to go willingly."

Pharis snorted. "Not necessarily."

Larissa gave him a sidelong glance, ignoring the comment. "Your training can't begin until you go back."

"What training?" Aurianna continued to bite her lip in bewilderment, dreading the answer to her question, yet somehow already having an inkling of what it would be.

Pharis sighed. "She means your Kinetic training. You don't realize it, *apparently*," he said with a another pointed look at her aunt, "but you're one of us. A Kinetic. That is a certainty, straight from the mouths of the Arcanes. I don't blame you for being shocked by all of this. You should have been told, especially since these powers would have shown themselves years ago and can be very dangerous if left untrained. Now my job is harder because I have a very short amount of time in which to convince you to go with me or drag you along."

Larissa blurted out, "I promise you, Reg—"

"Do not call me that. Not here."

"Okay, Pharis, I promise you my actions were for good reason.

I can't explain them to you, but please believe it's better this way. You have no understanding of how things are here. It's worse than I ever expected, but I've managed to keep her safe. That's the most important thing."

Pharis slowly nodded in affirmation. "What I really want to know is how you have an Aether Stone. And don't play innocent. I can only assume that's the purple stone you were referring to a moment ago?"

Larissa looked frightened for a moment, fidgeting with her hands. "I had an extra one when I came here. But it lost its magic over time. It doesn't work anymore."

He stared at her, confusion wrinkling his forehead. "I had to bury one before I left, in a place where we knew it could still be accessed in your time." He shook his head and narrowed his eyes. "I don't understand how you were able to bring an extra one across the threshold. I thought it was impossible. That's why we had to bury the one for my return trip."

"It was . . . it was part of the spell, I imagine." Changing the subject, she added, "Well, I'm glad you have a plan and a way back. Aurianna, dear, I need you to listen and understand how important this is. You were cursed because someone didn't want you around. They feared you and believed you to be a danger to them. Well, you may not be dangerous now, but hopefully you soon will be. Either way, he's right. Training is necessary, or else any dormant power could show up unexpectedly, and without proper training, that could be disastrous. And besides, there's a . . . prophecy. As ridiculous as that may sound, I heard it myself, straight from the Arcane who had the vision. The prophecy foretells of a woman who will end all of this. Someone who will bring the sun back to the sky. Bring back magic and everything that was lost. The Arcanes believed it referred to you, for a variety of reasons I'm sure you'll soon learn. You don't have to believe it right now, and it's far too much pressure to throw on you, but...if there's a chance you can fix this mess we're all in...could you at least go and find out? Perhaps you can save us all."

Aurianna had been listening with a barely concealed rage. She stood up, putting her hands on her hips. "Save us? How can I save us by leaving? I can't believe I'm even having this conversation. Why should I believe any of this? You say I have powers. How is that possible? Wouldn't I know about it if I did? It makes no sense!" At the corner of her vision, the candle in the window flared and sparked for no apparent reason, its flame threatening to engulf the curtains in a sudden but intense inferno. She remembered the incident the other day with the fireplace, something she hadn't really thought to question. Until now.

Closing her eyes, Aurianna willed her emotions down, down, deep within that black hole where everything she felt eventually landed. Just in case.

Pharis leaned forward, placing his elbows on his knees. "No, you're right. It doesn't make any damn sense! It doesn't make sense that I'm sitting in a hovel wasting my time trying to convince a girl to let me steal her away and take her back to literally just a few moon cycles after her own birth. To live as a twenty-year-old." Laughing bitterly, he added, "It makes no sense at all. If it were up to me, this whole prophecy business with the Arcanes...you must understand the people revere them and never question any of it. No matter how ridiculous it sounds, their word is...well, it's *not* up to me, so here we are. And, frankly, I'm tired of trying to convince or explain it to you. My mission is to bring you back. Either you get your things and follow me, or I'm throwing you over my shoulder and walking out the door." With those words, he stood.

Despite being fairly tall herself, Aurianna noticed he was almost a head taller than she was. His bright-blue eyes were piercing, glinting with a firm resolve to keep his word.

She swallowed before speaking. "I want to know why."

Pharis frowned at her words. "Hell if I know, girl. They believe in this prophecy, the Arcanes and everyone else, I guess. Personally, I don't think we need a savior. What we need is something else entirely. But it's true that without training you could be a danger to yourself and others. All I know is I have orders to return with you *tonight*." Now his eyes were pleading with her. He did not want to force her, but he would if necessary.

Thinking back to his words from a moment ago, Aurianna gasped with a sudden realization. "You said you were taking me back to a few moon cycles *after my own birth*. When exactly did you bring me here?" This last was directed at her aunt, but the woman didn't answer for a moment.

Just when Aurianna was about to lose her patience, Larissa said, "I ran here with you on the day you were born. The curse was put on you the moment you came into this world, so I had to leave immediately in order to fulfill the counter-spell."

"So my mother..."

"She...she wasn't able to bring you herself."

Died. Died giving birth to me.

The grief was overwhelming, even though she had never known her mother or even what she looked like. The same for her father. But now she knew at least a part of the truth, no matter how much it hurt. A wave of guilt washed over her, and she sobbed silently. Her aunt reached out to her, but Aurianna pulled away, the guilt taking her to a place inside her head where she wanted to be alone. She hardly ever showed this much emotion, and the sensation was strange. She let herself feel it for a few moments, sighing away the remorse like wisps of smoke.

When she was able to speak again, she asked, "What about my father? You never talk about either of them. I want to know."

"Your father was a great man. I can tell you that much. That's all I know."

"Was he there when I was born?"

Larissa shook her head.

"You don't know if he died?"

Another shake of her head.

Aurianna eyed her aunt, but the woman seemed to be telling the truth. She sighed. "Auntie, I . . . I'm sorry I yelled. You keep telling me to control myself, and I lost control just now in so many ways. But you have to understand how incredibly overwhelming all of this is. You can't expect me just to nod my head and follow along with a stranger. I can't bear the thought of leaving my home and . . ." She had almost said *my friends*, but the sentiment didn't ring true in her head.

A sudden realization hit her full force. "Wait! Aren't you coming with me?"

"No, I'm not. But I'll be waiting right here when you come back."

"But I don't want to leave you! I can't!"

Larissa smiled ruefully. "I know, sweetie. I know. I'm sorry to have to ask you to leave the only home you've ever known. But if you don't go, this future—our present, our lives—will only become worse. You must fix this. You must fix the past in order to save the future and our world. And, yes, I know that's an awfully heavy burden to place on you, but I know you can do it because the prophecy foretold it. No matter what you believe, or what Pharis believes . . ." Larissa sighed then looked beseechingly into her face. "Aurianna, you don't have to believe it. Just believe me." She stood and hugged her fiercely, adding, "I don't know how long you'll be gone, but it will only seem like a moment for me. When you're done becoming whatever you're meant to become, you come back to me here. I won't have time to miss you."

"But I'll miss you."

Her aunt stood back, smiling. "I know. Now, we must get you on the road. Don't worry about taking anything."

Aurianna wiped her tear-streaked face with the back of her sleeve, trembling with her unspoken goodbyes. "I can't do this. Larissa, please come with me. At least give me that comfort. I can't do it alone."

"You must. And you will. I cannot come with you. I'm sorry."

Pharis looked at the older woman in confusion, but he remained silent. Aurianna tried to control the emotions overtaking her, tried to stop the flow of tears, the gasping sobs wracking her body with each breath she took. *How can they not see that they ask the impossible?*

Larissa sat back down on the couch and stared off into the distance, into some unknown and unseen region of the sky that the Darkness blotted out with an inky black hand. As Larissa sat lost in thought, Pharis paced the room, his jaw clenched in impatience. Aurianna thought about every wrong thing in her little world. She thought about the bodies and the burning pits, the biting cold and the Darkness.

She had once tried to leave, but she'd been stopped by those she thought were her friends. They had done it with good intentions perhaps, but the result was the same. Her body was permanently scarred by the incident, as was her mind. She hated that mark as much as she hated the Darkness. But it accurately described what she was: a runaway. She had wanted to leave, to run away, to find out how to make things better. She had wanted to explore the world, and she had planned on doing it without her aunt. So why was this any different?

Deep down, she had known then that she would return home at some point. Despite her aunt's assurances, Aurianna had no way of knowing if she would ever return from a trip through time itself. There were just too many unknown factors.

Yet she had run the risk of possibly never being able to return when she had chosen to head into the unknown of the Darkness. Was that any different?

No. Her fears might be warranted, but this was her chance to do exactly what she had wanted to do for a long time. She had a chance to fix things, to make them right, to stop the Darkness and bring back the light. How to do that, she had no idea, but deep down she realized she wanted to try.

"The man we saw, the Kinetic, I . . . he wasn't the only one. There was a landing this evening, and I followed them to the Consilium."

"You . . . what?" Her aunt's voice was barely a whisper as she snapped her head around to face Aurianna.

"I know, I know. It's just . . . I can't keep watching things like this and not do something. It's not right, and you know it, Auntie. You said it yourself. The things they do to those people . . ." She paused to take a deep breath, the tears threatening to spill over once again. "It's worse than I ever imagined. The Praefects are draining their powers. I think that's where the electric power is coming from. The Kinetics might be dangerous, but they're still people. How can the Consils let this happen?"

"Let? I'd bet they're the ones ordering it," Pharis said.

"Either way, I can't let it continue. When I got there, I saw the cages they keep them in. And I spoke with one of them. He was frightened at first. I can't say I blame him, considering what we're doing to them. He told me about a prophecy, one that would make all of this go away. I don't want to think about the implications of changing the past, but if what you say is true and we're both from that past, then it seems like there must be a connection. I want to help, but I doubt I'll be any kind of savior, at least not in a grand sense. I do want to do this, though. I want to help in some way."

The stillness of time, the slow realization of what she was about to say, felt like the soft edges of a waking dream abruptly sharpening into focus. A dream she felt she'd been living for her entire life, only now finally becoming clear. Mind reeling from the implications of her sudden clarity, Aurianna stared at her aunt for a moment, willing herself to have the courage for her next words:

"I'll go."

Her simple answer caught the others off guard. Larissa struggled to her feet, and Pharis stopped pacing.

With an intense look of pride, Larissa took Aurianna's face in both of her hands as she kissed the girl's forehead. "I know you can do this. Fear is never a bad thing. But the brave face their fears and overcome them." She turned to look at Pharis. "Take care of my girl, Pharis."

"Great. Let's go." His gruff reply embodied the frustration he was only halfheartedly attempting to hide.

Directing her hard gaze at Pharis with a look of uncharacteristic intensity, Larissa said, "Tell them what it's like here so they understand." When Pharis started to interrupt her, she held up a hand. "Yes, they already know, or else you wouldn't be here. But knowing and understanding are two different things. They need to understand just what the cost will be if you fail."

Pharis gave a swift nod.

Aurianna said, "I swear I'll come back for you. Stay right here, okay?" The tears were again forming in her eyes, a hazy film blanketing her vision and blurring her view of the woman who had not only raised her but had sacrificed everything to save her life all those years ago. She wiped them away with her sleeve and offered a rueful smile. "I haven't thanked you for saving my life. I promise I'll do the best I can to help everyone and make you proud. Thank you. For everything."

Larissa enfolded her tightly in her arms. She whispered, "You've already made me proud, child."

After one last hug, Aurianna started to turn away, to follow the man who had moved to stand by the door, eager to leave and return to his home. Then she remembered.

"One second. I have to get something."

She raced to her room and opened her jewelry box. There, in the bottom drawer, was her mother's necklace, the one with the dark sapphire stone.

Some of it made no sense at all to her, yet so much was now clearer in her mind. Aurianna had always known she didn't quite fit, like something about her was out of place. Now she knew it was the time and not the place she was out of sync with. And her mother's necklace had always reminded her of something right at the edge of her memory. If her mother had died in childbirth, what had become of her father? She wondered if he would still be alive when she traveled back to the past, or if he had died before she was born. Before today, Larissa had never spoken of the details to her, just that her parents had died a long time ago.

A long time indeed.

Now she had a piece of the puzzle. A small piece, but it was a start. She might get the answers she had always been seeking and find out more about her family. Aurianna loved her aunt and appreciated everything she had done for her, but a part of her craved more. She wanted to know what had happened to her parents and maybe even find other relatives. Maybe.

Either way, she was leaving the only home she had ever known. And she wasn't entirely sure if she truly believed they were going to travel through time. Aurianna felt silly even thinking about it. But maybe it wasn't so silly. Maybe.

She picked up the necklace, her spirits lifting, and slipped it on, tucking it under her shirt. Turning her back to the mirror in the corner, Aurianna looked over her shoulder at the reflection as she pulled down the corner of her tunic. She gazed for a moment at the image, the small patch of dark, puckered skin staring back at her with its text transposed by the mirror.

Effugere.

In the reflection it looked like nonsense, but the meaning was still the same: *runaway.* Only now, just like the reflection in the mirror of the branding etched into her skin, she was running backward.

She was running back to her beginning.

The idea of traveling alone with a strange man was also a bit frightening. His walking in on her in the bathing room had created an awkwardness between them. Or maybe it was just her.

Maybe.

The man her aunt had called Pharis was several years older than she was, perhaps even in his midtwenties. If he was telling the truth about his mission, then she supposed she should be perfectly safe with him. He seemed a bit grumpy, but otherwise he wasn't nearly as terrifying as she had imagined in the alley.

And thinking about that incident made her blush. Running away must have looked so ridiculous to him. But what could anyone expect from a young woman who meets a strange man at night in the street? It was perfectly logical for her to have been afraid, even if her fears had nothing to do with what one would expect in that situation. She had been terrified of the things the man in the cage had told her. Now, here she was, doing exactly what she had been afraid of, setting things in motion for her world—her time—to change, perhaps drastically. But anything would be better than what they had now. The Kinetics were right. Something had to be done.

She threw on a coat and rejoined the man who would take her to all the answers.

Chapter 7

AURIANNA

They left after another round of tearful goodbyes and started walking.

Aurianna said, "Where are we going?"

Pharis pointed into the distance. "To the Imperium. That's where we buried the Aether Stone." Without a light source, she could barely see his arm in the Darkness, much less whatever he was pointing at.

"The...what?"

"Aether Stone. E-THER. Do you not listen? We explained this back at your home. It's how we—"

"No, I heard you about this *Aether Stone* thing. I meant the other thing you mentioned," Aurianna said with no small amount of trepidation.

For a moment, Pharis looked confused, then realization took over his face. "The Imperium? That giant building across the bridge."

"You mean the big creepy place on the island? We got in trouble for going there when I was a kid. It's a death trap. Why would you bury it there?"

His sigh of frustration was eloquent. "In my time, that *big creepy place* is my home—and home to a lot of other people. It's the Imperium, the residence and school for Kinetics, where they're trained and where many of us live." He added with a hint of indignation, "And it's not creepy."

"Oh," was all Aurianna said in reply. They continued to the edge of town and started to feel their way carefully across the bridge. She was deep in thought for a while, a fear growing within her core as she remembered the flash in the distance after her harrowing experience at the warehouse with Faethe. She asked, "Is this the spot where you landed?"

"What? Yes, why?"

"Because I saw you fall," she whispered breathlessly. Coming here was a very bad idea.

"Yeah, so?"

"Well, if I saw you, so did they."

"Who is 'they,' or do I even want to know?"

Aurianna shook her head. "No. You don't. But you'll get to know them really well if we don't leave this place. Now."

Her sharp, staccato words seemed to unnerve him. He asked warily, "What does that mean?"

"It means they're going to be on the lookout for you. I don't understand how they didn't already find you."

"You keep talking nonsense. Explain what you mean."

"The . . . the Carpos," she sputtered. "They're a special force within the Praefects, chosen by the Consils. Their job is to hunt your kind down when they fall. They know and see everything. And the Carpos always catch them. Every time. I have no idea why you weren't caught. The flash was definitely further out than I've ever seen. Maybe they weren't looking out this far. Your people normally land near the warehouse on the hill."

"Probably because I landed in the water. Hard, I might add." His disgruntled tone was unmistakable, and it only made her bristle more. At least now she understood his bedraggled appearance.

"Look, Pharis, I didn't ask to be collected, I didn't ask for a babysitter. So don't get mad at *me* because *you* were sent here. It's not my fault you got stuck with the job. I'm just trying to help. They will kill you if they find you! And me as well, I'm sure, for even being with you!"

As she spoke the words, her frustration brought her almost directly in his face, and Aurianna was close enough to see the changes in his expression. For a moment, Pharis looked sheepish, but then his familiar condescending demeanor took over. Aurianna had begun to wonder if he had any other look. "If they were going to find me, they would have. I assume that's why the Arcanes stressed to not use any powers while I was here. That's probably what attracts these Carpos of yours. The other Kinetics are most likely tapping into their small reserve of control over Air. Aerokinetics are scarce, but fully trained adult Kinetics have enough control to slow a fall. There's no one here. Let's go." He dragged her by the arm for several yards before she pulled away and continued to follow him reluctantly.

After crossing the bridge, Pharis stopped just outside the main door into the massive structure. Part of the surrounding wall was destroyed as if from an explosion. He felt along the wall, seeming to measure from the doorway, then sat down and began to dig with a tool he pulled from inside his cloak. Trying to peer inside, she remembered her brief adventure as a child, cut short before they'd gotten past the first room. She couldn't believe her curiosity about the place might be satisfied.

A few minutes later, he moved over several inches and began digging again. Aurianna wished he would hurry. Tired of waiting patiently, she once again tried to examine the inner walls of the room. It was impossible to make anything out. The Darkness obscured everything.

Just as she was about to ask if she could do anything to help—since Pharis was now on his fifth hole and was obviously having issues—he shouted out his success as he pulled an object from the hole in front on him.

She sidled closer and could barely make out a small glass bottle containing what appeared to be a rolled-up piece of paper. Not a stone.

"I thought we were looking for a purple stone, not . . . well, whatever that is." Aurianna was beginning to think this was all a joke after all. She reached for the paper in his hand as he stood and began dusting himself off.

"Just exactly *what* are you doing?" Pharis pulled the paper away before she could get a grip on it.

"I want to know why we just spent precious time digging up some old papers when we're supposed to be finding this Aether Stone and getting the hell out of here. Before we get captured or killed. Or both."

"And that is precisely what I'm doing. This *old paper* is a map to where the stone is buried."

"So, you don't actually know where it is?"

"No, not exactly. But the Arcanes didn't want to risk the location being lost if something happened, and they didn't want to send it with me in case I was captured. So they buried it and told me where to find the map."

"But . . . if something happened to you, no one would know where the map was."

Pharis said, "Yeah, the hope was, I think, that I could at least get a message to you. It would be easier to explain the location of the map than the location of the stone."

"So they just hoped I'd figure it out on my own? Oh, wait, let me guess. It was destined for me to return, so I must have found a way, right?"

"Something like that, I'm sure. I didn't question the Arcanes."

Aurianna shook her head, smiling cynically. Then she thought of something which sickened her to her core. "They were willing to lose you in order to find me?"

At her words, Pharis grumbled, "Seems that way. Come on, let's keep moving." He spun around, trying to look at the map, but there was no light by which to see. He took off into the interior that was darker still.

Aurianna watched as Pharis pulled a small torch from his belt, along with a metallic box. He ran his thumb up the side, flicking the lid open. Another small movement of his thumb caused fire to burst forth. He lit the torch in his other hand, causing a small shriek of fear and wonder to escape Aurianna's lips.

"Quiet! Do you want to meet these . . . Carpos of yours first-hand?" Pharis gritted his teeth, his nostrils flaring.

"No! Sorry, I . . . That's incredible. How did you do that? Is that magic?" she exclaimed with delight.

Pharis stared at her for a full eternity before looking to the hand still holding the object, flipping it back open and causing the fire to appear once more. "Yeah. Magic." His eyes held an amusement she suspected was at her expense.

"Will I be able to do that?" Aurianna remembered the incident with the fireplace, along with a dozen other seemingly innocent occurrences. The idea both terrified and excited her.

"Use a lighter? Sure," he replied. At the confused look on her face, he burst out laughing and continued laughing all the way through the front room and into the first hallway without looking back.

* * *

Pharis led Aurianna through a series of doors leading further and further into the castle-like structure. They soon entered a massive room with giant pillars lining the side walls and a wide staircase at the far end. Before she could examine the room more closely, he stopped just inside, turning right and entering a door covered in dust and cobwebs. Apart from that, she could see very little of her surroundings.

Pharis was right. She would have never been able to find the stone on her own. The entire place felt like a maze to her. The pace he set was making her dizzy. Still, she followed behind, unsure of where they were going or how long the path to the stone was. Just ahead of them, on the other side of the door, was a winding staircase inside a very narrow space. The stairs extended in a spiraling pattern in both directions. They began to descend.

The walls were made from rock, just like most of the structures in town, but dust covered everything and pooled in every corner. What little light they had was just enough to keep them from tumbling over one another in the darkness as they made their careful way into the depths.

As they traveled, she tried to ask Pharis questions about the place that would be her new home. He grunted or gave short, unhelpful replies each time. She began to ask about her past and her family. She wanted to learn as much as she could because the little she knew was still a confusing mess in her mind.

"Sorry to disappoint you, but I don't know anything about you, other than your name and the fact that you were born three moons ago as far as my timeline is concerned. And yes, that's weird. But so is all of this. Deal with it."

"But you keep mentioning this prophecy—"

"I mentioned nothing."

"Well, Larissa did, and—"

"Do you ever stop talking?"

"Do you ever give a straight answer when asked a question?"

Pharis sighed for what felt like the hundredth time. Turning to face her, he stopped so abruptly she almost ran into him. Backing up just enough to avoid a collision but not enough to ease her discomfort, he said. "I don't give two damns about some prophecy. I told you that. They're always really vague and could honestly mean a million different things. But the Arcanes speak and we listen. They said the prophecy speaks of you. I think maybe we don't need a savior. At least not some girl from a hovel who just found out two seconds ago she's even a Kinetic—"

Raising her hands defensively, Aurianna replied, "I don't know how I feel about that part. But you don't have to be so rude to me."

"And you don't have to ask so many bloody questions!" He turned around and trudged down a narrow tunnel. The ground and walls in this passageway were covered completely with dirt and nothing else.

"How is this possible?" Aurianna wondered aloud after a few moments.

"What is it now?"

"I was just wondering how this area exists without protective barriers. In the bottom level of the Consilium, we have special walls and flooring made from a type of stone that protects us from the magma. Except for the hole where the burning pit is, of course."

Pharis stopped. "Bottom level?"

"Yes, where I found the prisoners."

"What prisoners?"

"Right before you found me in the street." She flinched internally and blushed again at the memory of running away like a lunatic. "I was at the Consilium, remember? I told you about this earlier. I snuck in and found the other side of the bottom level, the side we're not allowed to enter. I found a long row of cages with Kinetics trapped inside them. I spoke to one of them, and he's the one who first told me about the prophecy." She paused and looked down. "I couldn't do anything to help them." She certainly wasn't savior material. She couldn't even save those people from certain death.

Pharis responded, "In my time, I've never seen a bottom level at the Consilium. I don't think it exists yet." He started walking again, speaking over his shoulder, "Let's go."

Aurianna realized he hadn't answered her original question. *Why is there no protection from the magma here?*

The tunnel became narrower the further in they went, causing Aurianna no small amount of discomfort. She wasn't used to being confined to small spaces, especially not deep under the ground. The feeling was nauseating.

"Do people in your time enjoy being trapped in tiny little passages underground? If so, I think I might reconsider this journey and go back home."

Pharis ignored her and continued walking.

When they reached a more open intersection, Aurianna breathed a sigh of relief. Then she noticed he had stopped to stare at the map again, trying to hold the torch as close to the paper as possible without setting it alight.

Oh, wouldn't that be just peachy?

"Are we lost? Please don't tell me we're lost. I am not going back through that tunnel again."

The moment the words left her lips, Pharis whirled on her,

grabbing her left forearm with one hand while squeezing the map with the other. The torch hit the dirt floor with a quiet thud, somehow managing to continue its steady burn.

His face was inches from hers, a flood of rage dancing wildly in the blue of his eyes, but the torment there didn't reach his grip on her arm. His touch wasn't soft, but there was a stiff hesitation in him every time he seemed to lose his cool. Something was upsetting him greatly, and she didn't think it was all about her.

Tilting his head to the side, he spewed out, "If you don't shut your mouth," sharply punctuating each word, "someday someone's going to shut it for you." The intended hostility behind the implied threat dripped from his lips, but his eyes continued to betray his true emotions, a sadness under the fury, sadness rooted so deep she almost felt sorry for him.

Almost. None of it negated the fact that he had grabbed her and basically threatened her. But for some reason, although his grip was slack enough and she could have easily wrenched herself free, she didn't pull away.

He held her like that for the space of a silent forever—neither of them moving or speaking—until his nostrils flared, and he suddenly let go of her arm. A momentary flash of guilt washed over his features, passing so quickly she might have imagined it. "Let's go," he said, his voice a low rasp, barely audible. Picking up the dropped torch, he stomped away without looking back to see if she was following.

Aurianna stood silently for a moment, absorbing the shock of his emotional outburst, a small amount of fear hitting her amid the pity she had felt for a moment. This man was not her friend, that was certain. She followed without a word, keeping her eyes on the ground, watching as her feet took her further and further away from the safety of home.

Just when Aurianna thought they would end up walking on forever into the bowels of the earth, Pharis suddenly stopped in front of her and pulled out his digging tool again. The ground was hard packed, reminding Aurianna of her earlier unanswered question about the magma. However, she held her tongue and decided to hold onto the thought until she could ask someone else. Preferably someone who wasn't a complete ass.

The further down he dug, the more concerned she became with the whole issue. Was there no magma level on this island? Could he conceivably dig indefinitely and never hit anything but dirt and rock? Surely not. But as soon as she thought this, he reached down into the hole—at least a forearm's length deep—and brought out a frayed and dingy bundle of rags.

"That's what we came here for? A dirty piece of cloth?"

Slicing his gaze in her direction, Pharis flared his nostrils but ignored her comment. He unwound the tattered fragment of material, layer by layer, until nothing was left but its luminous contents—an oblong, amethyst-colored object.

The Aether Stone.

It looked very similar to the one her aunt Larissa had shown her, the one she vaguely remembered from her childhood. Only...this one was still glowing.

The light emanating from the stone was strong enough to illuminate the entire area, so Pharis threw down his torch and stomped out the dwindling fire, looking around for a moment before saying, "Yeah, this should work well enough. I think."

"You think?" Aurianna uttered the words before she realized she had spoken. Immediately, she bit her lower lip and looked down, that same fear flowing through her once again. She was pretty sure he wouldn't harm her.

But still.

Either way, a part of her still feared his reactions and didn't want to risk any further altercations while alone with him. After all, she had no knowledge of his background or inclinations toward violence. Better to err on the side of caution, even if it irked her pride a bit.

Pharis didn't seem to notice her sudden reaction and merely replied, "You want to go back home?"

Aurianna shook her head vehemently. Returning home was not an option for her now.

"Okay, then." He sighed. "I only meant that I don't know if its power has been protected or not. The Arcanes said that burying it would be enough, but I don't know what they were trying to protect it from exactly, so I can only assume it's working since it's still glowing." Thoughts of *the Darkness* were a bitter mantra scrolling through the back of Aurianna's mind at his words. "If, for some reason, you're correct in thinking we're being followed, we need to do this quickly. Otherwise, the power this thing puts out will *definitely* have them crawling in our direction. No doubt we'll be putting up a signal all the way to the sky, even this far down. When I tell you to, grab the stone with me. Don't hesitate."

She nodded, not knowing what else to do. Pharis held his hand out, the blue stone in his grasp, and began to speak loudly.

"In the name of the Essence, we ask for safe passage back to our time, back to our home." Sparks of something like electricity began to shoot from his closed palm. He opened it, and more slivers of bright purple current snaked out in random intervals, filling the whole of the area as if trying to escape.

He continued speaking aloud. "Take us back to when I left, and we will neither disturb your realm nor attempt to stay."

The power of the strange orb became overwhelming to her senses, a strange noise growing in the silence, and Aurianna noticed

Pharis's hair was sticking straight out from his head. Frightened, she began to back away. He held out the stone. "Now! Touch the stone!"

She hesitated, continuing to back away.

"Damn it! You've got to touch it, or you'll be stuck in here alone!" he screamed in frustration.

Pausing only a second longer, Aurianna swallowed her fears, stepped forward, and gingerly placed her fingertips on the stone.

The world dissolved with a clap of thunder.

PART TWO

THE UNSEEN PAST

The roses dying, dying in their bed;
A thankless death to purge the unseen past.

CHAPTER 8

AURIANNA

Light and shadow, swirls of blue and purple dripping with starlight and an ethereal otherness.

She waited.

Aurianna reached out into the void, hoping for something to hold onto, something to steady her revolving mind and body, but she found nothing. Then she began to realize that *she* was not what was spinning. The world around her was turning circles, crashing in upon itself.

And she was aware of Pharis beside her. Only not. She knew he was there, but she could see nothing of his form nor feel his hand. Or her own, for that matter. Her breathing became erratic, her skin trying to crawl inside itself even though, according to what her eyes told her, there was no skin. No body. No substance.

But still she could feel him there. Aurianna felt herself being pulled in all directions at once. Then, as suddenly as it had begun, it stopped. Pharis stood beside her, looking impatient. She looked down. Her own form had taken shape again, much to her relief.

But where were they? The spinning had stopped, yet the backdrop of color-tinged light remained.

Just as she was about to ask, Pharis spoke. "This is the Aether, the realm of the Essence. We're allowed passage through to the other side, but we cannot linger. That door will close any second. We must hurry." Aurianna looked up and saw the opening to which he was referring. It wasn't a door in the conventional sense, but a hole—no trace of anything beyond a thick veil of darkness—closing in on itself, more and more by the second.

Pharis tugged on her hand, unceremoniously yanking her through the opening. The first thing Aurianna felt was the nausea and confusion of everything, once again, falling into a spinning nothingness.

The second thing she felt was the icy, cold slap of water as she hit with a force hard enough to make her lose consciousness.

As her senses returned, Aurianna was vaguely aware of Pharis pulling her through the water, up and over a ledge of some sort, and positioning her on her side on the hard ground. A coughing fit seized her, expelling the water from her lungs with a fierce intensity that made her shudder, increasing the shaking of her nearly frozen form.

When the choking sensation fled her body, she closed her eyes and lay back down, trying to get her breathing back into a normal rhythm while still trembling from the cold.

Aurianna opened her eyes.

And stared.

And continued to stare in wonder and bewilderment at the expanse before her.

The waves rolled and crashed around her, their noise hidden behind the silence of her mind in that moment.

Despite her shock, Aurianna pushed herself into a seated

position. She forced her legs—now trembling from something other than cold—beneath her as she attempted to stand.

The *sun*.

The sun's rays were beaming down on them. The sky was an infinite blue interspersed with soft white and voluminous shapes which drifted through the air like nothing she had ever seen before.

Because she *had* never seen any of it before, not like this. But Aurianna knew what it was, what all of it was. There was no mistaking something that breathtaking, that magnificently warm and delicious. The cold was already beginning to seep from her bones as she stood basking in the light, a ridiculous grin plastered on her face as she continued to gaze about in wonder at the miracle above them.

I must be dreaming.

Her concept of "sky" was an unbroken sheet of gray gloom, a blanket of mist with the slightest hints of some far-off dregs of light that barely managed to illuminate their daily activities. Older people, like her aunt, had described their memories of blue skies with distinct clusters of billowing clouds, but the startling intensity of the vast azure expanse and the sheer enormity of the roving white masses were almost more than her overwrought mind could handle.

Turning in a circle, she took in the entire landscape as far as her vision allowed. They appeared to be on a small rocky piece of land in the middle of the water. All around, the steep cliff faces marked the world as she knew it. Only this wasn't the world as she knew it.

Her world was atop the cliffs and below a sky vastly different from the one her eyes now beheld. But the witness of her eyes wasn't enough.

This can't be real.

Off in the distance on a slightly rising hill, a city lay sprawled in a familiar pattern, the town she called home. The looming structure Pharis had called the Imperium was sitting on its tiny island, the back side of the building facing them, but with a much brighter—and less creepy—feel to it than her earlier experience. To her left and right, the cliffs rose and continued into the distance behind them, with the promise of other possible towns and people along the way. Pharis had dragged her out of the water onto a small indentation of crumbled rock at the base of a tall spire jutting up out of the water. The top of the rocky structure was at least forty feet above their heads.

Reluctantly pulling her eyes away from the view, Aurianna looked over to see Pharis staring intently at her, an odd expression on his face. She pointed at the spiky rock tower looming over them. "What is this? Where are we?"

For a moment, he seemed confused, then answered, "You don't pay attention well, do you? This is my home. Your home. A century before the time when you lived here, but it's the same place. We're just a little off, space-wise, is all. But that was expected."

"I don't understand. Why didn't we land in the same place?"

Pharis huffed, fumbling in his pockets for something. "Because, you silly girl, the world is constantly spinning. Traveling through time is one thing. Taking the position of the space into account is something else entirely. The Essence allow traveling through their realm, but they decide the exact specifics." He pursed his lips, pausing his movements as he turned to frown at her. "We couldn't predict exactly *where* we'd land even if we knew the *when*. Traveling through the Aether involves traveling through time, not space." His hands continued their search as he patted his clothing with increasing urgency. "As far as the Aether is concerned, space is relative to where we were in relation to the world, not where our feet happened to be touching the ground. The world kept spinning over those hundred years. We didn't. Got it?" He finally managed to pull an object from his pocket. It, like the magic flame, was made of metal, but it was much larger and had a completely different shape.

Horror inched up her spine. "Are you saying we could have ended up stuck *inside* this rock instead of beside it?"

Pharis shook his head. "The Essence wouldn't let that happen."

Nodding, she was about to ask him what the object from his pocket was, when Pharis surprised her by lifting the thing with one hand, pointing it straight up. A blast of noise that rocked her eardrums erupted from his hand. She winced as a burst of light flew up into the air.

"Flare gun. It's a signal to let them know we're here, so someone can come pick us up."

"Do they have a boat or something?" She had been fascinated as a young child by a tiny replica of a boat inside a bottle belonging to one of their neighbors. Aunt Larissa had said they were used for traveling the waters long ago.

"Or something, yeah. Come on. We have to climb to the top." Pharis began walking up the spiraling slope that wound up the side of the rock, Aurianna following closely behind. She was close enough to hear him mutter, "And I'm *not* taking another swim in this blasted water for the rest of my life."

When they reached the top of the spire, Aurianna didn't even notice her exhaustion from the events of the last several hours. The sun held her full attention, the world around them so incredibly bright and filled with color that she wasn't sure she would ever be able to look away. This was better than any magic.

At the top of the spire, they both clung to the jagged tip to avoid falling into the crashing waves below. They couldn't stand properly but Aurianna braced her feet against the rocky slope.

After a few moments, something in the distance caught her eye.

She saw movement atop the Imperium, but she couldn't tell what it was. It looked like a puffy oblong ball with a giant wooden tub attached underneath, but it was too far away for her to be sure. As the structure moved toward the closer edge of the Imperium's roof, it seemed like it was going to fall over the edge.

After a moment's pause, it did in fact fall over the edge, causing Aurianna to cry out.

Pharis nudged her with his elbow. "Stop that! It's fine, I promise."

As she watched, the tub seemed to slow its descent significantly. Once it passed the top edge of the island's cliff face, the tub's downward path slowed even more, eventually leveling off some distance above the water's surface as it began moving toward them.

Aurianna had no idea what she was seeing, but it did not look normal or natural to her eyes.

The object drifted closer, and she was able to perceive more detail, the air seeming to carry it along without any friction.

What she had originally taken for a tub she now recognized as a long, somewhat narrow boat suspended by a bunch of thick black ropes from what could only be described as a massive elongated bubble. The bubble, which appeared to be constructed from some kind of sturdy fabric, looked fit to burst.

After only a few minutes, the strange transport arrived beside them, hovering in the air in a way that completely unnerved her. Pharis grasped the wooden edge of the contraption and swung himself into the boat, but Aurianna was too scared to move.

"Get in the damn ship!" Pharis yelled at her. She shook her head, wide eyes staring at him.

The man who had been steering the boat—*ship?*—held his hand out to her. "Come on. It's perfectly safe, dear. I promise." He had a large black mustache and matching eyebrows but no other hair on his face or his head. His features were gruff looking, but his eyes seemed kind to Aurianna, and she smiled at his words. Reaching out tentatively, she allowed him to take her hand and pull her slowly toward the "ship". Impatiently, Pharis sat down on one of the wooden seats along the edges, refusing to help or look at her, turning his eyes toward home.

Once she was settled, having taken a seat away from her grumpy companion, the man went back to the helm and started turning them around. He looked at Aurianna as they took off in the direction of the Imperium.

"You've never been on an airship before, have you?"

"I've never even seen one. This is…" She was unable to finish her sentence, the words floating off into the air around them as she felt the sensation of flying across the water.

The man smiled. "Amazing?" he offered.

Aurianna smiled back. "Yeah. Amazing." The world around them danced in her vision—she realized she was holding her breath—as she tried to take it all in at once.

"The balloon up there"—he pointed a meaty finger above her head at the giant bubble—"it's filled with Air and moves wherever I tell it to. I'm an Aerokinetic. Not too many like me." He laughed, puffing out his chest. "What's your name, girl?"

"Aurianna."

He smiled again, turning the wheel slightly with one hand and waving the other in front of him as they dipped close to the waves below them. "Nice to meet you. My name is Argo, and this here is my airship, the *Minya*." Smile widening, he gestured ahead. "The town in front of us there"—he nodded his head to point—"including the Imperium, is all part of the capital city. Welcome to Bramosia, Aurianna."

* * *

Climbing out of the airship onto the roof of the Imperium, Aurianna felt her legs tremble to have stone once again beneath her feet. It was a strange sensation considering the fact that this should have been the most normal thing in her experience. But the ride across the water had done something to her, scrambled her senses.

Slowly, her equilibrium normalized as she stood and stared at the small delegation of people waiting for them. Head swimming, knees buckling, she suddenly realized just how dizzyingly high up they were. Argo had taken the airship on its earlier path in reverse, back up the side of the Imperium, an experience Aurianna was not yet able to comprehend. The entire thing was ludicrous, yet she had been a part of it.

Water glided by on both sides of them in gushing torrents, a never-ending flow of liquid glass. The rapids cascaded over the side of the Imperium, disappearing into the depths below. Yet the water continued to flow across the top of the building. Where did it come from, and where did it go?

None of it made any sense to Aurianna, but just then her immediate thoughts were of her surroundings. Further in the distance, across the expanse of water below, a tiny figure stood atop a high cliff, leaning dangerously close to the edge. Gazing at the form that seemed so close yet so very far away, her vision expanded, and Aurianna saw the full reality of the world she had lived in her whole life. The entire landscape before her was one long cliff that curved away in both directions. She'd had no idea the cliffs continued on for what seemed like forever. Despite occupying the same space, her known world of one simple town surrounded by a vast open nothingness seemed so very small compared to the one now standing open before her in the light of a sun she had never known.

An enthusiastic grin spread across her face. Nothing would stop her now. The world was hers to explore.

The sound of footsteps trailing away brought her out of her reverie. Afraid of being left behind, she followed Pharis as he began to walk toward the group, noticing the people were dressed in both subtly beautiful and bright colors she had only seen on some of the Consils in her time. The future. Their future, her present. Or was it her future now too? It was too hard to wrap her head around any of this, so she gave up trying.

Pharis stopped in front of the group. One of them addressed her, saying, "Welcome to Bramosia, the capital city of Eresseia. I realize this must all be very overwhelming right now, but I assure you we are here to help in any way we can." The man turned to Pharis. "The Magnus has requested we take the two of you straight to the audience chamber. He is waiting for you."

She couldn't be certain, but she thought she saw the slightest twitch to Pharis's lips. He replied, "Of course."

The colorfully garbed group led the way to a door in a corner of the rooftop. Silently following behind, Aurianna noticed each corner contained a door of its own. The door they went through opened into a stairwell winding down in a steep spiral for what looked like quite a long way, making Aurianna wonder if they were traveling all the way to the bottom level of the building. At the last minute she turned and, as the door was closing, waved goodbye to Argo. Grinning widely, he waved back.

They eventually left the stairs, veering right onto a short metal platform that took them to another door. Aurianna gasped when she was led inside.

A vast, open room spread out in every direction, flowing patterns and colors that took her breath away. The interior of the structure was made mostly from stone, just like the exterior had appeared to be. But everywhere she looked, the bursts of color took over her senses. Reds, blues, violets, and purples covered much of the floor and walls in the form of fabrics in intricate patterns. Some adorned the wall in vertical lines, some covered areas of the floor beneath them. Even the wide staircase on the opposite side of the room was covered in a perfectly cut piece of scarlet with swirls of bright yellow and orange.

The uncovered parts of the floor looked somewhat familiar, and she realized the marble floors resembled those in the Consilium back home (and presumably in the one now as well). The patterns were different, but she still felt a strange connection to this place. To Aurianna's unaccustomed eyes, the overall effect was too much to take in at once.

And there, right in the center of the space, a massive piece of stone architecture depicting what looked to be a battle scene. Water flowed out from all around the bottom of the scene into the giant stone basin in front. Aurianna gaped.

Then she realized what she wasn't seeing. There were no candles. Looking up in wonder, Aurianna saw what was making the room so bright.

Electric power.

Light was raining down on them from a multitude of sources high on the ceiling. She recognized them from the Consilium back home. This was the same power they used to provide electricity to the building, lighting its rooms and corridors. But she had never seen so many of the light sources before, never seen a room so brightly lit.

Her frozen stance must have caused concern because one of the group, a short but powerfully built female with light-brown skin and small metal circles jutting out from various parts of her face, asked, "Are you all right?"

Peeling her eyes from her surroundings, Aurianna said, "Oh, yes! Sorry, I just . . . I've just never seen so much color and light."

The girl's eyes flicked down to Aurianna's drab attire, so she added, "Yeah, we don't have access to colored fabrics where I'm from. I mean *when* I'm from. Or...I don't know. It would be when, right?" Time travel semantics were going to be an issue, she decided.

The girl laughed. "Yes, I guess so."

The group continued across the room as Aurianna took in the rows of columns leading up both sides of the space, which arched and met in the vaulted ceiling far above. Each pillar was massive, with what looked eerily like the head of some sort of creature protruding from the top. Murals were painted on the ceiling and on some of the walls, but most of the wall space was either bare or taken up by the beautiful fabric creations. Aurianna noticed many of them had symbols that seemed to repeat across multiple tapestries, and she made a mental note to ask about them later. She had far more pressing questions she'd like to have answered first.

Aurianna followed them over to the fancy staircase she'd noticed from the other end of the room. With a wide entrance and a massive handrail in the middle, sectioning off the left and right sides, the structure made Aurianna feel certain she was headed somewhere very important. They ascended the stairs that swept majestically in both directions to circle around to the upper floor. Stepping through an entrance with guards on either side, they were standing in a room directly above the one they had just left.

The upper room was similar in width but half as long as the one below, with even more fabric lining the spaces along the walls and floor. At the far end, opposite the staircase, sat a man in a large chair. He wore robes of a deep purple, the silver lining thick with embroidered designs along every edge. He had a high collar, and around his neck he wore a plain silver pendant. On his head was a small silver band. Despite its lack of ornamentation, the headpiece seemed to imply this man was very important.

He was surrounded on both sides by men dressed in identical brown robes. Juxtaposed with the vibrant colors of the man in the chair, their plainness was accentuated. They neither moved, nor smiled.

Behind them was a closed doorway that presumably led to the rest of the level. Aurianna wondered what lay beyond that wall.

As they drew close, Aurianna could see her initial assessment had been correct: the man sitting in the middle was obviously someone highly valued or respected, as his clothing and demeanor suggested. He sat with his back perfectly straight, his chin slightly tilted into the air, eyes watching her with a keen sense of something hidden, some secret he kept.

As they approached the dais, the ones who had guided them from the roof moved aside, allowing her to move ahead with Pharis. Aurianna felt more than a small twinge of fear pass through her as she glanced among them. Once he reached the area directly in front of the seated man, Pharis briefly bent at the waist, lowering his head. Aurianna, following, wondered if she should do the same, but before she had the chance, the seated man turned to her and spoke.

"Greetings, Aurianna. We've been waiting quite a while for you."

Pharis's head shot up, his body straightening and shoulders tensing at the man's words. His entire demeanor changed, blue eyes flashing and all pretense of humility gone. He stepped forward with teeth clenched. "What do you mean, a *while*?"

The man in the chair sighed and shifted uncomfortably, looking sideways at one of the robed men standing beside him. Hesitantly, he said, "Well, Pharis, as you know, the time travel mechanism is at the whim of the Essence. You were just brought back a little later than expected is all."

"How much later?" Pharis asked, his teeth still clenched.

The man stared at him before replying, "Fifty-nine days."

Silence filled the room for what seemed an eternity before Pharis suddenly turned around and stormed back the way they had come.

"Pharis, wait!" the man yelled after him. When Pharis didn't stop, he added, "As your Magnus, I command you to stop!"

Pharis halted. Turning back to face them, he calmly replied, "As you wish, *Magnus*." His caustic emphasis on the last word left an uncomfortable feeling in the air. Still, he returned to his previous spot in front of the Magnus.

"I am sorry for it. I truly am. We had no idea the Essence would refuse to honor your request." The Magnus hesitated before asking, "You did ask for the correct day, did you not?"

"You mean did I follow the instructions pounded into my head a thousand different times in a thousand different ways by your dutiful friends here?" He gestured to the robed men surrounding the Magnus.

Aurianna had been certain that Pharis could not have looked angrier than he did before, but somehow his coldness in that moment seemed far more deadly than anything she had ever witnessed. It reminded her of the night her friends had betrayed her and the devastation she had felt in knowing how alone in the world she truly was. A coldness had crept into her heart that night, one Aurianna had been unable to shake completely, no matter how many times Faethe had apologized. The sad truth was her friend wasn't sorry for what she had done. She was only sorry Aurianna was so bitter about it.

"Pharis, I…" the man began.

"Of course I asked for the correct day. The day after I left. The day I expected to be coming home." Pharis was practically seething in his anger. Clearly, this was not something any of them had been prepared for, despite their supposed knowledge of time travel and the Essence, whatever that was.

One of the robed men on the dais stepped forward and cleared his throat. "We can only assume the Essence had a reason for this. No one knows their minds or their reasons, so we must move forward and focus on the plan."

"Ah, yes. The plan. I had almost forgotten about *the plan*." The cynicism in Pharis's voice was beginning to unnerve her, so she slowly began to back away from him and the man called Magnus. She felt a hand on the small of her back. One of the young men from the group had stepped up to stop her moving away from the spectacle.

"Don't," he whispered in her ear, his mouth so close his breath felt intensely hot against her skin.

"What?" she asked in what she hoped was an equally low volume.

"Shhh," he whispered against her hair. Her insides tingled, causing her to twitch slightly. "Don't say anything. Just walk back up there." With a gentle shove at her back, the man returned to his previous location as if nothing had occurred. Aurianna walked slowly forward until she was standing beside Pharis again, realizing she had missed some of their conversation.

"And what about our guest?" the Magnus inquired, looking in her direction with an air of mild curiosity.

She started to cringe under the scrutiny but refused to let him intimidate her. Lifting her chin, she replied, "What *of* me, sir? I have no idea why I'm here, other than the fact that my aunt insisted it was necessary to 'save the world,' as silly as that sounds when I say the words out loud. I've been dragged, threatened, and verbally berated across time and space, and I'd like a little more explanation than just the idea that I'm 'destined' to be here."

Competing looks of frustration and something akin to admiration seemed to battle for dominance over Pharis's face. The man he had called Magnus, on the other hand, looked sharply at Pharis upon hearing her words.

"Threatened? By whom?" His tone was pure menace.

Pharis sighed in exasperation. "The girl was refusing to come. You said, 'one way or another,' right? Well, one way wasn't working, so I tried another. It turns out she was willing to come along with merely *threats* of violence. I swear I didn't touch a hair on her pretty little head." Bowing his own pretty head, he added, "So, if you'll excuse me, I'll be going back to my room to prepare myself for tomorrow. Whatever tomorrow is now." Despite his parting words, his anger seemed to have somewhat dissipated into a reluctant resignation.

Before he could stalk off, the Magnus said, "It sounds like she has a lot of questions left unanswered at this point."

"Questions I was instructed not to answer. And others for which I *have* no answer. Let your Arcanes respond to her incessant interrogation. I assure you she does love to hear herself speak."

"Fair enough. But I need you to escort our guest on a tour of the Imperium and grounds. She'll need to acclimate herself to a completely new environment fairly quickly as her training begins tomorrow."

"What do I look like, a servant? Have one of your welcoming party handle—"

"I will have you handle it, Pharis! Her questions can be answered now, by you, and anything you are unsure of can be cleared up tomorrow. Understood?"

"Understood." The pause was only slight, but the still-smoldering anger in Pharis's tone was unmistakable.

Aurianna couldn't stand for people to be talking about her as if she wasn't there, but a part of her was too frightened to speak. When the Magnus dismissed her with a flick of his hand, she followed Pharis as he left the room and went back down the stairs, the group that had met them on the roof trailing behind. As she started down the staircase, a voice followed her.

"Welcome to your new home, Aurianna." The voice belonged to the young man who had stopped her from trying to back away earlier. Hearing the words directed at her, Aurianna glanced back to get a better look at her secret helper. Tall—slightly taller even than Pharis—with a thin build and hair that fell halfway to his shoulders, hair so white it was practically silver. The man's deep brown eyes twinkled devilishly and contrasted dramatically with his alabaster skin. And his lopsided smile gave the impression he was amused by something—her? It was impossible to tell. He looked young, probably younger and certainly no older than she was, and every bit as friendly as his voice had sounded. Aurianna was immediately suspicious. No one was that friendly, in her experience.

They reached the bottom of the wide staircase and strolled across the room toward the building's entrance. "What's the look for, honey? I'm just trying to be friendly." His eyebrow shot up. "Am I making you uncomfortable? I just thought you could use a smiling face after all those sour ones back there."

"Ambrogetti! Why don't you get back to class, huh?" Pharis had turned sharply to address the young man.

"Well, now. Settle down there. I'm just trying to help the young lady out after you and your father did your best to terrify her with your let's-see-who-has-the-bigger-pair routine back there," came the slow drawl from her unsolicited companion. Everyone had stopped moving, the others in the group looking more than slightly uncomfortable at the exchange. The two men stared at one another without blinking.

"Excuse me?" Pharis said with distaste. He looked ready to explode, crushing his lips together into a thin line.

Aurianna noticed the friendly woman from the welcoming group with whom she'd briefly spoken earlier. She stood apart, her eyes focused elsewhere and glazed over as if daydreaming.

"Look, I'm just here because—"

"You'll show some respect, Javen Ambrogetti, or I'll make sure you're still here, waiting to graduate a year from now."

Nostrils flaring and jaw clenched, Javen glared at Pharis for a moment. "No offense intended. I was just trying to keep things nice and simple. As I was saying, the only reason I'm here is because the Magnus thought it would be good to have some Acolytes her own age in the welcoming party. Obviously, as you pointed out, I'm one of the few that fit the description." Javen turned to Aurianna, smiling with genuine warmth as he extended his hand. "I happen to have the afternoon off from classes in order to be here. I might as well make myself useful. If you'd be willing," he gestured with an open palm motioning toward their surroundings, then turned back to Pharis. "I'd be happy to take the young lady around the place and show her everything she needs to know. Seems I'd be better suited for the job, seeing as I know more about the training side of this place." He raised his eyebrows meaningfully at Pharis, a gesture that didn't go unnoticed by Aurianna, though she couldn't be sure what he was implying.

Eyes flashing for an instant, Pharis regained his composure, straightening and raising his chin in the air. "So be it. I have work to do." He veered left and took off toward the door they had used earlier. Javen, still holding his right hand out, waited patiently for her to accept his offer and his help. She still didn't want to trust him, but getting her away from Pharis had been one point in his favor. A tour and some answers were both on the agenda, it seemed.

She felt the urge to acquiesce and give him her hand, but she resisted, instead nodding up at him with a slight smile. "Lead on."

His confident gaze faltered for half a second before he returned her smile. Refusing to be rebuffed, he grabbed and tucked her hand into the crook of his arm. She was not at all comfortable with the intimacy of the connection and stiffened, refusing to move forward with him.

His lips quirked in wry amusement, and he drawled, "No?" She smiled back, despite herself and shook her head, pulling her arm back. One corner of his mouth lifted up in amusement, and he drawled, "I was merely being polite. You can just follow me if you like." Smiling back despite herself, she nodded.

Shrugging, Javen led her to the right, in the direction of an identical door to the one Pharis had taken in the other corner of the room. Aurianna stayed in step with him as they approached the door that opened into another spiraling staircase leading up into the dark unknown. She felt this world was already swallowing her whole.

CHAPTER 9

AURIANNA

"The room we just left is the main hall. The room above, filled with the grumpy old men, is what we call the throne room, even though the Magnus is not technically a king, nor does he have a throne. Technically. But that's another matter entirely. It would more properly be called an audience chamber, I suppose." Javen was gesturing in the general direction of the room as he spoke. Aurianna felt herself smiling despite her reservations about Javen. He seemed kind, but she knew better. Even the closest of friends could turn on you. Besides, this place, this time…it all felt like a dream.

Or a nightmare. Either way, she wasn't about to let her guard down to anyone, let alone a complete stranger.

They continued up the stairs, the metal resounding in muffled echoes with each step they took. The handrails felt smooth to the touch, no sign of rust or deterioration. Then she remembered.

"What about the lower levels? Do they exist here? Well, I guess they must, or else Pharis wouldn't have known about them." At the mention of the other man's name, Javen flinched. "Or would he?

I'm so confused about how this time traveling works. How is it you have things like that ship and ... and time travel, and we don't? Can you go anywhere, anytime you like? Are those stones the only way to do it? How does it work? What is the Essence? Is the Aether—"

Javen laughed. "Hold on a second there." He paused as they reached a door two levels up from the main hall.

Before he could answer any of her questions or lead her further, she asked, "What's the deal between you and Pharis?"

His smile drooped and, nostrils flaring, Javen dropped the hand he had raised to push open the door. "His sister disappeared not too long ago. He thinks I was involved."

"What? Why you?"

"Because it's no secret I have no love for their family and what they represent. He thinks I'm involved with the resistance movement."

"Resistance to what?"

"To the whole setup. Just people tired of being under the thumb of Kinetics, being reliant on magic for everything. No one knows if they even exist as an organized group."

"Oh." She opened her mouth to ask another question as Javen opened the door into a large room. Aurianna paused, mouth open and stunned as she gaped around the room. *The Consilium has nothing on this place*, she thought. She slowly took in the ostentatious display. Javen nudged her to precede him, and they entered the hall.

Eight long, narrow tables with cushioned benches stretched the length of each side with a few shorter ones scattered in a nearby corner. Aurianna could see people standing in a line, holding things in their hands, as others sat at the far end of the long tables, eating and talking quietly. There didn't seem to be many people, particularly for the amount of seating available. Only a handful seemed to notice their presence, and those who did quickly went back to their conversations once they saw nothing interesting was happening.

"This," Javen gestured grandly, "is the dining hall. Not many people are eating the midday meal at this hour. It's still pretty early for most groups, but those who work the second shift around here are sort of forced to eat pretty early."

"Shift for what?" Aurianna asked.

"Depends. A lot of them are city guards. Some have jobs in the area. Some Kinetics work outside of the capital, so they eat wherever they're stationed for most of their meals. Everyone has a routine, even if it's not *routine*, so to speak." He flashed what he obviously thought was a disarming smile, but Aurianna, while tempted to find him charming, was not about to let down her guard.

"Hmm," she replied noncommittally.

Not discouraged in the slightest, he continued to smile at her until she began to feel uncomfortable. "What is it?" she asked, trying to keep the acid from her tone.

To his credit, his grin only faltered slightly. "I just... I can only imagine how strange this must all seem to you, considering where you're from." He paused. "Or when, I guess I should say."

"And just what exactly do you know about where—or when—I'm from?"

Javen shrugged, running his hand through the back of his ice-blond hair. "Not much, to be honest. I know things are different in your time. Much different. No Kinetics, no power, no structure. Just a small community left, and not really enough food to go around. The Arcanes briefed us—*us* meaning your welcoming party—on the basics. Based on what you're wearing, I'm guessing they weren't exaggerating about the limited resources, either."

One eyebrow shot up and her voice went flat. "What... I'm wearing."

At least he had the decency to blush at her tone. "Well, I mean …well, you know it's…it's just different is all. No colors, no shape. Just different, see?" As he spoke the last part, he gestured around to those who were walking past them in the dining hall, a flurry of bright colors and garments that looked as if they were made specifically for each individual. Maybe he was right, but still.

She decided to change the subject. "So, who are the Arcanes? I mean, they exist in my timeline as well. But who are they, exactly? I've always wondered about them." As she spoke, a particularly large woman in a bright green robe with a tall brown collar stepped between them, forcing Aurianna to back up. The woman looked at Javen, smiling and waving in an odd way as she passed by, seemingly trying to appear flirtatious. He returned both gestures, albeit half-heartedly, a look of discomfort on his face.

Once she had passed, Javen's smile wavered again as he narrowed his eyes. "You have them in your time?" When Aurianna nodded, he said, "No one knows much about them, honestly. They keep to themselves and stay underground mostly, down in the Imperium's lower levels. Except when they're summoned by the Magnus, of course. They don't usually welcome visitors to their rooms, except the Magnus or the Regulus. The Arcanes advise the Magnus on matters of importance, but mainly they just stick to themselves doing…whatever it is they do."

"So, their job is just as cryptic here as it is in my time?"

"Yeah, I guess so. Are you hungry? We can take a quick break if you like."

Aurianna smiled sheepishly. "No, I'm afraid I'm a bit too worked up from all the excitement right now. Thank you though."

Javen led her back to the staircase. She followed him down until he exited through yet another door. The floor here was untiled—a mixture of dirt and stone—the walls unadorned. They were standing in a small alcove, surrounded by several passages branching off in different directions. Aurianna looked about in wonder, recognizing the lower levels she and Pharis had traveled through on their way to the Aether Stone. The memory did not sit well with her.

"The Imperium isn't used in the future, so the Arcanes are actually housed under the Consilium instead. I wonder why." She paused to look around, adding, "I've seen this place back—(*forward*? she thought)—in my time, but what is it for?"

"This is the beginning of the lower levels. The Arcanes are in that direction." He pointed down one of the passages. "We're below ground level right now, so the underground chambers are much larger than the floors above. Not sure why, but maybe to accommodate all the Voids, though I don't know how long it's been like this. I'm not exactly a historian." Javen's smile had returned full force and, despite her best efforts to stop her face from betraying her, she could feel herself smiling back.

She looked at him expectantly for a moment. When he didn't get the hint—just continued to smile at her—she sighed. "Okay, I'll ask. Voids?"

"Ah. Well . . . Voids are those who didn't quite make it through training, so to speak. Sometimes a child will display powers that never fully manifest themselves. They can occasionally show Kinetic abilities, but it's purely by accident and only on rare occasion. Problem is, by the time they find out, they've already been taken from their home and brought here, probably already trained for a good amount of time. At that point, their family has already accepted they aren't coming back, and to be honest, going back isn't really an option. Being a Void isn't exactly something to be proud of, let's just say. They're called 'Voids' because they are considered empty of power, empty on the inside." Javen couldn't hide the bitterness from his tone, his eyes looking off into the distance at some remembered pain.

Something about what he'd said was bothering her a great deal. "So, they take Kinetics as children? Just take them away from their families and keep them here? Can't they at least go visit?"

As he answered, they began walking the length of one of the corridors in the vast underground network. "Powers typically begin to manifest just before puberty, around nine or ten years of age. That's the normal starting age for training, so they must come here or risk their powers controlling them. Having your child almost burn down your home is a pretty good incentive for most people. That isn't to say it's not difficult, and visiting is off limits for several years until they get some sense of adjustment. But things have been this way for long enough people are sort of used to it. Once upon a time, having a Kinetic in the family was a source of pride for most people."

"Meaning now it isn't?"

Up ahead, Aurianna saw an open expanse situated at the intersection of several of the passages, a large group of children standing in a circle, all of them intent on an oblong pit of glowing magma. Here, at last, was something she found familiar, despite the undercurrent of fear that came along with the memories of the burning pits back home. She suddenly realized this was where she had asked Pharis about the protective walls for the magma. Was it not all around them? How were they not burning up?

She stood mesmerized as some of them raised their hands in the air, the intense red liquid following the arc of their arms as the Kinetics swayed their fingertips in time to some unheard beat. The magma flowed through the air as if by magic (*well, it was a sort of magic, wasn't it?*), curling tendrils of heat floating in the midst of the people gathered there. None of them were burned, and none of them seemed concerned in the least. She made a mental note to ask more about this later, though she felt certain the answers would only bring more questions.

"It's complicated. Many of the villagers are unhappy with the way our current Magnus is running things. The system's been in place for many generations, so being dependent upon Kinetics isn't a new thing. But the Magnus tends to push new developments requiring the rest of the world to have more reliance on *us* and less on *themselves*. Some people don't take too kindly to it and want to do more within their own communities. As it stands, Kinetics run most everything. We provide most of the things they need to survive, like heat, Energy, irrigation for crops, you name it."

"Energy?"

"Energy, uh . . . it's what gives off light, among other things. It's one of the Kinetic elements."

"Oh, the electricity! I see. So, why is that a bad thing? I wish our Consils had done more for us."

"That's just it. The Consils are the representatives for the regions, a way for non-Kinetics to have a say in how things are run. They're supposed to play a bigger part in running Eresseia as a whole, but the Magnus keeps stepping up his role little by little. A lot of people don't like the idea of being at our mercy for so much of what they need. They'd like to do more for themselves. But too many have gotten lazy and don't mind letting Kinetics do all the work."

"You have Consils here as well?" Aurianna asked.

"Yes, well, the other Consils are supposed to work in conjunction with the Magnus."

"The Magnus is a Consil as well?"

"Sort of. Yeah, I mean, he's supposed to be one of six. He's meant to be more of a figurehead, a leader and representative of the Kinetics. But it seems more like he's running the show lately from what I've seen. In addition to the Magnus, each of the five regions has a Consil."

"There are *five regions*?" Aurianna's voice was a whisper filled with wonder.

"Six. There's Vanito—that's where I'm from—and Ramolay. Plus Menos, Eadon, and Rasenforst. And the Magnus represents Bramosia and the Imperium, making six Consils in total."

"You don't like him much, do you?"

"I wouldn't necessarily say that. I've got nothing against him personally, but I don't like all of his policies." Winking at her, he added, "Just don't mention that to anybody, you hear?"

"Is it an unpopular opinion to have?"

"Around here? Sometimes. Most Kinetics don't mind having a job, a purpose for their training. Seems a waste otherwise. But some think about their families back home and wish things were different for them."

Javen stopped in front of a small, wooden door on the left side of the hall, pointing further into the looming passageway only partially lit by the sparse candlelight. "That way leads to even more tunnels. This place is a maze, but I think this should be the last stop on our tour for today." He pushed the door open into a tiny version of the dining hall upstairs. Men and women in dull gray robes were sitting at the tables, eating, or milling around in groups. The moment they noticed the open door, all conversation ceased, and all eyes were focused on them. No, not them. Just her.

For a moment, no one moved or spoke, the air thick with an unvoiced question. Then Javen closed the door with a soft bang, breaking the spell of silence, for she could hear the voices begin speaking again behind the door.

He answered Aurianna's questions before she could ask this time. "That's the dining hall for the Voids. They have their own routines and run their own schedules, but essentially they have shifts like the adult Kinetics."

"So they're guards as well? Why do they dress differently?"

Javen looked taken aback for a moment. "No, no. Not guards. They run the Imperium's day-to-day tasks, like cooking, cleaning, serving in the upstairs dining hall. Remember, they have no powers. Not truly anyway. The robes mark them as Voids, so no one forgets they are second-class denizens of the Imperium."

"So . . . what? They're forced to work here for the rest of their lives, cooking your dinner and scrubbing the floors?"

"Basically, yes." Javen's two-word answer contained all the information she needed. The idea made her more than a little uncomfortable. Even knowing what her people did to the unfortunate Kinetics who escaped to the future didn't diminish the reverse problem she saw here. The irony was not lost on her.

Sensing Javen had something to say, she turned to him. For a moment, he looked on the verge of speaking but eventually shifted his expression and merely asked, "How would you like to meet some friends of mine?"

Chapter 10

AURIANNA

Javen led Aurianna back upstairs, up the winding staircase, across the main hall and through the massive double doors she had noticed earlier. She realized these were the same doors she and Pharis had entered, in her time, on their way to finding the Aether Stone. Of course, then it had been too dark, the ravages of time masking the characteristics of the hall despite Pharis's torch.

This was the main entrance to the building—but the gateway to this new world. Would she be allowed to leave of her own accord? Could she explore this familiar, yet unfamiliar, world without having to sneak away? Did she have a curfew here? Were there Praefects watching and dictating her movements? Freedom was an idea she felt unaccustomed to, and she suddenly realized just how much of a prisoner she'd been her entire life.

She looked about, taking in the bright day and colorful gardens. People were walking around the grounds, some with a purpose, some merely strolling along at a leisurely pace. And it was easy to see why.

Breathing deeply, she noted how much more pleasant the smell of the water below appeared to be. Perhaps it was all in her head, but this place—this *time*—presented itself as a reprieve from her normal life, despite the confined feeling she had inside the Imperium. This was not her normal life, but it was for these people, these figures running along in their daily duties, coming and going, tending the gardens, which stretched before her to the left and right. They went about their normal lives as if people weren't dying, as if the world wasn't going to hell in just a handful of generations. Aurianna reminded herself that none of these people knew that fact, and none of them had the ability to change one bit of it. That was supposed to be her job, though how in the world she was expected to accomplish it, she had no idea.

Thoughts racing through her head at breakneck speed, she gazed out into the immaculately tended gardens, the rows of colorful blossoms of all shapes and sizes, the ivy lacing its way up the walls of the castle-like structure with still more blooms seeming to reach the sky. Somewhere up there she knew the twin rivers of flowing water ran down the back side of the Imperium before cascading into the water below.

Aurianna followed him around the side of the structure. Entering the gardens to the left, she looked off into the distance at the coastline that disappeared into the horizon. Running all around the edge of the cliffs were metal rails, a rusted anomaly in her time, ignored as a useless vestige of the past. Judging from the ones nearby, they appeared to be in pristine condition now, which sparked an intriguing thought. Could the trains she'd learned about from the books in her time be in existence here? The concept of a machine so complex and intricate, so massive and powerful it could literally carry people from one destination to another seemed almost as wondrous as magic.

Across the expanse of water, she could just barely make out the tiny dot of rock rising from the depths, where she and Pharis had "landed" in this world, when the blazing glory of the unabashed sun had wrapped light beams of euphoria against her skin, across her vision, blinding her as it opened her eyes to the new world in front of her. The rocky pinnacle stood almost dead center between the two sides of the elevated coastline stretching off into the distance in a half-moon shape, the cliff face white and gleaming in the midday rays, the sheen glinting off toward the distance before disappearing into the horizon.

Basking in the sun, Aurianna gazed at the endless possibilities as she tried not to think about how high up they were. Strange how it had never bothered her back home, never even occurred to her as anything more than a *thing-that-was*, a fact, a truth. They were never supposed to go near the Imperium or the cliff's edge, unless instructed or required to do so. Her people merely existed, not looking beyond the view from their front door, and she had been just as guilty as the rest of them.

Only she hadn't. Not always. She had tried to leave, hadn't she? They may have stopped her, beat the idea right out of her head, but she had at least tried. Why had she not tried again? Was her fear of them so great? Ah, there it was—the truth that made her just as complicit as the rest of her people. The truth was . . . her courage had died alongside her trust. No, she had not attempted her journey again. She could have done it if she hadn't told anyone what she was doing. That had been her mistake the first time. But couldn't she have left without a word, and no one been the wiser until morning?

Javen interrupted her thoughts by stepping in front of her view, blocking out the cliff faces and the tiny dot and the water churning far below. Blocking out the memories that were, and the dreams of *what if.* Her attention was brought fully into the present when Javen grasped her upper arm and shook her slightly.

"What?" She jerked her arm away and frowned.

At her outburst, Javen lowered his head and sidestepped away from her burning gaze. Aurianna instantly regretted the harshness of her tone, sighing loudly and adding, "Sorry...Javen. I was lost in thought, a million miles away. Or years perhaps. My anger wasn't directed at you." When he peered back at her from beneath long pale bangs, fierce points of darkest brown held her gaze for just a moment longer than she felt comfortable with, forcing an involuntary chill to creep up her spine and down to her toes. Whether from fear or excitement, she wasn't sure.

"Okay, yes, it was directed at you. What I meant was it wasn't intentional. I'm just angry about a lot of things back home. Y-You j-just"—she stammered as he continued to stare into her soul—"You just startled me is all."

A slight curve at one side of his mouth told her he was amused at least. "Ah" was all he uttered. As he began to walk away from her, she followed in silence. When at last they reached the far back corner of the Imperium grounds, Aurianna could indeed see—and hear—the rushing waters flowing incomprehensibly down the back side of the building and down into the depths below.

Javen walked over to a young woman dressed in clothing similar to several others who were standing around the cliff edges. Dark gray dominated most of the outfit, with black trim and black boots. A dark gray cape hung across one shoulder and around her neck, the ends joined together by several large buttons. It flowed down almost to her knee and sporting a large sigil on the front, presumably something marking her position. Aurianna could only assume it was a uniform of sorts. One piece of her outfit was different, compared to others who wore the same livery. Under the cape, but over the regular tunic, she wore a secondary shirt—or what looked like part of one—joined together at the chest with thin pieces of rope, and a solid black belt at the waist.

On Javen's friend, the over-shirt stood out among the dark blues and greens, the light creams and blacks of the other uniformed people. Hers was a deep rich fuchsia, and in total conflict with the rest of her clothing. Yet, somehow, she made the color work. The woman was petite but extremely muscular, with obvious definition beneath the uniform and an hourglass figure over which Aurianna felt a twinge of envy. Her medium-brown skin with russet undertones was complimented by dark-brown hair, neatly tied up in a ponytail.

Waving her over, Javen waited for Aurianna to approach before gesturing to the woman beside him. "This is Sieglinde Hellswa—ow!" He ducked his head and attempted to block her hands as the small woman punched him over and over. Finally, he grabbed her wrists and said, "Sigi, I've told you before not to do that. You hit harder than you realize, woman!"

Sieglinde began to pummel him again, replying, "Yeah, and I've told *you* before not to *call* me that!" Aurianna stared in bewilderment at the pair until Javen finally backed away and threw his hands up in what appeared to be mock defeat.

"All right, all right. Sorry. Aurianna, this is my friend—" He paused for effect as he gazed sidelong at the young woman, her head tilted in a gesture that could only be threatening further bodily harm to him. "*Sigi* Hellswarth. She's from Rasenforst, a region on the far side of Eresseia," he continued, pointing off into the distance. "Sigi, my dear, my darling friend, this is Aurianna."

Sigi's face shone with genuine enthusiasm. "Nice to meet you, Aurianna. Don't mind this guy." She jerked her thumb at Javen, who was grinning mischievously. "He just likes to get under people's skin sometimes. I hate my full name, and he knows it. Just call me Sigi. *Please.*" Frowning, her brow furrowed as she squinted her left eye in confusion. "Why haven't I seen you before? You seem about my age, right? But you didn't graduate with us. I'm sure of it." She threw a quizzical glance at Javen then looked Aurianna over from head to toe with eyes of blue-gray steel which contrasted spectacularly with her skin tone. Her scrutiny was intense but devoid of hostility.

Aurianna turned to Javen, unsure what to say. He sighed and answered, "Sigi, it's a long story. Aurianna only just arrived here."

"I don't understand. Where are you from?"

Aurianna replied, "Here. I'm from this town."

"Bramosia?" Sigi's look of concern and confusion made Aurianna regret her answer, but she wasn't sure what she was supposed to be telling people. Was she supposed to keep her identity a secret from everyone? Clearly that wasn't going to work if she was to be constantly questioned. Some rule unknown to her had been broken, but she had no idea what it was or how to fix it. "Javen?"

Sigi stared at the young man until he finally responded. "Like I said, it's a long story."

Several bands of black encircled Sigi's legs and torso, holding an assortment of weaponry. Aurianna couldn't identify them all, but she had no doubt—these items that seemed to crawl across the woman's entire torso were deadly. They were made of a similar metal to that of the fire-making device Pharis had shown her. And although they were shaped differently, she assumed they had a similar purpose to the long but thin cylindrical objects she had seen the Carpos wield as they chased down the Kinetic, the edges shining in the tiny dying veins of light from their diseased sun. This woman's accoutrements were larger and bulkier, and Aurianna was suddenly afraid. She wore other items that also seemed like weapons, but she had no frame of reference for them.

Then there was the weird contraption around her neck, two pieces of glass fused together with metal. What was that for? Not to mention the dark branding that twisted down the right side of her neck and disappeared beneath the collar of her tunic. Did they do that here too? Punish wrongdoing with a permanent physical reminder? What had she gotten herself into?

"She's not…you didn't bring a…Javen, please tell me you didn't. I'll have to report this, you know." She shook her head, her long dark hair bouncing with the gesture despite the band around it keeping it off her face.

Javen's eyes grew wide with shock. "No, no. Nothing like that. She's one of us. Just not trained yet."

"What do you mean *not trained yet*?" Her skepticism was replaced by an undercurrent of anger, although Aurianna had no idea why the girl would have any reason to be angry with her, and she suddenly felt the urge to leave. Quickly.

"Relax, girl. It's all on the up and up. Pharis brought her here actually, and it was all approved by the Magnus and the Arcanes. Promise."

"Pharis . . ." She sighed. "Please don't call him that. He . . . he brought her here?" The look of uneasy but thinly veiled disgust Sigi gave her at those words made her think perhaps the anger was preferable. An uncomfortable feeling creeping up her spine, Aurianna began to back away from the conversation.

Javen rolled his eyes at his friend, a loud sigh escaping his lips. "Sigi. No, not like that."

Her brow raising, Sigi said, "Like what then, Javen? For what other reason would he be allowed to bring a strange girl to the Imperium?"

Realization began to dawn on Aurianna, her choked reply sounding like a gasp. "Are you serious? You think I'm here for *that*?"

"Well, he does have quite the reputation, I'm afraid."

Javen interrupted their exchange, saying, "She's untrained, remember? I'm pretty sure that's why she's here. But she is a Kinetic. I know it sounds bizarre, and I know you're just doing your job, Sigi. But ask the Magnus if you don't believe me."

"I have a responsibility as a member of the City Guard, Javen. Don't take it personally."

City Guard. *Well, that explains the uniform.* And she noticed that Sigi periodically glanced about her in an alert-to-her-surroundings way as well.

She turned to Aurianna, who was still inching away. "I apologize for the insinuation, Aurianna. My job is to protect this place, and I must admit this is a first for me. I've never heard of someone our age not being trained. Were you hidden by your family? That's a serious crime."

Javen put his arm at the small of Aurianna's back, bringing her back to stand in front of Sigi again. By pure instinct, she almost jerked away from his touch but, deciding the gesture was meant to be comforting, she begrudgingly allowed it.

Not knowing what else to say, she replied, "Well, that explains all the dangerous gear you're wearing."

"What?"

"I mean you being a City Guard. It's why you have so many weapons, right?"

Javen laughed, startling Aurianna. "I'm pretty sure the 'guard' part is just a bonus for her. She'd be strapped even if she was working the mines." When Sigi slapped his arm, he continued, looking at Aurianna as he spoke. "Sigi's family makes weapons, so she kind of grew up toting metal around like a baby bottle. You could say she's a bit of a fanatic when it comes to weaponry."

The woman blushed, conceding the point. "Yeah, I guess I am.

121

Been carrying guns and swords of all shapes and sizes since I could stand up with the weight. Forging 'em too. My papa is the best metal smelter in all of Rasenforst. It's just my brothers helping him now. Mama passed a long time ago." Aurianna heard the sadness in the girl's voice. "My sister Hilda is here at the Imperium. Both of us girls got the flame, so to speak. None of the boys did though."

Javen smiled gently, winding his arm around his friend's shoulder and squeezing her against his side in a comforting gesture. "It was nice to see you, Sigi, but I think we need to get going if I'm going to show our new friend here around the rest of the place. Seriously though, go speak to the Magnus or one of the Arcanes. Hell, go ask Edelina. She was with us when Pharis brought Aurianna in. She'll tell you."

Sigi admonished, "Javen, stop calling him that. It's disrespectful."

"So? He was being a total ass to me earlier."

"And I'm sure you did *nothing* to antagonize him, as always." Scrunching up her nose, Sigi added in a singsong tone, "Not really the point though, is it?" She smiled at Aurianna. "Good luck with your training. Perhaps we'll be able to meet up for a meal in the next couple of days. You could tell me more about yourself."

Aurianna returned her smile. "I'd like that. Thanks."

Waving to his friend as he turned away, Javen led Aurianna back inside the Imperium. Looking back, she could see Sigi had already returned to her station and was staring resolutely out into the unknown, her hand barely grazing the tip of one of her weapons. The young woman obviously took her job very seriously.

Just before entering the building, Aurianna looked up and saw a giant clock at the very top of the facade, something she hadn't noticed when they had walked out. Once inside, they turned back to the spiral stairwell and continued up, farther than they'd gone before, past several levels including the dining hall they'd visited earlier. As they walked through the door at the next floor up, a long, narrow hallway greeted them with a series of doors on either side at regular intervals. A corridor directly to the right split into rows of other hallways down that side.

"This is the dormitory area for all Acolytes, anyone still in training. To the right are hallways identical to this one, to maximize the space and fit as many rooms in here as possible. They all run parallel to one another, and there are other levels above us set up the same way. This floor is for females, the next one up is for males, and the levels above are strictly for full-fledged Kinetics who work here at the Imperium, like the instructors and guards like Sigi."

"So...I'll have a room as well?"

His mouth curved up at one corner at her hesitation. "Of course. I'll have to find out where you've been placed, but you'll have a private room, I'm sure. Some of the younger Acolytes have to room together, but I highly doubt they'd make you share."

She was grateful and said as much. When her stomach began to grumble, Javen took her down to the dining hall to grab something to eat before figuring out where her room was. And she was so incredibly exhausted, the idea of a bed sounded more interesting and attractive than anything she had seen yet. With a sudden real-ization, she calculated it was the middle of the night by her own internal clock, despite being barely past midday here. The events of the last several hours made her head spin.

Javen invited her to sit down at one of the long tables as he went to make her a tray of food. When he returned with a platter piled with bread, cheese, and two steaming bowls of some sort of stew, Aurianna wanted to cry. Despite her earlier comments about being too wound up to eat, she knew she shouldn't have passed up an opportunity to eat. The rations back home hadn't become miserable yet, but she had never seen this much food at one meal before. She grabbed one of the goblets filled with a clear liquid she hoped was water, downing it in only a few gulps. She quickly began devouring the food in front of her.

Javen stared at her, a quizzical look taking over his face. "Earlier you said you couldn't eat, but…you're starving, aren't you?"

Cheeks flaming in embarrassment, she replied, "Um, we have food and water and all. Just not this much. And it's been a long day. I don't think my body knows what it wants, to be honest."

"Hmm," was all he said. In her mortification, she made a point to slow down after that.

Javen finished his stew first and left her to continue eating as he went off in search of someone in charge of room assignments. When he returned, she was utterly sated and ready to fall into bed and not wake up for many hours.

"I got your room assignment, but they said you'll get your training schedule tomorrow. The room is indeed a single, and as long as there aren't any issues, your schedule will probably remain the same until you reach another level of training."

"I'm certainly tired. I hope it's not too early here for me to sleep. It would be the middle of the night back home."

He smiled as they climbed the staircase back up to the dormitory levels. "It's kind of early, but it's understandable. You'll probably want to familiarize yourself with everything in the room. Clothing and linen should be in the drawers somewhere, as well as soap and things like that. All the rooms are cleaned and set up by Voids. They're usually very thorough."

When they reached the appropriate floor, Javen led her to the hallway on the right and handed her a strange metallic band.

"Wear this on your wrist at all times. No one can get into your room without this, and it's keyed to your identity for use with other areas as well. You just hold it up to the screen beside the door."

"Thank you. For everything. I'm sorry again for snapping at you earlier. I just need some time to adjust."

He gave her another smile and a think-nothing-of-it wave of the hand then changed the subject. "We do get some days off, so maybe I could show you around town one day?"

"I'd like that very much." Her return smile didn't feel forced at all. His charm seemed genuine. She was still wary about these strangers, but he'd been nice to her so far. Letting her guard down was certainly not in her nature, yet...

"Well, get some rest, and I'll come by in the morning to walk you down to breakfast if you like."

As he stood with his gaze darting everywhere but at her, enshrouded in awkward uncertainty, she replied, "Sure. Good night then. Um, good afternoon, I mean."

"Sleep well, Aurianna." He turned to leave.

Holding the bracelet up to the screen beside the door, she heard a whirring sound and watched as the door began to open, the noise no louder than a whisper despite the entrance being made of the same thick metal she kept seeing. When she looked back, Javen was already gone.

As she stepped through the opening, Aurianna searched for a way to illuminate the room. Surely they didn't expect her to stumble around blindly in the dark. When she turned around, she spied a series of buttons on the wall just inside the door. Using the small amount of light trickling in from the hallway, she could just make out the outline of each protrusion. Pressing the first one she felt, Aurianna jumped when the room was flooded with light from overhead. She looked up and saw more of the light sources she had noticed in the main hall downstairs and all around the building.

Experimentally, she pressed each of the other buttons in turn, discovering several other sources of light around the room. She marveled at the simplicity and cleanliness of the space. There was a small bed in the corner, with a tiny table next to it. A small electric light stuck out from the wall just above the table, and she noticed several books stacked there. She picked one up and read the title to herself. *A History of Eresseia.* It sounded incredibly boring. Nonetheless, she was grateful for the opportunity to learn more about her world.

A dresser sat against the wall beside the table, perpendicular to and just beside the door. Aurianna opened the drawers and found a collection of linens and underclothing, as well as several outfits in colors that almost made her squeal with joy. Real colors. Clothing that might actually fit her shape. She held one of the outfits up to her frame, determining that it would fit almost perfectly. How they managed it, she had no idea, but she was overwhelmed with a feeling of euphoria. She couldn't help it. They were just clothes. But combined with everything else, it was more than she could have ever imagined.

Turning back to the buttons on the wall, Aurianna continued pressing them. One lit up an alcove in the back corner across from the foot of the bed. Hesitantly, she walked over to the opening. And gasped.

A bathing room. But not just any bathing room. A tub took up one wall, something that resembled a privy (though a far more complicated affair than anything she'd ever seen) sat in another corner, and towels and soap products filled some shelves.

And sitting at the back of the tiny room was something she had never seen in her life. But she knew exactly what it was.

Aunt Larissa had described them in so much detail over the years that Aurianna knew beyond a shadow of a doubt it was a shower stall. Her aunt had bemoaned the loss of the contraptions, stating a bathing tub was just fine when one wanted to sit in their own filth.

A shower, Larissa had said, was like a little piece of divinity, a breath of fresh air when getting clean was your goal. Now Aurianna had one. And not just that. She had a shower of her own, and no one she had to share with. Larissa would never believe this.

Thinking about her aunt made Aurianna well up with tears. Her body began to shake with uncontrolled sobs. Telling herself she was merely exhausted, she tried to stop, but the tears continued to flow. She slid down the wall and sank to the floor, giving in to the overwhelming emotions. Hugging her knees to her chest, Aurianna rested her forehead on her arms and let the tears fall. *This is all too much*, she thought with a sudden burst of panic. What had she been thinking? She was all alone in an unfamiliar time and an equally unfamiliar place.

This wasn't her home. This was a nightmare.

Pushing herself up off the floor, Aurianna went back into the bedroom, stripping off her frayed tunic and pants. Something bulged within the pocket of the pants—the stone her aunt had given her. She had forgotten all about it. No light emanated from it, and there was no magic within it, but she felt the connection to home.

Grabbing what looked like a nightgown from the dresser, she slid the stone under the clothes in the drawer and turned off the lights after she dressed for the night. Pulling back the thick linens from the bed, she crawled in, admiring the softness of the material despite her continued tears.

Sleep did not come for many hours. When it finally took her in its grasp, her dreams were filled with shadows and light, dancing together in undulating patterns that held many secrets she had yet to uncover.

Chapter 11

PHARIS

The man was insufferable.

No, that didn't even begin to describe the vicious bastard who was currently droning on, unaware of Pharis's fury.

Pharis distracted himself by watching the pre-dawn sky through the window as the barest hint of light teased its way over the treetops. The sun was not yet ablaze with the hope of the day, the hope for a savior who would rescue them from a fate that had not yet come to pass. A fate that, had he not seen it for himself, seemed ridiculous to even consider. But he *had* seen it and could give testimony to the standard of so-called living those people experienced and struggled against every day. Even the poorest residents in this time had more.

The Magnus, surrounded by a silent cadre of Arcanes, continued to speak, unaware Pharis was currently imagining ways of killing the old man in his sleep.

If only. The problems resulting from that particular action would hit too close to home. The mere thought of himself sitting on that seat of power made his insides curdle. Looking down, he ran his hand down the front of his crisp blue tunic, the hue just a shade lighter than the blue of his eyes. How he had missed his wardrobe, even for the few hours he'd been forced to dress like a common Kinetic for his mission. But compared to what that girl had been wearing...

Aurianna. Her eyes had *shone* in the darkness. Glowed almost. He'd never seen anything like it. But compared to the drabness of her wardrobe, perhaps any color would have seemed bright by comparison. Of course, she had worn that necklace when they left, the dark stone somehow lighting up her features, despite it being a blue so deep it was nearly black. The girl though... Aurianna. Shame hit him full force when he thought about how he'd treated her, how he'd spoken to her throughout the trip back, not to mention before. Pharis had known it wasn't her fault, had known she was just as much a pawn in this as he was, but still the rage had overwhelmed him, choking off his sense of reason.

She couldn't help who she was. But her very existence brought about a fury Pharis could not contain. And the incessant talking hadn't helped one bit. She had been able to get under his skin in a way few could, but he blamed the man in front of him for that. His hatred should be directed there.

With a jolt, Pharis came back to reality when he realized the Magnus could make things infinitely worse for him if he happened to miss some crucial detail amid all the insanity. The old man was saying, "And I know this has been difficult for you, but until you begin to understand the sacrifices involved with leadership, you will never be ready. We often must do things we find uncomfortable or unpleasant for the sake of the greater good."

Pharis uttered a low chuckle, but no mirth reached his eyes or his words. "The greater good? You can't be serious. You and I both know you wouldn't have sent for the girl if you didn't have some plans of your own. Savior? Really? At least have the decency not to throw that in my face. I'm no fool. This is your own personal agenda, and I refuse to be a part of it." He quickly turned and strolled out of the room, the guards near the entrance unsure whether they should stop him or not.

Good. Let them think about the man who sat behind him on the dais, barking orders at Pharis to stop. Let them question themselves, question if their loyalty was misplaced.

"Boy, you will obey me in this."

Pharis smirked, the corner of his mouth rising as he narrowed his eyes and cocked his head to the side. He turned to look back, simply staring at the man.

One of the Arcanes stepped forward to stand closer to the edge of the raised platform, even though Pharis was now on the other side of the room. The robed figure sighed and, not even needing to raise his voice, said, "This isn't about you, or any of us. It's about the future of our people."

Pharis huffed. The group of men were now staring at him intently, willing him back toward them with their eyes. He resisted, replying, "And which people would that be? Kinetics? What about all the others who claim this gods-forsaken land as their home? Would they care if the Kinetics were wiped clean off the planet? Somehow, I think they wouldn't be bothered by the future I saw. At least they'd be free from all of this."

A saccharine smile crawled across the face of the Magnus, but Pharis saw real menace in his glare. The early morning rays from the window now cast strange shadows on the men posed around him. He pointed to the staircase. "Get out."

"Gladly." Pharis stormed across the room, nearly shoving a guard out of the way as he headed down the stairs.

He knew it had been a mistake to argue. What was the point? The outcome would remain the same no matter how much he fought it.

He stormed down the stairs, across the main hall, then out the front doors. He marched across the bridge and into the city beyond. Bramosia had been little more than a half-empty village in the future that now seemed so surreal. And Aurianna had lived under those conditions. What could've happened to create such a horrifying state of affairs? The darkness in the streets had been palpable, clinging to his skin in ways that had made his spine tingle. What did the Arcanes know that they weren't telling them? They may have convinced themselves this girl was their salvation, but he would bet his entire inheritance the Magnus was using the situation to his own advantage, his own little slice of revenge for the past events that time could never erase, at least not for their family. And Pharis almost felt sorry for the person on the other end of that wrath.

Almost.

Thoughts of the tragedy that had plagued his family reminded him of how much he missed his sister, the only other person with the guts to stand up to the man who had made their lives a living hell from the day they were born. Mara had always been stronger in mind than he was, more willing to push boundaries and test their father, pushing him to just short of his breaking point. She had been born mere seconds before him, but he'd felt he was trying to catch up to her his entire life.

Until she had disappeared. Until the day his heart had been torn out by the loss of her presence in his life. Losing their mother had been hard on both of them, but losing his twin had been even more devastating. What made it worse was the not knowing, not understanding. Had she left on her own? The idea was preposterous, and yet...

She had been voicing opinions about the resistance movement for quite some time. Usually only in his presence, but someone could have overheard her, reported her. Was the Magnus capable of harming his only daughter, the heir to the only seat of power that mattered? Now that title belonged to him. And he loathed it with every ounce of his being. Mara had been the strong one, the leader. Hell, she had *ideas*. Ideas that could have changed the world, changed the way things ran, changed the way others saw them. The rest of the world may put on a pleasant face for the Kinetics, but he knew many of them despised being coddled. Despised the "leadership" offered by his father and, to some extent, every Magnus before him.

Pharis himself had listened to and agreed with many of his sister's ideas, offering to help her in any way he could. But then she had disappeared without a trace. Whether it was their father, the Arcanes, or even members of the resistance who thought to destroy the Magnus by stealing away his daughter, he didn't know. After all, the man had another heir, another puppet for the Arcanes, to be thrown in the metal chair and have that crown placed upon his brow. A heavy weight he did not yearn for, yet he would accept it in a heartbeat, if only Mara would be brought back, alive and unharmed.

Javen Ambrogetti was another issue. Pharis was convinced the bastard was involved in his sister's disappearance in some way, if it was indeed the resistance who had taken her. The boy was far too vocal about his hatred for their family.

He needed her guidance right now more than ever. Would she tell him to accept his fate and move on? No way in hell would she let their father get away with this. But what could he do? He was just as bound to follow orders as any other being in Eresseia, no matter that one day he would be the one giving those orders.

The familiar nausea at the thought threatened to engulf him, a tidal wave of panic hitting a crescendo as he suddenly realized . . . he was standing in the middle of a bustling Bramosian street, onlookers staring at him in concern and confusion. He had walked out of the Imperium without a single guard on his heels.

Interesting.

Perhaps they had been so stunned by his outburst no one had realized he'd left. Perhaps they were just hiding in the shadows? But he didn't think so. His bodyguards were always two steps behind him, no matter where he went. In fact, his little "trip" had been the first time he'd had a chance to truly be alone for an extended period, albeit not as extended as he would have liked. Perhaps he should thank his bloody fool of a father for demanding that he go. But that part had been the Arcanes idea, as they'd insisted it was his part in the destiny that was to unfold. Well, that and the other thing. There was no way his future happiness and freedom were going to be dictated by their vision of a destiny he wanted no part of whatsoever.

Destiny.

He made his own destiny.

After realizing he had absolutely no idea where he was going, Pharis turned around and marched back to the Imperium. He was going to have a talk with the Arcanes. A private talk, away from his father's prying eyes.

He walked determinedly to the lower levels and stood outside the door to their sacred area. He knew better than to barge in, but knocking was awkward, especially when someone always opened the door the moment your hand grabbed the metal knocker. Frankly, it was unnerving how quickly they answered.

He could have sworn the door was creaking open a second before he made contact, but the small man on the other side merely smiled at him in that dispassionate way they had, like nothing surprised or worried them. The Arcane asked in a soft voice, "Yes, Regulus, how may I help you?"

His nostrils flared. They had to know exactly why he was here. Pharis decided he wasn't going to play games right now. He replied, "You may help me, yes. I'd like to speak to whomever is available."

The man's short stature did not diminish his presence as he stared at Pharis, scrutinizing him like he was some common Kinetic. After a moment, he gestured inside the room, and Pharis quickly entered.

The space was deceptively large, but most of it couldn't be viewed from the foyer. Pharis looked about at the stacks of books and rows of bookshelves filling most of the room. He often wondered what secrets those tomes held, but no one apart from the Arcanes was allowed to view them—not even the Magnus himself.

Several of the robed men joined the one who had opened the door. They stood in front of him, their hands clasped in silent question, waiting on him to explain the nature of his visit.

As if they didn't already know.

Drumming his fingers against his side in nervous anticipation, Pharis began speaking in a subdued voice, trying to keep a lid on his simmering anger. "You know why I'm here. I'm requesting you tell my father to forget about the other part of this plan. Whatever end you are seeking, do what you must in regard to this girl. But I respectfully decline any further part in the affair."

One of the men—not the one who had opened the door— smiled at Pharis. It was not a comforting gesture. "We understand your hesitance, sire. But none of us can stop the hand of fate."

"Fate is not the determiner of my life. No Magnus or heir has ever been forced to do something not of their own choosing. The idea is ridiculous, especially since you're basing it off some stupid prophecy that reads like a drunken riddle!"

"Please calm down, sire. We are certain you will find yourself in favor of the idea once you spend some time—"

"I've bloody well spent enough time already! I can assure you, while I do feel sympathy for her situation, nothing will ever be enough to change my mind. I tolerated her for the sake of getting us both back here, but I want nothing further to do with her. And if you don't tell my father to stop this nonsense, I swear to you I will spend all my days as Magnus working to make your lives a living hell." He stomped away, slamming open the door and heading back down the hallway.

Ridiculous. Absolutely ridiculous was the only way to describe it. They had never done this to anyone in the past. Why now? Why him? He would simply refuse—his father be damned.

Chapter 12

AURIANNA

Aurianna awoke to an awareness of a strange energy. She could detect nothing with her eyes, but she felt it all the same.

After taking several seconds to recall where she was, Aurianna decided to brave the unfamiliarity of her new room. Throwing back the covers, she sat up and reached over to a small button on the wall above the table. Sometime in the night, when she'd gotten up to use the privy, she'd noticed the button and realized it looked like the ones by the door. Sure enough, it had turned on the light on the wall above the table.

How convenient.

A hot shower seemed like a grand idea, but she was worried the contraption would be too difficult to manage without some guidance. Her fears were unfounded, however. It was the simplest thing to adjust the controls and resulted in one of the happiest moments of her life up to that point, the water so warm she thought she might start crying all over again.

Wrapped in the softest towel she had ever known, her coppery

136

brown hair dripping water down her back, Aurianna sidled up to the dresser, opening one of the drawers and eyeing the clothing once again. Compared to a lifetime of shapeless clothing made of monochromatic fabrics, the strange tunics and cloaks were colorful, yet not garishly so, form-fitting with the occasional sheen of a fabric unknown to her. The sleeveless cloaks were almost long enough to hit the floor and had places for the arms to fit, just like a tunic.

Brilliant, she thought.

Grabbing the first set of undergarments she saw, Aurianna dressed quickly, appreciating the soft inner material of the clothing almost as much as the colorful yet practical exterior. The tunics were a little odd, she noted as she slipped one on, trying to figure out the trick to tightening and tying the cords that laced up the front. Once she had managed well enough, Aurianna started to slip her mother's necklace under the tunic but decided she wanted the comfort of being able to touch and see it. She needed that comfort, especially today.

She walked over to the full-length mirror on the bathroom wall, but her reflection was obscured by a layer of steam. Wiping it with her towel, she stood back, admiring herself in a way she never had.

Nice.

Brown pants and a dark greenish-blue tunic, together with one of the sleeveless overgarments in a brown slightly darker than the pants. Boots and belt—both discovered in the bottom drawer of the dresser—to match the cloak.

Very nice.

It wasn't like her to worry so much about something so superficial, but it certainly improved her mood to know she would have access to nice things, at least in the way of a wardrobe.

A sharp buzzing at the door interrupted her reverie.

Javen.

After only a moment of panic while trying to figure out how to open the door from the inside, she found the mechanism hiding on the panel directly under the buttons for the lights. When she opened it—with no small amount of trepidation and sudden incomprehensible shyness—she found herself looking directly up into his now-familiar, smiling face. He seemed genuinely excited to see her. Aurianna felt a tingle of excitement as well as a twinge of uneasiness that snaked back into her mind. *Easy, girl.* She couldn't forget where she was and why she was here.

Out loud, she said, "Good morning, Javen."

"Good morning yourself." He stood with his forearm propped against the door frame, his grin showing off teeth so white they didn't seem natural. He stared without speaking for several seconds then seemed to come back to himself, offering her his arm. "Ready?"

"I guess so. I hope I'm dressed appropriately."

Javen looked her up and down several times, his eyes lingering at her neckline and the jewelry shining there. Just when it started to feel uncomfortable, he offered his arm again. "Most definitely."

* * *

Upon entering the massive dining hall, Aurianna was caught off guard by the sheer number of people who now shared the space with them.

The entire area was littered with breakfast-goers, every table at least half full, and some without a vacant spot to be seen. Javen led her to the back of the line waiting to get their trays.

"Well, well. I see the rumors are true."

They turned to find a young woman, exceptionally tall and elegantly thin, with shoulder-length whitish-blonde hair similar to Javen's. Her eyes, however, were bright blue—almost clear—with a sparkle in them Aurianna could only assume was directed at her. The young woman was slightly taller than she was, making Aurianna stand up straighter. She got the feeling this girl was not someone to trifle with.

"Laelia! Good to see you, as always," Javen said in answer to the cryptic greeting.

"What rumors?" Aurianna couldn't help herself.

The girl called Laelia smiled at her bold move, yet her eyes held nothing but ice as she replied, "I see you've had the pleasure of meeting dear Javen, but I think you have me at a disadvantage. I don't believe I know your name."

Aurianna bristled. "What rumors?" she repeated.

"Laelia, don't start." Javen's retort was terse but pleading.

"What? I'm just trying to introduce myself to your . . . what exactly is she now?"

"Laelia."

"Javen." Laelia mimicked his warning tone.

"Is this really necessary? Her name is Aurianna, and she's new here. She needs training, and I was asked to show her around yesterday. I thought she could use a friend, and who wants to eat breakfast alone? I mean, besides you, of course."

Laelia's smirk slowly warped into a full-fledged smile that looked almost genuine.

"You know I can't resist juicy gossip, Javen."

"What rumors?" Aurianna was practically shouting.

They both turned to her, surprise at her outburst showing on both of their faces.

Biting her lip sheepishly, Aurianna apologized. "Sorry, but I'm kind of tired of the types of 'rumors' that seem to be following me around. Let me start again. My name's Aurianna, and I'm just here at the request of the Magnus, I guess. I'm supposed to be trained."

Concern wrinkled her brow. " 'Supposed to be trained'? Trained for what?"

Javen saved them from any further awkward conversation by pushing Aurianna up in the line ahead of him as they moved to the first containers of food. She heard him whisper to the other girl, "Come sit with us, and we can discuss it."

Relieved at the respite from the discussion—however temporary—Aurianna looked at the various offerings in front of her, mouth watering in anticipation. It had been quite some time since their early dinner the afternoon before.

A man with sandy brown hair, slightly graying at the temples, was staring directly at her from behind the lines of food, the broom in his hands momentarily idle. It was not in a curious who-is-the-new-girl kind of way. This look was one born of some intense emotion she couldn't identify but had never felt directed at her before. Unsure of what to do, she continued to steal glances at the man. His dark robes were the color of ash, like those around him. He was dressed like one of the Voids.

Hurrying to fill her plate with anything that looked remotely familiar to avoid the molten intensity of the man's gaze, Aurianna waited for Javen to lead the way to a table. Once they'd grabbed drinks, he steered them all the way to a spot in the far back corner, nearer to the door but away from most of the curious ears.

And they certainly were curious. Every single person in the room, try though they might to hide it, had been watching at some point or another since they'd arrived, both before and after her unfortunate spurt of anger in the food line. She knew this was something she was just going to have to get used to.

Sitting down with their food, the three of them stared at one another until Laelia broke the spell and started eating her breakfast as if nothing unusual was going on. Her movements were utterly graceful, each action flowing into the next. She smelled of jasmine, Aurianna noted, with pale-as-ivory skin like Javen's, creamy smooth and with rosy cheeks.

"Okay, listen." Javen hesitated, shoving a bite of food into his mouth, and Aurianna wondered if he was debating on how much to tell this girl. Was she friend or foe? Surely they wouldn't be having breakfast with her if the two of them weren't close. But the girl's words had seemed so hostile back in the line. Aurianna wasn't sure what to think at this point. "I don't know what we're supposed to be telling people and what we're not. The Magnus and the Arcanes had Pharis bring her here... from her home. This is all on them. I'm just trying to help her out, seeing as she's a bit out of her element here, so to speak. Attacking her isn't very helpful, Laelia, and you know exactly what I mean. No one needs your patent bitchiness right now."

One of Laelia's eyebrow shot up. "Why, Javen. I'm hurt. Really hurt. I thought we were friends." She immediately began eating her breakfast as if the conversation had never existed. This girl was anything *but* hurt, it would seem.

"Laelia."

"Yes, Javen?" came her breathy reply.

"Stop."

"Stop what?"

"You *know* what. That's exactly what I'm talking about. I'm trying to tell you something maybe I'm not supposed to, and you want to play games."

Laelia raised her eyebrow again, a feline smile registering on the girl's face. "But it's fun. You're so easy to rile, darling."

Javen shook his head and continued eating, blatantly ignoring both women and refusing to look up from his plate. Laelia began to do the same. *What is wrong with these people?* Aurianna didn't know how to continue, didn't know what to make of his friend. She supposed she needed friends as well, but things weren't off to the grandest of starts.

Hesitantly, she asked, "Where are you from, Laelia?"

Surprised at being addressed again, she replied, "Vanito. Same as Ambrogetti here." She gestured at him with her spoon, and he glared at her from under his pale eyebrows.

"Are you one of the—I've forgotten the word now—are you in training?"

"An Acolyte, you mean? No, only poor Javen here is left of our little group. The rest of us graduated already. You have to be at least twenty for that, though, and the poor dear made the mistake of befriending people just a tad older than himself."

"Don't flatter yourself," Javen offered.

"I would never."

"Good."

Beyond all comprehension, the two of them smiled at each other.

Smiled? Seriously, what is wrong with these people?

Picking up the thread of conversation, Aurianna asked, "So, what do you do then?"

"I'm a Sparker and an Emissar, liaising and transporting electricity between the Imperium and the regions," Laelia responded, as if that answered everything. Aurianna's confusion must have shown on her face because the other girl said, "You . . . have no idea what I'm talking about, do you?" When Aurianna shook her head, the girl did the same. "Javen, really, what's going on?"

"I told you. She's not from here. She doesn't know anything about our world. She's . . ." He sighed and put down his utensil, wiping his mouth on a napkin. "Look. If I tell you this, you have to promise—you have to *swear*—you'll keep it to yourself and not run around like the gossip you normally are, telling everyone what I'm about to say."

The girl could tell this was a really juicy secret. Excitement lit her pale blue eyes. Leaning forward, arms crossed on the table in front of her, Laelia nodded, smiling that feline smile again. "I swear."

"I'm serious. You absolutely cannot tell anyone until we know it's okay to do so."

Laelia nodded again.

Exhaling audibly, Javen said, "The Magnus and the Arcanes sent Pharis to go get her and bring her back here. They gave him an Aether Stone. She's actually from the future."

Blinking rapidly, Laelia only stared for a moment. Then she laughed. Loudly.

Several people around them turned toward their corner at the abrupt sound.

When neither of them joined her, Laelia stopped just as quickly. "You're serious?"

Javen nodded.

"She's from the future?"

"It's not like the concept is new, Laelia. It's what the Aether Stones are for, you know."

"Yeah, but no one's used them in a long time. Why would they suddenly want to bring some girl from the future back here?"

He shrugged. "Don't know. Don't care. I'm just trying to help her find her way around. She just got in yesterday, and they're already expecting her at training this morning."

"Training for what, Javen? She's too old. How's that going to work? And what region is she even from?"

"Again, I don't know. She's from Bramosia, she says." He pursed his lips then said, "Yeah, I know, so don't look at me like that."

Zeroing in on Aurianna, Laelia asked, "How in the world are you from Bramosia? No one's actually *from* here. People just come here to live sometimes. Your parents have to be from one of the regions."

"In my time, Bramosia is all there is." At the look of naked fear and wonderment on the girl's face, Aurianna wondered—too late—whether she should have kept that part to herself.

Anger flashing across her face, erasing the fear from only a moment ago, Laelia uttered her next words with clenched teeth. "What does that mean?"

"I don't know what it means. All I know is something bad is going to happen."

"Bad how?"

"Bad as in catastrophic. But that's what we're trying to fix."

"Oh, well, as long as someone's on it." Laelia's flippant reply belied the knowing look behind her eyes.

The prickling on the back of her neck alerted Aurianna that a new and powerful presence had entered the room behind her. She turned and saw Pharis, dressed in deep blue fabric that drew the eye and a pristine, collared tunic that singled him out from every other being in the room. "What's his story?" She nodded in his direction.

"Who?"

"Him. Right there." A blank look from Laelia was the only answer she received. "You don't see the man standing in the corner, speaking to one of the... Voids?"

Sputtering, Laelia replied, "You mean the Regulus?"

"Regu-who?"

"The Regulus. Son of Darius Jacomus, current Magnus of Eresseia?"

Shaking her head in confusion, Aurianna let the words sift around in her head. *Pharis is that man's son?* "But I thought—"

"You thought you had your eyes on something tasty? Well, that he might be, but he's still the crown prince."

Too many thoughts were whirling inside her mind. "He's a prince?" *But it makes no sense,* she thought. Sending *him* back to get her? Of all people? And he certainly hadn't been dressed like a prince then.

"Well, not exactly. Not really. That's what we call him though—behind his back of course." Laelia's smug grin held some inner secret. "His official title is the Regulus, and his dad is officially the Magnus—"

"But everyone knows the old man would rather be called King," Javen interrupted. "He sure thinks he's one, anyways."

Laelia rolled her eyes at him and continued, "Magnus is just the title of the person in charge of the Kinetics. He's supposed to be our leader, but frankly"—she threw a meaningful look at Javen—"the position's been abused more and more each generation, at least according to those who've been around long enough to know. Yes, Javen, Darius does seem to imagine himself a king at times, but he's just one man. The Consils are the ones we need to watch out for. That kind of power is what can really do damage if they decide to disregard the needs of their citizens."

Javen shook his head. "The Consils are chosen specifically to protect the citizens of their region. Alone they wield little power. Together they can't agree on what type of tea to have for their morning meetings, much less anything important."

This made Aurianna laugh. "So, the Consils each have the same amount of power?"

Laelia nodded. "Yeah, but there have been alliances in the past. In theory, the Magnus has the same power as any of the other Consils, no more, no less. He's ambitious, sure. But the rest of Eresseia—the non-Kinetics—wouldn't be okay with him disbanding the Consils or anything like that. They'd revolt for sure." She paused a moment. "But to get back to your original question, the Regulus is like the equivalent of a crown prince, if the Magnus were a king. He's just the heir to the title of 'Magnus.' "

Irritated, Aurianna glared at Javen. "Why didn't you tell me who he was before?"

"What do you mean? I *told* you about the Magnus."

"I *mean* Pharis!" she said in a low voice through gritted teeth.

Laelia raised her eyebrows, leaning forward and propping her elbows on the table as she rested her chin on her hands. "You're on a first-name basis with him, are you? I thought only Javen dared to call him that." Her smile was threatening to split her face.

Javen scowled at Laelia before turning back to Aurianna. "I just assumed you knew his identity. After all, you came in with him."

Her eyes now wide with glee, Laelia responded, "Where exactly did you *come in* with the Regulus, dear Aurianna?"

But Aurianna was staring daggers at Javen. "Well, considering all he did was yell at me and sneer in my direction the whole time, asking him if he happened to be the crown prince must have slipped my mind," she said flatly.

Laelia laughed. "Yeah, now that *does* sound like our Regulus."

"What do you mean?"

The girl shook her head emphatically. "Nah-ah. Not until you tell me what you were doing with him."

Aurianna sighed. "He's the one who brought me here."

"Why would the Regulus take on a courier mission?" She added, "No offense. But it just seems odd the Magnus would send his son out on a mission like that."

"That's what I've been sitting here trying to wrap my head around. I didn't know who he was at the time."

"So you've got an 'in' with the Regulus. You might be my new best friend."

"Trust me, he hates my guts."

146

Laelia gestured dismissively, waving her hand. "Oh, he hates everybody, or so they say. But I've also heard he's got ways that can make a girl forget all that. For a while, at least." Javen looked more and more unhappy with each passing second. "Oh, but we would never forget our resident charmer, Javen. We Vanitians gotta stick together, right? I think you've got your eye on someone else though, don't you?" Nudging him and winking in a highly suggestive manner, Laelia made him blush.

Ah, subtlety. Aurianna was not amused. She merely said, "I only asked about Pharis—I mean, the Regulus—because he had such a chip on his shoulder yesterday. Now I guess I know why, if his dad made him go get me instead of sending someone else. Still doesn't quite explain the level of hostility, though."

"Like I said, girls tend to overlook his somewhat gruff exterior. He's always like that to some degree. Trust me. I've heard stories from a few of the girls over the years. Nothing bad or anything. He's certainly not violent or careless. But apparently, he's very moody and doesn't talk much. Not that I blame him. Most of the girls around here aren't very interesting. Present company excluded, of course." She smiled her feline smile again.

"Well," Javen said, getting to his feet with far too much enthusiasm, "I guess we need to get going."

"Have fun in *class!*" Laelia exclaimed, emphasizing the last word like a thinly disguised insult.

"Ha-ha. You are such a bitch."

"Love you too."

As she headed back upstairs with Javen, Aurianna realized she was about to face the biggest unknown in all this craziness: Kinetic training.

* * *

Heart racing, hands trembling, Aurianna was somewhat under-whelmed by what she saw: blank-walled hallways to their left and their right. She could see at least one door farther down each of the two branches, and lots of students milling around, but not much else. Javen led her to the left, and they started to walk down the long passage.

"The classrooms basically form a rectangle," he explained. "The entire shape is surrounded by the hallway we're in, which goes around the perimeter and back to the beginning where we entered. The rest of this level is divided up into four equal-sized classrooms with two doors on the outer walls of each room leading back into the hallway. Most of the rooms also have inner doors leading to the rooms adjacent, but only Magisters—instructors—can use those."

Nodding, Aurianna wasn't sure what to do next. Javen, however, walked up to the nearest open door and asked a woman where they might get Aurianna's schedule. The woman pointed down the hallway to her right, so they continued walking until they came to the next door. In this doorway stood a much older man than any she had seen yet. His overgarment was fire-red with a yellow tunic over and black pants beneath. His hair was white, and his eyes seemed tired, but they did not look kind.

"You're a little early today, Javen. Who is this?" Aurianna saw the recognition dawning as his forced smile died. Obviously, the instructors would've had to have been told at least something to explain her sudden appearance. She wondered what exactly they had and hadn't been told.

"Magister Daehne, this is Aurianna. I'm sure you were told about her. That's why we're here. Do you know where we might find her schedule?"

"I...uh...think we may need to call the Magnus up here. There seems to have been a misunderstanding."

"What's going on?"

"Well, when we were told a new student was being brought in suddenly, a student who we were told would need training starting with the basics . . . of course, no one thought we'd be dealing with a . . . a woman."

"What's that supposed to mean?" Javen asked before the same words escaped her lips. Why would her being a woman matter to these people? There were plenty of both male and female Kinetics around this place.

"Oh! No, no, I didn't mean it like that!" Flustered, he babbled on. "What I meant to say is that she is, in fact, scheduled for Energy training first thing this morning."

Javen frowned. He looked at Aurianna and explained, "They apparently have you scheduled with the Youngers."

"What are the Youngers?"

Magister Daehne cleared his throat, visibly uncomfortable. "They are the beginner Acolytes, starting with the preteens who first come to us around ten years of age, all the way up until they turn sixteen. After that—until they graduate—they are known as Olders." He looked at Javen and began to stumble over his words again. "You have to understand, if she needs training starting at the beginning, she'll actually have to start *at the beginning*. And we just assumed it meant she must be a bit . . . younger."

Aurianna's eyes were glued to the man's face as she tried to glean the meaning of his words. "So . . . you're saying I'm taking classes with little children?"

"That was the plan, yes. But obviously something is going to have to be done because having a grown woman in classes with the Youngers just isn't appropriate. I'm not sure what to do though since it wouldn't do you any good to be in classes with the Olders like Javen. You still need to learn the basics, and I don't know if we have the time for one-on-one sessions." Putting on a fake smile, he said, "For now, let's just go with what we have, and I'll contact the Magnus to get this all straightened out. I imagine he will have an answer if he's the one who wanted it done."

A little numb, but still not quite sure what the significance of it all was, she allowed herself to be led down the corridor, around two sharp corners and down the passage on the opposite side. Here another man stood, greeting students as they entered the room. Very young students.

His look of confusion morphed into one of understanding in a matter of seconds. To Aurianna's amazement, the man started laughing.

"Well then. It seems we are in a bit of a predicament. Good morning…Aurianna, I presume?"

Javen intercepted the greetings. "Good to see you can find the humor in this, Magister Martes. I don't think Aurianna is quite so amused. Neither was Magister Daehne."

"Clearly Magister Daehne can't see this for what it is."

"And what exactly is it?"

"This, my dear Javen, is a blessing in disguise."

"How do you figure?" It was Aurianna's turn to feel confused. She added, "Sir."

"Either you will profoundly succeed, and so quickly as to defy all of our logic and understanding of how the Essence work in our world, or we'll have to break from tradition and allow you to remain with the younger Acolytes, or…we'll have to find another way to train you."

Aurianna smiled faintly at the man, feeling herself warm to the instructor a little.

Clapping his hands together, he smiled back. "Well, no matter. Come on in and join us, Aurianna. I'm sure Javen needs to get back to Magister Daehne and his Fire training." As Javen waved to her and walked away, Aurianna had no choice but to follow Magister Martes into the classroom as he chuckled to himself and muttered, "Definitely going to be an interesting day."

Aurianna couldn't help noticing the eyes of every single child in the room staring straight at her as she gazed at her surroundings. One small boy, in particular, seemed to be gaping at her presence.

Magister Martes, resting his right hand gently on her shoulder, announced to the students, "I would like you to meet the newest addition to our class. This is Aurianna, who will be joining us today." As the students began murmuring among themselves, he attempted to speak over the noise. "I understand this is out of the ordinary, but Aurianna here didn't have the benefit of receiving training when she was a Younger. I'm going to ask that everyone be kind to her and do your very best to make her feel at home."

He led her over to a spot on the other side of the room near the front. Aurianna sat down, noticing the one boy still staring at her, a slight smile on his face. She smiled back. As soon as she did, shock took over the boy's features, and he immediately looked away.

As the instructor began speaking, Aurianna tried to pay attention, but she had no idea what the man was saying for the most part. She'd been handed a book to follow along, just like the other children, but most of it didn't make sense to her, and she was already beginning to feel defeated.

The subject in this class was Energy, or electric power as she had come to know it. These children seemed to be learning about the principles of Energy, and she wondered how long before they would be given the opportunity to try out some of their powers. Not that she was complaining. The idea of having to show any inkling of the power she wasn't sure she even had was both frustrating and nauseating to her.

Throughout the hour, as she struggled in vain to comprehend the Magister's teachings, the boy kept sneaking glances in Aurianna's direction. The furtive gestures might have gone unnoticed had her full attention been on the lesson, but as it was, she found herself distracted as her focus was pulled toward different points around the room. The classroom was rather large, and a multitude of items decorated the walls, most of which she did not recognize. The diagrams and symbols were unfamiliar to her.

Aurianna's thoughts came back into focus when the bodies surrounding her began standing up and moving away. Quickly getting up to follow them, unsure of where to go next, she was stopped at the door by Magister Martes.

"I had hoped to capture more of your attention with my lecture, but alas, it might not be so easy to entertain the mind of a young woman in the same way one holds the attention of younger children. I wonder . . ." His thoughts trailed off as he seemed to be contemplating something.

Blushing at being caught daydreaming, she responded in what she hoped was a lighthearted and self-deprecating manner. "I'm so very sorry, sir. It's just that I don't really understand any of this, and it's a bit overwhelming, to say the least."

"Indeed." His smile returned. "I wonder if we might be able to find a solution to this predicament. In the meantime, continue following your current schedule. Some individual reading of the textbooks might benefit you, obviously, but I'm thinking we might arrange something better. Let me speak to the Magnus, as well as the other Magisters, and see if we can figure it out. Perhaps the Arcanes might even know of some way to speed up your training. Or at least these beginning stages."

"I would appreciate it."

He nodded. "It's imperative you gain some knowledge of the

logistics of the elements involved. I'm sure you've at least had some education on the history and culture of Eresseia."

"No, sir. I haven't. Not in the way you mean, at least."

Aghast, he stared at her for a moment. "You can't be serious." When she nodded her head, he added, "You've had no education whatsoever?"

Irritated at the insinuation that she was perhaps completely ignorant, she replied, "Yes, of course I've had an education. But my education consisted of more practical issues. I didn't have the luxury of strolling around a castle and eating as much food as I wished. We had to struggle just to provide for ourselves, and I worked hard every day. My aunt taught me a lot, even a little history, but I wasn't given any kind of preparation for this." The look on the Magister's face made her pause. She suddenly realized he had no idea what she was talking about. "You don't know where I'm from, do you?"

"Well, I thought I did. But apparently, we've only been given a small piece of the bigger picture here. My apologies if I offended you. What you're describing simply isn't possible for anyone living in Eresseia, yet you seem to be sincere."

"And why, exactly, would I be insincere?"

"The real question is *who, exactly, are you?*"

"I wish I knew the answer to that."

He surprised her by laughing at her response, a reaction she wasn't sure how to deal with. "Don't we all, Aurianna. Don't we all. That is your real name at least?"

"Yes, that is my real name."

"Well, off to Water training you go, then. I'll have a chat with the others. For now, please be patient with us. This is uncharted territory, for us as well."

Tell me about it, she thought, as he led her to a second door on another side of the classroom and directed her to her next class.

CHAPTER 13

AURIANNA

Aurianna crept into the large, overcrowded dining hall, unsure if she should just wait in a corner until she saw someone she knew. Considering that included all of maybe three people right now, she decided that plan probably wouldn't pan out.

Throughout the morning, the magisters had, each in turn, seemed flustered by her predicament, had promised to find a better solution, then had seated her in the front of their classroom, and dumped a book in front of her. After lunch she'd spent an hour in "Study Hall" trying to wrap her head around some of her book assignments. She'd finally been told she could do as she wished until dinner was served. "Free time" they'd called it. Taking a detour back up to her room, she had unceremoniously deposited the textbooks on her bed, resolving to get a bag of some sort to carry them around in future. Then she had roamed the building for a while, looking around the open areas and the different levels until she realized it must be dinnertime and joined a stream of people headed for the dining hall.

Joining the back of the food line, she stood up straight, facing forward, willing everyone to leave her alone and not attempt to make conversation with her. Today had been hard enough without more questions, more stares. Nothing about her life made sense now. Her mind wandered back to her life in another time, and she thought about Larissa, about the home she was missing terribly.

Out of the corner of her eye, she caught a flash of dark-as-night hair. She turned but saw nothing and no one familiar. She remembered there was, in fact, one other person she knew here, albeit not in the best of ways.

That wasn't fair though. Pharis had been thrown into this just as much as she had. However, the fact that he had been given at least a little more preparation wasn't lost on her.

And no one was expecting *him* to save them all.

I'm the one who needs saving.

She grabbed a tray and began moving up the line. But when a warm hand touched her back and a voice whispered, "There you are" in her ear, her instinctive reaction was to swing around, almost taking Javen's head off with the tray.

"Hey! Whoa there! Sorry, didn't mean to startle you." He'd thrown his hands up in defense, ducking just as the tray came around near the side of his head.

And now people were staring. *Perfect.*

Aurianna merely glared at him, her eyes icy with hostility at the audacity, the familiarity. Perhaps she needed to distance herself from Javen, if only to clear up any misunderstandings about their extremely new, extremely tentative friendship.

Interrupting her thoughts, he drawled, "Seriously. I'm really sorry, Aurianna. I was just worried when I didn't see you around upstairs, so I thought you might have gotten lost or something. I was just glad I found you. Didn't mean to startle you.

Maybe she was overreacting. He probably didn't realize just how close he'd been, or maybe he was trying to avoid other people overhearing him.

But still.

"Well, don't do that again."

Javen was staring off behind her at the tables nearest the food line. "Sigi's here, so she might be done with her shift. Maybe she's working second shift and got her dinner break a little early. Either way, we can sit with her, if you like."

Better than Laelia, she thought, but then she remembered Sigi's initial reaction to her and internally cringed a little.

Javen must have sensed her discomfort because he smiled warmly as he added food to his plate. "Sigi's good people. She just needed to feel like she was doing her job, is all. You have to admit your story is a bit outlandish, right?"

Smiling ruefully, Aurianna said, "Right. Yeah." They continued filling their trays with an assortment of foods, some familiar, some she had never seen but which looked worth trying. One thing she made a point to pass over, simply because it looked a bit grotesque, its top covered in a dark-brown liquid of some sort. Javen grabbed one and saw her staring at it.

"I'm guessing you don't have chocolate cake where you're from?"

"I don't even know what that means. But that thing doesn't look edible."

"You're going to eat those words in a minute." Javen led her over to a table nearby, where Sigi sat talking to another guard—or so she assumed from the uniform—who looked up at them quizzically, suspicion creeping into his gaze.

Sigi, however, smiled at them as they approached. With a twinge of hesitation in her eyes, she turned to her companion. "Ellery, this is Aurianna. She's a...new friend of Javen's."

Despite his wary gaze, Ellery was polite in his reply. "Hello, Aurianna. Don't think I've seen you around." Before anyone had a chance to think of a reply, he turned to Sigi, saying, "Well, I've got to be off. My break is over in a few minutes, and I've still got to run downstairs to pick up a new weapon before going back on shift." He left, making room for them to deposit their trays on the table in front of Sigi.

Sigi looked at Javen, exasperation on her face. "I don't know how to handle this. Do I tell people? Do I not tell people?" She'd been weighing the words in her outstretched hands but dropped them the moment she finished speaking.

Javen's answer was quick and decisive. "You tell what you have to, and no more. I think they want to avoid a panic."

The girl turned to her. "But what information do I even have to give them? *Why* are you here?"

Aurianna felt the tension within herself as well as around her. Nearby, the man from earlier that morning, a broom in his hands, was again staring with a scrutiny bordering on fascination. This wasn't normal curiosity, and she was starting to freak out. He did indeed appear to be one of the Voids, and she had no idea what she was supposed to think of them.

"That man over there. One of the Voids. He keeps staring at me. He was doing it this morning as well." Aurianna's voice was barely a whisper, even though there was no way he could hear their conversation from where he stood on the other side of the food line, well into the confines of the kitchen area. When they started to turn their heads, she exclaimed, "No! Don't look!"

Sigi and Javen both looked at her in exasperation. Sigi said, "How am I supposed to see who you mean if I can't look?"

"Just... I don't know... look casual."

The two Kinetics slowly turned their heads at different times, trying to look like they were merely glancing around the room. By then, the man had gone back to sweeping the floors.

"I don't see anything, Aurianna."

"Okay, fine, but he was staring, and it's creeping me out."

"It's probably because you're new. We're not used to seeing new people our age. And speaking of which, how about we go back to my question?"

Aurianna cleared her throat. She explained as well as she could, with short interjections from Javen, where and when she was from, including all that had occurred to return her to a time just a few moon cycles after she had been born. Sigi's eyes widened, a look of empathy crossing her face at the revelation. Aurianna included everything she had been told by both Larissa and Pharis, as well as the events of her meeting with the Magnus the day before. Careful to keep her tone light when it came to the bit about the prophecy, she tried to make it clear she found the idea to be ridiculous, but Sigi had a completely different take on it.

"You're saying the Arcanes sent for you? Aurianna, they hold the key to everything related to prophecies. Anything like that always comes from them, and they never lie. There must be *something* to it. What does the prophecy say?"

Only then did it occur to her no one had ever volunteered that bit of information. "I'm not entirely sure, to be honest. I haven't actually heard it."

"Well then! That settles it. Tomorrow during your free time in the afternoon, I can take you to have a chat with the Arcanes. They should be able to give you some answers. I'm on first shift this week, so I'll be off duty about the time you get done with weapons training."

"Weapons training?" Aurianna asked, starting to panic.

"Oh," Javen responded, grinning sheepishly, "yeah, about that.

She's not in classes with the Olders, Sigi. She's gotta start at the basics, you know? And they didn't realize she'd be...not a Younger."

"She's in classes with the little ones? Why can't they do individual sessions with her instead?"

"It was mentioned, but apparently no one has the time."

Sigi scoffed. "So she's just supposed to continue classes with kids half her age?"

Aurianna answered, "Well, Magister Martes mentioned the idea of me doing some of the book work on my own. At least the stuff I could just read and go through without much help. I'm guessing I'd eventually start to understand some of it, but right now I just feel kind of lost."

"Seems like that's something the Arcanes could help with as well. Then it's settled. I'll take you down there tomorrow afternoon."

Javen looked more than a little put out by his exclusion from the excursion, but he didn't say anything. He was staring at her again, and despite his friendly nature, it made her uncomfortable. His gaze dropped to her neckline again, and she realized he was probably looking at the necklace. She hadn't seen anyone here wearing jewelry besides earrings and the occasional metal loops around the eyebrows and mouth, like the girl who had been a part of her welcoming party.

Before she could give any affirmation of her consent to the plan, Javen jumped into another conversation altogether. "What's that?" He indicated a torn envelope sitting on the table beside Sigi's elbow.

"Oh, yeah. Dad wrote me again. He's still going on about that weirdness with his neighbors and all the recent arrests in town. I don't know. Drunk and disorderly isn't completely out of the ordinary as far as Rasenforst goes, but he says it's getting worse. I keep meaning to send a letter to one of the town guards to ask what's really going on."

"Probably nothing, Sigi. A bunch of drunk locals is nothing to worry yourself over."

"I hope so. Still, it's weird."

Aurianna decided to ask the guardswoman about her family. She had mentioned a sister who was also a Kinetic.

"Well, Hilda's in training here as well. You've probably seen her since she's in your classes. She's twelve, so she'll be jumping up to the next age level soon. She's a phenomenal Pyro. Hell, she'll be better than me before long."

"You mentioned other siblings?"

"Yeah, my brothers are all still back at home working for our dad. He's one of the local weaponsmiths."

"How many brothers do you have?"

"Six."

"*Six?*"

The russet undertones of Sigi's skin became more noticeable as she blushed. "Uh, yeah. There's eight of us total. Dad's had his hands full since Mom died."

"Oh. I'm sorry." Feeling awkward, Aurianna didn't know what else to say.

Sigi stared into the space before her and sighed. "It was almost ten years ago. She died shortly after my youngest brother was born. Mom got sick and passed away pretty quickly, so she wasn't suffering long."

"Still, I'm sure it's hard." Aurianna frowned. "I have no memory of my mother."

"My dad took it pretty hard. Me and my older brothers were kind of in shock for a while. I tried hard to help him out afterward, so I got really good at weaponry and such. Always wanted to prove to him I was one of the boys." She smiled at some hidden memory. "Now I feel like I'm doing just the opposite most of the time. The men around here see me as one of them, all right, and that's about the extent of it."

Javen huffed. "Sigi, I think you're wrong. No one could miss that bright pink lipstick you wear."

She punched him in the arm. "Yeah, well, no one's expressed their thoughts on it."

"Maybe they're scared you'll bazooka them in the face."

She laughed, but it didn't reach her eyes. "Yeah, maybe."

Aurianna thought perhaps she hadn't given Sigi enough credit. The girl had a strength (both internal and external) she had to admit she admired. And Sigi wanted to help. But she still had her loyalty to the Magnus, and that made Aurianna somewhat nervous.

Javen had finished his meal and eaten half of the brown oddly squishy thing he'd referred to as *chocolate cake*. Pushing the plate over in her direction, he nodded and gestured with his eyebrows for her to try some. This was perhaps the thing she'd been the most skeptical about since her arrival. It was just food though. Food was food. Where she was from, you ate what you were handed. Why was she hesitating now?

Without giving herself time to reconsider, Aurianna shoved a tiny bite of it into her mouth.

Her mouth was not prepared.

She shoveled in two or three more bites before Javen, laughter in his eyes, said, "Ready to eat those words now?"

"How does something like this even exist? It doesn't even make sense." When Javen started to pull the plate back, she grabbed her side and held on, making a threatening gesture with her eating utensil. "I didn't say I didn't want it."

Both of their faces broke into grins. Sigi looked back and forth between them with a knowing look in her eye.

When they had finished eating, all three rose from the table at the same time, depositing their now-empty plates as they left the dining hall. Sigi waved good night as she continued up to her dormitory level two floors above Aurianna's. Javen lingered in the stairwell for a moment as he stared at her necklace again. At least, she hoped he was staring at her necklace.

"Well, I guess I'll see you tomorrow some time," she offered.

Seeming to come back to himself, he nodded. "Breakfast?"

"Sure. Good night, Javen."

He smiled, waved, and continued up the stairs to the next floor, she assumed. She opened the door and strolled down the hallway. Once inside her room, she collapsed directly onto the bed. Exhaustion snaked through her limbs, her muscles, and settled into her very core, despite the fact that she really hadn't done much of anything all day besides listen to lessons on things she didn't understand and attempt to read books about concepts completely foreign to her.

Forcing herself to get up and shower first—and she was glad she did once the hot water hit her—Aurianna got ready and climbed back into bed. She fell headlong into a dream world filled with visions of tiny children dancing around her, pointing and laughing.

Perhaps tomorrow she would get some answers.

But more than likely, even more questions would arise.

* * *

Arriving at her classes the next day, Aurianna received some heartening news: She would be working individually from now on, at least for a little while, until she had a good grasp of the basics of the world and the magic within it. Most of this would involve reading on her own, but she didn't mind at all. Eventually it would have to start making sense, she told herself. She just needed to start at the very, very beginning.

She also learned that she would be meeting with each of the Magisters for short training sessions in the evening. No one had mentioned anything about Air training, so she assumed it wouldn't come up unless she somehow started to display characteristics of the rare power. No one had explained why that specific element was so underrepresented. The other four—Fire, Earth, Water, and Energy—would constitute her training for now, but the book work was the focus until she mastered the information within. Four elements, half an hour each. Not too overwhelming. She hoped.

Walking back to her room with the pile of books she'd been handed, Aurianna suddenly felt the loneliness creeping back in. She normally didn't mind being alone, but being here made it feel different. The world was a much bigger place, and she felt that much smaller as a result.

One of the instructors—Magisters—had recommended adding *A History of Eresseia* to her reading list, especially since she already had the copy sitting on the table in her room. She trudged back to her quarters, throwing the bag filled with heavy tomes on the bed and flopping onto the blanket. Opening one of the books at random, she settled against her pillow and delved into *Kinetic Energy: The Magic of the Elements*.

Though she was sure she'd read a good deal, Aurianna found herself startling awake, a thin line of drool dribbling down her chin and onto her tunic.

Gross.

Then she realized what had woken her—someone was pressing the buzzer to her room. She pushed the button to answer on the intercom. "Yes, who's there?"

"It's me." The voice added, "Sigi."

Could that much time have passed? Had she slept the day away?

"Okay, hold on a sec."

Pressing the button to open the door, she put on a smile for her visitor.

Sigi was dressed in a simple blue tunic and overgarment with brown pants that complemented her terracotta skin and bluish-gray eyes, her dark hair full and loose, no longer pulled back. This was the first time Aurianna had seen the girl's bare arms, and the sight was impressive to say the least. The muscles of her arms were incredibly well defined and sculpted, clearly able to take on any weapon she needed to in her line of work. Despite her short stature and powerful arms, Sigi somehow maintained an air of soft femininity. She was wearing even more makeup than usual now, but it looked nice on her. And she smelled of orange blossoms.

Aurianna took all of this in as Sigi stood smiling back at her. "You were asleep," Sigi said dryly. It wasn't a question.

There was no point in lying, so she sheepishly explained how her morning had gone, gesturing behind her to the books on the bed.

"That...is a lot of books." Sigi nodded.

"Yeah. I'll be spending my days chugging down coffee, it seems."

"I'm guessing you missed lunch?"

"I was reading for quite a while, at least I think I was. But yeah, I must have slept straight through lunch."

"Well, then let's get a move on. Maybe afterward we can go early to dinner. Ready to go visit the Arcanes?"

* * *

They took the stairs all the way to the bottom level. Traveling through the vast length of tunnels, Aurianna was suddenly nervous about the prospect of speaking to an Arcane, something she never would have dared in her own time. As they walked, she asked, "Are you sure this is a good idea?"

"Why wouldn't it be?" Sigi gave her a sidelong look.

"I mean, they kind of keep to themselves, right? Aren't you supposed to not bother them?"

"Bother them? Answering questions about the mysteries of life is part of their job, Aurianna."

"Oh." They stopped outside the large metal door, Sigi grabbing the metal knocker without a moment's hesitation. Before she could use it, however, the door open, pulling the knocker out of her hand.

A tall robed man opened the door. "Yes?"

"We're here with some questions for you." Sigi didn't seem the least bit afraid or intimidated by him.

"Of course. Come in."

Sigi seemed surprised at the easy invitation, even though she had seemed full of confidence about their welcome just moments before.

Walking into the room, Aurianna spied rows upon rows of bookshelves lined up in the middle of the space. Dust covered most of the surfaces she could see, though several tables were in use by the robed men wandering about and hunching over giant tomes. Peering into the secret lives of the Arcanes was beginning to sound more and more appealing. With all this potential knowledge, the answers to everything must be down here somewhere.

As she tried to see farther down the rows, another of the men came out from behind a counter and walked up behind her. "Welcome, Aurianna," he said in a soft voice.

Startled, she jumped several inches into the air, gasping. "Oh, hello."

"I apologize. I didn't mean to startle you."

"No, no, it's fine. Um, so ..." her words trailed off, hovering with an awkward expectancy.

"So you'd like to know more about your role in all of this prophecy business?"

Sigi smiled. "That's part of it, yes. She has a lot of questions for you," she responded on Aurianna's behalf.

"Of course she does. We've been expecting you." He looked back and forth between the two girls hesitantly. "Maybe you'd prefer we speak alone?"

For a moment, Aurianna considered his words. It was true she barely knew Sigi, and there was no telling what she would learn from this encounter. Did she want an audience, particularly someone who had proven her loyalty to the powers-that-be, the people she wasn't sure she could trust?

She wasn't being fair. The Magnus would presumably be privy to anything she might learn anyways. Keeping this in mind, she told the Arcane, "No, it's okay. I want Sigi here. I think I'm going to need a friend for this."

Never would she have anticipated the look of sheer unadulterated joy on the girl's face. Maybe Sigi needed a friend as much as Aurianna.

Surprisingly, the Arcane was smiling as well. "All right then. Let's go find somewhere to chat, shall we?"

He led them over to a table situated under a lamp in a corner of the room. Clasping his hands together, elbows on the table, the man introduced himself as Simon and asked where she would like to start.

"No idea, honestly," she replied, sighing heavily and adding, "but I guess let's get the crazy stuff out of the way. So, this prophecy... um, yeah, let's start there."

"Well, that is perhaps the best place to start, although certainly not the easiest. The thing is, prophecies aren't just some words that get thrown around." Simon gestured to the shelves around them. "These books contain all the knowledge of both our history and our future here in Eresseia. We're only the keepers of this knowledge.

We have no control over what and when information is ready to be known. The words become known when they're needed."

Aurianna and Sigi stared at him, then at each other, sharing a glance that communicated their identical lack of comprehension.

Finally, Sigi said, "Forgive my ignorance, sir, but I've lived here my entire life, and I have no idea what you're talking about. I can't imagine Aurianna does either."

He nodded. "I understand this is confusing. It's why we don't really try to explain ourselves to the general populace. We're not trying to be cryptic, but it's the truth. We are the disseminators of information deemed relevant at the time by the Essence."

Aurianna chimed in, "Pharis—the Regulus—he mentioned the Essence, but I don't know what that means."

It was her turn to receive a look of surprise from Sigi. "Really? You don't know about the Essence?" When Aurianna shook her head, Sigi said, "The Essence created this world. We get our power from them, so to speak, and each element has a deity. Caendra is Fire, Terra is Earth, Unda is Water, Fulmena is Energy, and..." she halted, looking at Simon for a moment before she added, "and, um, Caelum is Air. But we don't have much of a connection left to him."

"Is that why Air powers are so rare?"

"Yes," Simon answered, "that is why. We keep the temples to the deities in good shape, but the old ways seem to be dying out. Not many non-Kinetics visit the temples, but we still pay homage at all our ceremonies and throughout the training process. And they, in turn, provide the Kinetics with their abilities and guide me and my fellow Arcanes to do their bidding. Prophecies are tricky things. Sometimes they might have different meanings. That's the way prophecies work. My job is to protect the knowledge in this room from reaching people before its intended time or place."

"And the Essence determines that time and place?"

"Exactly."

"Well... can I see it? Or... Or hear it? Or whatever it is you do?"

Simon's gaze was intense. He finally responded, choosing his words carefully. "This is highly irregular, but I think you need to read it yourself. No one outside these chambers has seen the actual written words, and no one knows of their existence other than the ones who heard them spoken and the ones we have told. It's important you see it with your own eyes." He stood, motioning for them to stay seated as he picked his way over some stacks of books and disappeared between shelves. He returned within minutes, carrying a large green tome. The edges were frayed, and the entire surface was dashed with dark spots and flecks of discoloration.

Simon carried the book over to their table, laying it down gently in front of Aurianna. Sigi stood and walked around to look over her shoulder. As Simon opened its pages and began flipping through them, he stopped on one page, practically bare except for a collection of words written as lines like in poetry she had read:

> When the red sky at morning
> Bursts forth to cleanse the land,
> Beware the dragon's warning,
> For the end is close at hand.
>
> Rising up to heights unknown,
> Burning forth to scorch the sky;
> Beware the infernal stone,
> For the end of all is nigh.
>
> She will steal your life,
> For the world to burn and bend.
> Beware the silent knife,
> For she will be your end.

Speaking became a foreign concept as Aurianna stared at the words in front of her. *Dragon? End of all?* What in the world did any of it mean? And how could anyone assume it was in any way related to her?

Sigi found her voice first. "So...umm...what does that mean?"

Simon cleared his throat. "It means that we are all in a lot of danger."

"Danger? From what?" Aurianna finally said.

"That is the real question. When Azel was given the vision—"

"Vision?"

"Yes, when the Essence are ready for us to know some piece of information, one of us is drawn toward the book containing it. When he opens to the words, he is presented with a vision of a possible scenario."

"Possible?"

He sighed. "It's complicated. Whether a vision can be prevented from happening, or not, is dependent upon a number of factors, most of which would be beyond your understanding. But when Azel received the vision, he saw something that made him insist on running to your mother's bedside as she was giving birth to you. Unfortunately, he was killed in the process, so we don't know which version of things he saw. We only had the opened page."

Narrowing her eyes, Sigi replied, "Killed? Where did this happen?"

"It was an internal issue, nothing to do with the City Guard. He was killed by supernatural means, and as we know, Aurianna was saved from the same fate."

Stunned, Aurianna sat in silence. After a moment, she spoke her quiet words into the silence of the room. "My mother didn't die from giving birth to me, did she?"

Refusing to look her in the eye, Simon nodded. "You see, when you were born a few moon cycles ago, someone very evil cast a spell on you. A curse, actually. That isn't something most Kinetics can do. In fact, it's the only time I've ever seen that kind of ability outside Fae magic. The woman who took you into the future to protect you was a midwife during your birth. She and the other two women who were assisting your mother were each to give you a gift. Now, I can't tell you what they were because, as is the way of things that come from more ancient sources of power, they would disappear if I spoke of them. But these were very simple things that have helped to make you who you are. Larissa was the last to give you her gift, but this evil entity cursed you before she could. I'm sure she told you a little about the curse. You would have died had Larissa not used her gift to change the curse. Instead of dying, you had to leave this place for the hundred years it took for the curse to be over."

Sigi was staring at her, eyes wide with disbelief and awe. "Really?"

Aurianna shrugged. "As far as I've been told, yeah. I just assumed from what my aunt had said that my mom had died in childbirth. Not..." Trailing off, she stood up and began pacing the small alcove full of the shadows of ghosts she'd never known. She abruptly stopped as a thought occurred to her. "But how do you know all of this? Were there other witnesses?" She couldn't hide the hope in her voice, the hope someone could tell her more about her mother.

Simon frowned and shook his head. "No. We have the Book of Histories to tell us that tale."

"Book of Histories?"

"It's the book listing everything that has happened throughout our history. The Essence update it, or at least that's what we assume. Anytime a major event occurs, the details are added to the record the next day. It's always been this way. We check it regularly, and that's what the book described for the night of your birth."

"Can I see this record?"

"I'm afraid I cannot show you the Book of Histories. The Essence would forbid it."

Sigi's voice rose as she chimed in, "Hang the Essence! Most Kinetics don't even visit the temples anymore."

"That is a sad fact, for sure. But it doesn't change anything. I cannot show you that book." Simon appeared to be contemplating something. "I know how this must sound."

"Do you?" Aurianna challenged. "Because I don't see anything on this page that even remotely points at me."

"That's because it doesn't. At least not in the way you think." Her confusion must have shown because he immediately added, "The Magnus believes the prophecy is speaking of the one who cursed you. He believes it to be a Kinetic who did so, the Enchantress who lives in the tower across the bay."

"Wait, what? Then why am I here?"

"You, Aurianna, were brought here to stop her."

CHAPTER 14

PHARIS

Seeing her walking back toward the stairs with that look of fear in her eyes, Pharis realized the Arcanes must have told her everything. *Everything.*

He almost felt sorry for her. Hell, he *did* feel sorry for her. But he couldn't bring himself to approach her. She was still what she was, and as long as things remained as they were, she was a problem he wanted nothing to do with. He had bigger problems to handle, like trying to find a way to make his future position less of a heated subject for the people.

So why had he followed her down here?

The guardswoman who had accompanied her was lost in thought as well, clearly in on the secrets tearing his life apart. That made things more complicated. The woman turned to look at Aurianna, saying something he couldn't hear, and ascended the stairs on her own. For some inexplicable reason, the girl wasn't following her. She must be in shock. Her eyes held both amazement and trepidation in their depths, the amber glow once again catching his attention—did no one else notice how incredibly uncanny the girl's eyes were?—and he found his feet stopping of their own accord before he reached the staircase in the adjacent corner, the one dedicated for the use of the Magnus and his family.

Perhaps he could speak to her, get her on his side. *Who am I kidding? She hates me.* Not that she didn't have good reason to, considering how rude he'd been to her on their journey here. But he had every right to feel the way he did. Having her on his side would be mutually beneficial. Surely she would see that.

Without thinking it over any further, Pharis walked over to where she was still standing. Upon hearing his approach, she startled, spinning toward him.

"Oh, it's you," she said in a tone that held everything unspoken between them in its grasp.

"Yeah, um . . ." He had lost the ability to speak. What should he say? Where should he start? Then he had a sudden unnerving thought: what if she thought he was in on it?

Aurianna swallowed loudly, her eyes still sparkling in the darkness and—he now saw—lined with unshed tears. "Regulus, I'm . . . I'm really sorry you were dragged into this."

What?

He studied her a moment with narrowed eyes. "You're sorry?"

"Yeah, I realize the mission was far below your station. Obviously, I didn't know who you were at the time. But they shouldn't have sent you, and I honestly don't know why they did, but I get why you were so angry."

Pharis frowned at her, clenching his jaw. "Don't presume to know or understand me, girl. You know nothing about me. You weren't supposed to know who I was then, and I don't care what you know—or think you know—now. I was horrified by the things your Consils were doing to my kind, and I certainly don't want anyone to suffer like that, but nothing is ever that simple. This plan of theirs will solve nothing. We need to present a united front, and we need to do it quickly."

"I have absolutely no idea what you're talking about, Pharis." She didn't seem to realize she'd slipped back into calling him by his name instead of his proper title. He didn't correct her.

"I'm saying we need to address it now, before it gets out of hand."

"Before what gets out of hand?"

Exasperated and gesticulating wildly, he threw his hands up. "The wedding plans."

Time stopped.

Her body stiffened, spine going completely straight as her nostrils flared and her eyes widened. She seemed to be struggling to breathe. A long series of deafening silences chained together into an infinite moment that had him questioning all his assumptions. Was it possible she didn't know?

A breathy whisper reached him in the enclosed space which seemed to get smaller and smaller by the minute. "Whose?"

And that one word summed everything up. They clearly had left that part out of whatever information they'd just dumped on her back there.

Well, shit.

"I . . . I . . ." he stammered, struggling to find something—*anything*—to say. He hadn't wanted to be the one to tell her. He'd just assumed that was why she was so freaked out.

"Whose wedding, Pharis?"

"Well, um . . . Well, it's . . . it's . . ." He ran his hand roughly through his already disheveled hair in agitation, finally stumbling over the last word. ". . . ours."

She was nodding as if it was the most normal thing for him to say. "Okay, yeah. Well, of course it is." Her voice was rising higher and higher in pitch, and he was worried people would hear her. "I mean, I totally remember you asking me to marry you, Pharis. Must have been right after we fell in the water, right? Or was it when you were biting my head off for trying to understand the crazy that had just become my entire life? When was it, Pharis?"

And now she was hyperventilating. *Great.*

"Aurianna, please listen. It wasn't me. I had nothing to do with this. I told him it would never happen. That's why I came to talk to you. I just thought you already knew. I mean, you seemed upset after talking with the Arcanes, so I figured they had broken the news to you. I was under strict orders not to mention it before we got here. My father . . . this was *his* plan, and the Arcanes agreed. But I am completely against it, I assure you."

She was still staring at him with a wild fury, but some of the heat had seeped away. He took that as a good sign. After a moment of silence, she said, "So, your father—the Magnus—wants us to get married. Why?"

A sardonic smile formed on his face, but Pharis hoped she could see it wasn't happiness etched on his features. "He doesn't just *want* us to get married, Aurianna. He made an official decree. He just hasn't shared it with anyone other than me and the Arcanes. They seemed to jump at the idea. I have no idea why any of them think this is a good idea." *Liar.* But he continued, "If we speak to him together, tell him we refuse to go through with it, he'll have no choice but to drop the whole thing. No one else knows yet, so it's not like he can't take it back."

"And you knew about this the whole time?" Her anger was coming back, and now it was directed at him full force.

"Yes, but understand he isn't just my father. He's the Magnus. I have no choice but to follow a direct order, so I didn't say anything to you. It was an easy order to follow, unlike the wedding itself. I didn't know you, you didn't know me, and I had hoped he would change his mind by the time we got back." Bitterly, he added, "No such luck."

"I need to sit down." On the bottom step of the stairwell, Aurianna collapsed in a heap, putting her head between her knees and breathing deeply.

"I...I'm sorry for breaking it to you like that. I just thought you already knew." He thought for a moment. "Why were you so upset then, if it wasn't about this?"

"Why?" Hysterical laughter bubbled up to the surface, twisting her features into sharp focus. "Maybe I'm upset because the Arcanes seem to think I'm here to destroy some kind of evil, to stop some Enchantress who lives in a tower." He stilled at her words, felt the blood rushing from his cheeks. She didn't seem to notice and continued ranting in frustration. "They seem to believe I have the power to do that. Yet they can't tell me how or when I'm supposed to accomplish this task. And the prophecy..." Her hands, which had been gesturing in the direction of the Arcanes' room, settled down onto her lap. She looked defeated.

"The prophecy is a bunch of misunderstood words thrown together with a nice little bow tied around it. They have no idea what it means, so they can't tell you anything. That's why they can't answer your questions about it."

"Have you seen it?" she asked flatly, her tone derisive and suddenly beginning to grate on his nerves again.

"I don't need to. I've seen them before. They never mean much of anything, and the Arcanes are usually wrong about them anyways. Often nothing at all happens, and when it does, it's never what they seemed to imply would happen."

"Have the ones you've seen ever spoken about the end of the world?"

"End of . . . they told you it was the end of the world? And you believe that?"

"I don't know, Pharis!" she exclaimed. "I don't know what to believe. A few days ago, I didn't believe I'd ever be traveling back in time. Just a few minutes ago, I didn't believe I was engaged to be married." Snorting, she added, "Funny how truth can change your whole belief system."

Focusing on the floor, at his feet planted on the solid ground, with the world around him spinning off into madness, Pharis began to laugh.

Her eyes narrowed, Aurianna clenched her teeth then asked, "What's so funny?"

"It's just good to see you're as upset about all of this as I am."

"You're laughing because I'm upset?"

"That's not what I meant!" He exhaled in frustration and lowered his voice. "I just mean I'm glad we're on the same page. That we can present a united front to my father and get this straightened out."

"I couldn't care less about a 'united front' as you call it," she said, "because I don't belong here. He may be your father, your *Magnus*, but I plan on leaving once all of this is straightened out anyways."

"You think he'll just let you leave?" Actual horror filled her eyes at his words, so he corrected himself. "What I mean is, you'd have to fulfill what you came here to do before he'll let you go back. And part of that is the marriage." Realizing what he was saying, he added, "So yeah, looks like you're not going back."

"Over my dead body. I don't know what the prophecy refers to exactly, but as soon as I can figure that part out and perhaps make some solid progress in my training, I will return home. I promised Larissa, and I plan to keep that promise."

Pharis sighed. "Before I was sent to find you, the Arcanes had tried to prepare me for what to expect, but I couldn't believe those stories were true. We think maybe the Consils in your time are trying to replicate what they see as magic, not understanding it really doesn't work that way. We don't possess power within us, at least not more than a tiny piece of each element that flows in our bloodstream after a first successful attempt at using that power." At her quizzical look, he shrugged and added, "That's how they explain it during training. But Kinetics can only manipulate the elements. We can't create them from nothing."

"I guess that's why they only had a little bit of electricity, not enough to do much with. It took draining an immense number of Kinetics to make a very small amount."

"That just makes it all the more disgusting. And they're still doing it even though they're obviously getting nowhere." Didn't she see there was nothing for her to return to, even if she succeeded in fulfilling this ridiculous prophecy? As soon as they found out she possessed those same powers, her life would be forfeit. How could she not see that?

"But isn't that what I'm supposed to be preventing?"

"How exactly are you supposed to do that? You said yourself, the prophecy doesn't really explain anything."

"I don't know yet. But I'm sure I can figure it out." Aurianna waited in silence for a moment, chewing on her bottom lip as she stared off into the distance, lost in thought. A devious smirk stretched across her face. "I think I can solve one of our problems though. Take me to the Consils."

* * *

A tour around Bramosia was *not* the way Pharis had planned on spending his evening.

And spending it with her . . . well, that was just the icing on the cake. But she seemed to have some sort of plan to get them out of the whole marriage problem, so for that reason alone, he had consented.

Now he was regretting that decision as he tried desperately to keep moving, while Aurianna kept stopping to stare at everything, asking question after question until his head began to ache.

"What in the world are those people doing?" she asked in wonderment.

He sighed. Again. "They're cliff diving. It's kind of a recreational activity around here, at least for some."

"Have you ever gone cliff diving?"

Pharis couldn't help but laugh as he remembered his dip into the freezing lagoon the night he had come to get her. "Intentionally, no. I was never allowed to do things like that. Can't have the heir risk hurting himself, now can we?" His tone was sardonic. He increased his pace in frustration, not realizing he was doing so.

"Then why were you sent back to get me? Wasn't that even more dangerous?"

"That is a great question. Good luck getting an answer because I haven't been able to, neither from my father nor from the Arcanes."

Chewing on her bottom lip, she frowned and continued following him. She was struggling to keep up with him now, so he slowed back down. He had an image to maintain anyway. The Regulus didn't hurry anywhere, at least not when people were watching.

Out of the corner of his eye, he could see her looking around in awe, taking in the sights and sounds that were ordinary to the people who lived there, himself included. Vendors lined both sides of the main streets, selling anything from sweet treats to tunics. They didn't usually approach him, but Aurianna was telegraphing interest, gazing at the selections like she'd never seen most of them. Which he guessed she probably hadn't.

They were in the heart of the city, the thriving center where life was all around and commerce was king. He was constantly fascinated by the fact that here, in this particular aspect at least, these people were able to be so self-sufficient despite being right under the nose of the Imperium, so close to the man who held the constant noose around their necks that tightened every day.

Aurianna was looking across the sea of bodies, however, over to the temple area. She asked him, "What are those buildings for?" and pointed in the direction of some small but highly decorated buildings.

For a moment, he wondered what the structures had been in her time. Probably empty. "Those are the temples to the Essence," he replied.

"Simon explained them to me, but he mentioned the people here don't really worship your deities anymore. At least, not like they used to."

"I guess that's true, yes. They're very strict about keeping the temples maintained and the fires and such going, but not many people truly go in to pray anymore. Non-Kinetics never do."

"We don't even know about them in my time, so I guess the practice was completely wiped out somehow."

Gritting his teeth, Pharis said, "Yes, I guess so."

"But you seem to believe in them. I mean you called on them to help us time travel. Does everyone believe in them at least?"

"Difficult to say. I think most people believe in them to some extent. Kinetics definitely do because they're the embodiment of those elements. You have to believe those powers come from somewhere. And without them, we would never be able to travel through the Aether, considering it's their realm."

"Only Kinetics can travel with Aether Stones?"

"I don't really know how it works, but that's my understanding."

"What kind of Kinetic are you? I mean, what element do you control?"

"It is not considered proper to ask, and we are not supposed to discuss that sort of thing."

Expecting a snide remark, Pharis looked back. He saw her face fall as they were nearing the home she'd grown up in. He had to admit—to himself—it must be difficult to handle that sort of disconnect, to see your childhood home in a completely different time with a completely different set of people occupying it.

Aurianna began to slow down as they walked by, all her attention on the building, so he stopped and waited for her to decide what she was going to do. People passed on all sides, but she was frozen, gazing at the only shred of familiarity that was left to her. No fear marred her face, only longing and sadness.

The moment passed. She turned back to him, nodding to the hill toward the Consilium in the distance. She was ready to move on.

Walking beside him, her eyes focused forward now, she asked, "Are all of these people Kinetics?"

"No," he replied, "only about half, maybe. The other half are those who decided to move here for one reason or another or who are just passing through."

"So, the non-Kinetics get along with the...with us?"

"Define 'get along.' I mean, yeah, I guess so. No intermingling is allowed beyond Bramosia, so the people who live here are already making the decision to live among each other."

"Intermingling? You mean like...like couples?"

"Yes. Kinetics aren't encouraged to pursue relationships, but if they do decide to dally, it's forbidden to do so with non-Kinetics outside of Bramosia. They both have to move here if they want to do that. The whole thing is frowned upon, but everyone knows it happens. Absolutely no children though, not when a Kinetic is involved. Too dangerous, they say. Kinetics coupling with their own kind isn't encouraged either, but since all Kinetics have to check in here from time to time, they'll both receive the birth control on a regular basis."

"Wait…what?"

"Birth control herb? It's in the water supply here in Bramosia and at the Imperium. Everyone knows about it."

"Well, I didn't!"

The corner of his mouth turned up as Pharis looked at her, raising an eyebrow. "Were you planning on starting a family right now?" As soon as the words left his mouth, however, he realized the implication of what he'd said and quickly looked away.

"No, of course not! But you can't just drug someone and not tell them." She thought for a moment, her brows knotted in indignation. He saw the moment the realization dawned on her. "But what about the…you? You were born here, right?"

"Yes, well, the rules are different for the ruling family. The Magnus doesn't use the same water supply for drinking. One day, I guess I won't either." He sighed.

"Oh." She seemed to be speechless at his revelation. *Finally.*

They walked the rest of the way in silence.

* * *

When they reached the Consilium, Pharis guided Aurianna through the main doors leading into the public conference hall. Most days, the Consils could be found there when they weren't in meetings. A surprising number of issues were brought to them by the townspeople, by both Kinetics and non-Kinetics. His father always complained when he returned from his time with the Consils, unused to actually listening to people's complaints with a sympathetic ear.

Pharis was curious about the bottom level Aurianna had mentioned before. As far as he knew, it didn't exist in this time, but it seemed an odd addendum to an already-established structure. Did the Consils know something about it? And what would they be using it for at this point?

When they reached the interior of the conference hall, a Praefect was standing by the empty dais. She told them the Consils were, in fact, in a meeting in the back rooms. Normally he might be inclined to use his position and storm into those rooms, demanding to be seen. But it was entirely possible his father, whom he would prefer to avoid, was here. And he thought making a good impression on the Consils might be the key to obtaining their help.

After several minutes of waiting, Aurianna began pacing back and forth across the marbled floor as she chewed viciously on her bottom lip. Her golden eyes were alight with some hidden fire, probably fueled by the same indignation he himself felt over the whole marriage issue. Absentmindedly, he pulled the metal lighter from his pocket, flicking it open and shut, open and shut, until Aurianna glared at him.

"What?" he asked.

"Do you have any idea how annoying that is?"

Quirking up one eyebrow, he glared back at her, a slight smile on his face. "Right back at you."

"Huh?"

"Exactly." He knew he was intentionally getting under her skin, and now was perhaps not the best time to do so, but he couldn't help himself. Just to push a little further, he opened the lighter again and ran his thumb down in one smooth motion. A small flame ignited, causing the girl to stare at it in wonderment. He remembered her mistaking the object for actual magic and began to laugh despite himself.

Her brows wrinkled in frustration. "What's so funny?" Despite her obvious confusion, she somehow knew he was laughing at her.

A part of him wanted to continue the joke, if nothing else just to amuse himself. But considering he still needed her help with their current problem, it probably wasn't the smartest move.

He sighed. "It's not magic, Aurianna." He closed the lid, opening it back again and flicking the flame once again. He motioned her forward.

"I don't understand." She started toward him, hesitantly at first, but her curiosity eventually won out. Aurianna reached her hand out and gingerly closed the lid of the lighter. He handed it to her, and she opened the contraption, looking down into its interior as best as she could, clearly trying to decipher the riddle of the flame. She then made several attempts to light it by mimicking his earlier movements. When she finally succeeded, she jumped back from the flame, accidentally dropping the lighter onto the tiles. Picking it up, she stared at it for a moment then looked back at him.

Finally, she said, "So, it's just a regular flame then?"

Nodding, he responded, "Yeah, it's just metal and stone rubbing together, which ignites the oil inside. No magic involved." He suddenly realized he'd never wondered before, so he asked, "How did you create fire back home?"

"We didn't, most of the time. Just reused the hot embers in the fireplace and threw some tinder on it." She thought for a moment. "Occasionally you'd have to restart one from scratch, but that was a pain, to be honest." She smiled at him.

"Interesting. Well, this lighter makes it much easier, I promise." He returned her smile.

"So...you can't control fire then?"

Now he felt uncomfortable with the line of questioning. "Um, no, I can't. But even those who can prefer one of these to wasting their energy on something small. Elemental control takes a lot out of a person and calling up raging hot magma from beneath the ground is a bit of overkill just to light a small fire."

"Then what do they use it for?"

"Depends on the element. They'll show you in training, but for instance, with Pyrokinetics, a lot of them are used for heating entire towns. Industry, factories, mining. Stuff like that."

She looked as if she might respond, but at that moment, the doors at the other end of the room behind the dais slammed open, and a group of men and women came storming out. When they saw Pharis, everyone slowed their pace, pasting smiles on their faces and sitting in the ornate chairs in a row along the wall.

"Regulus, what a pleasant surprise. How may we assist you today?" This statement came from Margery Rigas, Consil for the region of Menos. She was a heavyset woman with rosy cheeks and the typical laid-back attitude of most of her countrymen.

He bowed. "Madame Consil, thank you for seeing us. I would like to introduce you to Aurianna." He waved in her direction, prompting her to step forward.

Their facades dropped only slightly, refusing to betray their confusion. Cormick Lowe, the Consil for Eadon, said, "Welcome, Aurianna." He turned to Pharis, adding, "And who exactly is she?"

"She is the girl from the prophecy. I know my father told you about it, but perhaps he didn't mention he sent for her."

Five equally baffled looks stared back at them now. No one spoke for a moment. Finally, Consil Rigas cleared her throat. "Excuse me? What do you mean *sent for her*?" Bafflement was turning into barely concealed anger.

"I mean the Magnus sent me forward in time with an Aether Stone to retrieve her in the hope of having this prophecy taken care of sooner rather than later. I'm sure he had the best interest of all regions at heart. No one wants a disaster of any sort, no matter who it involves."

"Indeed," said Anson Glaeser, the Consil for Rasenforst. "Well, it would have perhaps been a better welcoming had we known she was coming. I trust the Arcanes have filled you in on all of our concerns with regard to this prophecy and the possibility of a civil war on our hands?" The last part was clearly directed at Aurianna, who had been standing still throughout the whole introduction, looking like she wanted to disappear through the floor.

She stammered, "Ye-yes, sir. Well, no, actually. I don't know anything about a civil war, per se. I just know that I'm supposed to stop whatever it is that causes things to turn out the way they do."

"The Arcanes have assured us that a war between Kinetics and non-Kinetics will happen if things do not change from their current course. We are charged with protecting our people. Non-Kinetics do not want our world ripped apart by conflict any more than Kinetics do."

"I see. Well, I just recently arrived, so I have a lot to learn at this point." She was chewing on her lip again, eyes darting around to each of the five figures in front of them. "And that's actually why we're here. I don't know how I feel about all of this yet, but from what I understand, your positions are designed to be of equal weight to that of the Magnus, no?"

Genius. Now he saw her plan so clearly. Absolutely brilliant.

He could see the hesitation on the faces of the Consils as they said, practically in unison, "Yes."

She continued, "Well, it's been brought to our attention that the Magnus plans to have me marry his son here. Quite against our will, I might add. The only reason I can think of for this is he recognizes the extent of my powers and wants them for himself. The easiest way to control me would be through a marriage union, I imagine."

The extent of her powers? This was turning out to be quite amusing. She was, of course, lying, putting up a pretense of arrogance he knew she didn't really feel. It was contrary to her nature, as far as he'd seen at least. But it was the best plan for getting the Consils on their side.

And she had known that. Why hadn't he thought of it?

The Consils were still staring at her, either incredulity or outrage displayed with every look, every line of their features. When Consil Rigas spoke again, it was in a quiet voice full of simmering anger. "And what would you have us do about it?"

"Well," Aurianna said, "we had thought you of all people would want to put a stop to this, seeing as he's clearly going behind your backs on this to gain an extra bit of power for himself."

The Consil scrunched up her face. "Indeed." She nodded. "All right. We will speak to the Magnus and make sure this union does not happen under any circumstances. In the meantime, good luck with your training, Aurianna."

The dismissal was clear in her words and her eyes, so they turned around abruptly and left the chamber.

Chapter 15

AURIANNA

Weeks passed, but Aurianna couldn't bring herself to tell the others about the Magnus's attempt to foist an engagement on her. Somehow, she knew how Javen would react, not to mention the look of pure devilish delight she could imagine on Laelia's face. She wasn't sure why she hadn't told Sigi though, considering they were now having many of their meals together, with and without Javen. There was no reason not to include her in the secret, but some part of Aurianna knew the whole marriage deal was more complicated than it looked. She felt certain Pharis was still lying about or holding something back. She could see it every time their eyes met across the crowded dining hall. Some fire still burned there. Perhaps, some deep-seated passion born of anger or contempt?

Today was not for those kinds of thoughts, however.

A gentle breeze floated across her skin as she stood on the bridge, looking down the coastline and out across the bay. The water below caught the early morning rays, orange and golden hues scattered in prisms across the azure sky. Puffy white clouds floated on the breeze—their destination unknown, uncertain, unlooked for in the lazy dawn light. She had never seen anything so lovely. As she gazed longingly at the natural beauty strewn across the heavens, she heard Javen walk up behind her and stop, so very close to her she almost lost her breath. Was she really doing this now, allowing him to have this effect on her?

Yes, yes she was.

And her heart skipped another beat when he whispered in her ear, "Beautiful." She got the distinct impression he wasn't just talking about the sky. Tingling set in against her skin—tiny pinpricks of hot and cold in intermittent bursts.

"Yes," she whispered back. Aurianna turned to face him and, attempting to put more distance between them, she stepped back and looked up at the structure they were leaving behind that day. The Imperium shone with a brilliance belying the rough exterior, the sunlight casting only the slightest of shadows among the various nooks and corners and caressing the clock face with a blinding flash that made her eyes water.

He was smiling, and she wasn't sure if she should be irritated at the gesture, if it was perhaps at her expense. But he only said, "Come on. The train will be leaving soon."

It was then she realized the beauty about her had completely distracted her from noticing the enormous machine sitting directly across the bridge from where they stood. Beyond the giant metal contraption and through the thick plume of smoke rising from its uppermost protrusion, the capital city of Bramosia lay spread out like something both foreign and familiar. She wanted desperately to visit the town again, to see what she might recognize, but a part of her also railed against the idea, fearing what she might *not* recognize. She had been so tempted to knock on the door of her old home, half-expecting Aunt Larissa to open the door and welcome her in. What would she do when a stranger was staring back at her, an unfamiliar being wrapped in the trappings of a familiar scene?

She was honestly afraid to find out those answers.

But today they were going to visit one of the nearby regions, taking the trip by steam train, which was another frightening thought for her but seemed the most common mode of transportation for people in this time. Larissa had told her about steam power and how it had once been a key component of life here in their world. But the story and the reality were very different things, and the colossus in front of her was a testament to the power these people wielded, power she had no grasp of whatsoever.

She wanted to believe she would eventually understand—and perhaps even master—that power, but each day brought more and more frustration, and little to no improvement in her personal explorations into the elemental world.

But at least she had begun to grasp the dynamics of the world and the processes by which the elements worked. She knew Kinetics were able to wield control over one or more elements, but they did not, in fact, have the power to create it. They could move the magma just below the planet's surface to a different location, and they could combine it with other elements, but they could not create the element out of nothing. It was, supposedly, just a matter of bending each element (Fire, Water, Earth, Energy, and, in a small way, Air) to one's will, coaxing it to move where one desired it to move and in the manner needed for the job at hand.

The maps had certainly been helpful, though the regions themselves were still, as yet, completely foreign to her. The landmass was shaped like a nearly contiguous ring of adjacent regions. However, a big chunk of the landmass—the part directly opposite Bramosia in the ring surrounding the lagoon—was separated from the rest of the loop by two narrow straits. Part of the ring looked like it had broken away, creating an island separated from the mainland by a narrow strait on either side. The straits connected the calmer waters of the lagoon to the dangerous swells of the *Mare Dolor*, or Sea of Sorrow, beyond. The island was on the far side of the lagoon, opposite Bramosia and the Imperium. The maps labeled part of this island as the region of Vanito, Javen and Laelia's hometown, though there seemed to be a lot of uninhabited territory behind it on the outer side of the landmass, an area covered in forest and wildland from what the maps told her. Nothing suggested what it might be used for or why it seemed untouched.

The land rose high in sheer cliffs from the water's edge, both on the inner lagoon side and on the surrounding ocean side. The island also rose high out of the water. The violent waves of the Sea of Sorrows pounded the outer cliffs, but the relative calm of the lagoon allowed the people of Eresseia to pursue sailing and fishing—not to mention cliff diving.

A long time ago, some brave souls had undertaken the task of cutting steps into the cliff face at various locations across Eresseia to provide access to the lagoon below. Sigi had told her about these when they were discussing cliff diving a few weeks ago, pointing out that the water was simultaneously both a novelty and a source of fear for the people of Eresseia.

As Aurianna and Javen crossed the bridge to reach the waiting train, she tried to avoid looking into the city itself and the place she'd once called home. Instead she focused her gaze directly at their destination.

The train was a marvel unto itself, but its track structure was nothing short of miraculous. The entire lagoon was outlined along its edges by the rails built upon giant metal supports that began somewhere under the depths of the water and climbed up to the height of the land far above. Each region supposedly had a stop where people boarded or disembarked, depending on their destination. If one desired, the ability to ride the train all around the circle and back was always an option, albeit a journey that would take most of a day to complete.

Nearing one of the train cars, they climbed the steps into the interior of the train. Aurianna turned right and looked around, trying to take in every detail of her surroundings. Javen gently prodded her forward, but the corridor in front of them seemed to stretch on beyond her vision, though she knew each car was mostly self-contained. She wasn't sure how far to keep walking, but when one of the compartments on the right was empty, she looked at Javen questioningly. He nodded, and they entered the small space, each taking a seat on the bench along one side. Javen allowed her to sit closest to the window, pointing things out through the glass until the train started to move, beginning the journey into the unknown, into the beyond.

"So, you'd really never seen the sun before you came here?" he asked her.

"No, I really hadn't. Not like this."

"That's a shame," he said, smiling with a glint of some unknown thought behind his eyes. After that, he stopped speaking, and they enjoyed the rest of the train ride in almost complete silence.

The main benefit of sitting on this side of the train was the ability to see the landscape as they passed. She was given a basic visual tour as they chugged along the tracks, seemingly suspended in midair. The land to their right bestowed all its wondrous scenery. Hills and valleys gave way to olive groves and vineyards bursting with color. Horses raced alongside them, stopping short as the undergrowth thickened. Sheep grazed in vast pastures, their fuzzy tails waggling in excitement as they nibbled at the grass.

Aurianna was entranced by everything—the colors, the sights, all of it winding into one long story set to pictures now ingrained in her head, playing over and over again.

She never wanted it to end.

But, eventually, the train came to a slow, chugging halt at a rather out-of-the-way area that spoke of farming people and a distinct lack of hurriedness. Javen led her out of the station and over to a nearby stable.

Horses. Oh, dear goodness. They were going to ride *horses*.

The thought made her both nauseous with fear and giddy with enthusiasm. She had never dreamed she'd ever be riding a horse. The only ones they had back home were used purely for farming and were always tied up to something, whether it be a cart or a plow.

"Where are we?" she asked.

"Menos. Home of the Geokinetics—Earth Kinetics. Or Dusters as we like to call them."

As Javen spoke with the stablemaster, Aurianna meandered around the stalls, looking at each beast in turn, curious as to what they might be thinking. After passing four or five of the animals, she noticed one standing back in its stall, large glassy dark-brown eyes staring at her knowingly. They exchanged a moment of understanding, the horse's gaze unflinching even as Aurianna unhooked the door to its stall, oblivious to the shouts from both Javen and the stablemaster.

Here was a true thing of beauty, its coat black as night and shining in the minimal light cast from the overhead electric bulbs. Just as she was reaching out to touch her coat (for Aurianna knew it was a mare), the man in charge stumbled over to her, exclaiming, "That's not a good idea, miss. Oracle's not very good with people."

"Well, good, 'cause neither am I." After a moment's pause, she added, "Wait. Did you say her name is *Oracle*?"

"Yes, ma'am. Oracle's always letting us know how things are gonna be, whether we like it or not."

"You're joking," she said flatly.

Laughter came billowing from behind the man. Javen's amusement rolled out in uncontrolled chuckling that had him wiping the tears from his eyes.

Despite herself, she started laughing as well, rubbing her hands down the animal's mane and along its side. Oracle wasn't thrilled that everyone was having a laugh at her expense. The mare kicked the back of her stall and shook her mane in protest, garnering a sharp gasp from her new master. But Aurianna sidled back up to the creature, petting her whether she wanted the attention or not. "It'll be alright. He's not that bad," Aurianna whispered in the horse's ear. Oracle whinnied, sharing a laugh with her.

"Oracle," Javen repeated, shaking his head and walking back toward the front of the stable. The stablemaster shrugged and quickly followed.

They worked out a deal, and Aurianna was allowed to take Oracle, providing she could get the horse to cooperate. But any worries were unfounded as the beast stood still, allowing Aurianna to climb ungracefully atop her massive back and slide her feet into the stirrups with more than a little help from a couple of grooms.

With their belongings tucked away in saddlebags, the two adventurers trotted off into the midmorning sun, eager to be on their way. She felt a rush of excitement like she'd never felt before, even since arriving in this past version of her reality. Being outside in the clean, fresh air, with a sky more beautiful and enchanting than anything she'd ever known, Aurianna had a moment of unexpected euphoria, feeling everything around her as if it were a part of her, the edges of her vision blurring as she stared into the distance toward the adventure awaiting her.

They passed vineyard after vineyard, the greenery rolling out across undulating hills and countryside. The lush vegetation was mainly confined to the neat rows of olive trees, grape-bearing vines, and the occasional set of fig trees dotting the landscape. Javen patiently pointed out these things, teaching her in a way that felt more beneficial, more *real*, than anything she'd thus far gleaned from the books she'd been given.

After far too brief a time—though she had to admit her thighs and bottom were killing her—they stopped in the middle of a small clearing. "Why are we stopping?" she asked as they dismounted, Javen taking her hand quite unceremoniously as she slid down Oracle's side. Oracle shook her mane and nickered. She could have sworn the animal was laughing at *her* now.

They seemed to be in the middle of nowhere, no discernible landmarks in sight, no buildings or structures of any kind.

"He should be around here somewhere, though it's rather difficult to pinpoint his exact location when he's out hunting."

"Who are we looking for?"

"My friend, Theron. He's a Duster, but he prefers hunting to anything else. He's from this region and provides meat for the locals. His parents' house isn't far from here, which is how I know he should be in the area, but they wouldn't have any clearer idea than I do as to where he is exactly." His eyes twinkled. "Don't worry though. He'll find us. Theron's an excellent tracker."

As they stood in the small clearing, letting the horses graze freely, Javen retrieved some of the food he'd stored in the saddlebags. She accepted some dried meat and fruit, grabbing her canteen from her own saddlebag. Deep in thought, Aurianna munched happily as she stared off into the distance.

"This is the furthest into the land I've been. Still seems like the coastline is never-ending."

Javen nodded. "Yeah, it can feel like that sometimes, but once you've traveled the entire place from end to end, it begins to seem a lot smaller."

"What's beyond then?"

"Beyond? Beyond Eresseia?"

"No, I mean what's beyond the regions here? This big ring, I gather. But what about out there?" She waved her hand in the general direction of the ocean still far outside her vision.

"Out there is nothing. This is it. This is Eresseia, and that's all there is."

"But there *must* be more. Has anyone bothered to explore beyond the lagoon?"

"Too dangerous. The Mare Dolor is called the Sea of Sorrows for a reason, Aurianna. A long time ago, people did try going out further, but no one made it back alive. Perdita Bay is bad enough"

"Perdita Bay is the lagoon, right?"

"Yeah. Perdita means 'lost things.' I'm not sure when it started, but people tend to lose items in the lagoon quite frequently. The creatures down there must have caves full of hoarded treasure from all the years of things dropping into the water."

"What creatures?" Apprehension skittered across the back of Aurianna's neck.

"What? You haven't read about the monsters that inhabit Perdita Bay. Well, I better not spoil it for you. I'm sure it'll come up in your studies."

"Hey, that's not funny! I thought people go cliff diving into that water!"

"Yep."

"And it doesn't bother them that there are monsters down there?"

"Guess not."

"You're messing with me."

He laughed. "No, I'm not. Look it up yourself when we get back to the Imperium."

"Speaking of getting back . . . where is this friend of yours? Don't we need to head back soon?"

"It'll be fine. Trust me."

Trust you, she thought bitterly. What a novel concept. Trusting anyone seemed an impossible task for her now. She had seen what trusting others got you, and that was in a world where she knew the rules. Who knew what kind of punishments were doled out in this place of incomprehensible magic and mysterious creatures who inhabited a realm beneath the waves? Lost in thought again, she realized she was subconsciously rubbing her shoulder.

Javen looked at her with a note of concern on his face. "Are you in pain? The ride can be a bit much if you're not used to it."

Blushing in embarrassment, and not wanting to divulge the secret of her marked skin, Aurianna merely replied, "No, not really. Just a little sore is all. I'll be fine."

As soon as the words left her lips, they heard a rustling behind them, the shrubbery around that side of the clearing swaying wildly in the gentle breeze. Or was something moving in the thick undergrowth?

"I don't think that's your friend," Aurianna whispered.

"I don't think so either," he rasped with a tremor in his voice.

They waited in silent anticipation, praying the horses wouldn't make any sudden noises or movements. She noticed then that Javen had grabbed her hand. She started to pull away but suddenly realized it might be a bad idea if she got separated from her only way back home.

Home?

Home? This wasn't home, was it?

But it didn't matter in that moment because a figure emerged from the bushes, clothed head to toe in tans and browns, and a forest green cloak with a hood draped so far forward that the face was completely hidden.

Javen let out a breath she hadn't realized he'd been holding. "Theron! So glad it's you. I think something's nearby."

"That would be my quarry," came a soft-spoken, but very deep, voice. The man peeled back his hood to reveal long dark-blond hair and eyes somewhere between green and blue, the colors swirling together in a mixture that spoke of both intelligence and compassion. The way his keen gaze took her in made her suspect that this man was an observer, someone who said little and knew much.

"Theron, this is Aurianna. She's just arrived at the Imperium for training."

"A Kinetic then?" That familiar look of confusion crossed his face. "Why now?"

"It's a long story, my friend. How about we head over to your folks' place and talk over a proper meal."

"Working on it, Javen. You may have scared it off, however."

Just then, a massive beast with tusks at least the size of her arm came rambling into the small clearing, its fur matted with blood from several cuts across its torso and back.

"What...the hell...is that?" Aurianna shrieked.

Metal flashed, and in the blink of an eye, Theron was pointing a weapon behind him. He squeezed the trigger and, without missing a beat or turning to look at his prey, replied, "Dinner."

"I am not eating that...that thing! What is it?"

"A wild boar. Well, it *was* a boar. Now it is dinner."

Another rustling behind them had Aurianna scrambling backward. A small animal with reddish fur, pointy ears, and a white underbelly scampered out of the brush and ran toward Theron.

"Ah, late to the party as usual, I see."

The animal seemed to frown at him.

The young man tucked away his weapon. "Don't look at me like that, Rhouth. You know it's true." His dark-blond hair fell well past his shoulders, and a golden symbol hung from a chain around his neck. Aurianna was pretty sure she'd seen the image somewhere before.

A small but sharp yelp came from the creature just before it settled down at Theron's feet and began to lick itself clean like she'd seen cats back home do.

Hesitantly, Aurianna came closer, asking, "What is it?"

"She's a red fox. Never seen one?"

"No. She's kinda cute, I guess." Rhouth jerked her head up, staring indignantly at the source of the affront to her reputation as a fearsome hunter.

Theron laughed. "Not sure she'd agree with you."

And without another word, he hoisted the carcass onto his shoulders and strode away, his furry companion trailing behind.

Javen and Aurianna had no choice but to follow the hunter as well, leading their horses behind them.

* * *

Theron led them to a cottage which squatted amid a massive field of lush green. He dropped the dead animal unceremoniously on the ground in front of a small building to the side, calling into the opening. When a young man appeared, covered in grime and sweat, Theron pointed to the carcass and gave the man some instructions. The next thing she knew, the animal was being carted off into the small structure to be cleaned and prepared for cooking.

So, Theron wasn't joking. It really was for dinner.

When the man returned a moment later, he took the horses from them, leading them off into the barn. Theron motioned them over to the cottage. A woman appeared in the doorway. She was older, and plump, with light-brown hair flecked with gray, and tanned skin like Theron's. She called back into the cottage in a surprisingly low-pitched voice, "Jerry! Company," then waved them all inside.

"Welcome! Come in! Come in!" The woman's cheeks were flushed, her skin slick with sweat as she wiped her hands on a towel hanging from the waistband of her apron. Judging from the fresh stains on the apron, Aurianna assumed the woman had been cooking when they arrived.

Theron was just introducing them to the older woman, Nerina Panago, when a tall man with thinning white hair stepped into the room. Rhouth the fox promptly wrapped herself around his legs as he tried to walk. He was thin but powerfully built, clearly a man who worked very hard for a living. "And this is Jerry Panago. These are my parents. Mom, Dad, you know Javen. And this is his friend, Aurianna."

"You are most welcome, dear," Nerina said, looking at Aurianna. "You'll stay for supper?"

"Oh, well, thank you, but I don't know. I think we may be late getting back as it is."

Javen smiled at her. "I told you not to worry. It's still early. And we don't have classes tomorrow since it's a holiday. I had Sigi pack you some clothes and such for the trip in case we decided to stay the night."

And when had she been asked about this?

Instead, she replied, "You might have told me earlier."

"It was kind of a surprise, and I didn't want to freak you out since you hadn't been away from the Imperium overnight before." He frowned and added softly, "Sigi thought you'd appreciate some time away from the place."

Sigi was right, but she still bristled a bit at the decisions being made for her. There was no point in arguing about it now though. Theron's parents seemed like nice people and didn't seem put out by Javen's declaration in the least.

"Well, that's settled then," Jerry said. "I'll go see about dinner."

"I just sent Peter off with a boar. He should be working on it," Theron told him.

His father nodded and left to help prepare the animal.

Nerina said, "I'll have the extra rooms made up. You kids can make yourselves comfortable anywhere you like and rest up before we eat. Might be a few hours. Can I get you anything in the meantime?"

"No, ma'am, not right now," Javen replied. They all followed the woman back into the kitchen as she continued her work, the little red fox curling up in a corner for a nap. Aurianna sat on a small wooden chair facing a back window of the house with a full view of the sweeping landscape that stretched off into the horizon. Perfectly spaced rows of greenery covered the rolling hills.

"So, this is a farm?" she asked Nerina.

"Well, yes, for our own use. But mainly we run a vineyard. That's how we make a living."

"Is that what those rows are? What exactly is a vineyard?"

The woman stopped in the middle of kneading a mound of dough to stare at her. "You don't know what a vineyard is?"

Javen jumped in. "Aurianna's new around here, and she's in a bit of a unique situation."

"Just what does that mean?" Nerina's sharp tone caused Rhouth to raise her head in irritation, her impromptu nap interrupted. But the fox settled back down and closed her eyes once again.

Javen seemed unperturbed by the woman's outburst, however. "Miss Panago, I know Theron has told you about the issue we're facing. He's not one to spread rumors, but I'm sure he's explained about the issue with . . . *her*." His emphasis on the word made everyone in the room bristle.

"Well, yes, everyone's heard stories about that woman. They say some of the shipwrecks were caused by her . . . that she lures those poor people to the rocks around her tower and smashes them all to pieces." She nodded her head at Aurianna, narrowing her eyes. "But what's that got to do with this girl here?"

Theron chimed in with, "Yeah. I'd like to know that as well."

"The Arcanes brought her here because she's supposedly the one who's meant to stop her. Apparently, they have a prophecy and everything." When the other two continued to stare at him, he added, "She's from the future."

"The . . . future?" Theron seemed more than a little suspicious of Javen's words.

"Yeah, you know, we have those Aether Stones they go on about, the things they used to use for the Essence and stuff. Well, they sent Pharis to go get her."

"Pharis?" Sputtering, Nerina added, "You mean the *Regulus*?"

"Yeah, yeah, him. He brought her back, and now they're training her." When Aurianna glared at him pointedly, he shrugged. "Nobody said we couldn't tell people, right?"

"Yes, well," she replied, "I don't think it's easily digestible information, if you haven't noticed. Especially for people who don't even know me."

Nerina wiped her hands on her towel, eyes fixed on Aurianna as she walked around the table to stand in front of her. "So, it's true?"

"Which part? That I'm from the future? Yes. That I'm some sort of savior from a prophecy? I don't know. Doubtful. But I'm here, so I might as well do what I can in the meantime."

Theron cocked his head to the side and pushed himself off

the door frame he'd been leaning against. The movement caused Rhouth to jump up and run to his side, in preparation of some perceived danger based on his body language. She was clearly very tuned in to her master. Aurianna wondered how long they'd been hunting together. When he didn't speak for a moment, she started to say something, anything to fill the awkward silence. But suddenly he said, "So you're not from here at all then?"

"Here as in Eresseia, yes. My home was . . . is . . . will be in what you call Bramosia. But the world I lived in is a far different place. We had no sunshine to speak of, for one. And things were pretty meager and all, especially food and clothing."

"It's true then?" Nerina was almost whispering now. "The world falls apart because of whatever that woman does?"

Aurianna shook her head. "I don't know. Something happens, that's for sure. This world looks nothing like the one I'm from."

They were all staring at each other now, Nerina and Theron giving each other a look that held some purpose Aurianna couldn't quite grasp. Rhouth was licking herself again, looking for all the world like a cat. The image made Aurianna smile. Out of the corner of her eye, she noticed Nerina returning the gesture.

"So," the woman finally said, "you've never seen a vineyard?"

"No, ma'am, I haven't. What is it for?"

"Javen, you haven't introduced this young lady to the finer points of wine drinking yet. I'm surprised, considering the company you normally keep." With a wink, she walked to a back door, opening it and gesturing everyone outside. "You boys show her around. I'll get to work on preparing the wares for a little taste testing when you return." The gleam in the woman's eye made Aurianna somewhat nervous, especially considering her cryptic words, but she followed the men and the diligent fox to the back of the house.

Chapter 16

AURIANNA

After a brief tour and a little bit of information about running a vineyard and how the product was made, the three of them returned to the kitchen, sweaty from the afternoon sun and ready for a pre-dinner snack. Nerina had already laid out some finger foods, along with a pitcher filled to the brim with a dark, purplish-red liquid.

The older woman smiled at them as she continued with her bread making on the table in the middle of the room. "Enjoy your tour, dear?"

"Oh, yes, everything is so beautiful here!"

"Thank you kindly. Food is ready and a pitcher of wine for you to taste if you three would please wash up. We can save most of it for dinner, but we tend to pour freely around these parts."

Theron had warned her to be careful, that the wine had a way of altering your mind a bit. That didn't sound appealing in the least to Aurianna, but she had agreed to at least taste the wares, the life-blood and livelihood of his family.

They sat down at the small side table and nibbled on chunks of meats, cheeses, and bread. Aurianna hesitantly sipped at her wine, unsure how she felt about the taste. After a few tries, she felt her tongue adapting somewhat to the flavor, though it still had an odd aftertaste.

"Is Peter your brother?" she asked Theron.

"No, Peter just works for Mom and Dad. I come around to help out when I'm not working for the Imperium. Normally my hunting efforts go straight to the locals or the Imperium. But when I'm off, I tend to stick around here. Peter picks up the slack when I'm gone."

Nerina was smiling at her son. "Theron's an only child, I'm afraid. Took us forever to be blessed with him. Jerry thought we'd never have kids." A faraway look entered her eyes, but she quickly blinked it away. "Theron here was our little miracle. And we almost lost *him*, so I count us lucky."

Theron interrupted his mother, saying. "Um, so, have you guys been preparing her for the Volanti?"

The what?

Javen squirmed. "Well, no, not yet. But she hasn't had any weapons training, so there's really no point in upsetting her over it. She's had a lot to absorb, you know?"

"You don't think that's kind of a big thing?"

Aurianna interjected, "What's the Volanti?"

"They're enormous creatures that show up every few moon cycles or so. Terrifying things to anyone's mind, especially on first sight." Theron aimed a glance at Javen before continuing. "Kinetics get called out to fight them, but elemental magic does nothing to them. The only possible way to hurt one is with an actual weapon. The guns are powered by our magic, but the output is different from our Kinetic abilities. The weapons all use ammunition. The monsters take tributes, some Kinetic, some not. Seems indiscriminate, but we're trying to figure out where they come from and where they

take the people. Doubt they're still alive, but if we can stop them…"
He trailed off.

Speechless at this sudden revelation, she swung her head back
and forth between Javen and Theron. "Are you seriously telling me
real monsters come and snatch people and eat them?" Her voice
gradually rose in pitch and volume.

Javen replied, "It's not an issue as long as you stay indoors when
they come. Some people don't listen."

"What do they look like?"

Now Theron's mouth was curved up in a crooked smile, a wicked
gleam in his eye. "Oh, they're quite horrifying. Over twenty feet
tall, with fleshy wings and gigantic jagged teeth."

"You're joking," she said flatly.

Nerina sighed. "It's no laughing matter. And no, he's not joking.
They are quite grotesque from what I've seen, which isn't much. We
stay far away and inside when word comes."

"These monsters just show up randomly, and no one is freaked
out about it?"

"Of course we're freaked out. But what can we do?" the woman
asked.

"Well, where do they live?"

"That's what we can't figure out. We've had scouts out to watch
for them since the beginning. They aren't living anywhere in our
known lands. It's gotta be well across the Mare Dolor, and we don't
have the technology to get that far out."

Aurianna realized she was gulping down her wine at this point,
her nerves slowly loosening despite the goosebumps crawling
up and down her skin at the thought of something so monstrous
showing up to eat them.

Theron watched her intently for a moment. "How much traveling have you done?"

"This is the first region I've visited outside Bramosia." Aurianna noticed a slight delay between her thoughts and her words. Somewhere deep within her mind, she knew she should be concerned about this, but she just couldn't bring herself to care.

Javen said, "I'd like to show her some other regions, but I figured one step at a time."

"Hmm," was Theron's only response.

"Have you heard anything about this weird stuff Sigi's been going on about?"

At the mention of the girl's name, Theron's entire posture straightened, and his face took on a strange look. "Weird stuff?"

"About Rasenforst. She said her dad's been sending her letters about strange behaviors and people acting crazy."

Theron's lopsided smile returned. "We *are* talking about Rasenforst here, Javen. The town is practically crawling with weird and crazy. Drunken antics are a nightly occurrence there."

Nerina clucked her tongue, adding, "Those people don't know how to handle their alcohol."

Theron threw a sideways glance at his mother from the corner of his eyes. "Big difference between wine and hard liquor, mother. They tend to prefer their drinks to have a bit more kick."

"That's true," Javen replied, "but it seems like there's more to the story. Not the normal kind of antics. These are more of a violent nature."

"Yeah, I've heard some stuff," Theron said. "Haven't seen it for myself yet. I don't really have an opinion, but maybe I should go check it out next week when I'm over that way."

"Maybe."

No one spoke again for a moment, but Aurianna began to feel incredibly sleepy and more than a little lightheaded. Something must have shown on her face because Nerina looked at Theron and said softly, "Perhaps our guests would like to rest before dinner. Maybe you could show them to the guest rooms."

Aurianna was incredibly grateful to the woman. She followed Theron to the back of the home, Javen trailing behind them hesitantly. When they reached a bedroom in the corner, she nodded her appreciation to Theron, who pointed out the location of the privy. She fell onto the bed in a heap, vaguely hearing Javen say something about returning to the kitchen with Theron.

Her thoughts faded into nothing.

* * *

Shades of night borne of nothing more than her overactive imagination, the dream which had kept her in thrall faded slowly as she awoke from the brief forever of her wine-induced nap. She had slept fitfully, dreaming of a giant creature which battled a group of people, all cloaked in shadow. It was a nightmare of epic proportions that seemed ridiculous now. Obviously, the story of the Volanti from earlier must have fueled her darkest fears.

Then she remembered where she was. She must have cried out upon waking because, at that moment, Javen poked his head into the room to check on her. She tried to smile at him, but her entire face felt on fire. He'd come to bring her along to dinner, but her head was beating like a thundercloud.

Nerina came in after that, offering her some tea mixed with a headache remedy, which she gratefully accepted in her desperation. The pain subsided after several minutes, at least enough to allow her to have dinner with the others. Dinner was delicious, but uneventful, and she had been careful to take only small deliberate sips of her wine during the meal.

Afterward, Theron led the way out to the back porch to relax in the rocking chairs. They sat in silence for several minutes, enjoying the sounds of nature and continuing to sip their wine. Aurianna closed her eyes, relishing the absolute peace she felt in that moment.

When Javen went inside to top off his wine glass, Theron was the first to speak. "So, you're going to save us, huh?"

Aurianna opened one eye, glaring at him from her position two chairs away. "That's what they keep telling me."

She could see his understated smile from where she sat, even in the darkness pervading this area so devoid of unnatural light. At least the moon held sway here, unlike the night sky back home. It had a beauty all its own, even if it was no match for the glory of the sun. "Ah, yes. The elusive 'they.' The Arcanes." He hesitated. "Do you not believe them?"

"Why should I? What can I possibly do? How is a random person like me so involved in this story?"

"What makes you think you're random?"

The thought made her pause before answering, unsure what exactly he meant with his cryptic words. "I mean . . . I'm just a girl who grew up in a village that doesn't really exist until way into the future. I'm as far removed from your supposed enemy as I could possibly be."

"So?"

"So?" She sputtered. "So I'm just here because they brought me here. I wouldn't be here otherwise."

"And you think that means it's random, do you?"

"Well, yeah. That's pretty random if you ask me. If you'd read the prophecy like I did, you'd understand how vague it all is. It mentioned absolutely nothing that even remotely describes me or my situation."

Theron sighed, leaning forward and propping his elbows on his knees, head hanging down. His chair had stopped rocking, and Aurianna sensed something in the air.

Speaking softly, he said, "When I was young, my parents were overprotective of me. They'd tried for so long to have a child, and when I finally arrived, they were terrified of losing me. It used to drive me mad, all the hovering and the rules. One day, when I was six, I took off into the deeper part of the forest past the boundaries of Menos, further down the coast. I got lost. More than lost, really."

"That sounds horrifying!" Aurianna said.

He nodded. "It was. Children in Menos are trained from a young age to navigate the land, and we learn how to survive in the wild. It's just part of our culture. But it did me no good that day. No matter what I did, I kept going in circles. I couldn't find any water or anything to eat, and I knew I'd really messed up. Finally, I gave up, found an abandoned cave, and settled in for the night. All I could think about was how terrified my parents must have been." His voice hitched on the last sentence, all the past emotions showing on his solemn features.

"Well, it must have worked out okay if you're sitting here now."

"In a way. My father found me the next day. Walked right up to the cave entrance and called my name. I ran out, and he hugged me. Took me home without a word. They weren't even angry, and I couldn't understand it. Not until my mother told me what had happened while I was gone."

Chills ran down her spine as she waited for his next words.

"The Volanti had shown up the previous day, shortly after I'd left the house." He gestured into the distance. "Right in the middle of our town. One of the neighbors lost their son that day. After that, the creatures had prowled toward the open fields, and my parents were frantic. Mother said . . ." he trailed off. Tears in his eyes, he sighed. "She said someone—or something—appeared out of nowhere at the front door. Told them exactly where I was and how to find me. That's how my dad was able to locate me so quickly."

"That's . . . that's . . . wow. Just wow."

He shook his head. "That's not the most important part of the story. The day I left, I wasn't just running away from my overprotective parents." Theron paused before lifting his head to stare intently into her fixed gaze. "Someone told me to go."

"What?"

"Someone showed up in the field while I was checking the vines and helping out my father. She told me to leave immediately and to head into the forest until someone came for me. I know it sounds crazy to follow the advice of some stranger, but something in me told me I absolutely had to do it. Something just felt right. And that advice probably saved my life. I know I would've been taken by the Volanti had I not been far away. That's why I feel so strongly about—" and as he reached for the necklace with the strange symbol on it, Javen walked back out on the porch.

"Your mother still loves to talk, Theron. It wasn't easy to get away. Took the liberty of grabbing the wine pitcher and bringing it with me though." He smiled and sat back down. "What did I miss?"

"I was just telling Aurianna about my necklace."

"Ah, yes. Theron here is quite the religious man. Always wears that thing everywhere he goes. No idea why, but it's very important to him."

Has he never heard Theron's story?

Aurianna decided not to bring it up if Theron wasn't going to, so instead she asked, "What does the symbol stand for?"

Theron answered her, "It's the sign of the Essence. Each of the five have their own symbol, but this is the one that represents them in total. The Essence as a complete and intact whole. Five as one."

"Phar—The Regulus told me the Essence aren't worshiped much anymore."

Javen bristled at the mention of the man's name, but he said,

"They aren't really. Not anymore. People have better things to do with their time these days."

Theron gave him an odd look and added, "But we can't deny their existence. That's how we get our powers. The Essence deem who is worthy to wield them and bestow the powers accordingly."

"Spoken like a true believer, Theron. But you forget about the Voids. Why would a group of deities choose someone to wield that power, only to take it away?" She didn't fail to notice the hint of thinly veiled irritation in his tone.

"The Essence have their reasons, I'm sure. No one truly understands the Voids, Javen. Until we do, it's difficult to say what they are, or why."

"You're right, of course," Javen's lips thinned in a forced smile.

They sat in silence for a while, Theron slipping occasional glances in Javen's direction, a hint of concern on his face, Aurianna contemplated all she'd learned that day.

When it was finally time for bed, Javen walked her back to the room she'd rested in earlier, lingering in the doorway long enough to make her uncomfortable. He didn't say anything as she stared back questioningly, so she bid him a good night, thereby dismissing him and giving him no choice but to head off to his own room.

After he left, she rested her head on the pillow, surprised to discover she was still incredibly tired despite her earlier nap, and fell asleep almost immediately.

* * *

She was awakened by a light tapping on her shoulder. Opening her eyes, she started to panic at the darkness of the room and the tall figure looming over her. Before she could scream, a voice whispered, "It's okay. It's just me. I didn't want to wake everyone else just yet, but I have something to show you."

Javen straightened back up, offering his hand, which she could barely make out in the moonlight filtering through the curtains of the small window. She took a moment to shake the confusion from her head as she sat up, wary of his proximity in the dark.

"What's going on, Javen?"

"You'll see."

She detected a small smile on his face, his boyish features alight with some hidden secret he seemed overly eager to share. "Where are we going?" she asked warily.

"Just outside. Trust me, okay?"

She almost laughed at that but followed him out of the house, trying to be as quiet as possible to avoid waking their hosts. When they reached the front yard, he led her to their right, up a giant hill whose top loomed ahead of them, she asked again, "Where are we going?"

"Just up this hill."

"You said we were going 'just outside.' Now it's 'just up this hill.'" She stopped walking. "Explain what's going on."

He turned, looking down to where she stood lower on the incline. "Aurianna"—he sighed—"I have a surprise for you. Please just trust me. We are stopping at the top"—he pointed to the apex of the hill—"just there."

She glared up at him for a moment but followed. When they reached the top, it flattened out somewhat, creating a natural sitting area large enough for a decent-sized crowd. But at the moment, they were alone in the space. She raised her eyebrows expectantly.

Javen pulled out a blanket he'd been carrying (how had she not noticed that?) and spread it out on the ground before them. He gestured for her to sit, which she did. When he joined her on the blanket, she looked at him expectantly. "Just wait and watch" was all he said and pointed off into the distance.

So they waited. And she watched, staring in the direction he'd pointed. For a few minutes, nothing happened. Just when she began to feel irritated once more, about to demand an answer from him, it happened. Ever so slowly, but it happened.

And it was glorious. Like nothing she'd ever seen, even in her brief time in this brighter, more beautiful world. She had thought the sight of the morning sun was breathtaking to behold, the bright, bold hues of orange and gold radiating across the sky. But that seemed an afterthought of the event she now witnessed.

The gray sky was melting away, the barest glimpse of those now-familiar colors starting at the horizon and edging their way across the landscape. Red, orange, yellow, pink, purple—endless myriad hues that left her breathless. Speechless.

They sat in silence for an infinite moment in time, her mind all at once both racing and still. Realizing she had tears—actual tears—in her eyes, Aurianna made a quick swipe at them, not wanting to obstruct her vision for even a moment. Who or what could be responsible for something so incredibly majestic? The magic, in that moment, was palpable.

"Beautiful," she finally whispered, still trying to catch her breath.

Javen wasn't looking at the horizon. Both eyes on her, he said, "Yes. Beautiful."

She turned to face him, forcing her eyes away from the sunrise still inching its way up the sky. Unsure of what to say, Aurianna sat, trying to find the words to show her appreciation for this gift, this moment that was sure to remain in her memory until her dying day.

And then words were unnecessary as he leaned in closer, their breaths entwined, dancing on the air between them. His eyes dipped lower, staring unabashedly at her mouth, his intention written clearly in those dark orbs.

Aurianna found she didn't care then. It should have bothered her. It should have made her close back up and walk away before he could break down that wall. Shocked at her own internal mutiny, trying desperately to break her body's betrayal yet knowing she couldn't, Aurianna almost imperceptibly leaned in closer.

That was all the cue Javen needed as he closed the gap between them. His hand reached up to cup the side of her face with the gentlest of touches as he brushed his fingers against her cheek. Lips barely touching, a hint of need, anticipation dancing on the air—electric sparks made from a different kind of magic.

Just when she'd closed her eyes, about to lean in further, he pulled back, and it was over. But when she opened her eyes again, he was smiling at her, face beaming with pure joy. "Sorry. Couldn't help myself. Your enthusiasm is a bit catching, I'm afraid, and more than a bit endearing. We tend to take things we're accustomed to for granted, I guess. And...you are quite beautiful."

Blushing furiously, she looked back out to the sunrise to avoid his gaze. "Thank you," she whispered, hoping he knew she was talking about more than the compliment or the moment they had shared. The scene in front of them was continuously shifting, colors rearranging against a backdrop that lightened with every passing moment.

"You seemed so in awe of the midday sunlight. I figured you would want to see this," he continued. "Besides, you can imagine all the other regions from here, even if you can't see them. You said you've been studying those maps. Helps to get a visual of the land."

"Will I be allowed to visit the other places?"

"At some point, I'm sure. Takes a bit more time to get further out. A full circle on the train is about an eight-hour ride with all the stops, give or take. Theron does it a lot for his hunting since the two main hunting spots are here and all the way on the other side of the lagoon, south of Rasenforst, on the way back down to Bramosia."

"His job is just to hunt and provide food?"

Javen smiled. "Pretty much, yeah, along with tracking. He's damn good at it though. Him and Rhouth have this system that defies logic sometimes. That girl is smarter than all of us, I think."

"Where does an animal like that come from?"

"Theron said he found her wandering out of the woods one day. She followed him home, and that was that."

"So . . . Sigi's a guard, Theron's a hunter, and Laelia mentioned something, but I didn't understand, so I've forgotten now." She leaned back on her elbows, basking in the brightness of the morning.

"Laelia's a Sparker—Electrokinetic, you know, since she's from Vanito—so a lot of them are Emissars for the Imperium." He followed her lead, laying on his back and closing his eyes. "The Emissars have to take electric Energy out to the regions on a regular basis. Each region has these gigantic batteries so that everybody has continuous power, but the Sparkers have to replenish them fairly often or the batteries will die out."

"Laelia's a Sparker . . . but you're not?"

She glanced over to see a look of contempt cross his face, but it was difficult to tell with his eyes closed. A moment of silence passed before he responded, "I should be."

"I don't understand."

"I should have that power, but I don't really. I honestly do okay with fire, which isn't unheard of even though I'm not from Rasenforst. My natural affinity should be with Energy. It's frustrating that I can't do what I should be able to do. I guess that's why I empathize with the Voids. I almost was one."

Aurianna was stunned at the revelation, unsure of how to respond. "I'm sorry" was all she could think to say.

"Don't be. I'm a damn good shot, and my Pyro abilities are pretty good, though nowhere near as good as Sigi's, considering she's from Rasenforst and all. It's in her blood. My power is just a fluke." Bitterness oozed from him in tiny invisible rivulets, and Aurianna suddenly felt a chill in the air that tempered the warmth from the rising sun.

Aurianna decided to change the subject. "What about the area beyond Vanito? You grew up there, so you must know something about it."

"What do you mean?"

"The unmarked area north of Vanito on the maps. The entire rest of that island isn't labeled. Is that a hunting ground or something? I just assumed it was uninhabited since it's unmarked."

Javen sat back up, narrowing his eyes at her and squinting in the approaching daylight. "You mean Fae territory?"

"What's Fae territory?"

He waved vaguely, indicating the direction of the area in question. "They say the Fae used to inhabit that area. No one goes there." At the look of confusion on her face, he added, "Fae . . . as in Faerie. The Fae folk. Shape-shifting creatures who walked the land long ago, back when they say the deities did as well. Everyone's scared of the stories, so no one goes there."

"Shape-shifting. That sounds terrifying."

He shrugged. "Maybe." He stood up and reached for her hand to help her up.

They went back to the Panago home and ate breakfast before their return journey to the Imperium. They would ride the horses back to Bramosia rather than take the train, which only traveled counterclockwise around the loop.

Aurianna wasn't keen on giving up Oracle now that she felt she'd bonded with the animal, but she knew she couldn't keep the horse at the Imperium. When she mentioned this to Javen, he laughed and said, "We've got stables in Bramosia some people use. We can buy her, if you like."

"But I don't have any money." She had seen the people in Bramosia exchanging the coins they used here for trading, but she didn't have any herself, nor did she know how to get any.

"Don't need any. Not on hand anyways. Kinetics have a line of credit that gets billed to the Imperium at very deep discounts seeing as we're considered vital to the communities. A horse might still cost a good bit, but you haven't used any of your allotment I'm guessing, so you should have enough. The stabling is free in town for us."

This was a new concept to Aurianna, and she was ecstatic when the stablemaster in Menos nodded his head at them and agreed to bill the cost to the Imperium. Even at a "deep discount," Oracle was costing her about a moon cycle's worth of credit, according to Javen.

Javen rented his horse for the trip back across the plain to the Imperium, and Aurianna happily mounted Oracle, lovingly patting her neck beneath her mane and whispering to her about all the adventures they would have. The mare nodded its agreement.

The ride was exhilarating—and a little painful, considering her muscles hadn't recovered from the day before—and over far too quickly for Aurianna.

As they approached the stables on the outer edge of Bramosia, she was relieved to see the structure had a large grazing area comparable to the one in Menos. They left the horses with the stablemaster there, giving him Aurianna's information.

Heading back to the Imperium on foot, they were skirting the main sections of the town, but being so near to it again was still more than a little unnerving for her. Javen pointed out a few places of note as they walked, but she chose to keep her eyes focused in front of her on their destination. After a few minutes, Javen noticed her seeming disinterest and ceased his banter.

They walked the rest of the way in silence.

Chapter 17

AURIANNA

Frustration building, Aurianna shook her head to clear her vision, dizziness and nausea overwhelming her senses. Magister Martes, the Energy training instructor, was lounging on a nearby rock formation inside the small enclosure they were crammed into, watching her with an ease that was maddening. *How in the world is he able to remain so calm while we're standing here surrounded by sparks of sizzling death?*

Nothing had been happening for quite some time. Aurianna continued staring intently at the wall of Energy they were using for training, arms raised in an attempt to pull the strands of electricity toward her. This was fruitless. Nothing had been happening, and nothing continued to happen.

The room was beyond tiny, a far-removed hideaway for their one-on-one sessions that were far from secret. Yet the Magnus had insisted they keep to unused spots away from prying eyes during her training. At least they had all agreed to allow her some individual training before throwing her back in with the Youngers, something she was not looking forward to. Working with children should not have bothered her so much, especially considering she really was just a beginner, but deep down she knew it did. It was embarrassing, whether she admitted it aloud or not.

The smell of burning metal floated across the small space, increasing her dizziness. She felt as if she might get sick, making her even more determined to get this over with. Throwing up on the Magister was probably not going to make a good impression.

And of all the instructors, Magister Martes seemed the least put out by her presence so far. The others seemed far less patient. Continuing to focus on the crackling lines of Energy in front of her, she kept her arms up and as steady as she could. The heat in the room was becoming unbearable, and she knew they would have to give up for the day soon. She still had tutorials for the other elements before dinner, and the afternoon was the only time the Magisters had to spare.

After a few more minutes of nothing, Magister Martes said softly, "I think it's time to move on to your next instruction for the day. We can meet back here tomorrow. Same time?"

"But I haven't done anything. Nothing at all."

He smiled. "Did you really expect something to happen on your first try? It takes Youngers a couple of years to do anything of notice, and you are no different. Your age might give you a bit of an advantage in terms of focus, but your skill level is the same. Be patient. Give it time, and it will come. Stop worrying."

Easier said than done. But she followed him out of the area, up the stairs to the main level, and to the doors leading outside. Magister Jarden, a heavyset woman who showed little emotion, stood waiting to take her for Water training. Aurianna nodded her thanks to the Energy instructor and followed the Water instructor outside. They walked across the bridge into Bramosia.

They're not going to test me in the middle of town, are they?

But the woman took a sharp left at the other side of the bridge, heading away from the capital city. Off in the distance to their right and up the hill, the stable yard stood as a sharp contrast to the tightly packed buildings around most of Bramosia. Aurianna liked knowing her horse had plenty of room to roam. She cheered up a bit at the thought of visiting Oracle from time to time.

They stopped a short distance out, beside the banks of a small lake. Magister Jarden looked at her expectantly, neither a smile nor a frown adorning her face. She raised her eyebrows slightly when Aurianna just stared back. She wasn't sure what this woman was expecting her to do without any instruction.

"Well?" the woman asked.

"What is it I'm supposed to be doing?"

Magister Jarden harrumphed, cocking her head to one side. "Have you not been doing the reading you were assigned?"

Aurianna was getting irritated by this woman's complete lack of manners. "Of course I've been reading. Nowhere in those books did it tell me what my first lesson should look like. If that were the case, I wouldn't need you here."

The Magister's eyes widened a bit at the audacity in her tone, but Aurianna really didn't care at this point. She was hot, miserable, frustrated, and confused, and this woman was not friendly in the least. A complete change from Magister Martes. After glaring at her for a moment, the instructor said, "Dip your fingertips in the pool of water and swirl them around gently. Pull your hand back very slowly. Do this until the water follows your lead."

Follows my lead? Aurianna thought, her confusion growing. But she obeyed. With no choice for seating other than the muddy bank, Aurianna squatted down and placed the lightest of touches on the surface of the water, moving her finger in small circles for a moment.

Pulling her hand back from the water, she was disappointed but not surprised when no water followed her hand. She did this several more times, to no avail. She looked over at the Magister expectantly.

"You must keep doing that until you achieve success. Just keep practicing."

Aurianna was beginning to think the Magisters were really of no use to her. They were giving her instructions to stick her arms out, or stick her hand out, and... do something. How was that helpful?

But she continued, over and over until the woman cleared her throat, announcing their time was up, and abruptly turned to head back to the Imperium. She was clearly not happy to be spending her spare time training Aurianna. They entered the building, and Aurianna expected the woman to lead her to her next trainer, but Magister Jarden merely said over her shoulder, "Magister Garis will be here shortly for your Earth training. The Fire instructor was delayed this afternoon, so you'll be seeing him last today." And with that, the woman disappeared through a door.

* * *

She waited for almost half an hour before the Earth instructor showed up. The woman looked flustered and sincerely apologetic as she approached Aurianna.

"I am so very sorry, dear. I just found out Magister Daehne was delayed, so I rushed down as quickly as I could. Seems as if a Younger almost set himself on fire today." Aurianna assumed from her expression that the student hadn't been hurt too seriously.

"Oh my goodness! Are they okay?"

"Oh, yes. I think he gave Magister Daehne a fright is all. This sort of thing isn't completely uncommon, but it's still a bit harrowing for us old people."

Aurianna smiled but shook her head as she followed the

Magister. Back outside, they crossed the bridge and strode around the side of a rocky outcropping nestled against a small hill.

Gathering her robes, Magister Garis sat down on one of the smoother flat-topped rocks jutting out. She looked at Aurianna expectantly.

Aurianna sighed in resignation, once again lifting her arms up in front of her. She concentrated on the rocks just ahead, careful to avoid thinking about the one the Magister was sitting on.

To her astonishment, Magister Garis laughed. "Child, you don't have to try so hard. Just focus."

"Well, considering I haven't managed to move a single bit of anything today, I'd say I need to try quite a bit harder." Aurianna's frustration was creeping into her voice, her tone sharp. "No one will tell me what exactly I'm supposed to be *doing*, other than to tell me to 'focus.' How am I supposed to know what that means if I don't even know what it looks like?"

The woman didn't respond. Aurianna thought perhaps she wasn't even listening until the Magister raised her arms, staring intently at the ground in front of them. Suddenly, a fist-sized piece of rock broke apart from the rest and floated with far too much ease until it was hovering in midair about two feet in front of Aurianna's face. She was in awe, a chill climbing up her spine, but her irritation increased at the same moment.

"How am I supposed to do that? It's impossible." Eyebrows creasing, she threw herself on the ground and hung her head between her knees.

The Magister didn't speak for several moments. They sat in silence, and Aurianna could hear the faint wind whistling against the curve of the rock. Birds chirped somewhere far off, but there were no trees in their immediate vicinity. She was struck with the realization that she hadn't taken the time to appreciate the abundance of wildlife here, compared to back home. In her time, they did have a few birds on occasion, and all the livestock for farming, but not much else. There was so much to appreciate here, even if she couldn't master this one thing.

When the older woman finally did speak, her voice was small but weighty in the stillness. "Aurianna, you have been granted a gift, an *assurance* that you will, at some point, master this. None of us ever had that promise. Most of us get there, but it's never guaranteed. You have the knowledge that, no matter how long it takes, you will eventually get there."

Aurianna paused. She had never thought about it that way, but it was little comfort when all she wanted to do was scream. "But I *don't* have a guarantee. Just because they think I'm something, doesn't make it true." Realizing what the woman had said, she added, "So you know why I'm here?"

The Magister nodded. "We spoke to the Arcanes. You lack faith, child. Faith can take you places you never dreamed. The Arcanes wouldn't have gone to all this trouble if they weren't sure about you."

"I just don't understand the mechanism for how it works. What exactly am I supposed to be focusing on?"

Magister Garis smiled, her eyebrows raised as she stuck her neck forward pointedly and replied, "Yourself." She sat back, gesturing for Aurianna to continue her training.

Not a single speck of dirt moved that afternoon, but somehow Aurianna felt just a little bit more at ease.

When they approached the front entrance a while later, Magister Daehne was jogging toward them. He was out of breath and red-faced from running.

"I'm so sorry, Eleadora. That boy is going to be the death of me, I swear."

"No worries. Aurianna and I had a nice chat." Bowing slightly,

Magister Garis waved and said goodbye as she sauntered into the building.

The Fire training instructor was staring at Aurianna, a look of consideration in his eyes. Crossing one arm along his chest, he rested the other elbow on his wrist and tapped a finger to his lips in thought, pondering some unknown puzzle. If Aurianna was the puzzle, she had some bad news for him: even she couldn't figure herself out right now.

He hadn't been very nice to her on their first encounter, but she chose to believe it was mostly due to the surprise of the situation. He had been quite flustered by all of it, quite the opposite of Magister Martes, who seemed to take it all in stride. She wished she could be that calm through all of this. Frustration was rearing its ugly head again, but she tried to shake it off.

Finally, the man clapped his hands together and said, "Well. Let's head downstairs, shall we?" She had no choice but to follow him as he went back inside and took off down the spiral staircase. Aurianna had wondered why all four corners of the main hall had doors that seemed to lead to identical staircases, but it hadn't taken long for her to realize the ones in the far back corners were for Voids and guards, or anyone else who worked in those areas. The one they always took was for everyone else. Except for the Magnus and Regulus. The fourth spiral staircase was the only one that had access to the second level. Laelia had told her it led straight to the "royal" bedrooms behind the throne room. How she knew that, Aurianna decided she didn't want to know.

When they entered the underground level, the Magister led her off down one of the tunnels in the vast labyrinth. Her head grew dizzy with the twists and turns that ensured she would never find her way back out again on her own. The thought made her a little nervous, but this man was a teacher. She should be safe with him.

She hoped.

She was confused when they stopped briefly at an open doorway leading into a room filled with Voids. This was, presumably, one of their workrooms leading into the kitchens upstairs. Most of the food was prepared upstairs, she knew, but a lot of work went on behind the scenes down here. A few Voids also hunched over tables working on various non-food-related things.

"Can I get one of you to bring a few pairs of goggles and follow us to the training pits?" Magister Daehne asked the room in general.

One of the Voids, a younger man who looked to be in his midtwenties, nodded and ran off to grab the goggles from a shelf in the far corner of the room. He followed them a short way farther along the tunnel. They stopped at a more open area with a multitude of magma pits, long but slender gashes in the ground that seemed to frown at her.

The Void handed them each a pair of goggles before putting the final pair on himself. Now at least she understood the meaning behind the goggles so many of them—including Sigi—wore around their necks.

"I normally use my own pair, but I forgot and left them upstairs in the whole fiasco earlier." The Magister was putting his borrowed goggles over his eyes as he spoke. "The Youngers normally get much smaller experiences with Fire training than we're about to do. They don't get to come down here very often, except for special activity days. But you are a special case, as it were, so let's hope for the best." He motioned for her to put on her own goggles.

She placed the goggles over her eyes.

"The eyes are very sensitive to this sort of thing. Never forget your goggles, whether you are training or working with Fire."

She nodded and pointed her chin at the Void standing off to the side. "And what's he for?" None of the other instructors had brought anyone along.

"He is here . . . in case something happens, and we need someone to get help."

Aurianna wanted to be offended at the insinuation, but considering the day the man was having, she felt a little sorry for him. The fact was, she didn't expect anything to happen. Literally, not a thing. But she would try, nonetheless.

As before, she raised her hands in front of her, tilting her body to aim more for the magma peeking up at her from the ground. Concentrating as hard as she could, Aurianna was suddenly very glad for the goggles indeed. She focused on the bright orange-red liquid, arms straining, sweat beading on her forehead.

Her conversation earlier with Magister Garis had left her feeling slightly less defeated, but that was quickly wearing off, replaced once again by irritation, at herself and at the world. Why couldn't she figure this out? She knew she should be more patient, but the truth was, deep down, she truly wanted to be one of them, to be a Kinetic and show she could do something. To feel useful. Even if the prophecy wasn't true, she still believed she'd been brought here for a reason.

All her life, she had felt different, felt something was missing. Felt the need to go off in search of that missing piece of herself. Her own people had branded her for it, punished her for trying to do something good in the world.

The anger was building within her, but she couldn't stop it now. Aunt Larissa had always tried to teach her to control her emotions, but thinking about the woman only brought up more resentment. Her aunt had dedicated her life to protecting Aurianna, even saving her from a death curse. She missed her terribly.

Caught between sadness and rage, she felt a buzzing within her, a twinge of something both foreign and familiar, something she couldn't quite remember. The heat surrounding them became a part of her, gravitating inward like a spiraling ball of flame, pulling and pulling her inside herself until a buildup of energy emanated from her every pore.

A cry came from somewhere in the room, but her mind could only focus on the pull that was ripping her apart. The weight was excruciating, and she had no idea what to do. The choice seemed to be out of her hands as the buildup exploded outward, filling Aurianna with a sudden relief and a sense of emptiness she couldn't wrap her head around.

When her vision cleared and she looked up, silence filled the space. She thought perhaps her hearing had gone. The silence was palpable.

Magister Daehne had taken off his goggles to stare at a point to her right. The wall was covered in black scorch marks, a few red-hot embers still sizzling in the newly formed cracks and holes. Mesmerized, she stared for a moment as well, slowly turning her head back to look at the Magister. But he was now on the other side of the room, tending to the Void who was on the ground, convulsing.

Rushing over to his side, she dropped to her knees across from her instructor, unsure of how to help. He was holding the man's arms down, but the convulsions seemed to be easing. When the man stopped shaking, he looked at her with fear in his eyes, and she suddenly became aware of the fact that she might have injured him.

Speaking to the Void, Magister Daehne said, "Do you know where you are?"

The other man looked at him strangely. "Yes, of course. We're in the tunnel."

"How do you feel?"

"Fine now. I think I just . . ." He trailed off, looking back at her with that same trepidation—concern over his choice of words showing on his already pale and clammy face. "I think I panicked and started to pass out. I'm very sorry, Magister."

He looked back at her again.

"You weren't singed or anything?"

"No, I just got lightheaded is all."

The Magister did not look convinced. "But you were convulsing. Have you had this problem before?"

"No, but I think the shock just set it off. I feel weak and sick to my stomach, but that's all."

The instructor looked at Aurianna, decision weighing in his eyes. "Well, let's get you back to the others now. Our session is over for today." The two of them lifted the Void to his feet, taking his weight across their shoulders as they walked slowly back through the tunnel.

Turning around to survey the mess she had caused, Aurianna saw a giant ring of black where she had been standing when the world filled her up and exploded.

Part Three

AN UNKNOWN PATH

An unknown path I take through the darkness
To reach the grail I do not wish to seek.

Chapter 18

AURIANNA

More training was the last thing Aurianna wanted to think about, but several days later, she was informed she'd be joining the Olders in Weapons training. At least it seemed less harrowing than playing with fire.

Aurianna had told no one about the incident in the tunnels, and Magister Daehne hadn't spoken to her about it. He had given her several strange looks as they'd led the Void back to the room where they'd found him, dropping off the goggles and marching back upstairs, all the while, barely even speaking to her. A curt nod was her only dismissal in the main hall as he'd walked out the main entrance. Shaken to her core, Aurianna had gone straight to her room, refusing to leave even to eat dinner with the others. They must have known something was up, but no one bothered her.

Her training sessions for the rest of the week had been uneventful, but the damage was done. Aurianna was shaken to her core, and she was pretty certain Magister Daehne would have informed the other instructors about the mishap. No one mentioned it, however, and even Magister Daehne himself seemed to have moved on by the next day.

Today she was feeling a little better after finally getting a full—albeit restless—night of sleep. A messenger had arrived to inform her she needed to meet everyone down in the tunnels in the afternoon. She had no idea where to go, and the tunnels were a source of anxiety for her now. Still, she tried to get as much reading in as possible before returning to the maze of underground passages.

Once she reached the lower level, she noticed a group of people around her age and a little younger walking down one of the nearby corridors. She followed them in hopes they were going to the same place as she.

They stopped at a wide-open area, a large group of people already standing about. Racks of weapons stood off to one side, ready for use in the training session. Javen walked up to her from the throng, grinning from ear to ear.

"Ah, so she has decided to grace us with her presence once more," he said, bowing at her in a mock display of reverence.

"Funny," she replied flatly. "Who does the Weapons training anyways?"

"Someone on the City Guard usually does it. Sometimes a guard from one of the regions who happens to be in Bramosia. Just depends, but there isn't much to it. We practice our aim, work on conducting, and shoot a bunch of targets. That's about it." Still smiling, he led her over to the weapons rack, waving his hand at the metal display. "I'm to take you under my wing. Pretty sure I could teach this class myself. Take your pick."

"I just…take one?"

"Well, not to keep of course. But yeah."

She perused the rows, trying to decide between the significant size differences and varying style options. A few were slightly smaller, so she chose caution and gingerly picked up one of those, holding it like it might explode at any moment.

Javen pushed her hands down. "First of all, don't aim at *anything* unless you are ready to shoot. Keep your weapon aimed downward until you are literally aiming for a target. Second of all, it's not a wild animal. Just hold it like this." He demonstrated the proper way to handle a weapon, and she copied his movements.

"Good. Now follow me, but *keep your weapon pointed downward.*" They walked over to a row of wooden planks just as the instructor began speaking, directing everyone to choose their weapon and line up with a target.

Javen showed her how to stand, feet apart, both hands on the weapon to steady it. "It doesn't matter for the sake of firing since only one hand is needed for the contact to work, but it definitely helps your aim, especially in the beginning."

"And how exactly does one fire one of these things?" she asked.

"We're basically conduits, you know? The weapon will pick up any Kinetic energy you've got and fire the bullet when you squeeze the trigger. I used to struggle with this as well, but it just takes a small amount of elemental power—Fire in my case, since it's my only saving grace in the magic department." Bitterness crept into his voice again, but he was already looking ahead at the targets. "The one you chose is small enough to only need a very small amount, but I figure it doesn't matter much since you don't know what you have strength with yet."

Not entirely true.

But she only said, "So how do I make it work?"

Instead of answering, he assumed the stance himself, holding the weapon straight in front of him with both hands. He stared at his target for a moment, blowing out a slow and deliberate breath, before squeezing the trigger. A short beam of fiery red shot out from the weapon, so fast she barely saw it. When she looked back at the plank, she could see a rather sizable hole right in the middle.

Aurianna whistled. "Impressive, Ambrogetti." She smiled at him as he gave her a narrowed sideways gaze at the mention of his last name. "Yes, I remember things," she added, laughing.

Javen relaxed his stance and dropped his arms, saying, "Just be mindful of your ammo supply. If you don't have an extra clip, running out at the wrong moment could prove deadly." Her fear must have shown because he added, "A clip holds quite a lot of ammo though. Usually one is enough. I'm just saying though."

"Enough for what?"

He sighed. "You remember things, huh? Well, do you remember what we told you about the Volanti?"

"Yes," she replied hesitantly, drawing out the word.

"Someone's gotta defend the land against them."

"Meaning…us?"

"Yes, ma'am."

Not good, not good, not good.

But she only said, "Okay, then. Show me how to do this."

Aurianna resumed the position as he placed a hand at her wrist to help guide her aim. When his other arm slipped around her waist, the target in front of her blurred as her head began to spin.

Javen turned his face to her ear and whispered, "Don't forget to breathe. Breathe in. Breathe out. You got this."

She closed her eyes and tried to steady her breathing, to no avail. Pulling away slightly, she cleared her throat before focusing back on her weapon. When she glanced to the side, Aurianna saw a smug look briefly passing across Javen's features before he put an innocent stare back into place.

She was determined to ignore him. Breathing out slowly, she stared at the wood plank and pulled the trigger.

A small hole appeared just to the right of the larger one Javen had made.

He smiled. "Not bad…for a rookie."

* * *

It was several weeks before she could see any improvement from her training. Nothing was happening, but Aurianna began to feel as if the power were just beyond her grasp. A vague rumbling deep within her core, especially with Fire training. But no more "incidents" had occurred, for better or worse.

Walking into the dining hall one evening, Aurianna sensed eyes on her. Instinctively, she glanced toward the kitchen area, already knowing she would see him—the strange Void with the penetrating gaze that went far beyond mild curiosity. She thought about reporting it to someone, though she'd prefer to get to the bottom of it herself.

Just as the thought entered her mind, she heard her name being shouted across the room. The Void heard it as well and looked toward her friends at the same moment she did. They were sitting at the table on the far side, beckoning her over. She finished filling her tray and walked over.

Javen was practically pushing Laelia off the bench to make room for her. The girl was not amused and called him a word that made Aurianna blush.

A voice she didn't recognize, deep and resounding, said, "Ah, honey, I thought you were used to that kind of thing."

Laelia merely stared at the source of the voice. A man who looked to be a few years older than she was sitting at the table across from Javen. His skin was light in tone, though not as pale as the Vanitian ivory of Laelia and Javen, somewhat pinkish in hue giving him a youthful rosy glow to his cheeks that belied his age. When he didn't continue, Laelia finally replied, "And what's that supposed to mean, Leon?"

The man named Leon shrugged his massive shoulders, beefy hands clutching a fork and reaching for a plate of meat inexplicably sitting in the middle of the table, piled with more steaks than any of them could eat. He stabbed one and plopped it on his tray. "Men giving you the boot. Isn't that standard procedure once you're done rolling in the hay? I'm sure you've been kicked out of plenty of beds by now."

Aurianna was still standing to the side, the tension in the air palpable. She wanted to melt through the floor at the uncomfortable display going on. Clearly, they knew each other, but the look Laelia was aiming at the newcomer was enough to make Aurianna want to run away.

Eyes narrowed, a hint of a smile creeping across her face, Laelia cocked her head to the side. "Is that how it works? That what you do with your whores? I mean, right after you pay them, of course." Her smile took on its usual feline grace as she raised her eyebrows and continued staring at him.

Leon returned her smile. "Yes. I do make sure to pay mine. How's the free market working out for you?"

"I don't need to be paid. I'm not a whore."

"Not what I've heard. Giving the merchandise away for free doesn't mean you're not in the business. Just makes you a bad shop-keeper." He winked, his caramel-brown eyes twinkling.

Laelia abruptly threw her water in his face and continued eating as if nothing had happened. Droplets glinted off his dark-brown mane. Inexplicably, Leon merely wiped his face with his napkin and went back to his steak.

Completely bewildered by the surreal display, Aurianna continued staring at them as she slowly took a seat on the bench between Laelia and Javen. Sigi was nowhere to be seen, so she was probably on duty or asleep. She looked at Javen and let her discomfort and silent question show in her eyes.

He simply gestured to Leon. "Aurianna, this is Leon Bouchard. Leon, Aurianna."

She nodded and picked at her food, unsure what to say to a man with water dribbling through his sideburns and down his neck.

Javen continued, "Leon is my very closest friend. He left me behind a few years ago, but he's usually in Bramosia." He was interrupted briefly by a snort from Laelia. "Leon's a Hydro. He's from Ramolay and works with Bramosia's water supply. He has to travel some, but mostly sticks to Bramosia."

Laelia added, "Yes, he prefers the brothels here to any in all of Eresseia. I hear they have the best whores."

"Been asking around, huh?" Leon said. "If you're looking for work, I'm sure Madam Trudel would be happy to accommodate one more. No sparking the clientele though." He waggled his eyebrows at her, smiling as he waved his fork in her face. Laelia immediately snatched it from him and tried to impale his other hand where he'd unsuspectingly place it on the table beside him. He avoided the attack with astonishing speed, giving her a look of incredulity before shaking his head and returning to his meal. Bereft of his eating utensil, Leon picked up the steak with his bare hands and continued eating it like nothing had happened.

Seriously, what is wrong with these people?

Javen cleared his throat. "So, I've been telling him about your situation. Leon's got a lot of connections"—another snort from Laelia—"and says he can ask around about your parents and all."

Tears welled in her eyes. Aurianna had only mentioned her desire to find out about her parents once or twice to Javen, and only in passing. "Thank you," she whispered, not trusting her voice.

Leon looked up at her briefly as he picked up another steak from the pile in the middle of the table, his hands covered in the drippings. Licking the side of his palm, he said, "Sure thing, darling. I'm sure someone knows something, especially considering we're only talking about a few moon cycles ago. You being born and all, I mean." He winked at her and grinned, not the least bit put off by the oddness of that thought.

Returning his smile, Aurianna began eating in earnest, his seemingly endless appetite suddenly compelling her hunger to rear its head. The others at the table ate in silence for a few minutes as well. She watched as Leon picked up a third steak, still using his bare hands.

All she could think about were her people back home, not necessarily starving, but certainly always on the verge of it. His show of gluttony shouldn't have bothered her so much, considering this was an era long before and completely unrelated to her world. But the fact was it did indeed bother her, if only because she always felt she should be doing something, working toward fixing whatever this disaster was supposed to be.

Shaking the desperation from her thoughts, she turned to Javen. "So, how did you two become friends if he was so much older?"

Leon said, "Hey now. The word you are looking for is *wiser*."

Without missing a beat, Laelia added, "Or wanker." She waggled her eyebrows at no one in particular.

Javen glared at her but didn't respond. Instead, he glanced at Aurianna and said, "Leon's not that old. He's just a giant of a man. He's twenty-two. So yeah, there were years where we weren't in classes together. But we were bunk mates for a while as Youngers."

Leon said, "Pretty sure they regretted that for a long time. That hole still there?" At Aurianna's quizzical stare, he added, "Sometimes we'd get to wrestling. You know...boys. But one time, when I'd started to hit a growth spurt and didn't know my own strength yet, we were scrambling around the room, and I managed to pick Javen here up and throw him through the wall."

"It wasn't *through* the wall, Leon. I crashed *into* it. The wall had a big dent for years. I have no idea if they ever fixed it."

"Yeah, a Javen-sized dent." Leon had a deep chuckle that was natural and full of merriment. Despite his oddities, it was hard not to like the man, no matter what Laelia said.

"Hello, children." The voice behind them was light and familiar. Aurianna turned around and smiled at Sigi. "I see we are putting on our best behavior for the newbie. Congrats on not killing each other." She nodded, walking around the table to sit beside Leon.

"The night is still young," Laelia said with her customary feline grin.

"Ah, well, but I'd have to clean up the mess, and then there'd be paperwork…" Sigi sighed dramatically and reached across Leon to stab one of his steaks with her fork.

Indignant at her gall, he tried to stab her, then remembered he was no longer armed. Leon sat back, glaring daggers at Laelia, who twirled his fork in her other hand.

Sigi continued, "So, what are we up to this evening? Besides eating the better half of an entire barnyard." She was looking at Leon as she made the last comment.

"Just reminiscing about the 'good old days,' it seems," Laelia said.

"When exactly were those, again?" Sigi asked.

"Yeah, I really don't know. I wouldn't go back to those years for anything. I much prefer my life now."

"Agreed."

Aurianna leaned forward. "Leon thinks he might be able to find out some information about my parents." Not having a mother was something they shared and had spoken about several times.

Sigi understood her desire to find out more, even if the news was unhappy. Having closure was better than not knowing, but never having known her parents made it somewhat easier, at least compared to a situation like Sigi's.

"That's great news! Either way, I hope you can find out what happened." She paused to take a bite of her food. "Hilda says hello, by the way."

Aurianna had officially met Sigi's little sister at a few meals she'd shared with Sigi. She had gotten the impression Sigi only ate with Hilda when their other friends weren't with them, more likely for her sister's sake than for anyone else's. Hilda seemed to have plenty of friends her own age and didn't seem bothered in the least by the exclusion.

"Well, friends"—Laelia stood up—"and others. I must be off. I have an overnight trip to Vanito tonight. They requested an Emissar and a rather large shipment of Energy, so I'm guessing there may have been an outage of some sort. Something probably fried the storage containers."

"Will you stay to visit your family?" Aurianna spoke before she had a chance to consider her words.

Laelia's look turned dark and strained, her eyes narrowing, "No. I don't speak to my family." She turned and walked away with her empty tray, still carrying Leon's fork with her.

"Damn that woman," he mumbled after she'd moved out of earshot.

Ignoring him, Sigi looked to Aurianna. "Wanna go exploring this evening?"

Aurianna hesitated. "What do you mean by exploring?"

"You said you tend to get lost in the underground tunnels, so I figured we could go on an adventure. I've never gone through most of that maze. I doubt anyone has. We tend to stick to what we know, and from what I've heard, those passages lead off in all kinds of crazy directions." She turned her gaze to Javen. "Care to join us?"

"I mean, yeah, if Aurianna wants to go."

"What am I, chopped liver? Don't I get an invite to this shindig?" Leon's mouth twisted into a pout that made him look like a child. An enormous child.

"Shindig? Really? Yes, of course, you're invited as well."

"No, thank you. I've got business to attend to. And by business, I mean not yours."

They all stared at him. All except Javen, who continued eating as if he had already known what Leon was going to say. Sigi's mouth was gaping like a fish. She finally closed her mouth and shook her head, turning back to Aurianna and looking at her expectantly.

Aurianna realized everyone was waiting on her to respond. She had nothing better to do than go back upstairs and do some more reading, so she shrugged her shoulders. "Sure."

Sigi's look of enthusiasm was almost contagious. "All right, then. Adventuring we shall go."

* * *

"I'm pretty sure this doesn't quite qualify as an adventure, Sigi." Javen looked simultaneously distracted and bored. He had grasped Aurianna's hand as they'd left the dining hall. She hadn't pulled away.

Most of the tunnels were identical to one another, at least as far as Aurianna could tell. The dirt walls were varying shades of brown and gray and lined with tiny sconces. The lights seemed almost alive with Energy, their electric hearts beating out a constant buzz. She'd seen the ones at the Consilium back home, but they were everywhere in this place. She still found this to be fascinating even though the others felt it a simple thing.

It was easy to take things you were used to for granted, but she vowed to herself never to do so. She wanted to go back and talk to Larissa about all of it, to share her adventures with the only family she had left.

Doing that would mean fixing the problems here though. Perhaps not all of them, but certainly the one she was brought here for: stopping the Enchantress in the tower across the bay from doing whatever it was she was going to do. She'd never been out that way, but the tower could be seen as a very small structure in the distance, tall and slender. It felt menacing only because of the information she possessed about its owner. Otherwise, it would have merely blended into the landscape of this strange world.

The tower should have been visible to her in her own time, but for some reason, she couldn't remember having noticed it. Was it because it was part of the "outside world" she was forbidden to visit—therefore ignored by her brain—or had something caused it to be destroyed between the two time periods? Maybe it was taken down during the civil war between the Kinetics and non-Kinetics.

Aurianna realized Sigi was speaking. ". . . and sometimes we'd just get lost. I'm sure some of the Youngers have a more adventurous spirit than I ever did."

"You mean down here?"

Sigi smiled. "You weren't listening, were you?" As Aurianna started to protest, the other girl shook her head. "You had that faraway look on your face, so I thought you might be in your own little world. It's okay. Yeah, I was just talking about coming down here as a child. We did some exploring, but not near as much as you'd think."

Javen said, "Getting lost is a very real possibility, especially as a Younger. Plus, the Arcanes scared the shit out of most of us back then." He smiled at her as he gently squeezed her hand.

Aurianna laughed. "Really? Those old men?"

"Well, they were strange and mysterious, and you know how kids are."

They continued down the tunnels, Sigi and Javen pointing things out as they walked. When they came to the area where Aurianna had had her little "incident," Sigi's eyebrows shot up. "I wonder who managed to make that mess." She gestured to the blackened floor and walls.

Aurianna didn't say a word.

They kept going, but she was already feeling incredibly lost. After another twenty minutes of what seemed like mindless wondering, Javen suggested they head back up.

As they entered the main hall, two people approached, both dressed in the uniform of the City Guard. The male guard smiled shyly at Sigi as they approached. The other, a female, looked familiar to Aurianna. The woman's face was decorated with small metal rings that glinted in the light from the wall sconces.

"Edelina! What's wrong?" Sigi asked. *Edelina.* Aurianna remembered the woman as one of the people who had escorted her to meet the Magnus for the first time. She had seemed friendly enough. Javen had mentioned her name that first day to Sigi.

"Nothing, really. Noah was just mentioning wanting dessert, and I'm still stuffed from dinner. I thought maybe you could show him that late-night ice cream shop we talked about the other day. He's on break right now, but I have to get back to my shift." The man in question was blushing furiously.

"No, sounds great. I guess we're about done here anyways. Edelina, I guess you met Aurianna already."

"Yes, hello again. How are you settling in with everything here?"

"It's still a bit much but getting slightly better every day. They were just showing me around the tunnels, but it's a lot to take in."

Edelina laughed and looked over at Sigi. "Oh my Essence! Do you remember that time we scared the hell out of poor Magister Garis when we snuck out of Earth training and tried to steal some food from the kitchens down there?"

Sigi's face lit up as she giggled back. "Yeah, not such a great idea, in hindsight. The Voids were more terrified of her than she ever was for our safety. They were convinced she'd think they were somehow involved. I've never been literally shoved so briskly out of a room before."

"Then they locked us out, and we kept banging on the door until Garis showed up. I thought she was going to kill us for sure. That look on her face."

"Magister Garis?" Aurianna asked. "The Earth instructor?"

Sigi narrowed her eyes and licked her lips, hesitating. "Yeah, she's a lot more mellow now than she was when we were little. Not that she was ever as intense as Magister Daehne. I don't think anyone takes anything as seriously as that man does."

Aurianna couldn't disagree. The man may have kept her secret, but he was high-strung in the worst way over every little thing. Of course, having students blow up around you probably didn't create the most relaxing work environment.

Sigi continued, "Would you guys like to join us?" Aurianna saw Noah's face fall at the question. Something more was going on here, but she wasn't sure how to respond.

Javen saved her from having to answer. "I think Aurianna needs some help with one of her reading assignments. I promised I'd give it a go."

Sigi looked at the two of them quizzically, confusion etched on her face. "Oh. Why didn't you mention it before? We could have done our tour another night." A hint of pain flashed in her eyes, then was gone in an instant.

"No, no worries," Javen said. "It's related to some stuff my group happens to be doing in class right now, so I figured I might have it fresh on the brain, you know?"

"Oh, okay. Well, I guess you guys have fun with the homework. I'll see you later." Sigi waved to them as she turned and walked out the main entrance with Noah, his arms stiff at his sides as they took off into the night. Edelina shrugged and smiled brightly at Javen and Aurianna before returning to her post.

Aurianna started to ask, but Javen cut her off. "It's complicated."

"Clearly. But you lied to her."

He looped her arm in his, guiding her to the stairwell. "Well, you see, Aurianna, it's like this . . ." He paused for effect. "Noah's in love with Sigi."

Oh.

Oh.

"I see."

He shook his head at her. "No, you don't. And neither does Sigi. At least, I don't think she does."

They started up the stairwell, Javen following close behind her. A little too close.

Aurianna chose her words carefully. "Then . . . then why did she say yes to the . . ."

Javen finished her sentence for her. "The date? Yeah, see, I don't think Sigi sees it like that. Either she's too oblivious to notice when people want more than friendship, or she's too nice to be honest with them. And Edelina likes to play matchmaker far too much for her own good."

"And how do you know all of this?"

"Word spreads."

"So, how is it that Sigi doesn't know?"

"Like I said, maybe she does. But people here aren't assholes.

They're not going to go right up to Sigi and throw Noah's feelings under the train. To each his own, you know?"

"Or her own?"

"Yeah, that too." Javen laughed. "Well, this is your stop, so I'll say goodnight." He leaned in close, their breath mingling in the small space between their lips. Her heartbeat intensified, and she internally cursed the organ for giving anything away. "Love is funny. It can make you act in ways you probably shouldn't."

When he pulled back, she realized she'd been holding her breath. Letting it out in a rush, she looked at the floor, unsure of what to say or do. He lifted her chin and smiled. Placing the softest of kisses on the side of her mouth, he walked past her and continued up the stairs.

CHAPTER 19

AURIANNA

Aurianna awoke, sensing a presence in her room. When she opened her eyes, nothing was there. Still, she was unnerved and got up to search under and around everything in her small dorm room.

Even before looking at the time, she knew it was far earlier than she normally got up. The kitchens wouldn't even be serving breakfast yet, but she knew she wouldn't be able to go back to sleep. After showering and getting dressed for the day, she headed to the main hall and walked outside through the massive double doors at the entrance.

The sky was still dark, but the first slivers of light were creeping over the horizon. She immediately thought about the sunrise she had shared with Javen the other morning. The gesture had been incredibly thoughtful, though she wasn't sure how she felt about the *other* thing. Sure, it wasn't like when Damon had kissed her, but it still felt strange considering all the weight that had been placed on her shoulders. She wasn't here to develop relationships. She was here to develop her powers.

And save the world.

Yes, there was that as well. But she chose not to think too much about that part just yet. She tried not to think about the incident in the tunnels where she had scorched the stone and dirt, causing a Void to have a seizure. She felt terrible for having scared the poor man, but she had no idea what to do or say to fix it. She wasn't even supposed to speak to Voids unless it was in a professional capacity.

Her musings were interrupted by someone clearing their throat. Aurianna looked over to see Simon, the Arcane who had spoken to her in their chambers. The one who had shown her the prophecy. The one who had neglected to mention the whole marriage thing with Pharis.

"Good morning, Aurianna. I was wondering if we might speak for a moment."

When she nodded, he led her over to a bench near the cliff's edge, the perfect spot to watch the sun edge its way up into the sky. Already, the orange and red of dawn permeated the dark gray and blue of the night, forcing it into hiding for another day. For a few moments, neither of them spoke. They simply watched the colors blend and bend on the horizon.

Finally, Simon said, "Do you know anything about your name?"

"My name?"

"Yes. What it means."

"I didn't realize it had a meaning."

"Oh, yes. Larissa gave you the name for a reason."

"How do you know so much about my aunt?"

Simon smiled, looking at the ground. He hesitated briefly before he said, "I knew your aunt. We all did. And she knew what needed to be done, what needed to happen. That's why she named you after the prophecy."

"I'm sorry, what?"

"She named you Aurianna. It means *dawn* in the old language. Have you ever heard the little rhyme about the red sky?"

Red sky at morning, shepherds take warning.

Red sky. Dawn.

Oh. *Oh.*

Something was off. Instead of answering, she said, "So you're telling me I was named *because* of the prophecy, not the other way around. Not randomly. I wasn't destined to fulfill it. I was intentionally named to *look* like I was."

"Is there a difference?"

"Well, yes! Had she named me anything else, I'd still be back home, and none of this would have happened." She faltered as Simon raised his eyebrows and gave her a pointed look. "And no one would be fixing the problem." She sighed.

"Indeed. I think perhaps your view of prophecies is skewed by some misconceptions." He waved his hands in the air in front of them, gesturing toward the distant sky. "All prophecies originate from the Essence. Their will must be done. They decide the what, the where, and the who. We just have to determine the meaning. Your birth signaled the beginning of the prophecy. That much is certain, and the first line is most definitely about you. The timing, the circumstances, everything lined up. Azel received the vision when your mother went into labor, almost to the minute."

"How do you know that?"

"There are a lot of answers for you in this world, child, but you must discover many of them on your own."

"But why? Why can't you just tell me?"

"There are rules the Essence has set on how we Arcanes may interact with the world. Some things we aren't permitted to reveal, and you must discover for yourself."

"But how do you know that?"

Simon blew out a long breath, placing his elbows on his knees as he leaned forward. "I know you're angry. I know none of this seems fair right now. The only thing I can offer you is my absolute solemn vow that this is all for a reason. I wish I could say more, but please believe me: I can't. We can't go down this road again."

"Again?"

He looked agitated for a moment. "I just . . . If you want to fix things, keep doing what you're doing. Ask the questions. But look for the answers yourself. You'll find them. Maybe not in the time and the way you wish, but you will find them."

"Just tell me one thing." She hesitated for a moment. No one besides Magister Daehne and the Void knew about the incident in the tunnels, as far as she knew. Keeping it that way might be for the best, but she needed to know. "The other day, in the tunnels, I was doing Fire training with the Magister. Just like with the other elements, nothing was happening. Then something did happen, and I scorched the wall. More than that. It felt like I was catching on fire. I don't think that's supposed to happen. The Magister was really freaked out, and the Void we took with us went into shock or something—shaking really bad; it may have been a seizure."

Simon's eyes grew wide.

"I don't think anyone else knows. Maybe the other Magisters know by now . . . and maybe the Magnus? I don't know who he might have told. I'm guessing by your reaction no one informed the Arcanes."

"No. They did not." Jaw clenched, he stared at her for a moment, looking as if he might say more. The silence stretched on into the open sky, mixing with the vibrant colors of the awakening day. Finally, he faced her, saying, "Aurianna, the Darkness you left back home is always one step behind. Never forget that. Be careful of what you become."

"What I become? What exactly is the Darkness?" she said, adding, "And how do you know about it?"

"Arcanes know many things collectively, both past and future. Our job is to preserve this knowledge and use it wisely. I'm telling you this because it's important you understand the stakes here. The Darkness was caused by the loss of magic, combined with an evil that cannot be explained. If the singularity isn't stopped, the Darkness is the eventual inevitability." At her look of confusion, he continued, "The singularity is the event you must stop. It's the turning point on which everything will either change or remain exactly the same. Until that happens, time will play out as it always has. And the future you come from will be all there is."

"You said the Darkness follows me. If it's truly the absence of magic, why would it follow me?"

"It seeks to devour anything with power. It only wishes power for itself." He leaned toward her, looking her in the eye once again. "And it knows you have power. Just be careful how you use it."

"I don't even know what I did or how I did it. I can't control it."

Alarm filled Simon's face. "Yes, Aurianna, you can. You must. Control is the most important thing you can master right now."

"I thought magic was the most important thing. Isn't that why I'm training?"

He shook his head violently. "No. No. Control is everything. Without it, the magic is perhaps more dangerous than useful. You must stay focused on the present during your lessons. Don't think too heavily on the past or the future." He added, "Focus on the feelings, but do not dwell on them."

"I'm not sure I know how, but I'll try."

"You must. Think about everything I've said." Standing, Simon bowed to her slightly and said, "I'm always available if you need someone to talk to." He walked back toward the building.

Aurianna called back to him. "I choose my destiny. It does not choose me." His steps faltered for a moment, but he didn't stop or turn around.

As she watched him go inside, the imposing front facade of the Imperium gazed down upon her. Her new home seemed to loom over her, menacing and strange. But this wasn't home. The Darkness had merely followed her here, waiting to devour her whole.

After watching the horizon in silence for a few more minutes, she went back to her room, taking a hot shower to wipe away the lingering sensation of something vile. She had wanted to mention her recurring dream to Simon, but his revelations had pushed everything else from her mind. Was she just being played by everyone at this point?

No, she knew she had some kind of power. How or what, she wasn't sure, but the ring of scorched rock five levels below was proof positive something was writhing inside of her, waiting to get out.

Simon had told her that control was key. Larissa had often said something similar. Control of what though? Her powers? She wasn't even sure how she had done it, so how was she supposed to control it?

Sighing, Aurianna reached for the towel at the same moment a blaring siren began to wail in the distance.

Chapter 20

AURIANNA

Aurianna dressed as quickly as she could, throwing her still-wet hair into a knot on top of her head. She rushed down the stairwell, a crowd of people in City Guard uniforms pushing past her.

When she reached the main hall, everyone was piling into a side room she'd never been in before. They were all walking out with weapons in their hands, faces filled with a mix of fear and excitement. She spotted Sigi, who was strapping several different forms of weaponry on various holsters across her body. A massive weapon sat on the floor at her feet.

Sigi looked up and saw her approaching, a tight-lipped smile barely registering on her face. Nodding curtly at Aurianna, she said, "Well, moment of truth, huh?"

"What's going on?"

"Volanti." The creatures Theron had told her about. The nightmares that swooped in and took people from their homes, their families.

Aurianna knew her feelings must have shown on her features

because Sigi reached out a hand to steady her. "It'll be okay. We just need as much manpower as we can get. I'm not gonna lie though. These things are massive, and it takes a lot to even subdue one of them. I wish we could take one of the bastards down." Reaching down to pick up the weapon at her feet and hanging it off her shoulder as if it weighed nothing, the woman nodded toward the tiny room behind her. "Go grab a weapon. I'll wait for you."

On shaky legs, Aurianna pushed through into the space and grabbed the first weapon she saw. When she walked back out into the main hall, Javen was standing beside Sigi. He almost looked *excited.*

"Time to char us up some creature, eh?" he said by way of greeting.

Sigi ignored his comment and asked Aurianna, "Ready?"

"Would it matter if I said no?"

"Probably not. Let's go."

They exited through the main doors. Outside, chaos reigned. People were everywhere, both on this side of the bridge and in the town. Most held weapons. She assumed most of the non-Kinetics were in hiding. She felt a little selfish wishing she could do the same.

Aurianna followed the other two across the bridge. They took a right on the far side, joining a crowd of armed Kinetics, all heading to the outskirts of Bramosia in the opposite direction of the stables. She had never gone this way.

Up ahead, giant trees covered the area. But something was wrong. The trees appeared to be *moving.*

"What the hell is that?" She pointed at the shaking forest.

"They're coming through the trees. They're real close."

As the shaking in the trees intensified, so did her own. This wasn't normal, or okay, or anything she wanted to be a part of.

A deep voice behind them boomed, "Lovely day we're having."

The three of them turned to see Leon, looking far too calm under the circumstances. He was grinning from ear to ear, a cigar dangling from his lips and a ridiculously large gadget of some sort strapped to his arm.

He took a puff from the cigar, blowing out a cloud of foul-smelling smoke. He waggled his eyebrows and eyed the tree line behind them. Nodding in that direction, he said, "Looks like they're close." The idea made his face light up as he smiled with a child-like excitement.

Aurianna was baffled by this reaction, but she turned back around to face the unknown. A crowd of people had assembled in front of them, all waiting, their weapons pointed downward but ready to fire. The entire forest appeared to be violently swaying in every direction. Something flashed deep in the dark of the woods. Something that was not human, and definitely not friendly.

The next thing she could discern was the glint of razor-sharp teeth in the early morning light as one of the creatures thrust its head into the open air. As soon as it did, dozens upon dozens of shots were fired upon the Volanti. The creature ducked back to the cover of the trees.

But the reprieve lasted only a moment before the Volanti took a huge leap forward, landing very near the front line of Kinetics who were shooting at it. Clearly that had been its goal. Everyone started to fall back, even as they continued to fire at the creature who seemed unfazed by the hundreds of bullets ricocheting off its scaly hide.

The thing was beyond her wildest nightmares. Easily as tall as four or five grown men, the creature walked on its hind legs like a human. Everything else was as nonhuman as something could get. Aside from the teeth, massive claws stretched out from long, spindly hands and feet. The pinnacle of its height was accentuated by a pair of sharply pointed ears rising from the sides of the wide, bony head. Membranous wings lay flattened against its back. Angry red eyes. Teeth. Claws.

Shit.

Shit.

What god had created this creature of darkness, this demon from another world? Fear grappled with the instinct to flee. All around her, others were aiming their weapons at the creature, shooting an infinite number of bullets that seemed to be doing nothing to deter it.

Her friends joined in the fray, adding to the deluge of bullets sweeping across the ever-shortening distance between the Volanti and the crowd of Kinetics desperately attempting to stop it. Javen was aiming shot after shot, his face a solemn mask of concentration. Out of the corner of her eye, she detected the red-hot end of a cigar and turned to see Leon with his arm cannon aimed and firing a massive spray of bullets.

Without any conscious thought or awareness of her own actions, she raised her weapon, aiming for the middle of the Volanti's torso. No one had explained where to aim on these things, but no one seemed to be having much of an effect on the beasts, so maybe it didn't really matter. Still, she held the grip with both hands and blew out a breath. Hot metal shot from the barrel, red as magma, hitting the creature in its chest. Again. And again. But it would not be stopped. Not by her, not by anyone.

They were falling back, giving ground to the monster before them. Holstering her weapon, Sigi dropped to one knee. She yanked up the enormous contraption that hung by a strap across her back and balanced it on one shoulder. An explosion rocked the area as a large projectile burst from the gun, aimed directly at where the creature's heart would possibly be.

That seemed to do something at least. It paused to look down and stare at its chest, while Sigi seemed to be gearing up to fire again. Everyone who had stopped to watch her went back to firing their own seemingly insignificant weapons. Leon seemed to be having a small impact with his arm cannon. At least it was distracting the Volanti while Sigi prepared to try again.

Another boom shook them, smoke trailing from the front end of Sigi's weapon. It seemed to be working.

A thrashing noise to their left caught Aurianna's attention. Another of the nightmares strode from the forest on that side, looking to bypass the fray and go straight for the town. Half of the assembled Kinetics rushed to intercept.

Too late.

The monster was already nearing the outlying homes. Almost everyone was inside their homes or businesses, hiding until it was safe. Almost everyone.

Two men were valiantly attempting to ward off the creature with slingshots. Such an optimistic choice of weapon. Such a senseless way to die.

The Volanti leaped forward and snatched up the males in its giant claws. Without a second of hesitation, it took off into the air, the wings on its back whooshing out to catch the wind. It soared off into the distance. And then it was gone.

The other remaining creature seemed to be contemplating something as shots continued to beat against every inch of its body. After a moment, it reached over and grabbed the nearest Kinetic, taking off just as the other one had, bullets still whizzing through the air.

Then it, too, was gone.

Three people. Gone.

Gone.

Chapter 21

PHARIS

The flames on the altar candles flickered each time he swept by, threatening to snuff themselves out in protest of his fevered motions. Back and forth he paced, his mind a rush of thoughts and images.

Again. Again they'd come, and again they'd taken.

And no one seemed to care enough to *do* anything. Sure, they pointed their pathetic little instruments of death, hurling their tiny pinpricks of hot metal at the larger-than-life targets. But what use was it? They never stopped them. They had never taken one down.

But they continued to do what obviously wasn't working. There had to be another answer. A solution to the Volanti problem that continued to elude everyone, including him.

Here he was, in the sanctuary of Caendra, goddess of fire, the temple in Bramosia closest to the Imperium . He didn't dare visit the *other* one, the temple to Caelum, god of Air. The emptiness there was more real than in the others, the silence more pronounced and far from comforting. It chilled him to his very bones.

Here, the candlelight encroached into every corner, every crevice of the room, blinking and waving as one passed by, cheering on his thoughts of doom and gloom. Pharis had tried in the past to speak with the Arcanes about the mysteries surrounding Caelum. They offered him nothing but cryptic words and empty promises. No, he would have to figure this out on his own.

No one else seemed to care enough about the fading recurrences of Aerokinetics to want to find answers.

Tucked into the back corner of the temple, staring at the flame dancing in his vision from the altar against the back wall, he was abruptly ripped from his daydreams as the unholiest of sounds rang out, reverberating in his ears. Pharis turned swiftly in the direction of the noise, allowing his dark thoughts to awaken his deepest fears, terrified some creature had found its way into the sanctity of the temple. He wasn't hiding. In fact, his standing order was to stay in his rooms during these attacks. Can't have the Regulus snatched away by the monsters. Better to let the townsfolk suffer that fate.

The thought always sickened him.

As he turned, two things became apparent to him. The first was that the noise had been caused by the clattering of multiple metal trays which were now scattering across the floor after toppling from their perches on the holy altars of Caendra. The second was that the culprit was standing in the midst of it all, mortification coloring her skin and shock contorting her face as she covered her mouth with her hand.

Freckles. Amber eyes.

He sighed. Aurianna was the last person he'd wanted or expected to see today, especially here. People rarely visited these temples. That was why he'd come here—the solitude was a strange sort of comfort.

She was looking at him, eyes wide with terror, probably

wondering if she'd be stricken dead by some dormant goddess angered at her clumsiness. Not likely.

The deities had abandoned them long ago, long before any living generation. If only he knew why. Had too many Kinetics waltzed into their houses of worship, lazily knocking over altars and tripping over podiums?

The thought amused him for some reason, and so he laughed aloud before he even realized he'd done it. Aurianna's mortification intensified at the sound, and she slowly began backing away, still walking unsteadily but attempting to leave as quickly as she'd entered. The temple handlers had finally made it into the main room from wherever they'd been hiding, alerted by the horrendous noises they must have thought he'd made. They had probably been terrified to confront him about it. But now they saw who the real perpetrator was, and anger registered on their faces.

Pharis's amusement turned to irritation for some reason. The trays were made from nearly indestructible metal. Damaging anything in here would be very difficult to do. It should have been obvious to them simply by the look on her face that it had clearly been an accident.

Before they could speak, Pharis said, "Clerics, you may leave us." *There. That should stop them in their tracks.*

The two men looked baffled for a moment, sharing a look of concern before shrugging and turning around to reenter the back room. As Pharis watched them go, he caught the unmistakable sound of a long-held breath being released behind him.

He turned to the sound, suddenly unsure of why he'd intervened. This wasn't his problem. His problem was the very real fact that his future kingdom needed a serious overhaul, and his father was certainly not going to do anything about it.

Aurianna was staring at him, her expression a melding of

incredulity and gratitude. After a moment, she took a step toward him then hesitated. The corner of her mouth twitched with some unspoken truth, as if she wanted to say something, but the words seemed to be fighting against her speaking them aloud. But he could see the truth in her eyes.

When she finally spoke, the words chilled him. "They took three people." He should be used to this by now. Why did those words affect him so? This happened every time. But still, three. Three this time.

"Were any others hurt?"

"A few, yes. But they should be alright from what I could tell. I don't know. I ran. I've just…" Her words trailed off, but the emotion crawling across her face was clear enough, her horror and shock standing in the room with them just as certainly as if they were separate entities. She continued, "I've never seen anything like it in my life. With every problem, every issue we have in my time, nothing like that has ever occurred."

One eyebrow raised, he said, "Wishing you were back home away from this nightmare?" He couldn't blame her. Perhaps she was right. The future he saw was depressing, but the Volanti were a whole other level of hell.

"Well, yes. I mean no. I don't know. I just can't understand why everyone is acting like this is just how it has to be." Aurianna's expression and tone proclaimed her outrage. "They just snatched them up and took off. No one seemed fazed by that fact at all. Like it's just this thing that happens, so, oh well." She was chewing on her bottom lip, fury flaming her eyes to a molten gold, their depths shining with unshed tears.

She cared.

Not that the others didn't, he had to remind himself. They all cared, but no one cared *enough* to stop it.

Aurianna said, "One of them was a Kinetic. I didn't know her, but she was there, right there fighting with us. And then she wasn't. I didn't come here to guard the place from monsters. I thought I was supposed to be protecting Kinetics from this Enchantress, whatever it is she ends up doing."

He shrugged. "I don't know. I don't think anyone can save us. I told you that before. What we need is answers. We need to know how to stop the Volanti."

"We should speak with the Arcanes. Maybe they know something."

"They guard their secrets very well. They never tell us anything."

Aurianna stood straighter, squaring her shoulders. "Well, we'll just have to make them talk then."

* * *

The scenario was becoming all too familiar.

This time they were walking toward the Imperium instead of away, but just as before when they went to speak to the Consils, Aurianna was focused and on a mission. If the situation weren't so serious, he might almost find it humorous. The girl was walking faster than he could keep up with without breaking his measured gait. He tried to maintain appearances here at the Imperium, but he had to admit it had been nice to roam free during his little excursion to the future, no guards at his heels and no prying eyes to follow his every movement.

Here, it was different. Here, despite disagreeing with everything his father stood for, Pharis still respected his position and the prestige of who he was meant to be one day. He just hated what had been done in the name of that prestige.

Their little excursion was halted, however, when one of his father's guards stopped them at the entrance to the building and stated the Magnus wished to see him immediately. Something was wrong.

Aurianna took off ahead of him, quickly ascending the stairs at the end of the room, but he managed to catch up to her. The guards on either side of the entryway to the throne room glanced at one another as they saw her approach, unsure whether they were supposed to stop her or let her in. Once they saw him, however, they quickly moved out of the way to allow room for them both to pass.

The Magnus sat on his gilded not-a-throne and watched them as they strode purposefully toward the dais. No Arcanes were in attendance this time, and Pharis wasn't sure if that was a good thing or a bad thing.

The man presented them with his usual forced smile, the expression as fake as the words that followed. "Aurianna, my dear. To what do I owe this pleasure?"

Pharis sighed. "I was told you sent for me to come. Immediately."

An eyebrow arched as the Magnus replied, "Well, that would be the case. I was merely wondering why the girl is here as well." His smile widened, and Pharis realized his father had quite the wrong impression as to why they were here together. Clearly the Consils had yet to address the marriage issue with him.

Never mind. There were bigger matters at stake.

"Aurianna was with the others during the attack. I happened to run into her after the fact."

"Oh? And where was this?"

Ah. No getting out of this one.

"I was at the temple."

His father's face turned a delightful shade of purple before he even began speaking. "You left the Imperium during the attack?"

"Yes."

"Boy, how could you do that? How many times have I told you to stay inside when the Volanti come? We cannot risk losing the only heir to my title. How could you be so selfish?"

"Selfish? You want to talk about selfish? First of all, don't you dare call me *boy*. I'm older than you were when you took the title of Magnus. Selfishness is sitting on your ass while people are fighting to protect what they love. Those things are taking people. Every. Single. Time." Pharis was seething. He tried to maintain his composure but, as usual, failed. He had spent too many years suppressing his anger, and now his temper always seemed to be simmering just beneath the surface.

The Magnus was staring at him, eyes narrowed and lips crushed together in a thin line. The purple hue had segued into a milder red, but his thoughts remained clear on his face.

Leaning back in his not-a-throne, the man cocked his head to the side and licked his lips before speaking again. "And what, pray tell, would you like me to do about it, son?"

"Something. Anything. Send troops to investigate the far reaches beyond Eresseia. Follow them. Whatever it takes."

"You know as well as I do all of it has been done already. Our ships have gone out as far as they can, and no one can figure out where they come from or where they go."

"Then build better ships, damn it!"

"We simply don't have that kind of technology. The Mare Dolor is treacherous at best, and no one we've ever sent out that far has returned."

Aurianna saved him from having to respond to his father. "Magnus, something very disturbing has been brought to my attention recently, and I wish to discuss the matter with you." What was she going on about?

"Of course," he said to her, all the while his eyes never leaving his son's face.

The girl hesitated briefly, and Pharis wondered if she'd already lost her nerve. But he knew her well enough by now to realize she'd never let anything stop her from getting what she wanted.

"Well, sir, while it isn't anywhere near as horrifying as the current conversation, I've been made aware that you had planned to marry me off to your son. Presumably as some sort of calculated political move."

She clearly caught on quicker than he had previously thought. But there was no possible way she could guess the real reason, the true reason. His father hadn't even mentioned it aloud to him. He didn't have to; Pharis knew exactly what his father was doing and why.

But what was *she* doing? Why bring this up now?

The Magnus finally turned his gaze away from Pharis to stare at the girl in front of him. He hadn't been expecting this direct line of discourse any more than Pharis had. The man did seem to squirm for a moment before he cleared his throat. "And where did you hear that?"

Aurianna hesitated before answering. Pharis could see the internal debate clashing within her as her eyes flicked back and forth between him and his father.

"The Arcanes. I went to speak with them about the prophecy." *She lied.*

But his father seemed surprised at the revelation, not angry, so he must have bought the lie. "Oh? They told you." He hesitated, adding, "I see. Well, they have made it clear how important that matter is to the whole business. I'm just following their advice in this, I assure you. We must all play our part in stopping the approaching disaster. We know it is not far off, so we must be prepared. I had planned on giving you time to adjust to our world before springing that on you. But obviously the Arcanes know best."

"Yeah, I don't buy it. Something else is going on here, some motive you have in all of this."

"Why would you assume that? Pharis here is a charming young man, well educated, good-looking. I know I'm biased considering he's my son, but are you telling me you would turn down all of this?" He gestured around the room as he spoke, but Pharis was focused on Aurianna. His father was a compulsive liar, so his words meant nothing. Her response was all that mattered right now. The Consils might still save them, but this was her chance to let the Magnus know her feelings on the matter.

"Hmm" was all she said for several moments as they stood in absolute silence, the weight of it crushing Pharis's chest and making it difficult to breathe. When she finally spoke again, her words were the last ones he expected to hear. "Well, I guess I will take that into consideration. I need to return to my studies now and see if I might be able to get something to eat after all the excitement this morning. I seemed to have missed breakfast."

Aurianna turned and strolled back out of the room. He watched her go, wishing he could leave as well, but he knew his father had summoned him for a reason, a reason he had not wanted to share while Aurianna was in the room.

Rolling his eyes before turning back to his father, Pharis said, "Why am I here, then?"

"We will discuss the matter of your leaving the building later. Right now, I need you to go to Rasenforst and Eadon."

"Why?"

"Disturbing rumors have reached us. I don't know what's going on, and I don't care what you must do to fix it. I just want it stopped. Figure it out and report back to me."

"And are you going to inform me as to what those rumors are?"

The man hesitated. Something was seriously wrong. "Reports of people in Rasenforst acting very strangely. Running around aimlessly, violent outbursts for no apparent reason."

"Sounds like a typical drunken night in Rasenforst."

The Magnus slammed his fist on the arm of his chair. "There is nothing typical about it. I would call it a local matter, but the guards in the towns are having difficulty quelling this. Plus, it seems to have spread to Eadon as well."

"So Eadonites are acting like this as well?"

"No. Some of these Rasenforsters have shown up in Eadon. Same behavior, same outbursts."

"I don't understand."

"Neither do I. Just fix it. Take a contingent of guardsmen and act as my representative. Demand they cease and desist, or they'll face imprisonment. Any who have committed murder and been caught by the guards should be brought back here for trial."

"Murder? Are you serious?"

"Very."

Giving a stiff bow, Pharis quickly walked past the man and opened one of the doors behind the dais, doors leading to their private apartments. He went directly to his room, barely able to get the door open in his excitement, and gathered everything he might need for this trip: extra clothing just in case, his personal weapons, which he was rarely allowed to use, plus any personal grooming items he might need. The Magnus never let him out of his sight, never allowed him to do anything like this. Pharis wasn't about to waste the opportunity for a little freedom, not to mention a chance to show he could be a better leader than his father ever was and gain the respect of the soldiers he would one day be in charge of, men and women who probably saw him as little more than decoration at the moment.

He wandered back through the throne room, but his father was gone, presumably having retired to his own rooms. Lost in thought as he walked past the two guards at the entryway and began the descent down the wide sweeping staircase to the main level, Pharis was startled from his reverie when he came face to face with a familiar pair of amber eyes surrounded by freckles.

What the hell is she doing here?

"What the hell are you doing here?" he asked.

"I could ask you the same question. But I can clearly see you are headed off on some adventure."

"I'm doing no such thing. Now get out of my way."

"You mean you aren't going to investigate the weird things going on in the other regions?"

"What do you know about that?"

"Only what your father discussed. And I might have heard it mentioned before once or twice."

"My father ... You were listening?"

"Of course I was."

Of course she was. Her departure from the room had been far too easy, far too nonchalant.

He sighed, realizing he should have known. Pharis tried to walk past her, but she continued to block his path.

"What is it, Aurianna?"

"I want to go with you."

"Are you insane? Are you sure you were listening? This could be very dangerous, and besides that, it's strictly an official military contingent. No *Acolytes* allowed." He had meant for the word to be biting, but it didn't seem to faze her.

Still, she moved aside to let him pass. "Fine. Good luck then."

Pharis continued past her to give the order to the troops, but he glanced back, feeling a sudden wave of apprehension.

That was too easy.

Chapter 22

AURIANNA

Aurianna found Javen and Leon walking in through the main entrance to the Imperium. Hurrying up to her, Javen exclaimed, "There you are! We were looking everywhere for you. I started thinking maybe the creatures had returned or . . ." He didn't finish the thought as he grasped her in a fierce hug.

She allowed it for the briefest of moments, then pushed him away. She could see the hurt in his eyes, but she ignored it for now. There were bigger issues at hand.

"Where's Sigi?"

"Helping with the injured. Laelia's with her, I think. Why?"

"Well, I think she might want to hear about this."

"What? What is going on, Aurianna?" Javen shared a look with Leon, who had been uncharacteristically quiet during the exchange.

"What would they do if I just left for the day?" she asked.

"Left? Left where?"

"Let's say I took a train ride."

The concern on Javen's face eased a bit as he smiled. "Well, that can certainly be arranged. Classes are usually canceled on days like this. Where would you like to go?"

"I need to get to Eadon and Rasenforst."

"That's . . . very specific. May I ask why?"

"Remember the letter Sigi got from her father? The one about the people acting strangely?"

"Yes, I do." The unease was settling over his features again. "Why are you bringing that up? I told Theron he should go check on it, remember?"

"The Magnus has just ordered Pharis—the Regulus—to take some members of the City Guard to go deal with the issue." She lowered her voice. "It appears to have spread to Eadon as well."

"Eadon? Same behaviors?"

"No. I mean yes, same behaviors. But it's not the people in Eadon. It's people from Rasenforst who've gone to Eadon and are acting strangely over there. Terrorizing people or something, I guess. I really don't know."

"And you want to go *toward* the crazy people?" Leon said, snickering at his own words. "Man, you do know how to pick them, don't you, Javen?"

Aurianna frowned at his comment but ignored him. "I'm going then. With or without you. Any of you. But I think Sigi deserves to know about this, considering it's her hometown. She might be chosen to go with the official contingent, but if not, she might still want to go. If she can."

Javen sighed. "Let's go find her then, I guess."

* * *

The train rocked them with a gentle sway, rolling along on a steady beat that lulled Aurianna into a state of half consciousness. The excitement had worn off shortly after boarding the train with Sigi,

Laelia, Leon, and Javen in tow. Sigi wasn't chosen to be part of the group going with Pharis. She had had to beg someone to take her upcoming shift in order to go anyway with Aurianna. It had been her plea for her home and her family that had finally made someone feel sorry enough for her to take her shift.

Pharis would be right behind them, Aurianna suspected. He and his soldiers hadn't been ready to board this train, at least, but she assumed they would be on the next one. Two trains ran at all times, looping around in the same direction, but always on opposite sides of the lagoon. If the entire length of the tracks took about eight hours (including the half-hour stops at each of the six destinations along the way), he would be about four hours behind them. Plenty of time to investigate and leave before he ever showed up.

And yelled at her.

He liked to yell at her, it seemed. But no matter. They would be gone before the soldiers arrived.

After stopping at the sprawling countryside depot in Menos for passengers to board and disembark, they passed the forest where Theron had lost himself as a child. It was dense and massive, but after the trees ended, the landscape flattened out and provided nothing in the way of interesting scenery. The station at Ramolay was strange to her eyes. Some greenery around the top edge of a massive precipice spilled into what looked to her eyes like an open-roofed sea cave.

Aurianna realized the cave *was* the town.

Ramolay was the city of water, streets replaced by canals and waterways. It was built inside the cavern created in the carved-out cliff.

The train slowed once again, and she wondered how people reached the town below from the station. The train stopped, and she watched those who exited the train walk over to a metal box that lowered them down the cliff face. The front of the cliff face was open to the lagoon and the train depot, and far below she could see tiny dots, people moving along the water in narrow boats to travel from building to building within Ramolay. The concept was fascinating to her, and she made a mental note to visit the town whenever the opportunity arose.

Half an hour passed, and the train began its journey again, continuing to the next station. As the train came to a slow but steady stop at the entrance to the town of Eadon, Aurianna was amazed at how small but densely filled the place seemed. Menos had been massive in its expanse, but everything had been scattered out around the countryside. The landscape here was oddly barren, but closely spaced buildings littering the flat top of the cliff, the haphazard rows of structures leading down to the outlet to the Mare Dolor, the Sea of Sorrows. Here the cliff face had a far less steep incline, making its lazy way down to the water below. The homes were quaint, but plain, their simple colors dotting the cliff side. Everywhere in between was green—sparse, but green, nonetheless.

Aurianna decided it was pretty. It reminded her of home for some strange reason, far more than the current bustling version of her actual home did.

They left the comfort of the train, the wind whipping around them in gusts and making the air far colder than she was used to. They went straight to the local guard station. Sigi seemed to know the way the best, so the rest just followed as she wove through the buildings near the top of the cliff. Getting down to those located on the slope, however gentle the descent might be, seemed far more precarious. Aurianna hoped they wouldn't have to go that far.

Sigi walked into a small building on the outskirts of town near the top of the slope. Walking up to a desk located in a far back corner, she smiled at the man sitting there. He smiled back.

"Hello, Sigi. Been a while, huh?"

"Yes, Aldrik, it has. It's good to see you."

"How's your father?"

Sigi hesitated. "He's good. That's part of the reason I'm here."

"Yeah, I figured as much."

"You did?"

Aldrik nodded. "It's been quite strange around here. Haven't seen anyone we know, but they've all had the darker features associated with Rasenforst. We've got quite a few wounded, some severely so." His voice faltered. "I can't understand it, Sig. Can't wrap my head around it. It's like their minds are gone."

"So, this isn't some drunken idiocy?"

"No. No. They've gone mad, completely lost it. The things they do to the people they attack..."

"What? Aldrik, you have to tell me."

He was looking at the rest of the group, as if he'd just noticed their presence. "I don't think I should be talking about this in front of civilians. Captain said we should be keeping this quiet as much as possible until we know what's going on."

Leon stepped forward, resting his muscled forearms on the top of the desk and forcing his face closer to that of the guardsman. "And why is that, Aldrik?"

"Do I know you?"

"No, but you're about to real fast—"

Leon had stretched himself even further across the desk, but Javen and Sigi were pulling him back. Laelia looked on with an air of amusement but said nothing.

Sigi spoke again. "Aldrik, I think what Leon is trying to say is we need answers. Sweeping this under the rug won't help anyone."

Aldrik was silent for a moment before he said, "Sigi, do you not see the implications here? Rasenforst is attacking Eadon."

Sigi started as if someone had slapped her. After a moment of shocked silence, she shook her head in protest. "No. No, that's not possible. Rasenforst would never do that. None of the regions would. Why would they? It doesn't make sense, Aldrik. There's something very odd behind all of this, but I refuse to believe the town—any town—would try to start a war with any other."

"Then explain why a large group of them rushed in, full force, and started attacking the Eadonites."

Laelia had stepped around the side of the group, stopping to the left of the man behind the desk and laying her hand gently on his shoulder, sliding it up and down his arm in a soothing motion. "You said yourself they were out of their minds. That's not the work of a deliberate attack from Rasenforst." Her feline smile had taken on a flirtatious quality.

Leon rolled his eyes, but added, "Yeah, clearly this is not an organized group. Where are you keeping the prisoners?"

Aldrik seemed as if he might object to receiving orders from someone outside the Guard, but he simply said, "What prisoners?"

Sigi clarified, "The attackers."

"But we don't have any of them in custody."

"What? Why not?"

"Because . . . because they . . ." The man looked like he might be sick. "Sigi, they wouldn't stand down. They were *on top* of people, clawing at them and . . . doing other things." He was really about to get sick. "They wouldn't stand down. We had no choice but to shoot them. We couldn't get to any of them without being attacked ourselves. Bullets were the only thing stopping them. They weren't even afraid of the weapons. They just kept coming until enough bullets put them down. I think some of them got away, but in all the chaos, I can't be sure." There were tears in his eyes, but he didn't say anything else.

Sigi was staring into space, a look of pure despair on her face. She pulled herself together after a moment and said, "Right. Well, then thank you, Aldrik. I appreciate your help."

"No problem, Sig." He grabbed her arm as she started to turn away. "Sig, you find out what's going on, okay? Find out and fix it. If anyone can do it, it's you...and your...friends here." He nodded at the group.

When they were back outside, Sigi blew out a loud breath, then another. "Let's head on to Rasenforst then. There's obviously nothing we can do here. The train hasn't left yet. If we hurry, we'll make it. Otherwise, we'll be stuck here for hours waiting."

They rushed back, getting to the train just in time. As Aurianna watched the scenery once again fly by, she wished for a moment she was back home, with familiar troubles and familiar woes.

* * *

Rasenforst was cold, bitingly cold. Not like the cold of Eadon, where the windchill caused some discomfort. This was like the cold Aurianna remembered from back home during the season of Nivalis, only much worse. And she didn't have a warm cloak to wrap up in, or even a light jacket. The sleeveless cloaks they wore left her shoulders bare. At least the males had sleeves on their shirts. Looking at the other two girls, Aurianna realized they were shivering as well.

Laelia said, "Guess we were a bit hasty in our departure. Normally we would have brought cold-weather cloaks."

"Where would one find something like that, for future reference?" Aurianna asked.

"Should have been one in your dresser. Doesn't matter right now, though, does it?" Laelia's words were as biting as the cold.

Sigi once again took charge. "Let's head to my family's home.

There should be some extra cloaks we can borrow while we explore. It's not far at all."

They followed her to a modestly sized home with an attached workspace that dwarfed the house. A forge lay nestled behind a short wall, and they could see into the space, piles of weaponry lying around and hanging from the walls on the far side. Aurianna didn't have long to linger though, as they were ushered into the house at once. She wasn't going to complain considering she could no longer feel anything from her shoulders down to her fingertips.

Crowding around a large fire in the living space, the group focused on warming themselves while Sigi greeted her family with hugs, tears, and laughter. Aurianna felt somewhat uncomfortable witnessing such an intimate exchange.

Introductions were made. "This is my father, Johan. And my brothers Gunter, Emery, and Anton."

Sigi left the room and returned with a pile of clothing. They each picked out the warmest cloaks they could find from the stack. Aurianna thought maybe some of it had belonged to Sigi's mother. The girl was staring at the fabrics like they might reach out and speak to her. Aurianna knew that feeling. She used to stare at her mother's necklace, willing it to give up its secrets, to divulge the past. To give her answers.

She reached up, grasping the pendant. *Soon,* she thought.

Sigi's father had dark hair like his daughter, his skin a deep russet tone like most of the Rasenforsters they had seen on the way here. He also had the distinctive shorter stature of his people. But his arms were the size of small tree trunks, dwarfing Sigi's own impressive physique. The three brothers who were home were similarly built. They explained that the others were helping the town look for the missing citizens, the ones who had taken off in a frenzy.

Sigi sighed. "Dad, it's worse than you thought. The ones that left

…well, most of them are dead." Her father and brothers cried out in shock at the declaration, but she continued. "They attacked Eadon. Attacked *Eadonites*, Father. They were shot by the guardsmen there. There wasn't a choice. These people wouldn't let up, wouldn't stop. And they were too crazed or too powerful to be arrested. I think some got away, but I have no idea where they could be now."

A loud knock at the door interrupted their conversation. One of the brothers went to answer it. Theron was standing there, Rhouth crawling around his ankles as she nudged her head against his legs.

Sigi jumped up. "Theron! What are you doing here?"

The man stepped into the room, seeming to blush at her words, and he lowered his gaze to the floor as he spoke, slipping his hood off his head. "Hi, Sig. I was talking to Frederik down by the station about the attacks when I saw you and figured you'd head here first. You were right, Javen. Something very strange is going on, so I came to investigate. Checked out the local wildlife, and there's something odd happening there as well. Similar behavior, similar frenzy."

"What did Freddie say?" Sigi asked.

"Well, I mean, you know how your brother is." Theron smiled, looking back up at Sigi. "He's all for taking off right now to hunt those people down, but I convinced him we need to find the source of the problem first. At least, I think I convinced him."

"Doesn't matter anyways. Most of them were killed when they attacked Eadon."

"They attacked Eadon?"

"Yeah. In a massive way. There may be some out there somewhere though. There's just no telling where to find them or what to even do with them."

"Right. Which is why we need to find out how all of this happened. And why it's specific to Rasenforst."

Someone else burst through the door, gasping for air. From the resemblance, Aurianna guessed this was another of the brothers. "More. More of them." He tried to get the rest of his words out but stopped to catch his breath. Finally, he continued, "There's another mess of them, all junked up on something it seems like. They don't respond to our calls, even people we know. They're acting like lunatics, all zoned out and crazy hyped-up at the same time. Attacked one of the guards. Didn't kill him but came close. They're heading south toward the forest."

Leon asked. "To Bramosia?"

"Maybe. They'll get there eventually if they keep running like that. Sooner rather than later, I imagine."

Aurianna had a sudden thought. "Wait a minute. How did they get to Eadon? The land isn't connected on either side of Vanito, and I highly doubt they took the train all the way around unnoticed."

Laelia replied, "Or stopped to wait for the airship ferry. Twice."

"That's a good point. I didn't even think about that," Javen said.

"Swam," Sigi's father answered.

"*Swam?*" Disbelief clouding Laelia's words as well as her features.

"Yep. Cliff diving to an extreme. Then they took off at an impressive pace across the lagoon. Must have climbed back up the other side, though it doesn't seem humanly possible. Whatever's gotten into them, it's given them some kind of superhuman strength or something. There's some steps carved out for the divers near the area, so I imagine that's how they could have got back up. Though I don't know if their mental capacities allow for much rational thought, considering how they're acting." Johan shook his head, his own uncertainty a testament to the strangeness of it all. "I can't have all of you involved in this. Sigi, you at least…" He trailed off at the look Sigi was giving him.

"I'm a *guard*. It's my job!"

"But you don't all have to go. I'm not losing all my children in one night."

Sigi grasped her father's weathered hand. "Hilda is safe at the Imperium. And you're not going to lose us. This is what I'm trained for, and you must have faith in your sons to take care of themselves." She smiled. "You did raise us, after all."

All of Sigi's brothers were grabbing things from around their home, weapons and clothing, strapping as much of it to themselves as they could.

"No arguing now, Father. We're going to help. All of us. This has gotten out of hand," one of the brothers—Aurianna thought it was Emery—said.

Johan looked like he was about to protest anyway but conceded with a nod of his head. "We'll all go. Theron, are you joining in the hunt?"

Theron thought for a moment. "I would, but I think I need to explore the issue with the local wildlife. I can probably do more good here."

"Suit yourself. Javen?"

"Yes, sir. I can help. Leon and I will both come. Theron, you'll keep an eye on the girls?"

Sigi huffed. "Javen Ambrogetti, I really hope you're joking."

He winked at her. "Of course. You coming?" He drifted out the door, grabbing a weapon from one of the brothers.

Sigi looked at Aurianna and Laelia, biting her lip before saying, "Can you find your way around without me?" When both girls nodded, she said, "Alright then. We'll be back in a bit. Try not to get into too much trouble." She turned to leave, looking back at Theron and adding, "Happy belated birthday, by the way."

Theron's face turned a slightly deeper shade of pink. He looked down and mumbled his thanks.

The group left, leaving Aurianna with Laelia and Theron.

Laelia was the first to speak. "Where should we start?"

Theron said, "Well, what connection could there be between the affected animals and the people here?"

"None. Nothing I can think of, at least. Unless maybe they were bit by the animals?"

"No, doesn't work that way. It could make them sick, but not act like that. No, it's gotta be—"

"The water supply," all three of them said in unison.

"It would make the most sense. The one thing they share," Theron added.

Aurianna said, "But why is it only affecting some people?"

"That I don't know. But we should get a sample tested to find out if something is in it."

He led the other two around to the other side of town. As they walked down the main roads, Aurianna noticed how cozy and simple the dwellings were, yet sturdy and with their own beauty. Dark colors dominated, and the roofs were covered in patches of a material laid out in rows.

At the middle of one of the intersections, they stopped at a well. Cranking the rope pulley, Theron drew the bucket up. It slowly rattled its way up from the depths, arriving at the top just in time for the three of them to stare at each other in exasperation. They had simultaneously realized none of them had anything to put the water sample in to take back with them.

"Damn. Okay, new plan," Theron said, sighing at the two women as if it were their fault.

"Wait," Laelia responded. She ran across the street into a nearby shop, a pharmacy by the looks of it. Returning with a triumphant smile, she held up a glass vial.

"Excellent thinking, my dear."

"I aim to please." She handed the vial to Theron, who removed the stopper and dipped the container into the bucket with a gloved hand, careful not to let the water touch his bare skin. "Just in case," he added with raised eyebrows.

CHAPTER 23

PHARIS

Outside the laboratory, Pharis paced back and forth as he waited impatiently on the Hydrons within to determine what might or might not be in the water sample Aurianna and her group had brought back from Rasenforst that evening. The night had barely begun, but it felt like the light of day, and hopefully, enlightenment, would never come.

He had explicitly told the girl to stay out of it. Not only had she ignored his words, but she had also brought along a group of her friends, including a guardswoman who should have known better. He was their Regulus, their superior. They were supposed to obey him as their leader-to-be. And there they stood, the lot of them, pretending to ignore his seething rage at their insubordination.

When the doors finally opened, the group rushed up to the woman who walked out. Much to Pharis's delight, she ignored them and focused her attention on him, bowing slightly before speaking. "Regulus, we have determined the sample does in fact contain a foreign substance."

When she failed to provide further information, he raised an eyebrow. "And?"

The woman squirmed, wincing as she answered him. "Well, sir, it's . . . it's blood. Dragonblood, we believe. The samples we have are well preserved but date back to before our known histories. We are trusting the Arcanes' records."

Pharis was stunned. So, it seemed, were the rest of them. Incredulous, he asked, "Dragonblood?"

She nodded. "Trace amounts, so it wasn't deadly. But it does cause erratic behavior, violent and irrational responses, and, in some cases, brain damage."

This changed everything. It appeared the Arcanes were correct. The Enchantress was indeed behind it all. Who else had access to dragonblood?

He nodded absently as he thought about the implications. Either way, the woman in the tower needed to be stopped.

Aurianna stepped forward. "What does that mean?"

Ambrogetti was standing beside her, holding onto her arm with a strong grip to keep her from running into the lab. Javen was the last person he wanted to agree with, but in this case, he was right to keep her back. They had already risked exposure to the dragonblood as it was. Ingestion was, of course, the fastest way. But no one knew for sure if it were possible to be exposed through the air or skin.

The Hydron pursed her lips. "Only someone with access to dragonblood could have done this."

"So it was definitely intentional?"

"Yes, most definitely. And the only person who is thought to have a dragon is . . ." The woman's face was ashen, and a sense of unease rolled off her, coating the room in dread.

"The Enchantress," Pharis finished. "No one's certain about that, but some have claimed to have seen it in the past. The Arcanes already gave us advanced warning that she will attempt something, so I'd say it's a pretty safe bet she's behind this mess."

"So, this is the evil from the prophecy?" The question had come from the guardswoman—one of Ambrogetti's entourage, it seemed—but she glanced at Aurianna as she spoke.

The pale blonde girl with them was staring at him with an unnerving smile, showing far more familiarity than anyone ever dared to show him. His dark gaze only made her smile widen. When she licked her bottom lip in what was clearly a very deliberate act, he turned away before he lost his temper.

"Well, it doesn't specifically say *evil*. But yes, Sigi, I guess, perhaps, it is," Aurianna answered. "If what Pharis—*the Regulus*—says is true, then it looks like it would have to be her behind this." She whirled on him, asking, "She really has a *dragon*? As in, the winged things from picture books, that breathe fire and can rip people apart? I didn't even know they existed!"

He nodded. "Yeah, they exist. Or, at least, they used to. No one alive has seen a dragon, other than the few who claim they saw the Enchantress with one. They say she can control it. I don't know." Aurianna opened her mouth, but before she could interrupt him, Pharis added, "What I *do* know is we need to prevent this contaminated water from affecting anyone else." Pharis called for a guard from the outer hallway. "Send word to the towns, Rasenforst being the priority. Tell them to cease use of the town wells immediately. Have the kitchens provide some empty water vessels." He pointed at the Hydron who was still waiting to be dismissed. "Have your people fill the vessels as quickly as possible. I'll have them delivered directly to the towns for their use while we find a way to drain the wells." He started to leave the room but turned back at the last minute. "Oh, and take some empty vials to collect samples at each of the wells. Bring them back for testing as soon as possible." With that, he turned on his heel and made his way to his father's chambers.

This was not going to be a pleasant conversation.

CHAPTER 24

AURIANNA

"What do we do now?" Laelia asked. Aurianna and her friends were seated in a common area, the six of them staring at the ground as they wrapped their minds around the shocking news the Hydron had given them.

"We? Shouldn't we be asking what our new friend here will do now?" Leon asked. When everyone looked up at him in amazement, he waved his hand in Aurianna's direction and added, "I mean, that's why she's here, right?"

Javen glared at his friend as he spoke. "Leon, it's more complicated than that. We have an entire region that could already be poisoned. There's no way of knowing who could be affected or when. Or even if it's confined just to Rasenforst. We won't have any answers until they come back with the samples to test." Javen didn't notice how his words made Sigi's eyes glisten.

Aurianna could only imagine what the girl was going through. Some of these people were her friends and family. For all she knew, they might have already succumbed to the effects of the dragonblood. No one seemed to know how long it took, or why only some seemed to be reacting to it. Perhaps only certain wells had been poisoned.

She thought about all she had learned in her studies, in her training. None of it applied. None of it could help her. What had been the point of it all? How was she supposed to stop this woman?

"Maybe I could try speaking with her." The mouths of her new friends dropped open at Aurianna's suggestion.

"What?" Sigi asked.

"You can't be serious," Javen said.

But she *was* serious. She had always avoided speaking about her problems. Nothing good had ever come from her silence. She sat up straighter. "I am serious. I should try to speak with her and figure out why this is happening. Has anyone met with her?"

"No," Sigi said. "We don't even know what she looks like, except that she has hair like fire. As in flaming red, unlike any shade you could imagine, or so people who claim to have seen her say. Other than that, we have nothing but rumors and gossip. Like the dragon thing. I don't know if it's true, but I guess it makes sense for her to be involved if that's the only possible connection to a dragon that we know of."

"Then let me go to her. If no one knows anything about her, maybe I can find the answers by talking to her."

"It's too dangerous," Javen said. When she glared at him, saying nothing, he sighed. "It's late. Let's all get some sleep. It's been a very tiring day. Tomorrow we can see where things are, and maybe then we can make a plan."

Aurianna continued glaring at him. Javen seemed to think he was going to make this decision for her, but he obviously didn't know her very well. Still, she followed the others upstairs after bidding Leon and Theron farewell as they were off to Bramosia for the night. Everyone promised to meet for breakfast in the dining hall the following morning.

Aurianna had no intention of keeping that promise.

A few hours later, once she knew the others were probably asleep, Aurianna left her room, remembering to grab one of the warm-weather cloaks from her wardrobe. She had no idea where she might end up, so it was best to be prepared for anything.

A few of the guards glanced her way as she walked out through the main entrance, but no one attempted to stop her. She wasn't technically doing anything wrong, as far as she knew. Other than breaking a promise to friends.

But they had given her no choice. She had to try. Provoking a woman with unknown powers—not to mention a supposed dragon at her disposal—with no information on the enemy seemed a stupid way to go about things. They could be starting the very war she was supposed to stop. Her friends could be mad at her all they wanted. Something in her gut told her this was what she needed to do.

Aurianna's gaze went up to the front of the Imperium, to the massive clock face at the top. She was struck by how odd it made her feel. She couldn't explain why, not even to herself, but something about that clock unnerved her.

After making her way in front of the waiting train by the bridge, Aurianna realized the train would be going in the opposite direction from the tower, and delaying her plans by that many hours would not be helpful. Walking was also not a good option, as the tower itself was quite a long way from Bramosia, on the other side of the giant forest where they had fought the Volanti creatures. Had it only been that morning?

Resisting the urge to turn around at the thought of somehow facing those monsters again, she made a beeline for the stables.

Oracle was her best bet now. The horse was fast, and she felt a lot more comfortable riding her than she had at first.

The stablemaster looked at her strangely when she approached, asking to take Oracle for a ride so late at night. He hesitated for a moment as if he wanted to speak, but seeing as she was a Kinetic, he was conditioned to keep his mouth shut and simply comply.

Oracle dipped her head when she approached, allowing Aurianna to pat her neck under her mane. Aurianna realized she had missed the creature, missed the feel of the air on her face as they raced along the countryside together. The horse seemed ready to go, perhaps even more than she was, and she began to feel even more guilty for not having taken the animal out more often since purchasing her. Oracle didn't belong in a stable all day. The stablemaster and his workers let the horses roam within the pasture during part of the day, but it wasn't enough, especially not for a free spirit like Oracle. Aurianna made a vow to take the horse out as much as possible or find someone who could.

The horse seemed agitated, far beyond the excitement of seeing her. She was neighing loudly and moving around within her stall in frantic bursts.

Something was wrong.

Aurianna tried her best to calm the animal, but nothing seemed to help. Just as she was about to unlock the stall and get going, thinking she just needed to get Oracle on the move to work out her nerves, a noise in the far distance hooked her attention. All the horses were now acting strangely, bucking in their stalls and making a loud ruckus. She walked back toward the front of the stables, looking off into the distance for the source of the unearthly sounds chilling her blood.

At the corner of the building, movement caught her eye. Someone dressed entirely in white—the pale cloak stark against the dim illumination of the night sky—was walking toward the town. That fact, in and of itself, was not disturbing.

The fact that locks of flaming red hair were flowing out behind the figure was.

CHAPTER 25

AURIANNA

The woman, for indeed it looked like a woman, was walking slowly but deliberately toward the main area of town—and either the train or the Imperium. Contrary to how Kinetic power was supposed to work, a glowing flame lay nestled in the woman's palm, bright as day, and red as death. This wasn't magma being controlled to float up from the core. This was an actual flame, as if the fire had come into existence right within the confines of her hand. Which, again, was impossible for a Kinetic.

Aurianna watched the woman walk down the length of the train, stop at an open door, and disappear into the depths of the steam and smoke.

Without hesitating a moment longer, Aurianna ran back to Oracle and jumped on her back. She heard the unmistakable sound of the train's whistle, signaling its departure. *Damn it!* The woman—the *Enchantress*, for who else could she be?—was getting away. The train was about to take her off into the night without a trace, without them getting a single answer to any of their questions.

Aurianna had already left the stables behind when she realized something odd.

Oracle was already fully tacked up. Reins, saddle, everything. The horses were never equipped until their rider required it. Why was her horse ready to go?

There was no time to ask the stablemaster about it now. If someone else had borrowed the mare, she would have to deal with it later.

As she galloped toward the moving train, Aurianna suddenly realized the source of the hair-raising sound that had so spooked the horses. All across the horizon, from both borders, hundreds of forms were moving erratically, converging on Bramosia and the Imperium. How they had managed to get that far from both sides of the land in such a short amount of time was irrelevant. They were here—an approaching storm of blind rage and fury, dragonblood running through their veins.

Aurianna gasped as her thoughts froze. Oracle slowed as she, too, saw the approaching horde. The horse reared. Aurianna reached out to calm the creature, taking one hand off the reins to pat its neck and soothe its fears. A dangerous move.

The animal returned to all fours, neighing in fear at the sound and sight of the rampaging flood of human flesh running at them. Oracle tried to turn around and head back to the stable.

Aurianna spoke into the mare's ear. "I need you to be brave right now. I don't want to do it either, but if that train gets away, we'll never be able to stop any of this. You're fast. You can outrun them, and besides, they're running toward the town. They'll probably just run right past us and keep going. No one can catch you if you run like the wind."

With the greatest of effort, Aurianna managed to get the horse to a trot, keeping her nose pointed toward Menos, the next stop for the train. When they reached the front lines of the crazed horde, Oracle was already at a frenzied gallop, so none of them even glanced in their direction. Horse and rider flew past in pursuit of the train puffing away into the distance. The City Guard would handle the poisoned citizens. There was nothing Aurianna could do to help with that. Her goal was the train and its red-haired passenger.

They raced along for what felt like hours until Aurianna knew they were getting close to the train station at Menos. She had no idea what would happen there. She just knew she had to get on that train. Aurianna thought she heard hoof beats behind her, but she was too terrified to look back.

When she came up on the train, it was just slowing down at the station. Praying to the Essence or whatever gods might still be listening, Aurianna hopped off her mare and made a beeline for the back of the train. Lifting herself onto the platform of the last car, she opened the door.

The train suddenly lurched back into motion, throwing her against the railing. She reached out, grabbing hold of whatever she could. The metal bars felt ice cold beneath her hands, but she was focused on not falling to a watery grave, so she clung, half-sitting, half-prone, desperately trying not to lose her grip. Her sweat-soaked skin made it difficult, but she managed to maintain her position as the train once again threw her sideways. It seemed to have stopped once more, having only traveled a few meters.

Something was wrong. Instead of coming to a complete stop and waiting the typical thirty minutes before departing the station, the train seemed to have a mind of its own.

Aurianna quickly stood up and walked through the open door into the baggage car. The space was empty, save for some boxes stacked against the far wall. She made her way across the tiny space and exited back into the open air to cross into the next car.

Hearing a noise behind her, she looked back to see Sigi opening the door at the far end of the train.

How the hell did she get here?

Before she could speak, the train went back into motion and began picking up speed at an alarming rate within seconds.

She watched in horror as the sudden momentum threw Sigi backward, her friend desperately trying to grab onto something, anything. In vain.

The girl was swept through the door she had just entered and into the black night.

With a scream of anguish, Aurianna raced back across the car. The back platform was empty.

An ear-piercing screech pulled her vision down to her feet. Sigi was hanging onto the back ledge, dangling like a rag doll in the night. Aurianna lunged out, grabbing the girl's forearm with a sturdy grip.

Terror dripping from her voice, Sigi begged, "Don't drop me, okay?"

"Never."

Sigi let go of the platform with her other hand, reaching over to grab Aurianna's arm. The train made a sudden jerking motion as it accelerated. Sigi's hand swung wildly out, missing its mark. She was dangling by one hand, flailing in the open air, legs kicking in panic.

Aurianna began pulling her up, both hands now on the girl's left forearm. Her clammy skin was slowly sliding along Sigi's arm. She was losing her grip, her sanity, and she was about to lose her friend.

She felt the shape of the hand, the curve of fingers, and Aurianna knew she was going to drop the girl. There was little chance she'd survive from this high up, unless she used the tiny amount of Aerokinetic power most fully trained Kinetics possessed. Did Sigi have any such power? Even the most daring cliff divers were never more than a third of this height from the water. She was going to watch her new friend tumble through the air to her death. The water would swallow Sigi up, the waves enfolding her and tucking her body into the depths of the lagoon.

Clammy skin met with cool night air. Sigi's gaze as she fell backward was locked on Aurianna's, fear and resignation battling for dominance over her features. Aurianna turned away. She simply could not watch.

A thunderous cacophony reached her ears, forcing her to look back despite herself.

The train was plunging toward Perdita Bay.

No.

The bay was rising toward *them*.

It was incredible, impossible.

But it was happening.

A massive wave rushed upward, catching Sigi, cradling her like a mother would its cub. The sight was surreal. Sigi's look turned to one of bewilderment as she was swept sideways toward the land. The train was already leaving her far behind in its haste, but, in the distance, her bedraggled form alighted on dry ground. This wasn't Aerokinetic power. The water itself had come to the girl's rescue somehow.

Sigi was—inexplicably—safe.

The same could not be said of Aurianna. Desirous to have an end to this strange night, she raced back through the baggage area and crossed over into the first passenger car, hoping she could still find the woman she'd seen enter—was it a lifetime ago?

Three steps in, a massive figure hurtled into her from the left, tackling her into the side door at the end of the car. The door flung open, and she felt herself topple through.

Chapter 26

AURIANNA

Aurianna reached out and grabbed the ledge as her body slipped past it. *She* was now hanging precariously, holding on for dear life as the train continued to race along. She tried lifting herself up with her forearms. But the entire weight of her body was dangling toward the water below. She lacked the upper body strength. It was impossible.

Her eyes welled with tears. This was it. This was how she was going to die. Every unspoken word, every incomplete action, every source of regret in her life bubbled up to the surface.

Her arms were beginning to lose their grip, her strength ebbing, her will giving out. Above her, a loud grating noise echoed above the sound of the moving train. Aurianna looked up and saw the face of evil.

The figure who had sent her flying into the night.

The man's features did not proclaim him to be from Rasenforst, though she couldn't be certain which region he did belong to. None of that mattered, however. The look of scorn and rage on his face was quickly replaced by one of unmistakable glee. His eyes widened along with his smile, and Aurianna knew the danger was just beginning.

The man reached out suddenly, grabbing her arm. For a moment, Aurianna thought perhaps he was trying to help her. But as he lifted her up from the ledge, his other hand reached out to grab her throat. Twisting in his grip, she felt herself flail backward, and in the infinity that followed, everything seemed to move in slow motion. All she could sense now was the air enveloping her, enclosing her in a cocoon of imagined safety.

That illusion of safety would be short-lived, however. This was simply the calm before the storm when she plummeted to the lagoon far below.

The man reached out with a meaty fist, grabbing onto her by her necklace, the chain digging into the back of her neck with the sudden jolt. Aurianna flung her arms toward the man, her nails digging into his arm, clinging to him in a desperate attempt to pull herself up and into the train. Her fingernails inched their way up to his shoulder as he lifted her higher and grabbed a chunk of her hair with his other hand.

Aurianna jerked by instinct, the pain forcing the sudden movement. She felt the chain around her neck snap in that instant. A cry, and the pain in her scalp subsided. As his weight carried him forward, she twisted sideways and grabbed the metal bar on the bottom of the door, lodging her elbows onto the precarious ledge. Their bodies trading places, she watched as the man fell through the doorway and toward the waiting waters below.

She couldn't bring herself to watch the impact. Turning her head, she squeezed her eyes shut and pulled the rest of her body into the train. Once she was settled and convinced no more sneak attacks were imminent, she tentatively looked back.

Aurianna stood motionless, her gaze locked onto the lagoon far below, her senses frozen in time.

Her mother's necklace was . . . gone. The only connection she'd had to her family.

Not wanting to further contemplate what had just happened, she instead turned to face the inside of the train. The car was empty, but something was wrong. Whatever normally powered the interior lights was either turned off or broken. The only light in the space was the faint moonlight emanating from outside.

She hurried across the length of the train car, carefully opening the door at the far end before leaping to the next one. Aurianna turned the knob ever so slowly, peeking in before entering the next car.

All these cars were designed for passengers, yet up ahead in the moonlight, she could clearly see the outlines of objects stacked up across rows and down the aisle. She heard faint voices in the near silence, getting stronger as she stealthily made her way over to the cover provided by the stacks. As she got closer, Aurianna realized they were containers of some sort. She couldn't quite hear what the voices were saying. Getting closer was the only option.

But she had to see what was in the containers first. She lifted the lid of the closest one, gasping at what she saw.

Inside were rows of explosives. She might not have recognized them as such, but the label "WARNING: EXPLOSIVES" stamped on the side of each one was a pretty clear indicator.

This was worse than anything they could have imagined. What was this woman planning to do with explosives?

The train was traveling away from the capital city, but there was no way of knowing the true intentions of this Enchantress without getting close enough to hear.

Peeking around the boxes, Aurianna adjusted her vision in

the dim light. Up ahead stood two men who looked to be from Rasenforst. A snatch of white fabric was floating out the door just behind them as it closed. The two men were talking.

"And why do you think that is, you moron?"

"Hey! I don't need this shit, okay? I got my orders. The boss says, I do. But I didn't sign up to be involved in no kidnapping."

"You'll blow up a train, but you draw the line at taking hostages?"

"Yeah. I do. She's just a girl, and they say she's not even from here. Brought her here from the future, they did. Nobody on the train but us, and boss says we'll be protected. No one gets hurt."

"Then what is the point, idiot? If we ain't blowing nobody up, why are we here? You really are naive."

"I ain't ni-eve. I was paid to blow up the train, so that's what I'm doing."

Blow up the train.

These men were clearly not of the dragonblood-turned-zombie variety. Perhaps they weren't the most intelligent, but they could speak and reason—somewhat—and they weren't acting erratically.

"*The boss says,* huh? Well, did *the boss* tell you we're setting off the charges when we get back around to Bramosia? Pretty sure there's plenty of people near the station, all snuggled up in their warm, cozy beds. Beds we're about to blow to kingdom come."

Bramosia.

She had to warn everyone. But this train was speeding along on its one-way trip to destruction. Unless it stopped again, there was no way to get off.

She was trapped.

On a train with explosives.

Explosives destined to cause a lot of damage and possibly kill a large number of people. She might not know much about explosives, but judging just from the boxes she'd seen so far, it seemed certain they were aiming for a massive explosion. The Imperium *might* be far enough away to avoid much of the blast, but it would definitely feel some of it.

Her friends were asleep. Maybe Sigi would warn them. But Sigi didn't know about the explosives.

And not all her friends were staying at the Imperium. Leon and Theron were in Bramosia.

There was only one thing to do.

She had to stop this train.

The two men were coming toward her. The narrow aisle was mostly blocked, the sides of the car filled with individual compartments for passengers. Aurianna squeezed herself into a tight ball on the floor as the men sidled around the stacked containers and continued back toward the baggage car.

Once they were past, she hurried along the corridor and through into the next car. The passage here was empty, save for more boxes.

She continued through to the next car and the next, encountering more of the boxes of explosives, but there wasn't a soul in sight.

Strange.

Aurianna knew the woman had gone this way. She had to have more than two people working for her. They must be up ahead in one of the front cars. She wondered how all of this was related to the dragonblood. Was the Enchantress keeping these men clear-headed simply to blow them up with the train? Where did the men come from, and why were they helping the woman destroy their capital city, not to mention its people?

They must somehow be connected to the rebellion. Those people had no love for Kinetics, it seemed. But there were many non-Kinetics in Bramosia as well. Why kill your own people?

Why kill anyone? What did that solve?

There were Kinetics all over Eresseia from what she gathered. Kinetics ran the steam trains, Pyros in charge of keeping them running. The people would blame...

Oh dear Essence.

That was it.

They weren't trying to kill Kinetics. They were setting them up to be blamed for the explosion, for the deaths of so many people in Bramosia. The regions would revolt and go after Kinetics for this.

This had to be the singularity the Arcanes kept going on about—the catastrophe that would start a civil war—the thing that would force Kinetics to flee to the future in hopes of escaping.

To be tortured and drained of their power by a different group of people.

All for nothing.

This was why she felt the need to do something tonight, to get out of her room and seek answers to questions she didn't even know she had. She felt sure of it.

Maybe there *was* something to this prophecy business. But what could she do with the little training she'd had?

There had been the one time—the one disaster—in the tunnels. Clearly, she had an affinity for fire, but she'd been unable to duplicate the phenomenon. Magister Daehne had refused to look her in the eye since then, which led her to believe she must've done something incredibly wrong.

Almost spontaneously combusting must be frowned upon.

If only she knew what had lit the spark that day, what had knocked that poor Void unconscious and brought her close to blowing up her teacher.

Continuing through yet another empty compartment, Aurianna heard muffled voices in the train car up ahead. She couldn't tell whether a female voice was part of the mix despite straining her ears.

There was only one way to find out if the woman was nearby. Sneaking across the open-air platform to the next car, she ever so slowly slid open the door. Peeking through the sliver into the corridor beyond, Aurianna could see three men standing between her and yet another stack of boxes, presumably filled with those sticks of death.

Something wasn't right. The figures ahead weren't just standing still. They weren't moving at all. This was an unnatural stillness, and a sudden chill crept up her spine. Ever so slowly she pushed on the door, widening the gap and expanding her view.

A swath of colorless fabric flashed into that view, bright even in the dim moonlight streaming in through the side windows of the passenger compartment. It was a long cloak of pure white, the hood drawn up, the faintest glimpse of fire-red locks just below the edge of the massive hood. The robe was awash with a strange bluish glow. Aurianna couldn't see the woman's face, couldn't make out any other details. But the stranger was turned in her direction, almost as if expecting this moment, this meeting.

"Who are you?" Aurianna asked as she stepped into the room.

The woman's hands came up and ignited. Two small orbs of flame, simultaneously blue hot and bright red, lay placidly there on top of her outstretched palms.

Aurianna took another step, her voice rising in pitch and intensity.

"Who are you?"

The woman still didn't speak, but she began to walk slowly backward, ever closer to the door at her back.

The door swung open of its own accord, and the woman turned to leave the car.

Aurianna rushed forward, reaching out for the woman's cloak, but she seemed to move faster than was humanly possible. Aurianna chased her through the open door and into the next car, which turned out to be the coal car. Coal was stored on either side of the pathway until it was needed up ahead in the furnace.

She chased the woman through the next door and into the heat-filled engine room. The coal in here was normally kept hot and burning by the Pyros who worked on the trains.

But no one was here now. Where were the coalmen? How was the train running without Pyrokinetics?

The woman must be doing it somehow. She must, indeed, be a Kinetic, despite showing indications of something far greater. Those flaming orbs were beyond the scope of any Kinetic.

Who and what was she then?

She felt the anger in her rise, fury pounding a rhythmic pulse in her head and in her fingertips. A sizzle went up her arms, the sensation of fire and chill simultaneously battling for dominance in her veins.

The heat became unbearable. It felt as if the coals themselves were alight within her body, and a strangely familiar sensation began to fill her up. The feeling was, in one way, warm and comfortable, yet it also felt frightening in its intensity. The edges of her vision began to blur and turn hazy red, and in her mind's eye she saw flames engulfing the room around her.

All of this coalesced into a tiny ball of condensed rage, the symphony of sensations tensing inside her, ready to be let loose. She could still make out the form of the woman up ahead, but the figure was now leaning against the wall, attempting to stop herself from sliding down onto the floor. This scene disappeared as a dark cloud of emotion washed across Aurianna's vision.

She knew she had to end this, knew stopping the train by any means necessary had to be her primary goal. Some small part of her was overwhelmed by the need to find out more about this

"Enchantress" and discover her motivation for doing all of this. What was her purpose? Did she know who Aurianna was? Is that why she had planned on kidnapping her? Or was something even more insidious going on?

None of that mattered now as the train full of explosives continued to steam along at an insane pace, intent on its final deadly destination.

The woman half crawled, half walked to the open side of the engine room, thrashing her arms out in search of handholds. For a moment, Aurianna was unable to move, her feet seemingly glued to the floor. The other figure had found the ladder and was climbing up to the top of the train in haste.

Feeling her legs unstick, Aurianna rushed after her, fighting the sudden bracing wind accompanying her journey to the frightening zenith of the metal monster which continued to sprint down the tracks on its way to destruction.

The height was dizzying, and as she lifted herself onto the top of the train, her knees buckled. The woman, who had only moments before been crawling around weakly on all fours, was standing still and straight, patiently waiting for Aurianna to stand up.

For whatever reason, she wasn't attacking. Even out here in the open, the light was too dim to see much. The woman was backlit by moonlight, making it impossible to discern anything but the glowing white cloak, fabric billowing in the rushing torrent of air that threatened to knock them both from the train and into the deadly lagoon below. The Enchantress might be able to save herself if she truly was a Kinetic and had the foresight and some amount of Aerokinetic power to control a freefall into the darkness.

But Aurianna knew she herself had no such hope if she fell. She took a deep breath as she struggled to her feet.

As before, the woman conjured the flames within her palms, holding her hands out from her body.

When Aurianna attempted to walk toward her, the woman's hand flashed out, unleashing a line of fire at Aurianna's feet.

She jumped back, narrowly avoiding the flame and stumbling to her knees. Her kneecap sang with the jarring pain, and the anger she felt must have shown on her face because the woman began to back up, edging further along the top of the train.

Aurianna got back to her feet and raced forward again, the air around her working in her favor. The figure ahead was still facing her, still backing away.

They would be nearing the next station—soon, she feared. Even if they didn't stop, Aurianna couldn't risk the explosives going off near a populated area. She was exhausted but full of rage. She let the rage fill her up even more, relishing its comfort as the hum of energy once again ballooned within her. Running forward, she chased the woman down the length of the train, safety no longer her concern.

With blinding flashes, her vision switching between unfamiliar images, people she didn't know, places she'd never been.

A deafening noise behind her rocked the entire train as she continued to move forward, the metal under her feet warming up. She began to walk faster, the explosions behind her methodical and timed just as she passed each car.

Was she doing this? Was it the woman? No, that didn't make sense. Her plan was to blow up the whole of Bramosia, not one girl. But if not the Enchantress...

Chunks of wood and metal flew out in every direction, but all of it seemed to be happening beyond her current world, where only she and the woman before her existed.

The flames grew hotter, closer. She began to run again, chasing the figure ahead, who turned around and, staggeringly, began to run as well.

A final eruption, Aurianna's vision reduced to ash and fire, smoke and flame clouding the scene.

She let go. The power pent up within her released, and the world ignited into an inferno of wrath and flames.

Chapter 27

AURIANNA

A faint light behind closed lids. A muffled sound that grew louder every second. A slicing pain forcing eyes to open unwillingly.

Blinking.

Blinking.

Early morning dawn—dark hued and dripping with a blood-red stain—it heralded death and destruction amidst the natural beauty surrounding it.

"Hey! Over here," a voice called from the left. "She's alive!" Lifting her head to look around, the first thing Aurianna saw was a man in a small boat, a stranger staring at her in awe and wonder. The second thing she saw was the flotilla of charred wood floating and bobbing in the choppy waves all around her. And last but not least, the large piece of something beneath her, which was keeping her from sinking to the depths.

Where am I?

Water everywhere.

Perdita Bay. But how?

The man threw a rope to her and proceeded to haul her into the boat. A second figure sat there, a bucket of what smelled like fish at his feet. These were fishermen then. Had they been looking for her, or ...

She remembered. The train. The explosives. Sigi. Those strange men on board. The woman.

The Enchantress.

And the heat. The inescapable, overwhelming heat that had threatened to rip her apart. Whatever had happened to her, she knew she wouldn't be able to explain it.

The men dipped their oars into the water and began to row toward the side of the lagoon closest to Bramosia. Aurianna looked back to where the two men had found her, the wreckage from the train a testament to what she'd done.

And there was no denying what she'd done. For good or for ill, this was all on her.

The question was would they hail her as a hero for stopping the plan to blow up the Imperium and capital city, or would they condemn her for destroying their livelihood? The train system was their main mode of transportation, as well as their means of maintaining communication and stability for the entire civilization.

The *real* question was would anyone believe her story?

Far above them and out across the water behind them, she saw the evidence of her transgression in the distance. The structural beams of the railroad were missing a sizable chunk, and a large section of the tracks destroyed, not to mention the vehicle itself. Even if the other train was still running, the gaping hole between Menos and Ramolay made the train system inoperable and utterly useless until it could be repaired.

There was no telling how long that would take. Aurianna dreaded the inevitable conversations ahead.

The cliff face loomed ahead, getting closer with every passing second. The two fishermen hadn't spoken a word to her throughout the short trip, but they occasionally stole glances at her and then at each other.

They seemed almost . . . afraid of her. Well sure, she'd been floating among the wreckage of the train she'd somehow managed to blow up with glorious abandon.

When the boat docked by the steps at the bottom of the cliff just below the capital city, Aurianna jumped out before either of them had a chance to help her. They seemed loathe to touch her, and she preferred to grant that wish rather than see the look of horror on their faces if they had to touch her again.

Mumbling a swift "thank you" instead, she made her way over to and up the steps cut into the side of the towering landmass. It was a long and painful climb to the top.

* * *

The sun blazed brightly now, signaling a day unlike any other.

No sign of the horde.

They had been running straight for Bramosia when she'd galloped past on Oracle in the night. It seemed now as if they'd never existed.

The excitement of the exploding train must have died out already as well—*how long was I knocked out?*—for there was no one clambering out onto the grounds, no one peering off into the distance.

It should be a day of celebration. Why is no one celebrating?

As she approached the main entrance to the Imperium, Aurianna looked around. Extra guards in the area, at the doors. They glared at her incredulously. She must have looked a frightening mess in her bedraggled state. They did not stop her, however.

She entered the building, one of the guards following her inside.

He ran past her and up the stairs, presumably to inform his not-so-majesty that she had returned.

A shriek erupted to her left, and before she could turn to the sound, a small but exceedingly strong body bowled into her, almost knocking her to the ground. Within seconds, another figure, this one much larger, grabbed her and swept her off her feet.

Leon was swinging her around like a rag doll as Sigi chattered away, something about *dead* and *train* and *explosion*.

Aurianna untangled herself from the pair, noticing Laelia a few feet away. She was staring but made no move to come closer.

Laelia smiled slowly. "Good to see you're not in tiny little pieces." Sigi glared at her. Raising an eyebrow, Laelia asked, "What? Aren't you?"

"Of course I am." Sigi pulled Aurianna into another tight hug. "I've been out—*we've* been out—searching for you for ages. Everyone came running outside when they heard the explosion. Well, everyone not already dealing with the attackers, at least. I came back to get help after you saved my life, and then that blast, and I just thought—"

Aurianna shook her head. "Sigi, I'm not so sure that was me. I mean, I know it seems like it was, and I felt something happening, but the power behind it didn't feel…like it was me." She shook her head a second time. "I know that doesn't make sense. I mean, I'm not capable of blowing up an entire train on my own. I don't think any Kinetic is, are they?"

"Doesn't matter. We're both safe." Sigi frowned, stepping back. "How did you survive that blast? When did you get off the train?" She looked over Aurianna's hair—still damp with lagoon water—her bits of singed clothing… "What the hell happened out there?"

"I wish I knew."

Leon said, "You didn't see anything?"

"I *saw* plenty. I just can't explain any of it." She hesitated. Would they believe her? Did she even believe herself?

Sigi stepped closer, looking her dead in the eye despite being almost a head shorter. "Look, I was there. I almost died because I panicked, and something saved my life somehow. You can tell us."

"Before I do that, someone needs to explain what happened to the hordes of zombie-people I saw running toward the town last night."

Leon answered, "I heard the alarm go off at the Imperium, and by the time I ran across town to get here, the guards had a solid wall of rock and magma up on both sides of town. It was some crazy shit, I'll tell you. For a while, they kept trying to throw themselves at the barrier, but the Dusters and Pyros had it mostly handled, so the rest of us helped to restrain the horde. They're down in the cells, but nobody knows if they'll come back to themselves or not." He hesitated. "Or if they'll remember any of it."

"They just... let you take them in?"

"Let? No, it was pretty intense trying to get them all tied up. Even with half the Imperium helping out. The City Guard brought out the Energy disruptors after nothing else was working."

"Energy disruptors?"

"Sorry. They're these weapons that fire out a wire with a little hook in it that attaches to the skin. Then it shocks them."

"*Shocks* them?"

"Yeah, so they lose control of their movements and can't fight back." At Aurianna's look of bewilderment, Leon added, "Well, it's not like we use them very often. Only when absolutely necessary. They tried making some strong enough for the Volanti one time, but it didn't work. Anyways, once we got most of them onto stretchers and carried down to the cells, Theron took off to check on his family. Promised he'd be back to help search for you, but we haven't heard from him. It's a shame Sigi here was off following your stupid ass into the great wide open. We could've used some more muscle around here."

Aurianna turned to face her friend. "And why *were* you following me, Sigi? How did you know I would leave?"

The girl blushed. "I didn't. I was downstairs talking to Edelina when you walked right by us and out the door. I knew you hadn't seen me, and I worried about what you might be up to, especially after that speech you gave last night. I was just looking out for you. When I got near the stables, you were already flying out into the horde, completely in the opposite direction from where I thought you'd be going. Someone had just brought a rental horse back when I ran up in a panic. I think I scared the hell out of the stablemaster when I grabbed the reins right out of his hands and took off after you." She smiled to herself. "He didn't say a word when I returned the poor creature. I was soaked to the bone from my little near-death cliff diving experience. My shaking had more to do with what had happened than the cold water."

Aurianna had a moment of panic. "Where's Oracle? Where's my horse?"

"Don't worry. I brought her back with me. She's fine."

Leon took up the tale. "Sigi showed up, soaking wet, as we were transporting the zombie-people down to the prison. Raving about you and the train, and insisting we had to find you. We grabbed Javen, of course"—he looked back at Laelia, flipping his thumb in her direction as she glared at him—"and this one. We convinced the aforementioned stablemaster to lend us some horses at a steep rate. We were about to head out when the explosion lit up the sky." He chuckled. "Honey, it was something else, I tell you. A whole crowd came running outside again, but we took off to look for you. Sigi here was in hysterics at that point. Pretty sure Javen was as well."

Blowing out a breath she hadn't realized she was holding, Aurianna said, "Well, I heard these men on the train talking about blowing up Bramosia." A look of horror made its way around the group. "They had a shit-ton of explosives all lined up in the cars. There only seemed to be a few of the henchmen on board, but no one else, not even the Pyros who run the engine. Just her."

"Her?" Sigi asked.

"I mean, it had to be the Enchantress."

"She was there?"

"Yeah. At least I think it was her. Bright-red hair. Kinetic power, or something like it." A collision against her back made Aurianna gasp in fright... until she realized who it was. "Javen."

He turned her around, grasping her shoulders and burying his face in her neck. "Aurianna, I..." He squeezed tighter.

Leon spoke for him. "We've all been out looking for you since last night. Javen here refused to come inside to rest." Slapping the other boy on the back, he smiled. "Told you we'd find her."

Javen finally stepped back, holding her at arm's length as his eyes roamed over every inch of her, searching for signs of injury. His gaze stopped at her neck; a brief look of surprise flashed across his features before morphing back into relief. She had forgotten about the necklace in the chaos. Her mother's necklace. Sadness took over, and Aurianna felt hot tears spilling down her cheeks.

Laelia said, hesitation in her voice, "It's . . . okay to be upset. You've had a very traumatic experience."

Aurianna didn't correct the girl. She didn't want to have to explain that a piece of jewelry, no matter how special, was actually the cause of her tears.

Javen was still holding onto her shoulders. He pulled her into another embrace as her tears continued to flow, the moisture soaking through his shirt.

She finally pulled away, shaking her head. "I appreciate you all searching for me with everything that was going on, but I don't have the answers you're looking for."

Sigi's eyes widened. "Aurianna, we didn't go searching for you because we wanted answers. You're our friend, and you tried to save me, and I just…" It was Sigi's turn to shake her head. "We care about you, okay? I know you don't want to hear that, but—"

"There she is!" All four Magisters were striding across the hall toward them. Magister Garis, the one who had spoken, looked utterly relieved, as did Magister Martes, but the faces of the other two were hard to read.

Magister Daehne said, "We sent out search parties in multiple directions. We weren't sure where you might be, or if…" He seemed to collect himself. "You're here now though. The Magnus and the Consils would like to speak with you."

"The Consils want to see me?"

"Well, they are the governing body here. I'm pretty sure they'd like to know how and why their train blew up." His pointed look in her direction was filled with accusation.

Did he know it was her? Did he suspect? Was she even sure it *was* her who had caused the explosive surges?

Of course he suspected. He was the only person, aside from that one Void, with knowledge of her doing anything of the kind, albeit on a much smaller scale.

And of course it had been her. She had felt that familiar burning within her core, the need to release a power that seemed to come from nowhere and threatened to boil her alive from the inside out.

The entire group followed the Magisters outside and into the town. The day was beginning for most people, and shop vendors were carefully laying out their wares and setting up signs announcing the day's offerings and discounts.

Aurianna was forced to ignore it all as she was swept with the others up the hill to the Consilium.

They entered together, the Praefect standing duty informing them they were expected as he opened the door to the audience chamber. The young man started to block her friends from entering, but one look at Leon's massive form and fiery gaze made him change his mind.

Javen grabbed her hand and gently squeezed, then he didn't let go. They all walked into the massive room, stopping just short of the figures seated along the curve of the opposite wall. The Consils had their customary seats, and the Magnus sat in his at the end.

Another chair had been brought in for the occasion, and Aurianna was surprised to see Pharis sitting there beside his father.

He was glowering at her. *Fantastic.*

As Aurianna looked around at the faces of the Consils, one of them—a dark-haired but slightly balding man with fair skin and light-brown eyes—spoke up. "Since we are here to meet and discuss the events of the last day, we won't waste any unnecessary time. You have met with us once before, but we have not made proper introductions. I am Jonn Etling, the Consil for Ramolay." He nodded toward a woman who sat beside him.

She was a round woman with honey-brown hair and tawny, olive-toned skin. Clearing her throat, the woman said, "I'm Margery Rigas, and I'm the Consil for Menos."

The next to speak was a man who appeared to be much older than the rest, though his exact age was difficult to determine. "Cormick Lowe, Consil for Eadon." His deep golden-brown skin was wrinkled, but there was a keenness in his dark eyes. He had the physique of a scholar and salt-and-pepper hair that had probably once been a deep shade of black.

A woman with pale skin and hair, piercing blue eyes, and the most unfriendly expression of the group leaned back in her chair before speaking. "I am Giana Rossi. I am the Consil for Vanito." She was scanning the faces gathered before them as if looking for something.

The last of the Consils was a mustachioed male with deep russet skin and eyes that conveyed his impatient desire to get on with the proceedings. "Anson Glaeser, Rasenforst." He leaned forward in his seat. "It has come to our attention that our transportation system has been destroyed. Explain."

Abrupt. To the point. *Very well*, she thought. "Last night, I left the Imperium and walked over to the stables. I saw a woman matching the description of the Enchantress. The one you people keep insisting I'm supposed to stop." She paused for emphasis. "So I followed her with the intent of doing that." The Magnus was frowning at her in confusion, but she continued. "She boarded the train. I just knew something bad was going down, and I needed to get on as well. I took my horse and followed her to Menos. I boarded there, but the train didn't stop very long at all, and it kept slowing down and speeding up. Something was obviously wrong, so I snuck around and heard some men on board talking about sabotaging the train."

"Sabotaging?" Consil Etling from Ramolay, the man who had first introduced himself, seemed baffled.

"Yes. They had explosives on board and planned on blowing up the train as it passed back around to Bramosia."

The woman who had introduced herself as Margery Rigas from Menos spoke up. "You say these men *spoke*?"

"Yes, ma'am. This wasn't like the ones poisoned by dragonblood. You've obviously heard about that. It seemed the men were working for the Enchantress though. They kept referring to 'the boss.' " Cocking her head to the side, Aurianna glared at the woman. "Aren't you focusing on the wrong part of the story here? I said they were going to blow up Bramosia."

"Ridiculous," the Magnus said, squirming in his seat. "Why would anyone want to blow up the town?"

Sigi spoke up. "Perhaps someone trying to start a war between Kinetics and non-Kinetics? Ring a bell?" When he glared at her outburst, she added, "Sir."

Anson Glaeser from Rasenforst looked confused, and it was making him irritable. "So she decided to blow up the train early? Why?"

Hesitating, Aurianna looked at Javen, who was staring quizzically at her. He squeezed her hand again. "I don't think it was her. She was able to conjure orbs of flame in her hands, but—"

"Not possible," the Consil interrupted. "You clearly have no concept of how Kinetic power even works. She must have pulled up magma from a crack in the ground. That's what you saw."

"Conjuring is not something we do, young lady," the Magnus offered. "This isn't a magic show. *No one* has the ability to create elements. Only bend them to their will."

"Well, I know what I saw!" Her anger was seething just beneath the surface, like magma, ready to boil over. Her body warmed, the room suddenly too hot, and she closed her eyes as she took deep breaths. After a moment, she continued, "Look, I don't care what you think. The point is . . . these men had apparently been hired to kidnap me at some point later in the night after blowing up a good chunk of the capital. They said as much. She must know what I am."

"And what are you, then?" Consil Rossi's voice was quiet in the sudden stillness of the room, the coldness in her face intensifying with her words.

Out of the corner of her eye, Aurianna saw her friends' incredulity at that little revelation—the fact that she could have been the victim of a kidnapping plot. She had almost forgotten the man's words on the train. *Brought her here from the future, they did.* Who else could they have been talking about? It hadn't really mattered at the time next to the immediate issue of the explosives, but now that it came rushing back to her, the thought chilled her to the bone.

She sighed. "I don't know. I really don't. The words of the prophecy make no sense to me. But if this woman believes I'm a threat to her, then perhaps I am. Somehow."

"You haven't answered the original question, my dear. How exactly *did* the train blow up?"

Aurianna looked each of them in the eye in turn, saving Pharis for last. She had avoided his gaze throughout all of it because she hadn't wanted to see that disgusted look on his face. Now, it seemed to be mixed with concern, but he was still frowning at her. His gaze slid to Javen, and down to their joined hands. His frown reverted to a glare. Did he truly hate Javen that much? How could Pharis believe he was involved in his sister's disappearance?

That thought triggered another. On the train, she had wondered if perhaps this elusive rebellion was somehow involved. Maybe the woman wasn't a Kinetic and Aurianna had just imagined the flames in her hands. If she was working with the rebellion, it would explain the desire to blame Kinetics and start a war.

But she kept these thoughts to herself for the moment until she had time to mull them over further. Just now, everyone was staring at her, waiting for her answer.

The truth was not her friend, but it was all she had.

"I think...maybe...I did it."

Gasps of shock mixed with harsh whispers that echoed off the walls of the chamber. Throughout the ordeal, the Magisters had been standing off to the side. Magister Daehne stepped forward as the room took in her words.

He cleared his throat loudly to gain their attention before addressing the seated figures. "Magnus, Consils, I believe I need to interrupt here to explain something." He glanced at her, pursing his lips. "Several weeks ago, during our very first training session, something happened in the tunnels. It hasn't happened since, so I thought perhaps it was a fluke."

When the man didn't speak further, the Magnus prompted him. "Tell us."

Nodding, the Magister said, "We were working at one of the magma pits. She created a small explosion. Small, but far more than she should have been capable of her first time. And it wasn't like any explosion I've ever witnessed. There'd been an accident in class with another student on the same day, but his was the typical sort of situation when things go wrong. The magma usually creates more of a glow and erupts as it gets out of hand. In her case, I never saw what the magma actually did. All I saw was a bright light followed by the explosion. Blackened an entire section of the wall and the floor around her. I could tell something was upsetting her while she was focusing, but then that happened, and the Void who was assisting us reacted quite badly to the whole situation. He was frightened by it, and I guess he had a panic attack of some sort. We didn't speak of it again, and nothing else has happened, but she clearly has an affinity for Fire."

The Magnus looked at her with a small smile, as the others stared in wonderment. She hadn't told anyone about that day, not even her friends. Sigi was gazing with a puzzled look until her face lit up with some memory. Pharis was staring at her as well, his mouth agape to reveal his surprise.

Consil Rigas leaned forward, her next words spoken with great care and deliberation. "Are you suggesting this girl caused that massive explosion?"

"I believe it's possible, yes." Magister Daehne glanced between the Consils, nervousness mixed with apprehension, as murmuring erupted in the room. All were aghast at his words, arguing back and forth as if no one else were in the room.

All except Pharis, who stared at Aurianna with a strange contemplative expression. She felt laid bare before him, before them all. The irony was she had done exactly what she'd been brought here to do, yet they were angry and fearful at the thought.

Hypocrites.

The Magnus finally turned away from the bickering, the outer corners of his mouth quirking up, and said, "Well, it seems I was right, after all. The Arcanes will be pleased to know you've fulfilled the prophecy. We've found no other survivors from the explosion, so I'm guessing the Enchantress is dead. Or at least, I hope so. We'll scour the area to determine if any others are alive, but—"

"Hold on, Magnus." The Vanitian Consil was staring at Aurianna with obvious disdain. "This woman is claiming to have caused a massive explosion. No amount of fire in the train's furnace could have created an eruption of that size. Forgive me, Magister Daehne, but heating up a little magma is not the same thing."

"Did you forget about the explosives she mentioned, Consil?" Leon asked.

"No, Kinetic. I haven't. But I know the fire would have needed to reach those explosives. The coal in the engine is hot, but it's still a very small fire. It could not have reached far beyond itself."

Aurianna just stared at the woman. She had no explanation. What she had experienced defied logic, and she knew she would sound ridiculous if she spoke it aloud. But it was the truth—the only truth she had to give—so she chose her words carefully. "The fire didn't come from just the engine."

"Oh? And where, pray tell, did it come from then?"

"It started in the engine, but it . . . it expanded. I could feel it coming from somewhere else as well, but I didn't—I still don't—really understand it. Just felt like I was going to boil from the inside out, and the heat was unbelievable."

"You're telling me you pulled it from somewhere besides the furnace?"

"Yes, that's what I'm telling you. I don't know anything else. I just know the cars started blowing up, one after the other, as I was chasing her up on top of the train. Then everything went dark, and I woke up in the water. These two fishermen found me, but they seemed kinda scared of me."

"You blew up our central transportation system, and you don't even know if she's dead?" Cormick Lowe from Eadon asked indignantly.

"She has to be. Unless someone found her floating in the wreckage as well, I don't see how she could have survived. And those men . . . I don't know." Tears formed in her eyes at the thought, despite what they'd been planning. "I guess I killed them as well." She had never killed anything, let alone a person. Sniffling but determined to show strength in the face of this impromptu trial, she continued, "But there are other means of transportation. Horses, the airship ferry service. It might take a little longer to get places, but it should be okay until the railway is fixed, right?"

"Don't presume to tell us what is or isn't okay," retorted Consil Rossi. The Vanitian's glare was icy, almost cruel.

"I'm just saying it's worth it if she's been stopped, right?" Aurianna looked to the Magnus for confirmation.

He was nodding. "Indeed. If the prophecy has been fulfilled, all is well. The Arcanes can confirm her death somehow, I'm sure. Everything else is logistics." His smile widened even further. "Our business here is concluded then."

The Regulus threw a piercing gaze in his father's direction but didn't comment.

The Consils—after glaring at the Magnus for a moment—conceded and rose as one. They left the audience chamber, promising to send someone to verify with the Arcanes later in the day. The Magnus and the Regulus led the way out of the building. They traveled as a group back to the Imperium. Aurianna could only think about the stables. She needed to check on Oracle and see for herself that the horse was indeed okay. After some food and rest though. She was exhausted beyond comprehension.

Sigi was frowning and kept stealing glances at Aurianna. Finally, Aurianna slowed down, trying to pull her aside, and asked, "What?"

"Nothing." The girl kept walking and didn't look back.

Chapter 28

AURIANNA

When they returned to the Imperium, the last thing Aurianna wanted to do was more talking. Her brain could think of nothing but shower, bed, and food. In that order.

Javen kissed the back of her hand, promising to meet back up with her to get some food after she had rested. There was a sadness in his eyes, but he didn't say anything else. Leon gave her a lazy two-fingered salute to his temple and followed Javen back outside. Theron hadn't returned yet, so they were going to take some horses out toward his family's place to see what was holding him up.

Sigi didn't speak a word, just stepped into one of the guard rooms at the side of the front entrance. Aurianna realized Laelia was nowhere around. She couldn't remember seeing her in the Consil chambers either. Where had she gone?

Dragging herself slowly up the spiral staircase and to her room, Aurianna managed to find the energy for her much-needed shower, the hot water a balm to her fractured nerves. She stood still as it scalded her skin, relishing the heat she'd only recently been so keen to rid herself of. No release this time, the fire within her feeding on the steam and mist that enveloped her, comforted her.

Not stopping to change into nightclothes, Aurianna fell onto the bed, her hair dripping rivulets onto her pillow. Eyes closed, her body relaxed into a deep sleep.

Someone was calling her name.

She opened her eyes and rolled over, surprised to see an illuminated orb—swirling amethyst-colored eddies within—floating midway between floor and ceiling. Her mind and body were both drawn to it. Far off in some forgotten corner of the building, a breathy whisper continued to speak her name. Not only the name she'd known all her life. She could also hear the other.

Her true name. *Dawn.*

The two names alternating in a singsong voice.

Rising from the bed, Aurianna continued to stare at the orb.

The purple glow was mesmerizing, and she quickly forgot about the strangeness of the situation as she found herself following the moving ball of light out of her room and into the hallway beyond.

Aurianna followed the orb down the stairs and into the bowels of the Imperium. The purple orb floated down one of the tunnels, taking her far away from anything she recognized. She saw no people and heard no sounds beyond the insistent voice. Farther and farther she went into unknown territory.

Then…one minute she was walking down a tunnel, the next she was standing in a room filled with dark shadows, a room she had no memory of entering. The orb she'd been following expanded, stretching to fill the area and chase the shadows away. The light was no longer spherical but a giant crystallized shape topped with jagged spikes that protruded in various sizes from every surface of the object. It still glowed from within, the amethyst hue now blazing even brighter.

Something was indeed familiar about all of this, but she couldn't place it in her memory. It called to her, the light within beckoning, pulling her forward. Aurianna stepped further into the massive chamber, her hand outstretched before her. She didn't try to fight the tugging sensation that brought her closer and closer.

The glow intensified. She reached out with a tentative hand, aching to touch one of the jagged edges, unsure of why she had an overwhelming urge to do so.

Her finger inches from a colored spike, the silence in the room turned dense, her ears beginning to ache with the pressure. Cracks appeared in the air, like a shattered mirror, reflecting the light along its fractured edges. The light reached into the cracks, filling them up, then a blinding flash forced her to cover her eyes with both arms.

She awoke with a start, soaked with sweat. The light was gone. The glowing mass of jagged crystals was gone.

A dream. That's all.

But it had felt so incredibly real, and so incredibly familiar. But those tunnels were a labyrinth. She would never be able to find her way back to that room again, even if it were real.

A buzzing from the far wall. Javen must have come to check on her and bring her down to the dining hall. She donned a robe and opened the door. Javen was leaning against the door frame, a crooked smile on his face. He leaned into the room a little way, but his smile faltered when he saw how frazzled she was.

"I'm sorry. Did I scare you?"

"No, I . . . I just . . . need to get dressed." When he didn't move back from the doorway, she looked at him pointedly. Throwing his hands up, he backed away slowly, his gaze intense as she closed the door. Her skin was clammy and sticky from sweat. Another quick shower was definitely in order—a cold one this time.

Aurianna dressed quickly and went down to dinner with Javen. When they reached the dining hall and loaded up their trays, he led her to a table near the back of the room. Leon and Theron were seated there already, talking in whispers as they scarfed down mouthfuls of food.

Theron looked up at her and smiled as they approached. "Well, well, the hero has decided to grace us with her presence."

She scowled at his words. "Not funny."

He looked at her, contemplation settling in his gaze. "Wasn't trying to be. I'm serious, Aurianna. My parents owe you a great debt. We all do."

"Your parents? Are they okay?"

He sighed. "I went to check on them after the explosion. They weren't home. Turns out they'd left on the previous train. Dad was in talks with a guy in Ramolay who wanted to buy some of our farming equipment."

Aurianna took a seat across the table from Leon, by Theron. Javen grinned at Theron before elbowing Leon as he sat down beside him. "They taking up farming now in Ramolay, buddy? Not exactly the land of greener pastures. Gonna till up some underwater soil?"

Leon elbowed him back, his muscled arms plowing into Javen so hard he almost fell off the bench. "Ha-ha. We do have all that land up top above the waterways, you know. This guy owns some of it, I guess."

Theron nodded. "Yeah, and my parents had gone to talk to the man in person. They were staying at his home for the night, but they'd been up top only hours before that explosion. Had the train blown up closer to Ramolay, even the town below could have been in danger, especially if any shrapnel managed to land there. The man lives right on the bank of the lagoon, near the lifts."

"The lifts?" Aurianna asked.

"They're powered by electric Energy and take people down to the town when they arrive by train."

She remembered the metal boxes she'd seen from the train on their trip to Eadon. "I'm so sorry, Theron. I tried my best to keep the damage minimal."

"What are you sorry for? I'm thanking you. Without you, they might . . ." Theron couldn't finish his sentence.

She nodded. "I just wish I understood exactly what happened."

Theron's eyebrows raised. "I think it's pretty clear what happened."

"I don't know." She thought about the lives she might have taken. *Did I kill those men on board?* The one that attacked her must have fallen into the water—drowned or, more likely, been killed on impact—though she had been unable to watch. She knew it had been self-defense, but she still didn't like to think about it.

Or the loss of her mother's necklace.

Anxious to change the subject, she asked, "Has anyone heard from the Magnus? Has he spoken to the Arcanes yet?"

Javen looked at her strangely. "Not yet. Why?"

"I need to speak to the Arcanes as well."

"I'm sure he'll let us know what they say."

"No, not that. I need to know how they plan on getting me back home."

No one moved, but she felt their eyes on her. Did they not realize she would want to return home, to see Larissa again? To find out what changes had been made to the future, to the world she'd grown up in and the people she'd known all her life?

Leon spoke first, clearing his throat. "So, you're leaving then?" He threw a quick glance in Javen's direction.

"Of course. I came here on a specific mission. I completed that mission. At least, I think I did. My family is back home. My life is there. I want to see what my world looks like now."

Nodding, he continued, "Okay, then. Let's get you home."

* * *

No one escorted her down to the underground rooms of the Arcanes. This was something she needed to do alone.

The Arcane who opened the door led her into the main area. Simon was standing behind a counter, three of his brethren with him. He was smiling sadly at her.

"You want to go home."

She was surprised at his words. "Well, yes, of course I do."

Nodding, he stared at the table before him for a moment before looking back up at her. "Are you sure?"

"I'm sure. As long as everything is done." When Simon didn't respond, she asked, "Has the Magnus been to speak with you?"

One of the other Arcanes answered. "He called us into his chambers several hours ago."

When no further explanation was given, Aurianna looked at the Arcanes in front of her pointedly, aiming her gaze mostly at Simon, who was still refusing to look at her.

Still nothing.

Huffing, she said, "And?"

Another of the Arcanes shook his head. He hesitated before speaking, wringing his hands in front of him. "And we are aware of the entire story. The woman on the train is no longer here."

"So it's over?"

"Nothing is ever over." Simon looked back at her, sadness in his eyes.

"You said I was here to stop that woman. I stopped her. Why can't I go home now?"

"No one is stopping you. You may leave whenever you wish. It's important that you follow your instincts."

"What are you talking about, Simon?"

Gesturing for her to follow him, he led Aurianna off into the rows of shelving. The others didn't follow.

He seemed to be reading the titles as they passed the tomes, but suddenly he stopped and faced her. "Aurianna, there is nothing I can tell you that will make this any easier. The Darkness comes for us all eventually, seeking to turn us away from our destinies, but you must follow the path that feels right, that seems to lead to the best outcome. Perhaps this time things will work themselves out."

"I followed my instinct to go after that woman on the train. If I hadn't, a lot of people would probably be dead, and according to your prophecy, a war would have begun that leads to the future I know."

"You followed your courage. And that is all we can hope for."

She was shaking her head at his words. "No, Simon. That wasn't courage. I was *terrified*."

He smiled at her, his eyes lighting up. "Of course you were. But that's the point, isn't it? There is no bravery without fear. If there had been nothing to fear, anyone could have done it. You faced your fear." He leaned in closer, whispering, "And you faced your own Darkness."

"If that's true, then I can go home."

"If you wish."

She was getting nowhere. If the choice was hers, she already knew her decision. Simon was just playing mind games with her. Maybe the Magnus had put him up to it, still intent on marrying her off to the Regulus.

"And what of the Magnus then? What will he say?"

Simon's eyebrow shot up, bitter humor written on his features.

"You know exactly what the Magnus will say. But the decision does not belong to him, no matter what he thinks. Your ability to get home rests on the simplest of acts."

"And what is that?"

"Ask."

"But you just said he won't let me go."

"Not him."

"Who then?"

He lifted his hand, palm upward. "An Aether Stone is all that is needed." As he spoke, his hand was filled with an intense purple glow surrounding a small crystalline object, amethyst in color.

"How did you..." Aurianna bit her lip as she shook her head in frustration. She knew he wouldn't answer her. "So, I just ask the stone...and...I go home?"

Simon laughed. "You are not asking the Aether Stone for permission. You are asking the gods, the Essence. Only they can grant your wish to return. Just say the words 'In the name of the Essence, I ask for safe passage back to my time. I will neither disturb your realm nor attempt to stay. Take me back to the moment I left.' Hopefully, they will do exactly as you request."

"Hopefully?"

He shrugged. "They won't let any harm come to you, I promise."

Aurianna thought for a moment. "What about the stone that my aunt gave me? Why did she say it didn't work anymore?"

"Because it no longer contained magic. Over time, the Darkness took its magic. But that doesn't mean it cannot be healed."

"Then why are you giving me another?"

"The one you have may slowly regain energy as it pulls in power from this world, but it still needs a jump start." He held his hand out to her, offering the Aether Stone in his hand. "This one is ready now."

Nodding, Aurianna took it from him, turning it over in her hand, staring at the bright illumination within. Aurianna was reminded of her disturbing dream. Perhaps it was destiny's way of telling her it was time to go home.

Home.

* * *

Pharis was still glaring at her as if she'd done something to anger him, but she couldn't figure out what it could be. He should be happy that their marriage seemed to be dissolving far easier than they'd originally hoped.

The Magnus sat in his regal chair, his son standing beside him. Aurianna had known this part wouldn't be easy, and part of her had been tempted to leave without telling them, if for no other reason than to avoid this very conversation.

"Absolutely not. We have barely begun our investigation into the incident." The Magnus was seething, but he was doing a decent job of holding most of it in. She could see it in his eyes though—the rage at being outmaneuvered at the last moment.

She said, "The Arcanes say the woman on the train is gone. They gave me a way home." She stared at the man for a moment, willing strength into her voice. "I'm not asking permission. I'm letting you know as a courtesy. You cannot keep me here like a prisoner. You have enough of those to deal with already."

"That is completely beside the point! The people we are holding will be let loose the moment they calm down and can be interrogated. No one is trying to imprison you. I'm merely stating that we may still need you here."

"For what? To marry your son?" Pharis glanced at her sharply, as if he'd forgotten about that piece of the puzzle. "You may have your claws in *him*, but I am free to make my own choices. You aren't in charge of me. I come from a different world, and you can't stop me from leaving." Aurianna knew that wasn't entirely true. He could have her arrested and detained, but she was hoping that he wouldn't risk the public outcry. People in Rasenforst and elsewhere were already angry that their fellow citizens were still sitting in the cells beneath the Imperium.

The Magnus turned an interesting shade of puce at her last comment, but he merely stared at her for a long moment. Pharis—the Regulus—was looking off to a spot on the wall behind her, seemingly trying to pretend he wasn't even in the room.

At last, the older man said, "So be it. I ask that you give it more thought before jumping to any hasty decision."

"Of course." But she had already made up her mind. She planned on leaving as soon as she'd said her goodbyes.

Aurianna left the room and went down to the main hall, determined to find Sigi. She asked a guardsman at the entrance to the Imperium who told her Sigi was at dinner.

The dining hall was almost empty at that late hour, most Kinetics having already eaten. Sigi was probably scheduled to work third shift. She normally ate at this time when she had to be on duty at midnight. Aurianna spotted the woman at a table by herself, but as she approached, Sigi's face turned thunderous and she looked down at her plate.

What did I do?

Fumbling for something to say, she was surprised when Sigi spoke first. "I should have known that was you."

"What was me?"

"Down in the tunnels. We saw the aftereffects of your little Fire training stunt, and you didn't say a word."

"Shh!" Aurianna exclaimed, sliding into the seat across from her. "Well, I was kinda embarrassed."

"Embarrassed? That's freaking awesome! You're like some kind of super-Kinetic."

Aurianna shook her head vehemently. "No, Sigi, I'm not. I didn't do it."

The other girl's face dropped. "But you said—"

"I know what I said, and I meant it. It was my fault. But that power wasn't mine, not completely. I know that doesn't make any sense, but it felt very external."

"Of course it's external. That's how Kinetic power works. We don't have any internal magic or anything."

Gesturing with her hand, Aurianna said, "I know, I know. I just mean that it . . . Sigi, the only thing even close to magma on that train was the furnace full of heated coals. But the Consils were right. It was too small and too far away from the explosives and from me for the majority of the time. Whatever happened, it wasn't Kinetic. I'm sure of that."

"Doesn't matter, right? You destroyed her and her plans."

"Maybe." Aurianna looked at her new friend and attempted a halfhearted smile. "You're mad at me about something though."

"Maybe."

"Can you tell me what I did?"

"It's not something you did, Aurianna. It's what you're about to do."

"I don't—"

"Yes, you do. We both know you miss home. I get it. I do. But you never stop to think about anyone else."

"That's not exactly fair, you know. I left my aunt behind and came back in time to help people I didn't even know."

Sigi slowly shook her head. "No, you came here to find out about your past. Your parents and all that. Don't pretend that wasn't your main motivation."

"Well, yeah, that was part of it." Aurianna looked down, biting her lip. "My hesitation about my powers wasn't about me not wanting to help. I really didn't think I *could* help. But I did, somehow. And you're right. I do miss home. I miss my aunt." She let her gaze travel back up to meet her friend's questioning stare.

"And what about your friends?"

"I told you I didn't really have any close friends. They weren't real friends, anyways."

"And yet here you are, with a group of people who *want* to be your friends, and you still sit there with a chip on your shoulder about trusting people. We spent all night looking for you, you ass."

Aurianna was taken aback. Sigi had never spoken to her like that before. "There's no reason to be like that. What if you had the opportunity to see your mom again? Wouldn't you take it? Larissa is like a mom to me."

Sigi stood up, grabbing her tray. "But I can't, can I? My mom is dead!" With that, she stormed off, returning her tray and exiting the room.

That went well.

Trudging downstairs, Aurianna made her way to the stables to say goodbye to Oracle.

She questioned the stablemaster about the tack from the day before, but he was distracted by his work and seemed perplexed by her question, stating that he normally had nothing to do with the tacking unless he was personally renting out a horse. The man confirmed that Sigi had returned Oracle with another horse later in the night, dropping them off in a hurry.

"Them in the horde was a fright to the horses," he said. "I had enough on my hands as it was. But I did have to untack both the ones that guardswoman brought in. She just run off, yelling something about the train."

Realizing she was getting nowhere, Aurianna left the man to his duties and walked back to Oracle's stall, opening the door and entering the small space. It smelled terrible, but she assumed a person got used to it over time—maybe even took pleasure in it. Oracle seemed happy to see her, nuzzling her neck as she stroked the animal's face gently. She whispered her farewells in the only way she knew how, hugging her horse's neck as tears coursed down her cheeks.

Somehow, this goodbye was just as hard as she expected the others to be.

* * *

She didn't see Sigi again until the next day.

Across the horizon, the view of Eresseia was clear, the sky alight with the intensity of the midmorning sun. There was no train in the distance, no plume of smoke or piercing whistle to mark its arrival or departure. Those man-made sights and sounds might be absent for quite some time, but the beauty of the natural landscape was breathtaking, nonetheless.

Everyone had gathered at the front of the Imperium to say farewell to Aurianna before she returned home. Most of the crowd were just curious onlookers, but some of the Youngers were in attendance. The boy she'd noticed smiling at her that first day was standing beside Sigi's sister, Hilda. They all looked sad to see her go, despite barely knowing her. The Magnus and Pharis were there, a bit removed and wearing matching grim looks.

She spotted her group of friends, including Sigi.

The girl was standing off to the side of the crowd, arms wrapped around her torso, looking alone amidst the crowd. Even their friends seemed to be giving her space. Aurianna wondered if they'd been fighting. About her?

She sighed in frustration. This was not how she'd wanted things to end between them—between any of them. She understood Sigi's feelings, but going home had always been the plan. The thought at the forefront of her mind every day had been getting back to see Larissa and to find out if her actions here had made a difference in her world. Everyone had known this was only a temporary situation.

Theron and Leon came forward, entering the wide circle where she stood. Theron was customarily somber in his expression, but there was an ease about it that comforted her. Leon's smile was wide and...was he drunk? Seriously? At ten in the morning?

Leon sauntered up to her, invading her personal space with the ease of the extremely inebriated. "Looking fine this fine morning, darlin'," he slurred in a loud voice that sounded as if he meant to whisper but failed miserably. Everyone in the vicinity had probably heard him. The Magnus frowned even deeper, looking on with disgust. Pharis attempted to ignore them completely.

Aurianna blushed as she chewed on her lower lip. "Thanks. Good to see you too. I see you've had an interesting morning already."

Theron reached up to put a hand on Leon's shoulder. "Just a typical morning for our friend here. He's usually better at hiding it." He leaned forward, murmuring, "I think, with all the excitement, he went a little overboard last night."

"He's still drunk from last night?"

Leon said, "Wanted to send you off right, friend." His eyes were glossy and unfocused, but his speech was, surprisingly, only slightly slurred. "Planned on inviting you, but..." He stopped and looked around in confusion. "Guessing we forgot." He stumbled briefly, catching himself at the last minute.

A voice from behind his massive form piped up. "Wow. Early, even for you, man-whore."

Leon rolled his eyes as he whipped his head around to look at Laelia. "Didn't have a choice. That's the way your mom prefers it."

A dark look stretched across the girl's face. For a moment it seemed like she might hit him, but she only flared her nostrils and said, "Go to hell."

"You're here. Already there."

Laelia wisely chose to ignore him after that, turning to Aurianna. "Look, Sigi feels really bad about whatever you guys were fighting about last night. Said she's embarrassed and wants to know if she can come say goodbye."

"Of course! I didn't want to argue with her either." Not waiting to call Sigi over, Aurianna walked over herself and reached out to hug the other girl. Sigi's face lit up, and she grabbed Aurianna around the middle.

They both stepped back, still holding each other's arms, and stared at one another, eyes brimming with tears. Aurianna spoke first. "I'm sorry, Sigi. I didn't mean anything bad about your mom—"

"No, no, no. I know you didn't. It's just a touchy subject for me, and I overreacted. I'm sorry. And yes, if I could see her again, of course I'd go. You have to go. I'll just miss you. We all will." Sigi sighed. "But I know you have to go."

Theron, who had walked up behind them with Leon and Laelia in tow, said, "I guess we all thought you'd be here a little longer, but we're happy you get to see your aunt again and go back home. Who knows how changed your world will be when you get there?" He smiled, reaching out to shake Aurianna's hand. "I hope all your dreams for your future come true, my friend."

"Same to you," she said, returning his smile along with the handshake. "Please don't think any of this is easy for me. I wish I could take all of you with me, but my life is back in the future with my aunt and whatever plans life has in store for me." She looked around, suddenly registering who was missing. "Where's Javen?"

"Ah." Sigi threw a look around the group, frowning. "I think he's more upset than I am. He said he'd be here." She looked back at Aurianna sympathetically. "I'm sorry, Aurianna. I think you know how he feels."

"But he didn't seem that upset before."

"I know. He just hides it well. Javen's not usually this emotional, but I think he's having a hard time letting go."

Leon leaned in close, looking more sober than he had a few minutes ago. "Seriously though, I'll tell him you said goodbye." He suddenly grabbed her up in a dizzying hug that swept her off her feet, surprising not only her but everyone around them.

When Leon put her back down, he said, "I know I promised to find your parents for you. I'm sorry I didn't have the chance to answer those questions for you. If you could stay a little longer..."

Aurianna shook her head. "No, it's okay. I did want to know about my family, but Larissa *is* my family—the only family I've known, at least. I just want to get back to her."

Leon's characteristic grin was back, a cigar in his mouth that seemed to have appeared out of nowhere. He seemed to be having difficulties following the conversation as he said, "I can't believe you decided to go on an *epic chase* down the top of a *freaking train*. Awesome, by the way." Leon pointed at her as he spoke, only slightly slurring at that point.

Laelia rolled her eyes. "Yeah, that was pretty cool, I guess." She hesitated, standing awkwardly close for several brief seconds before throwing her arms around Aurianna's shoulders and squeezing lightly. Laelia stepped back before Aurianna had a chance to react or hug her back then crossed her arms like it had never happened.

Choosing to give the girl her wish, Aurianna simply smiled at the small group assembled around her. "I'm going to miss you all. Badly." She raised her voice to the crowd. "And all of you, thank you for welcoming me into your home and being so kind to me." A cheer erupted in the back and was echoed by all.

She turned around and walked back to the middle where the Magnus and the Regulus stood. The Magnus gave her a curt nod, not bothering to hide his pout. He quickly turned and retreated into the building without looking back.

She was left standing alone with his son, no one within hearing distance if she spoke softly. Pharis was staring at the ground, suddenly finding his feet incredibly interesting. She moved closer, feeling that leaving without a goodbye was just silly considering all they'd been through together.

"Pharis," she began, waiting for him to look up at her. When he finally did, she continued, "Pharis, I want to thank you for everything you've done—"

"Everything I've done. Really?" he asked snidely.

"Yes, really. I've—"

"Are we actually going to do this?"

"Do what?"

He huffed at her, nostrils flaring as he said, "You're kidding, right? You're just going to stand there and pretend..." Shaking his head, he reached into his pocket, pulling out a small metal object. "Here." He tossed the object at her. "I was planning on giving you that anyways. Have a nice life, Aurianna."

He stalked away from her, forcefully pushing his way through the crowd and back into the building.

What in the hell...?

She opened her hand. It was his lighter, the one he'd teased her about back in her own time, as well as here. Was this just another joke at her expense?

341

None of it mattered though. She was leaving—leaving all of this, all of them. Aurianna placed the lighter in her pocket with the old stone her aunt had given here, pulling the functioning Aether Stone from her other pocket, and gingerly held it up. She thought through the incantation as Simon had instructed her, remembering Pharis using similar wording all those weeks—*or was it entire moon cycles?*—ago. Time seemed to have frozen while she was here.

Yet in that time, she had learned a few things, not only about the world but also about herself. She was returning home a different person, one who had learned to not only trust herself a little more, but perhaps others as well.

She recited the words, lifting her face and voice to the sky. "In the name of the Essence, I…uh…ask for safe passage…um…back to my time, back to my home." The glow around the Aether Stone intensified. "Take me back to the moment I left."

The Aether Stone was shooting sparks of Energy in every direction, and a noise began to fill the silence of the gathered crowd looking on in awe. This was something they had yet to witness and, if she had done her job correctly, hopefully they never would.

She felt a prickling sensation in her scalp, and she knew her hair was standing on end. This time, though, she would not be afraid, even though she was making the journey alone. Aurianna smiled and waved to her friends. They waved back, a mixture of emotions revealed on their faces. The power and sound increased until the world around her disappeared with a resounding boom.

She was going home.

Excited for more of the Awakened Series?

The story continues in book two. Journey to the dark side with Aurianna and her friends in *Darkness Awakening*, the next installment in the Awakened series. Visit *lisamgreen.com/awakened* for information and links to retailers.

Turn the page for more information about the next book.

* * *

Expand the world of Eresseia with a free ebook

Sign up for a free ebook copy of *Daylight Burning*, an Awakened prequel novelette starring Leon Bouchard. You'll also hear about new releases and other updates from Lisa M. Green. Go to *lisamgreen.com/newsletter* for your free copy.

* * *

Enjoyed the book and want to show your support?

You are an amazingly awesome person! Thank you! Please take just a moment and post a review of the book on Amazon, Goodreads, Barnes & Noble, or anywhere you normally post reviews.

Once again, THANK YOU!

Awakened ~ Book Two

A savior has awakened. But she might just doom them all.

After Aurianna foils a deadly plot to destroy the capital city, the people believe she has fulfilled the prophecy and prevented the civil war.

However, when Aurianna returns home to the future, she realizes her attempts to thwart the catastrophe failed. Nothing has changed.

Now Aurianna must work to determine how and where the real event will occur. And she'll have to do it while still trying to control her elemental abilities. The fate of time itself is at stake if she can't learn to control her powers.

The timeline will be forever stuck in an endless loop.

Uncovering the shocking secrets of her own past threatens to shatter Aurianna's already fragile balance between power and self-restraint. These secrets have the potential to rip apart her connection with the people she now holds dear.

A tragic set of events leads to a battle of wills and a horrifying revelation that threatens to destroy her heart…and her home.

She might be the savior. But time is literally counting on her.

For more information about this book and others in the series, visit *lisamgreen.com/awakened.*

LISA M. GREEN

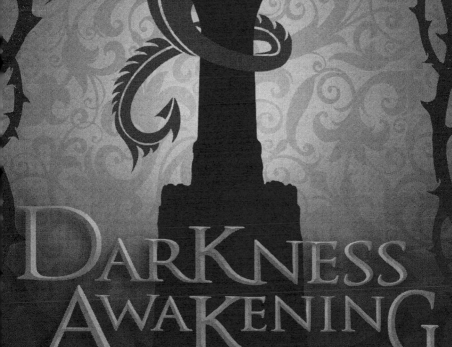

Darkness Awakening

AWAKENED ~ BOOK TWO

Glossary for the Awakened Series

Kinetics: those born with the ability to control or manipulate the elements, usually with an affinity for one element in particular based on their region of birth

Arcanes: a group of men who oversee the records and history books for all of Eresseia; they advise the Magnus on a multitude of issues but are loyal to the Essence (deities) above all

Consils: political delegates and representatives for the six regions of Eresseia

Magnus: leader of the Kinetics and the sixth Consil (representative for Bramosia); the other Consils are elected officials, but the title of Magnus is always a hereditary position

Regulus: the eldest son or daughter of the current Magnus and heir to the title

Magisters: teachers at the Imperium who specialize in training Acolytes in different elements

Acolytes: Kinetics who are still in training and haven't yet reached their twentieth birthday

Voids: those who are sent to the Imperium to train Kinetic powers which never manifest; they are shunned by others and end up working at the Imperium after failing to show any power

Praefects: people in Aurianna's future timeline who are chosen to do the bidding of the Consils (do not exist in the past)

Carpos: a special group of Praefects charged with tracking down, detaining, and torturing Kinetics who manage to travel to the future

Volanti: nightmarish creatures who attack the towns and take captives every few moons but are impervious to Kinetic weapons; they are as tall as several humans, with spindly talons for hands and feet, sharp fangs and claws, long pointed ears, a wide yet angular head, and membranous wings

Aether Stones: amethyst-colored stones of unknown origin that allow the bearer to travel through time via the Aether

LOCATIONS

Eresseia: the known world

Bramosia: one of the six regions and the capital of Eresseia; home to Kinetics and non-Kinetics alike

Imperium: school and home for Kinetic Acolytes, as well as home to some other Kinetics who work nearby; located in Bramosia

Consilium: political building for the Consils, located in Bramosia

Rasenforst: one of the six regions, connected to the element of Fire

Menos: one of the six regions, connected to the element of Earth

Ramolay: one of the six regions, connected to the element of Water

Vanito: one of the six regions, connected to the element of Energy

Eadon: one of the six regions, connected to the element of Air

Perdita Bay: the body of water within Eresseia's inner coastline

Mare Dolor: the ocean surrounding Eresseia (*Sea of Sorrow*)

The Aether: the realm of the Essence (the deities)

KINETICS/ELEMENTS

Fire: Pyrokinetics (nickname Pyros)

Earth: Geokinetics (nickname Dusters)

Water: Hydrokinetics (nickname Hydrons)

Energy: Electrokinetics (nickname Sparkers), the name for electric power

Air: Aerokinetics* (nickname Zephyrs)

*Aerokinetics are comparatively rare, though no one seems to know why. They are in high demand due to their scarcity.

DEITIES

The Essence: the collective name of the deities

Caendra: goddess of Fire, one of the collective group of deities known as the Essence

Terra: goddess of Earth, one of the collective group of deities known as the Essence

Unda: goddess of Water, one of the collective group of deities known as the Essence

Fulmena: goddess of Energy, one of the collective group of deities known as the Essence

Caelum: god of Air, the only male sibling among the collective group of deities known as the Essence

Acknowledgments

There is no way I can say thank you enough to everyone who helped make this book possible.

My husband deserves a slice of delicious chocolate cake and my undying gratitude for putting up with me and my special blend of crazy for the past several years, especially when I'm stressed to the max and ready to give up. He's my cover artist and website designer, not to mention the love of my life, who has helped in ways no one else ever could.

My gratitude goes out to my beta readers. Their insight helped me to weave a stronger tale.

Thank you to Kathryn Schieber at BFF Editing, my ever-tireless editor who somehow managed to make it through seemingly unending rounds of developmental, line, and copy editing. Without you, my story wouldn't be what it is today.

I can't forget all my loyal supporters and readers who have joined me on this journey by following my updates through the newsletter and social media. You've been here with me through it all, here at the beginning of all things.

About the Author

Lisa M. Green writes stories of myth and magic, weaving fairy tales into fantasy. She enjoys reading, writing, cooking, traveling, hiking, and playing video games that girls aren't supposed to like.

lisamgreen.com
facebook.com/authorlmgreen
instagram.com/authorlmgreen
@authorlmgreen

Made in the USA
Columbia, SC
20 November 2020